My Name Is Criminal

Jessica Shubert

First Edition

PAGE PUBLISHING, INC.
New York, NY

First originally published by Page Publishing, Inc. 2017

ISBN 978-1-64027-100-5 (Paperback)
ISBN 978-1-64027-101-2 (Digital)

Printed in the United States of America

Diamonds and gold, and dreams bought to be sold
Treasure has always been my way—
But to you, for the snow-white lie you've told,
I'd give all my treasures away.
The net you have snared me in stems the cold
And keeps the wicked truth at bay—
That my stolen dreams and diamonds and gold
Are naught but glass and painted clay.

—Maximilian Erebus, Plexusless poet and thief

<Daybreak One>

If I'm Not a Piece Of The Perfect Picture

- I -

Enemies of the Human Race

"Nobody's there," I whisper, trying to be heard over the deep city traffic while maintaining a sense of importance, as if anyone would be listening to a conversation of shadows on a roof. The two of us crouch by the edge and stare past the sidewalks full of people below and the glass walls barring off the streams of traffic, all the way to the residency on the other side. "Look, there's no mobile in the drive and he doesn't have a storage for it, and I know he's got no reason to take the bus with the wheels he's got." I turn back and grin at Vici, eyes glinting dangerously in the city lights. The things I'm implying scare even me, and I'm the one who's saying them, but there's no backing down now. "If we pull off this swoop, it'll get us both straight into the elite without so much as taking the lift, if you know what I mean."

"That is, if you fail to get us *killed*." Vici tightens her braid anyway, ready to go even though she's skeptical. "There are discipline and rapture operatives on every corner. I'll wager they've seen us already and are waiting for us to go on and give them a reason to shoot."

"They had a reason to shoot the second we stopped letting them control us," I snicker. "Now, let's go."

With one last glance, I slip off the roof and duck into the alley to check if the coast is clear before motioning for Vici to join me. We slip out of the alley and walk over toward the intersection of Brontide and Wicker with our hoods pulled up so the discipline ops, who stand at the corners for catching (read that as: killing) people like us can't identify us. I know, perfect disguise, look as suspicious as possible, but they can't arrest me for wearing a hood.

Not a meter away, mobiles of all kinds whip down the street, with the help of the MechTeamsters, of course. Almost nobody does any driving themselves anymore, that'd be crazy—one mistake and everything would go screwy. People err. Machines are flawless. I stare at the blur of color and sound through the ten-meter-tall blast shield that walls either side of the street. Everyone's going way too fast to see two hooded girls walking down the sidewalk, headed for the corner where the rushing rivers meet. One street dips under the other so that traffic is continuous, and we pedestrians've got these bridges humming with the vibrations of the rush under our feet.

Citizens pass us on every side, their eyes all flickering with the telltale glints, digital light. They're all using the Plexus, at least partly, every second of the day, even when they sleep, letting it "connect em and protect em," as it's said. You can see it in their eyes all the time unless they shut it off, and it seems they never do, and seeing it makes me sick. Me and Vici pretend to be joking about her shoes so we have a reason to look down so that the discipline ops can't take one look at our Plexusless eyes and get antsy and keep an eye on us and fire the second we put one foot outta line. They're wired as video display units too, so they're not about to miss. If they fire into the public and they hit someone, it's us they're going to hit, hands down. I'm not saying that they'll always get us or that it'll be lethal, but nobody innocent gets touched. We people who're classified strictly as non-innocent are the only ones to blood the gutters.

But we manage to get across Wicker Street without incident. Nowadays, that's a miracle for us.

Hooking a left onto Brontide Avenue, I pick my head up and get moving for the residency I was spying on. My heart is pounding. I know, I know, we do this every night, or at least I do, but this is special. This could mean the chance of a lifetime.

"Layout," I mutter, moving closer to Vici so only she can hear me over the traffic. But again, nobody's interested in us, anyway.

"Two-story residency: classic single-house setup, with living room in front right, kitchen in front left, smaller bathroom on back right, and bedroom on back left, with Center-Control in the middle. C-Con has additional ability to open panel to unauthorized cellar." She gives me a serious look. "In theory, that's where anything of importance should be kept."

Excellent. "And you can figure out how to work it?"

"If you can get me in." The questions are equally ridiculous. Vici can understand anything that runs on electricity, and me, well, I can get into anything that has an inside to get to. That's why she got picked to be my partner in crime tonight. I'll be honest: I'm a crook, if you couldn't guess. There hasn't been a residency, retailer, or organization that I've met that I couldn't get into, especially with Vici, who pretty much has the world of machines at her fingertips. She can mess with cameras and Center-Controls and all that junk I don't get so it makes my job a little easier. Her real name is Victoria Oile, but criminals don't call each other by the names they're born with. We use tags because someone once said that the criminal business is really kind of a giant play, where some of us get rich and famous on that stage and some of us only get the curtains and nobody is who they say they are so their real names mean nothing, but the tags, the name that you make for yourself, the *fame*, those mean everything.

Vici started making her name with minor hacks and heists that had no purpose but glory. The tag obviously comes from the whole "veni vedi vici" thing because of two interests: the idea of conquering stuff and Latin, which she's infatuated with despite her vast inability to pronounce it right. Thus she insists it is pronounced *vee-see*, and anyone that argues gets slapped so for future reference that's how it's "supposed" to sound.

That obviously turned her into a bit of a laughingstock right out the barrel, plus the unpaid raids—the gigs she did for fame without getting a fortune—left her in a pretty spot. Then I came along, and things changed for her.

I throw my protégé a little smile. Vici's started getting better known just because she's working with me. She's picking up tips, getting actual food in her stomach, and okay, I happen to be a really *popular* crook, so she gets her glory too. With some work and time, she's probably going to be one of the big ones, the crime lords out there that nobody can touch. They're the Next, we say, as in the next ones in line to exit the stage (everyone else is the Remainder—who knows where people got that from). That's the plan, to be untouchable, Next, with nothing to lose. But we're going to have to skip the whole time part and go straight to a lot of work because time is something that we criminals absolutely do not have.

The thing is, the Criminal Resolution Sector of our Adamantration (that's kinda like our government) has been cracking down lately. There've been more deaths nearby us this year than I've ever seen before, and everyone who isn't associated with a legend is probably gonna get swept under the rug real quick. So the only thing left to do is become a legend, because dying isn't exactly high up on my options list. Dragging a rookie with me on one of the biggest—scratch that, dragging a rookie with me on *the* biggest swoop I've ever attempted isn't high up on the list, either, but it beats dying.

So ready or not, we come up on the building—666 Brontide Avenue. Yeah, that's the address. I'm not kidding you, but I wish I was. There's no other residencies on the street, only a bunch of hollow husks of industrial things sitting around one resi with the sinister numbers standing sentinel above the door with such an ill air you get the feeling that they're watching your every move, and if you tried walking under them, one of the digits'd fall on your head. Then again, possessed digits would be the least of your problems if you tried walking through that door. I'm sure it's rigged.

No front door access, then. Obviously no windows. No big deal. I slip into the crack between 666 and 667, and sure enough, there's a vent frame for steam to come out from the distilling unit. Distilling units get on my nerves since they take up space, time and energy, and to be honest, they've got zero respect for privacy. There's nothing wrong with Sanitainer, otherwise known as the shower in a can, but hey, they need to make vents for these distilling units, and that gives me all the door I need. Silently I pull out my multitool and start unscrewing screws, pulling out bolts and even undoing welds. This isn't one of those swoops where you steal something and put everything else back into place and hope nobody ever notices, or notices too late and there's nothing they can do. This is the kind of swoop where you let the world know exactly who they're dealing with, so yeah, I can bust off this vent frame for good, and I'm not about to care.

"We're in," I hiss for effect, leaning the vent frame against the side of the building and taking off my boots before jumping up to the hole and squirming inside. Vici quietly worms in after me, toes resting on the edge of the tub of the distilling unit and crossing over to the other side so she can step down without getting her feet in the tub. We always do that if we have to enter over a tub since it might be wet in there. In this case, we do it because the tub is *full* of junk, dark, jagged junk that screams disaster and opportunity at the same time, depending on who's listening. This is the tub of someone who thinks spare material is more important than getting a distilling and doesn't turn up their nose at good ole Sanitainer. We're definitely in the right place.

Outside of the bathroom, the residency sits in inky darkness, but I don't need to use my flashlight because all residencies are nearly identical and I've memorized them. A few steps away is Center Control. The C-Con is what regulates all the temperatures, air levels and lights of the house. And for this house, it also opens and closes our door to seventh heaven.

We have to get there first.

Residencies for single people are kinda small, so it's only a matter of steps from the bathroom to the C-Con, so in a *normal* residency, it'd be simplicity manifested. However, this is, by no means, a normal residency. It is a monster with a casual shell, and it first becomes apparent when, one step past the sink, my toe hits something on the floor, something that lights up, nearly making me jump out of my skin.

It's roughly humanoid, but I can see it's missing key elements. A small dot on its chest beams light into the room, which is blinding after the darkness of the rest of the place, but I force myself to go still. Wires hang off the thing, and it's missing half of its arm, and it's got nothing above the shoulder line. A dot above the light source must be a camera, which must be watching me, analyzing me, but as I said, the thing looks broken.

It is, of course, a Mech. A MechMan, to be specific.

A Mech in general is any bit of machinery that performs some sort of task humans would normally be doing themselves, made by the Surgam tech company. MechTeamsters are boxes connected to the inside of mobiles that do all the driving if people tell them where they need to go, and I could go on and on about all the other special Mechs they've got for doing special junk. The MechMen are a work in progress, nothing so far but a bunch of rumors. They're not robots—they're too skeletal to do much manual labor, but nobody knows what they're supposed to do then. Become sentient and start a revolution? Sure, and I'll eat my hair. Still, there's potential for them. With their inventor, there's potential in anything.

The inventor's innocuous name is Jaden R. Steele. He is twenty-nine years old and he's the Adaman of one of the seven Sectors of the Adamantration. He's the most enigmatic man in Tersatellus. He singlehandedly created the design and programming for every Mech there is, plus a billion other inventions besides. He's our version of Chuck Norris, he's a miracle on legs, and he is currently being robbed.

How crazy do I seem yet?

Pieces of machinery dangle from the ceiling, reminding me of some sort of mechanical butcher shop, so me and Vici have to duck. I flick on the flashlight (hey, the MechMan has *its* one on) and look around a bit.

Sagging, outdated diagrams cover the wall, and two other semiconstructed Mechs lay around on the ground so that there's only a small path to walk down the center of the room. The medicine cabinet has one pathetic bottle of standard painkillers—the rest of the space is dedicated to cups and containers of various nuts or bolts or screws or rivets, all precariously stacked on each other so if I so much as poked one of the cups, they'd all crash down and really raise the dead.

When I find the light switch, I flip it, but nothing happens, which makes me frown. Vici gives me a disturbed look too, so I'm not alone. Before she can stop me, I'm trying the sink, the distilling unit, everything that's supposed to work, but nothing does. "So the Adaman that brings all the power and lights to the nation doesn't even have a working residency." I snicker to myself. Well, he's got several of these things. This is supposed to be some sort of workshop nobody knows about, a place where things can be done in total secrecy. So how do I know that it exists? That's a good question. Okay, moving on.

Careful not to touch anything else, I continue out into the hallway, Vici following close. Despite how the place has that dead feel of a powerless building and it somehow blocks the hum of the Plexus, the eerie mechanical energy made by all the Mechs and stuff is enough to bug anyone. It makes my head hurt, but I grit my teeth and ignore it.

In the hallway, more pieces hang down, tools, mechanical hands and feet, small contraptions I could never imagine the purpose of—they're unearthly spiders dangling by the gossamer strands of a web. They glitter in the light of the flashlight, twirling slowly as air currents or something moves them. It's haunting in a way that's almost beautiful if you look at it through the right eyes, like a whispered secret of humanity in a house that otherwise tries its best to seem as lifeless as possible.

Adamantration demand papers (Cielhomme, real paper!) with checks marked on them are stabbed to the walls with tacks along with tons of other business stuff, which overlaps with the blueprints and designs in some places. No wall is bare, which is freaky after a life of walls that are blank, because people can make walls look however they want in their own eyes with the Plexus. Vici looks closely at one of the Adamantration letters, and her face goes pale. "For Pete's sake," she breathes as she flips through some, and I can't help but wonder if Pete, Cielhomme, Blue Lou, Tsuneo and Geez are all related since everyone's always calling on them and doing things for their loves and sakes. "They expect one man to do all of this? I'm sorry, I became distracted." She lets the papers fall back in line and follows my footsteps again, so we creep together down the hallway, feeling watched even though the place is abandoned—we checked to make sure he was at his northern residency for some Adamantration meeting, and besides, if he knew we were here, he'd have come at us already, right? We're free to poke around.

In the room to my right, I can see a bunch of suspicious contraptions with their attention trained on the door, which is why I didn't walk in the front. But none of the contraptions stir, except a small whirring sound coming from where the bedroom should be. It's not a bedroom. It doesn't have the bed that all normal residencies have, just half a mobile. There's no couch or coffee tables in the living room, only a work desk with more projects and quota and plan papers waiting in the darkness for someone to come back for them. The kitchen's unrecognizable too, and there's no source of light anywhere except candle stubs and matches. This place isn't a home. It's not even a house; it's a prison, and I hate it more every second I'm here. "Rat? Center-Control's this way," Vici calls, and I meet up with her again, watching my step.

Yeah. My tag is Rat. Don't ask.

We make it into C-Con without breaking anything. What I expected, for some reason, was a normal looking C-Con, the computer in a closet deal that most people don't have to look at because they can connect to it with the Plexus. Silly me. Three out of the four walls are covered from floor to ceiling in computers of every kind, one of them taking up a whole wall, one of them with only nine buttons and small enough to fit in my pocket. "Welcome to Hedonshire," Vici mumbles, and I snort because Hedonshire's one of our real old-fashioned towns nobody thinks exists. She drifts over to the main computer, which is nearly buried, and starts moving her finger across the generic display unit (read: screen—I'm trying to sound smart), making it light up. "This room in itself is a museum. Full of antiques with no real value. We need something better. Is that correct?"

She halts in her analysis to look to me for confirmation. I might not be the brains of this outfit, but when it comes to knowing what to take and what to leave, I am the sticky fingers. I look around. "Yep. They might be valuable, but none of it screams 'Property of Steele,' see?"

She nods. "Listen for the hatch to slide open—it's supposed to be in the living room." Yeah, right. The constant whirr of machinery in the house grates against my ears loud enough that I couldn't hear her if I was standing outside the room. My fists clench and unclench, and I sway a bit under the mechanical pressure, so Vici glances at me. "I know, I know. Sorry. I'll try to go as fast as I can."

While I wait, I walk around the room, trying to find the best spot to avoid the pressure, and I, you know, kill time. "Rat," Vici sighs at some point without even looking at me, and I sulk and put the weird nine-buttoned thing back where I found it. "You can steal knickknacks later. This is serious."

"Yes, Mother." I roll my eyes. Even though Vici's a few months younger than me (which I love to point out on a regular basis cuz it makes me superior), she thinks she knows better than everyone else. And okay, I'll admit that she probably knows a lot *more* than most people know, but there's a reason she's considered the sidekick here.

Even at her fastest, Vici spends about ten minutes of tapping and sliding before I hear the sound in the living room. "That was too easy," she says nervously. For the record, that's about the longest it's taken her to get into anything, about three times over. "I thought I would at least have to... never mind. We're some of the only thieves out there, so he shouldn't have anything to worry about, and besides, this is a residency, not his real workshop at his headquarters or anything that important." I get the feeling she almost wanted more of a challenge, as if she loves his security so much she wants more of it, since this is probably one of the most secure establishments in Tersatellus. It's got a lock on the front door, which automatically puts it into the top hundred tightest residencies in the nation.

We sneak out of C-Con and into the living room. The hatch is open on the floor, slanted downward into a murky black hole that we've got to go into. Holding my breath, I clamp the flashlight in my teeth, get my multitool ready, and lower myself down the ladder. For every rung I go down, the temperature drops about two degrees, making me glad I brought a hoodie.

When we get down to the bottom, we're in a small room with metal flooring and a few chairs and some bookshelves stuffed with published books and notebooks and crumpled stacks of paper. I sweep the light around it all, making my eyes eat the sight. In Tersatellus, paper is pretty much extinct as it is, but books? Forget it. You've got the Plexus, what do you need *books* for? Yet here, the whole room is dedicated to the odd species, with the well-worn look and smell of use and care. I bet every book in existence is in here! Whenever Vici's observing something without touching it, I yank a book off a shelf and pull the yellowed sheets back to gawk at the legions of little dark words. The notebooks, which are kinds of books that people write in themselves, are full of ink, so most of it bleeds through, and the handwriting's so chaotic I can't read it in most places. It seems almost familiar for a second, but the feeling fades. I get that a lot. It's nothing.

Most of the books have bunches of colorful slips sticking out of them, so I flip open to one of the pages with a slip inside, and I find more scrawl on the slip and some underlining in the book. There's a little table already covered with books, and I pick up slipped ones that interest me, their leather bindings promising poetry and dramas from the ancients of Dostoevsky and Shakespeare to more recent Erebus and Chosovi. I scour the marked pages for that underlined stuff, soaking it up and holding it in the same way I breathe in that sharp, soulful smell of aged paper and hold it in my lungs.

In the corner, there's another oddity that captures my attention, and I set my armful of books down to go over to the weird contraption with the guess that it's some sort of cabinet. But when I lift up the top, there's only complicated strings in there, nothing worth stealing. Outside, the curvy box on legs has black-and-white buttons on it. Aha! It's some funky sort of keyboard. After sneaking a look at Vici, because she always tells me not to touch stuff, I push one of the buttons. Both of us jump when it makes a ringing sound, but before Vici can scold or stop me, I keep pushing buttons.

"Rat!" Vici hisses, but I run my hand all the way down it from right to left so it makes the sound of falling. Oh my gosh, we need to steal this whole residency right out of the ground! "For Pete's sake, Rat, it's a piano! They're a part of a band, which also includes sections such as brass, which are instruments made from brass and strings, which are . . . I mean, quit messing around. We can split one later if you want. We're here for a reason." I give her a smirk and abandon the thing. You can always tell when Vici's nervous because she starts explaining stuff she doesn't have to—a lot of people do it. You can tell she's a novice because nobody's here, and she's still nervous.

After I finish feasting my eyes on the piano and all the books, I notice an alcove in one wall where the bookshelves stop to make room for the alcove, and I walk over, curious.

Sitting inside is something that almost makes me puke right here and now.

It's a small square thing, thin as paper and no bigger than the nail of my pinkie finger. It's in two pieces, each of them looking the same: jagged and black, with tiny dark tendrils hanging off them.

For a long time, I can only stare, feeling some deathly flood of emotion rise up and threaten to swallow me whole at the sight of the one small thing that ripped my life to pieces. Then I choke it down.

"Vici, you should really see this."

She materializes by my side and gasps after stifling a gag. "Look, he snapped it," she breathes, taking the flashlight and examining the thing from every angle without touching it. Even from an extraordinary source, it's an ordinary mainframe, the kind you can find in almost every head in Tersatellus. And for all of us you can't find that chip in, odds are, we were ruined by the suckers.

The "us" in this point are very different from the "them" who still have those mainframes, I promise. We may look the same as you, and we may need the same needs and live in the same places, but we are not the same. We're not citizens; *they* are citizens. *We* are cutouts. And you, my friend, are somewhere in between, I think. You may not remember—it's been a few years, and I've learned not to trust memory—but at one point, when I tried to show you this difference, tried to show you whose side I was on, you wanted no part of it. But I believe in second chances, so if you're ready, I'm going to try and tell you something. I won't expect you to trust me—you didn't before, not when I needed you to. But what I am going to tell you is the truth, and what will be different this time is that I expect you to listen.

And if you are not who I think you are, if big red houses on the outskirts of cities and music boxes full of memories mean nothing to you, then I'd like you to know that this story is meant for a boy that used to be my brother. He's the one I talk to all the time, and you might think that's crazy, but all of us cutouts have loved too much and lost too often and let go of enough that we are all a little crazy. Besides, I think everyone has someone they write unsent letters to, someone they talk to even when they aren't really there. In my case, this someone is a boy named Statice.

Whoever you are, if you stick around for some reason and if you ever somehow meet this boy, could you do me a favor? Tell him my story, the story of my kind and how we love and fight and live, so he can no longer say that he doesn't know who I am. And tell him that when he's ready to come home, I'll be waiting.

Can you do that for me? Good. Now, I might as well start at the beginning.

Nobody actually knows for sure what started it or even when it started. To us, history begins on the day hundreds of years ago when, for some reason, people flocked to this forsaken place at the top of the world and made themselves a nation. Most of the outside world has never heard of this nation before because those people built this nation on ice and imported rock. They built it on ideals, but most of all, they built it on silence.

I walk up to a road map of this nation we made and stare at the many broken "islands" that make up the place, all separated by rivers and seas, gaps of ice, and surrounded by one thick line that represents the Divide, the great wall erected around our little world to keep it from floating away or leaking back out into the world. Beyond that is the blue Rift, a moat of ocean that was bombed into the outer reaches of the Arctic Circle to deny any close contact with land. This separation is defended by machines day and night, because this nation, called Tersatellus, believed it could be not only self-sufficient but superior to all other nations in existence.

Despite this pretense, though, Tersatellus had the common downside of any society: people, namely, people with their own opinions and ideas on the way things were supposed to be. What they decided to do to change that, to make everything better, was they started to implant these mainframes (I call them chips, even though they discourage that because it sounds weird) into everyone's brains before they were even born so that those tendrils snuggled in, and the whole contraption turned into a part of them.

Okay, they were really just supposed to help people communicate, and it started out innocent, and it is actually a good thing, but I'm a cutout, so I'm gonna be spiteful and suspect control, so bear with me.

These chips are run by a program called the Plexus, which is almost a kind of Inter-net since it's a code system that allows for connection and entertainment to everyone, but that's not all, oh, no. It lets everyone see the world how they want to with vision reforms. It hardly even monitors anything, just certain bodily functions to make sure you're not dying or upset in which case messag-es'll come to offer solutions. People nowadays can't feel pain, so if they trip on the sidewalk, they won't sting their hands, and if they get shot in the head, they won't feel that, either. They don't question the goodness of the Adamantration since it gives them this blessing; it makes everything better.

As far as I know, everyone honestly, doubtlessly, loyally, and wholly believes that everything and everywhere and everyone *is* perfect. And in a way, that means it is, isn't it?

The Plexus doesn't force citizens to feel or not feel things; it only blocks nerve signals that result in pain. It doesn't control or read or know what citizens think, and it doesn't miraculously erase problems; it just lets Public Prosperity see out of rapture workers' eyes to know if anything bad's going on around you so it knows to tell you the programmed response about how everything's under control. But whose control are all these problems under? Who gets to decide what's bad, what's painful? Whose version of the truth do you get to hear? And what on earth is *perfect*?

They knew that people would start to think these things, and they would start to rebel if they weren't heard. So a compromise was reached.

Around age twelve or thirteen—about the median between mature and uninfluenced thought—every kid gets the message that reminds them that they can have their section of the Plexus cut away and get this chip removed from their brain. Anyone can get extracted anytime they want, if they hear about it sooner or decide on it later, but people usually wait til twelve or thirteen and don't go after that because it's harder for kids and old people. Oh, and if they're faulty citizens, they almost *have* to get extracted early or else there's usually some bad side effect. "Faulty citizens" is the disgusting term for people whose Plexus codes got tangled or whatever so their chips don't work right (so much for perfect). Faulty or not, extraction makes someone's lifespan go from hundreds of years to only dozens, and they'll turn vulnerable to illnesses and negative emotions and sensations they never felt before, and they'll have no direct access to the Plexus, therefore becoming Plexusless cutouts. Some of them manage to live normal lives and just do it out of preference. Most of them become outcasts from society, forced to resort to other ways of sustaining themselves.

They'll be alone. That's something else that no normal citizen has to deal with, is the silence of not having the whole nation connected to them. It is that same silence that Tersatellus chose when it cut itself from the rest of the world, and we cut ourselves from Tersatellus for the same reason—for the chance to be better. To be free. At least that's what we tell ourselves to justify the decision.

The process alone is obviously not without its risks. Pasted to the wall above the alcove are the statistics that all of us cutouts memorize and keep in the backs of our minds: fifty-three out of every hundred die instantly during the removal because they pull part of the brain out or leave part of the chip in, and the rushed surgery couldn't save them. Of the forty-seven survivors, most of which still had complications but survived the surgery, eight more will die in the first day, fifteen more will die in the first week, and twelve more will die in the first year. That leaves twelve out of every hundred cutouts to live after that, though most don't get much further because of the complications and occupational hazards.

Because okay, okay, the main thing about being a cutout is that we're pretty much all a bunch of criminals. There, I said it, I embrace the stereotype. You wanna do things the easy way and refuse to pay for anything and get away with being bad? The first logical step is to get rid of the thing that allows the discipline ops to identify you on the spot.

I've lasted almost six years as a cutout and criminal, which is amazing to me. There is only one of us who has managed to get to twenty-nine years of age from his rumored extraction at age twelve, lasting *seventeen* years of being a cutout. And even to us cutouts who're lucky enough to make it five or six years, seventeen is almost unthinkable.

But sitting before us is proof that seventeen is not impossible.

"Do you realize that this thing is probably worth billions of euros to someone?" Vici shakes my arm. She still calls them euros or rupees even though the real term is *primes*, because they're just virtual numbers, points, fake money that only works in the Plexus or on special devices for cutouts. (They gave us the devices with the original intention of us using them to give us a normal way of transacting money and stuff, but that kinda flopped because people don't like to hire us, so the only transactions we get are by force or in the black market.)

I think about it. "Yeah, but it's about the size of a fingernail. We could walk out of here with that in our pocket. Maybe someday if we need cash, we'll come back for it, but right now we need publicity. Something to get us Next, remember? I don't care if we have to break it, drop it and run, that's fine too. So long as we really flare the discipline ops' nostrils, we're clear." I start looking around the room.

"As if you're not Next already," Vici says quietly.

My ego stirs a little, but I gotta be careful with this one, so I throw her a smile over my shoulder. "C'mon, snowflake, I said *us*. Our partnership doesn't even have a handle, does it? How do you say 'evil little suckers' in Latin?" She rolls her eyes about the snowflake thing. It's just something I call her even though she's even farther from snowy pallor than me. Let's just say we'd be real dirty snow.

Since she doesn't respond, I turn back around and keep looking. "Come out, come out, wherever you are... There's gotta be something. I mean, *maybe* one of those things upstairs would be *okay*, but I'm not sure..." Suspicion creeps up on me, and I walk over to an oddly large bookcase. "Help me move this."

"Oh, he *didn't*." Vici laughs and gives me a hand pushing the thing across the floor. There's no scuff marks or anything, but sure enough, there's a doorway behind the bookcase. "Classic. He has a stagey taste in doors, I suppose." She walks through the doorway with a gasp, making me tense and flick out the knife on my multi. "Cielhomme. And the ground floor seemed impressive." Light spills into the room from the doorway, so I shut off my flashlight and follow her in, wondering how a guy's supposed to get around this house of horrors if he only keeps one room lit.

If I were more observant, I'd notice a candlestick sitting in its holder on the bookshelf, smoke still dancing off its wick.

There's two tables and a desk. One table and the desk are coated in heaps of machines, but they're shinier than the ones upstairs, and each one I put my eyes on looks more complicated than the last. Somehow, they seem made more from desire than demand. "This one's meant to fly!" Vici pretty much squeals, picking up stuff and giving brief explanations of what it's supposed to do, and I pretend to listen as I look up at the light source for the room. It's slowly pulsating, and even though the color's off, I'm almost sure of what it is. Some whitened form of liquid lightning.

That, my friend, is the single most powerful substance currently known to humankind. It's generated by giant harvester orbs of glass high in the sky, usually on top of power buildings, filled with a special gas that was discovered/created about fifteen years ago. When it comes into contact with the lightning that strikes the orbs, it creates liquid lightning, a substance thicker than water with the vivid, glowing green color with the vividness of nature incarnate and the intensity of the heavens. One drop is enough to power a mobile for five kilos or kill a person without the shock-absorbing thing in a mainframe. These days, the stuff powers almost everything inside the Divide.

I've never seen it gathered up in its straight, undiluted form, much less a different color. It's blinding to look at the bulb, but if I squint, I can tell it's not even a mini version of a harvester, it's just a small glass sphere filled with the stuff, held in place by two small braces. If that bulb fell, it would mess up everything electronic within kilometers of here. My heart skips beats. He's using a veritable grenade as a light source. Some part of me wants to be nervous but I'm not that sensible.

"I think that this one is an updated MechTeamster! More durable. Look at this! Didn't I see the other half of this thing upstairs?" Vici's still lost in her own world. While I'm off thinking about the Plexus and all that stuff, she's probably listing off every wire in that machine to try and choke down the nerves. What basket cases we are. Before I accidentally open up my music box of memories to bury my fear under some other useless info, I whip my head around for something good to split.

"Hey, Vici? Check this out," I say, turning back around to the last table, the one that's not covered in stuff. This one has a blanket draped over it, white with a little logo on the corner. It's the symbol of Steele's company, Surgam, which is apparently Latin for something, but Vici can't find out what it is in the Plexus since the info always gets weaved out. But it's not the logo I'm interested in. A shape protrudes from the sheet, a shape that's not roughly humanoid but *exactly* humanoid, about my size.

Something worthy of being covered up is usually something very worthy of being stolen, and it's big enough that the discipline ops would see us making off with it. I'm already imagining it all over the Plexus: "The Cutouts Have Struck Again, Making Off with a Surgam Project That Was Set to Change the World!" The gangs will revere us. They'll protect us. Criminal Resolution and their discipline ops won't be able to look at us without finding themselves in a billion crosshairs. I reach for the edge of the sheet, tingling with apprehension. Vici watches with a rapt expression as I start pulling the sheet off.

Halfway off, the thing suddenly stops.

Vici's quit breathing, and I'm right there with her. Without a sound, I look over at the other side of the protuberance to see if the sheet caught on something, and sure enough, it's bunched up in one area, but less like it's caught and more like it's in someone's fist. This notion is really brought home when it starts moving, tugging the sheet back onto itself.

"Sticks!" Vici screams with her hand clamped over her mouth to mask the noise of the curse. Both of us stumble back away from the thing. It's living! Something's *sentient* under there!

But that's not the best part.

A vaguely annoyed knocking sound comes from behind us, and we spin around to see someone standing in the doorway. I barely get more than a haze of an image before my mind flies into rapid-fire mode, knowing that we are about to get caught.

I've never been caught before.

And this is the last place I'd pick for my first time.

"GO!" Vici yells, barreling toward the person to shove them to the side—with her adrenaline shot, she could probably take down a tank at this point, let alone some guy, but the thing is, he steps right out of her way, so Vici stumbles out of the room with nothing to push, leaving me alone with him. But even in the face of capture, I remember that we're here for a reason. My head jerks around, and I lock aim and let the rest of the world turn into background noise, quiet and fuzzy.

The guy's nothing but a blur as he lunges for me (or maybe he's going for the table behind me, I'll never know). He's fast, scary fast, but I'm freaking out, so I'm faster, leaping onto the desk and launching off with my feet, sailing *barely* above his head, reaching up, and yanking the glass orb out of the ceiling as I go. When the floor starts coming at me from one side and him from another, true panic sets in as some part of me reiterates what's going to happen if this bulb breaks. Hello, cutout here, no shock-absorbing anything! The bulb's bigger than a fist and icy, which isn't great for holding on to, but one hand manages to direct it to my pocket by the time my hang-time ends, and I slam into the ground in a roll, sending a jolt through my body. Ignoring it, I let the momentum carry me forward, scrambling in the sudden darkness since the light source is muted by my pocket. Words fall into my ears and stop there, unheard over the roar of my heartbeat. My hands find the ladder and I jump aboard, desperately trying to get up, but he grips my hood tightly in one fist.

Before I even make the thought, my multitool from my other pocket comes out and I'm slicing my own hood off with the knife. The force of that and the struggle to break it loose turns me around. It's free, but I'm not. I know if I try getting up that ladder, he'll grab my leg or something, so I stand my ground, back to the ladder, me with a knife, him with my hood still clutched in his hand.

His appearance is shocking. He's got pale skin, which stands out against the jet-black hair that falls gracefully back in a million thin barbs that look exactly like they're oily porcupine quills, arching down past his shoulders, which explains why everyone calls him the Porcupine. He's squinting slightly at me, trying to see inside of me with those eyes that have the color of sapphires and the depth of outer space. They almost seem to glow from the inside of his head. He's tallish also, sorta thin, which is common for us cutouts, but he manages it without looking fragile. In fact, watching him there with my hood caught in his long, spindly fingers, some part of me is wondering if he's going to kill me right here and now.

Oh, and he's wearing a once-white shirt and blue jeans, and I want to tell you that because that's the normal part, the standard, the ordinary. The part that isn't normal is the black trench coat he's got over it all, and I don't mean dark gray, I mean black. This is important: you don't wear black in Tersatellus. They don't make black clothes in Tersatellus. They don't make black buildings or black roads or black mobiles or black hair dye or black *anything* in Tersatellus, and they keep the lights on all the time, and people don't like anything so much as dark gray, so why does someone wear black?

Because someone ain't one of the average "they."

To wear black in Tersatellus is something only cutout does. It's our unspoken heraldry. It's the color we've taken from the knights for our own armor that means that yes, we're grieving and mysterious and everything that normal citizens could never be, but there's more to us than that. It's the lack of Plexus that defines us as a cutout, but it's our sable that says we're someone who's a defiance because we breathe, a rebel because we live, and an enemy because we're free. And it's true—you look at him and you don't think of an Adaman; you think of a warrior that, in past lives, ends up brutally murdered nine times out of ten.

All evidence to the contrary, I know exactly who I face. "You're Jaden Steele," I breathe, mostly because I don't know what my voice would do if it went any louder.

"So they call me."

It's a fitting first impression, considering it leaves me with less than no idea how to make any sense of him. So I do what I do with everything I don't understand; I take it as a threat and grip the knife harder.

"You're going to let me go now," I cue, not taking my eyes off him.

"Of course I will," Steele agrees in that same deliberate, threatening way. Then he stands back with a trace of a smile, the sly, lonely kind someone gives you when they're on the inside of some joke the rest of the world is outside of. Now I recognize the tone as careful, not ominous—I've hardly ever heard such a thing before, much less from any sort of politician, so I didn't get it at first. He's not setting me up and getting ready to shoot me, and okay, I'll admit it, that's the *last* thing I was expecting since I always had this hesitant dislike for the guy because even though he's a cutout, he's still the Adaman (or leader) of the Technology Sector of the Adamantration, and me and technology never get along, and the Adamantration obviously hates my guts, so I thought there'd at least be some guns out by now. Instead, he watches me expectantly.

Neither of us have any idea what to do. Great.

"Uh…you can keep the hood, if you want, if you let me go, I mean," I stammer, trying to bargain for my amnesty even though it's already been established. "I got what I wanted. My residency's pretty dark too."

He glances at the glow coming from my jacket then tosses the hood in question and catches it. "Well, thanks, though that's not what I—well, never mind," he says, actually laughing quietly to himself in that inside-joke way. The thunder of it rolls across the sky between the two of us before he locks eyes with me, as if to let me know that he understands a lot more than I think. This swoop means a lot more to me than some source of light, and I'm not the only one who knows it—in fact, he might understand more than I do.

"Maybe you don't know what you're really up to, but I do. You're aiming for the bay. Good courage out there. You'll need it," he warns before turning and drifting back toward the other room, the shadows of his cloak swimming in his wake. He takes the candle off the shelf then looks back over his shoulder at yours truly, who's still standing and staring—confused is an understatement. "Good courage out there"? I can understand "good luck," but I'm not even sure if his version makes a sentence, and it sure doesn't make any sense whatsoever.

"What bay?" I demand when I get my voice back. It sounds more desperate than I'd hoped it would. "Isn't the closest thing to one in Tersatellus just a sea or whatever?"

He looks back at me with a look of pleased surprise. "Gosh, you can go and you're still here, asking questions? You're still curious?"

Did he really just say "gosh" to me? I'm being messed with. My fists clench. "I just wanna know what you think you're talking about. I'm not going to any bays! There's none in Tersatellus, anyway, and even if there was, then I don't have any intention of going!"

"What's that matter?" he asks, feigning confusion, as if me going to this bay is unavoidable as nightfall. "It doesn't do to deny your cue back on stage."

"Cue? What stage?"

"The only stage worth playing on. Hudson Bay."

Hudson Bay. The phrase feels foreign and hostile as it sears through my mind in a flash of lightning. "Look, there are no bays out there anymore. What're you *talking* about, what's *happening*?"

"I think you know that," he says quietly, and my heart skips a beat before he goes on as if he hadn't said anything. "What should be happening is you leaving. Now that you 'stole' that, you're bad enough to qualify to go. You're Next—next back on the stage. They'll really need you gone once they know you can get in here, and nobody has to know you had help."

At first, all I can do is wonder if he's telling me that me and Vici are getting kicked out of Tersatellus for stealing a whacky lightbulb, but then the second part about getting help sucker punches me in the pride.

"Wait, you... you *let* us break in and enter?" I ask.

Steele nods, giving me the impression that he doesn't talk much. "Did you think I put up all that security as decoration, or did you really assume you could get in here without my say-so?" Now he shakes his head, making his quills sway back and forth, but his eyes never leave mine. "I'll only play victim for my own purposes."

Oops. I guess Vici's the smart one again for picking up that it was too easy, and I'm the arrogant one for thinking that nothing's too easy. Hey, all part of the charm, eh?

There's a few moments of silence where I try and put together what on earth he thinks I'm trying to qualify for, and why he wants me to qualify for it. "Oh, I get it, you wanted us to do something bad so your stupid Adamantration would kick us out into this Hudson Bay place, right? That's why you stopped me, was to tell me that you're going to have me killed officially, right?" This gets a "more or less" shrug that annoys me. "Then what's the rest of it?"

"I did want you to qualify, but the difference in our theories is that in mine, Rat, you survive." My mind reels, unable to grasp why this Adaman uses my tag or why he actually does believe in my survival. "You see, things are about to change, supposedly for good, but I'm not too good at leaving good enough alone."

"No, that's enough," I growl, drawing the line. "Nothing ever changes in Tersatellus, and if something ever did, I of all people wouldn't be able to do a thing, anyway!"

"And why not?" I recoil against the ladder as far as I can when Steele whirls full around to face me so I'm trapped in the bottomless wells of those blue eyes, where the shadows teem with dreams and nightmares, too big to hide but buried too deep to fathom. They search me for a moment, as if he judges which word to say by how he somehow knows I'll hear them—everything that comes out of his mouth has to go through this examination that makes it all measured and supernatural and made for you alone. "As a rare comrade in this bloody war we call freedom, you must know that it's always changing, so that we too have to change ourselves into people who *can* do a thing to keep on fighting," he finally tells me. A half-smile stumbles across his face. "And, um, watch who you tell that things don't change. It's sort of my job to see that they do."

Without so much as a wave, he disappears around the corner. Then there's a sharp clicking sound of a lighter that throws hints of candlelight and shadows into the room before the bookcase slides back and eclipses it.

Now that he's gone, my mind spins with all the haphazard things he somehow said so carefully, but the thing that really strikes me again was that it wasn't luck that he wished for me. Maybe because you don't need good luck to change into the warrior that wins that stolen tenth try.

Good courage, I think, feeling the gravity of the words sneak into me the same way faint candlelight escapes the corners of the bookshelf, telling me in a whisper that in this world suffocated with darkness and silence, one thing is for sure—things are about to change for good.

⟴

Vici's waiting for me outside, tapping her foot at me, when I fly into the alley. "Cielhomme, Rat, what the heck were you doing? What were you thinking?"

Panting, I take the glowing sphere out of my pocket. Her face goes slack. What I hold in my hand right now is not only a weapon of mass destruction but it could easily be one of the wonders of the modern world, because unlike the harvesters at the tops of buildings, there's no seams or holes or anything for the hostile liquid to go into, so its formation is a mystery. It's impossible, and there's only one Adaman that's famous for shattering impossibilities and also famous for everything to do with liquid lightning, so there's no question where I got this from. Since I took it down and it's going back to normal temperature, it's slowly started reverting to its natural color. It enchants me and Vici into staring at its wavering glow.

If that doesn't scream "Steele," then nothing will.

"You're a genius, Rat," she breathes. "A crazy genius."

"According to some poet guy I read about down there, 'Science has not yet taught us if madness is or is not the sublimity of intelligence.'" I'm tempted to toss it up to catch it, but that'd be stupid, so instead I shove my boots on while Vici holds the bulb.

"What did he say to you?" she asks as she gives the bulb an observation. I don't miss the jealousy in her voice.

"Well, basically he let me know we only got in cuz he let us, because... oh, he seems to think we're qualifying for something, getting Next so somebody kicks us out to some sort of bay, and he wants us to have courage, not luck, which probably means he doesn't care if we die or anything, as long as we're courageous about it." I grunt as I yank on the left boot. It's always been a bit tight, while the right one's all loose. "If I'm crazy, he's certifiable. Why's it always bravery, anyway? Nothing but glorified recklessness." Vici hands me the orb, and I stand up and peer out of the alley. "You ready for this?"

"What are we going to do with it?" Vici asks, gesturing to the bulb, and I think about it.

"You know what? I think I wanna keep it, y'know, as a souvenir. Let's make sure they know what we got and go home." Home. What a joke. Home isn't a house, it's wherever we love. You should know. You told me. Shaking the thought away, I pull off my jacket and wrap the bulb with it. "Now, are you ready for some orange juice?"

She nods to the code term and turns to the sidewalk. I take one last look at the residency. *What a strange guy*, I think before sprinting out into the mass of people that mill up and down Brontide.

With the lights on the glass walls, even loosely populated areas have the light of day, and most retailers are run electronically, and since people get "paid" by the Public Prosperity Sector for how much they exercise and take care of their bodies, they've all got to get out at some point. So at any given time of the day, there's still the same amount of people out as any other time, different ones depending on which music club is open. Me and Vici go out at night simply because we want to—we're what criminals call nocturnal predators. There's really no benefit to going out at night since the discipline workers all have junctioners, which are glasses that either allow for special kinds of sights and targeting or for communicating with other people, so their face appears in the lens, and their voice goes in your ear by the ends of the spectacles.

Junctioners are also one of the ways you can tell apart a discipline worker from a rapture worker. They're pretty similar people, but rapture men—they're almost all men—are the hands, feet, and most of all, the eyes of the Public Prosperity Sector, making sure everyone's happy, taking care of lawbreakers with the discipline workers, working as educators and telling the Plexus what needs to be corrected in society. They get different patches on their uniforms, and instead of junctioners, they get special implants in their irises that help them see any way the Adamantration needs them to see. We call em lasers because of it. It's fiberoptics-meets-eyeballs, and it's not pretty, I promise.

Somehow, those implants and junctioners can tell the difference between casual joggers and two girls dashing away from a crime scene. I'm sure the cries of "Come and get me!" are a bit of a clue, plus the bulb I wave around. We rip past a pair of ops at a corner, running across the bridge as they start shouting at us, getting the attention of the discipline men so everyone can work together.

Weaving through the crowd of people who don't even notice anything's going on, we pass by another pair, and I wave the glowing orb under their noses before bolting out of their way. "SPLIT!" Vici yells as they start shooting at us. The pedestrians still don't even bother to get out of the way of the discipline and rapture men. Because of their ugly, color-shifting eyes, the only way to tell they're angry with us is the snarls on their lips, and they are always angry with us, always trying to kill us the second they see us because of everything we are and all that we've done, but this takes the cake and eats it too. We've robbed an Adaman.

I'm still trying to figure out why he let us, though.

While Vici goes on ahead, I veer off to the left, wrapping the orb in my jacket again as I hook another left the second I can, trying to lose them. They know what we stole—that's enough. Now we have to make it home alive.

The orange juice trick is all about gathering attention and then abandoning it, going where they won't look for you. My next step is making sure nobody looks for me. I've lost their attention for a second, and that's all it'll take.

Someone passes me with a hat on, and I grab the hat and screw it onto my head, pulling the rim over my face. Take a scarf, snag something out of someone's shopping bag and yank it over my head, anything to help me blend. Suddenly, I'm nothing but a normal person who's out on a walk down Nox Boulevard, because even though the instant a discipline worker identifies someone as a threat and the threat shows up red in their junctioners-sight, they also go back to normal if they change description once they're out of sight. In this way, I slowly lose the attention of the discipline and rapture ops. They can't identify me as well, anyway: when I cut off my hood, I also gave myself a rude haircut. So with my jacket wrapped secretly around me under the new sweater and my hand in my pocket, concealing the bulb, I'm free.

I'm sure I make this sound easier than it is. Professional warning: don't try this at home.

Long minutes pass. My eyes scan the sidewalks all around for Vici as I turn on to our nearly abandoned street, Silhouette Court. It's closer to Farsia's outskirts but not close to one of the main outlets to the other cities, so there's much less traffic. The roads spread out the same way strands of a web do, escaping normal grid patterns when they get out here and break free from city lines, paving pale strips of gray across the hardened brown earth that they established into the tops of the flattened ice to make stuff safe for building on.

Light bursts in my vision from somewhere far ahead, light that isn't fake, and it makes my head jerk up away from my scanning. There are clouds in the north skies, and even though I see some bright flashes coming from them, you can't hear the thunder over the city noise, and besides, it never rains or snows, not really. Not when the hoppers suck all of it out of the sky before it can even get close to any of us down here. I see one of the massive hoppers floating slowly toward the thunderhead, and I wave at it, a habit I have because I seem to think that somebody on there's gonna see me, if there's anyone on there at all, which there probably isn't. They look like zeppelins, except they don't have any fans, so they don't make wind. Some of the tall buildings in cities are dedicated to them (they end up covering the cities; they're that big). Other buildings are for capturing, creating, and storing liquid lightning and its gaseous catalyst. Then there's all the business places and high residencies, where hundreds of people all somehow live in the same building together, with a scattering of random places, schools, warehouses, retailers, that sort of thing. And those are all the buildings in Farsia and any city.

The reason I'm telling you this is that you can't tell any of those buildings apart. They're all the same, concrete finger-bones sticking out of the grave without any decoration or windows or anything. No need for windows. Anyone inside can use a reform from the Plexus and make themselves a window with a view of a sunny meadow or proud mountains or the city if they really want to see it. Anyone outside can pick how they want the buildings to look, too, whether it's the classic glinting cityscape or it's everything in gaudy shades of purple. The sidewalks are blank, the mobiles are blank, and even the people all wear some shade of white because our world is a canvas that you use the Plexus to paint your perfect all over the off-white reality without intruding on anyone else's.

I have an idea about what they're seeing now because I've seen it before. I was there, was part of the perfect once upon a time that I can't remember but can guess at.

I'm sure it never bugged me until it started failing for me, and I figured out the hard way that things aren't as great as everyone thinks. Now, as I walk down this sidewalk in the dead of night toward one of many residencies I will never call home, I wonder if I ever thought any of this could be beautiful. Maybe I accepted it as fact. This was the way it always was, the only way all the Adamans said it would always be—all but one. I'm not sure what to believe now. It's ugly to me, but it's concrete, it's stable, it's *reality*, so it's impossible to think it could ever change. Then again, a lot of things I thought were impossible have happened in the last hour. A trace of distant thunder reaches me as I stride down Nox, chilling my spine and making me wonder, *What if I'm wrong?*

Of course I am. I think you know that.

The note crinkles in my pocket. It's real paper, and it's addressed to me. I've been carrying it for a few days since I found it in a box of hot cocoa mix I had specially ordered from Zenith (what, can't a gal splurge?).

It mentions no bay, no cue back on stage. It does mention a challenge. It asks me if I am still curious and if I want to know the truth. It invites me to find out. I know who it is from, and I denied that invitation. But after this encounter, I think the challenge is still there. And I'm starting to realize it involves more people and goes deeper than I thought.

It begins with the words, *Everything is about to change for good.*

I understand things have a tendency to do that. I'm not as stupid as I sound. But why's everyone getting so worked up about it? That can only mean one thing: there's trouble afoot. And I might not be inclined to trust invitations, but when there's trouble, I have a tendency to show up with a party hat and every intention of staying.

Since the Structure & Architecture Sector focuses on practicality and not being creative, our residency's got the exact same design as pretty much any other single-person dig. That's what you get for free, and by free I mean stolen. There is one thing that separates this residency from the others, though: the power hasn't worked here for years. That's my fault—I hate powered buildings. Seeing the darkness peeking through the cracks of the doorway makes me relax, since I've gotten used to the darkness. Then it reminds me of 666 Brontide, so I have to hurry inside to stop remembering that house of horrors.

Vici's sitting on the couch, talking to the Godfathers, when I step in. Her face breaks out into a smile when she sees me, and the smile gets even bigger when I pull out the bulb. "We got away with it, and better yet, they know it."

Godfather Outmode starts clapping slowly. He's not my godfather, and his name isn't really Outmode, but it's a cutout thing to reinvent yourself however much you need to to let go of the electrode (we call normal citizens electrodes) you used to be, cuz if you don't leave that life behind, it'll eat you. You'll start wondering how you ever picked being free over being numb, and the next thing you know, you're back in on the Plexus deal. Outmode got extracted a few years ago, which is amazing since he's a hundred and eighty something. Ever since he got extracted, his hair's been going white and falling out, and he's stooped, and his eyes've gone watery and sad (normal human beings don't live to be a hundred and eighty something—he's stopped declining, though, because normal Tersatellans are pretty tough still).

"Great," he sighs, relaxing against the couch. "I knew I could count on you for at least getting into trouble, Rat. Been handling that for years before us. Now, I haven't been so involved in this as you and Vici, so tell me I've got this right. The Adamantration will be afraid of both of you. DOs—alright, discipline operatives—will hesitate to apprehend you because they don't want to face the wrath of the Remainder who'll look up to you now. Okay," he says when I nod. "Great to know you criminal types all have each other's backs. It was a big risk, I'll tell you that, and it comes with responsibilities. You can't stop now, you're in this life for good, you're a Next until it's your cue to exit the stage—but it comes with the possibility of great rewards. This speech's mostly for Vici, you know the drill." He waves me off. Infamous little me gives a smile.

"Vici says there were complications," Godfather Craig says, all animated and leaning forward. Godfather Craig is, well, unique. He's really a faulty citizen, but he also happens to be a faulty rapture man. Rapture men are all Craigs because they don't have names the way teachers don't. People used to call them Rapture when they were addressing one personally, until someone started calling them Craig, and now all we cutouts do it, so now we have to call our Craig "Godfather Craig" because otherwise we get confused.

"The Porcupine showed up." I shrug, rolling the bulb around in my hands. "He let me go, though. It was no big deal."

My mind's already running on how I can get answers without talking about the note. I haven't told anyone about it.

"You got to meet him?" Godfather Craig is stunned. "Rat, that's a big deal! What was he like?"

"Oh, you know, exactly how you would and wouldn't expect him to be. He might as well've been speaking Latin, for all the sense he made." Both the Godfathers smile and nod, but I stop messing with the bulb and frown, thinking. "Something bugged me about what he said, though. I mean, everything bugged me, but..." Now, I'm not one to share my thoughts with people, but I've lived with the Godfathers for a couple of years now. I adopted Vici after stealing her socks, and she knew the Godfathers, and I let her bring them along, and here we are now. I wouldn't call us a gang or anything tight, but maybe one of them has a knack for translating nonsense, so I spill the facts. "He seemed to think I was doing something that even *I* didn't know I was doing, and if that wasn't enough, he said... What was it he told me?"

"Was it the thing about courage, Rat?" Vici offers. "Rat says the Porcupine doesn't want to wish us luck."

"Well, luck's never really worked too good for him," Godfather Outmode mutters to himself. I shake my head, because I can deal with people not wanting me to be lucky, considering I get shot at on a daily basis. Vici keeps going.

"Didn't you say he told you something about a bay?"

Godfather Craig straightens up on the couch, and there's something off in his voice. "A bay? What about a bay?"

I snap my fingers. "Oh, yeah! He said I was 'aiming for the bay,' whatever that is. Hudson Bay, he said." The Godfathers give each other a serious look, and my suspicion spikes. "What? You know what he's talking about?"

"Rat, there obviously are no more bays, not for us," Godfather Outmode snaps, getting to his feet to go get his blanket. "Tersatellus is surrounded by a wall. We don't have an ocean. We don't have a rest-of-the-world. It's nothing but Tersatellus, and that's all you'll ever live to see. Now, I'm going to bed, and I think you should too, not that you ever listen to me. You got what you wanted. Now that you've gotten into and out of a Steele residency alive, the Adamantration is afraid of you. They won't come hunting you down because you're too dangerous, and Vici's safe now too. As safe as it gets, anyway. You're at the top of the food chain now, and there's nowhere left to go, alright? Unless you want to be the Kill Switch, you're good enough." With that, he snags the blanket off the other couch, goes back to his, and curls up on his side.

"Um... yes, sir," I say, pocketing the bulb and drifting away, thinking that when we got extracted, "good enough" is exactly what we all ran away from.

- II -

Cause of Action

Vici runs to our bedroom as I walk into the kitchen and sit down at the table, putting the bulb on the top of the candleholder, where it's got no chance of running away. Now that it's green, it doesn't give off as much light, but the sight of it alone is energizing. When I jumped up to get it, I half expected myself to get electrocuted to death on the spot. That is a bolt of lightning, liquefied. I stare at it, mesmerized by the sluggish ebb and flow as it throws throbbing green light on me and the walls. It's green at standard temperature and pressure, but when I hold it in my hands, flecks of red flicker in the emerald glow. Steele must've been changing its temperature to make it go white, which would explain why it seemed cold to me when I grabbed it. How it goes from white to green to red, I don't know, so don't ask.

Vici floats back into the room and sits down across from me. We don't usually talk much outside of robbing, and I've only split (that means "stole stuff," in case you didn't know the criminal lingo—the actual act of stealing is the swoop and the whole plan is a gig) with her a couple times because I like working alone, but somehow, we've got this quiet understanding of each other. She gives me a shy smile. "We did it," she whispers, careful not to wake up the Godfathers in the other room.

"Yeah" is all I say, shaking my head. "I'll bet it's all over the Plexus."

"Of course not. The Adamantration may be concerned, of course, but the public is unaffected." She sounds as disgusted about the whole white-lie thing Public Prosperity does with the public as I am. They think that telling less of the story keeps everyone safer. The worst part is, they're right. "Still, it got the job done. I can detect shy traces of worry in the reports. It seems we're not the only ones taking this route. Our radical race is having a last hurrah of sorts as Criminal Resolution tries to snuff it out. This is good, Rat. They're panicking now. They're getting to the bottom of the barrel and finding us, the guck they can't scrape off no matter how hard they try. It seems the Next is the last."

I drum my fingers on the table, worried myself, and skeptic as always. "Yeah, I guess we did it. But..." Vici watches me intently while I work out the words, but I can't come up with anything eloquent. "I don't believe it. We can't be last, can't be waiting for our cue out. They cued us out a long time ago. The public doesn't even know we exit. And now?" The hint of thunder and greater things roll around in my mind. "It feels more like we're waiting for our cue to get back on stage to me, to show the world that this isn't it. I mean ... This can't be it. I don't believe it. Do you really?"

She looks at me gravely for another minute with a strange look on her face. "Rat. If this was it, if this was the end of the road, the curtain call, then what would we need courage for?"

"Don't tell me you believe that garbage," I scoff, even as I find myself believing it more every second.

Still not looking away, Vici pulls out her beacon and sets it on the table. I take the cue and do the same with mine. It's a thin silver disk the size of my palm with a blank glass screen on one side and a switch on the edge. It gives us news every day on anything that applies to us: a new deal on reimplanting the mainframes, a new incarceration technique, etcetera. This is all they gave us when they took away our mainframes. They welcomed our decision to be cut out. And they warned us not to do it for the wrong reason, that if we took the last step forward and cast ourselves with the wrong lot, then the Adamantration and its seven Sectors were no longer going to deal with us, that the only involvement they would have in our lives would be the end of them. That they would clean up our dead bodies after we starved away without their help, or that their discipline ops would put a bullet in our heads if we dared resort to crime to sustain ourselves.

I dared.

Five years later, here I am, with a stolen piece of Adaman property sitting in my candleholder.

Without even thinking about it, I flick on the beacon. It's something we do every night, look through what's going on, what big tags died today, whatever. I'm secretly hoping that our swoop gets on our news tonight.

The way Vici doesn't turn on her beacon tips me off that whatever tonight's message is, she already saw it. I squint at her for a second, wondering what she's hiding from me, as boring, normal news scrolls across the beacon.

Then something strictly unnormal happens. The screen flickers, and new words appear: SET DOWN. I put the beacon on the table, glancing at the living room nervously. Vici nods in support. The beacon beeps once, and then the compass rose comes up on the screen—it's our national symbol, and all the Sector symbols have some variation of it. There's an audio symbol next, warning that there's gonna be sound. Then the screen changes to that of a tiny video of some sort, where there are three important-looking people standing, and I know this video must be centuries old because two of them are dead or resigned by now, and one sucker's still holding on.

Absolon Vastate, creator of the Plexus and the only ever Adaman of Public Prosperity, mortal enemy of pretty much every cutout and especially me.

Vici holds her hands out to stop me from turning the beacon off, motioning for me to let it play.

"Greetings, offender," the guy to his left says. The cruddy audio hazes his voice, and I don't recognize him, but he's actually wearing the dumb yellow suit, so I can tell what Sector he belongs to before he says it. "My name is Honani Ways, and I am the first Adaman of Criminal Resolution, once the Integrity Support Sector before crime and criminals grew to a rate where it could not be handled so simply. If you have turned on this beacon and are receiving this message, that can only mean one thing: that too many of your unruly race have turned against the laws for whatever reason. There are many cases in which breaking the law is pardonable—situations of desperation, of helplessness, lacking control or sound mind, or another option to keep one's self alive, especially after deciding to extract one's self from society. However, some take this too far for reasons that are not to be taken lightly. If this society is to remain intact, people must adhere to the rules, yet this is impossible when there is such a supply of people willing to break them. It has always been this way, and as Adaman of the Criminal Resolution Sector, it has been my mission to thwart such rule-breakers. It was the suggestion of Honorée Jattends, first Adaman of the Technology Sector"—the woman in question nods—"and the sociological input from Absolon Vastate, Adaman of Public Prosperity, that led us to our conclusion."

Now he's gotta say something. "Many years ago, as I was trying to brainstorm ways to get rid of criminals such as yourself, especially the Next ones, which were threatening to overwhelm life as we knew it—as it must be so again now, if you are receiving this message—it occurred to me that the only reason that people resort to such crimes is if they want to either flaunt their freedom to sin or to sustain themselves after being cut out. In short, your desire for something you call liberty is what ruins society. As this came to me, I began to dream of a way to explain to you that the freedom that you are looking for is bloody and corrupted, while the freedom that I offer to all citizens is pure and perfect. I dreamed of saving those of you who were salvageable enough to someday realize this and get rid of those of you who are too stubborn to see sense."

My fists clench under the table. He's trying. He has to try to hate us. It has to be a conscious effort because that's who he has to be since he settled the Plexus and peace and prosperity, and we're everything on the outside of that, and then there's that little bit about salvageable people that slips out, and you can almost tell yourself he can't hate us as much as he tries to, but I refuse to tell myself that, refuse not to hate him, and I don't have to try. All I have to do is listen and not think about the handwriting on the note I found in the box.

The Tech Adaman steps in now, and I can tell this was her idea. "The simplest thing, in this case, would be for you to turn yourselves in to be retaught or executed in one great extermination that kills all the infective thoughts of freedom in your mind or all the rodents of wickedness in society. But since you are unpredictable and selfish beings abusing the freewill given to all people, there would be no way to get you to do this, because it would have no benefit for you. So I reasoned that if there is a possibility of benefit for you, then you would willingly give yourselves over. After thinking it out and working together, we have created a method of drawing you in, separating the auspicious from the hopeless, and returning what's left of you to society as good citizens once more."

Sir Adaman Ways takes another turn with, "During this special occasion, if you qualify to partake in it, some of you will be directly chosen, and more of you will be later chosen to take part within a stage we call the Hudson Bay. Only the most critical criminals in Tersatellus will qualify, so though you may not have known it, for every rule you've broken, you have pushed yourself closer to this occasion, shouldered yourself farther up the line until you might be, well, Next."

I close my eyes in a sickening shock of awe and fear. *Maybe you don't know what you're up to, but I do: you're aiming for the Bay.* Cielhomme, he was right.

It's Vastate's turn again. "The rest of the nation does not know about this competition, and that is the way it ought to stay lest the public take interest and skew the results. It is a race, designed to destroy the cruel and the weak and reward the noble and the strong. For every cutout that survives will receive on their beacons a thousand primes and a day. One thousand primes to do whatever it takes to become wholly Tersatellan again. One day of total Adamantration immunity to do it in. Yes, during the days that you earn, the rapture operatives will be blind to you, and the discipline operatives who have chased you so diligently will look the other way from everything that you do, whether it be illegally erasing your criminal record, having one last party before rejoining us peacefully, or indulging the last of your criminal cravings, if you have any left."

Me and Vici look at each other, eyes wide.

"And if you should win this contest? Prove that you alone are the greatest criminal lord in Tersatellus, the Champion over all the rest? Your prize is at least one million primes and Adamantration immunity for the rest of your life."

My heart stops, I'm sure.

"This message serves as a forewarning," Sir Adaman Ways says gravely. "If this is the path that you choose, make sure you understand that this challenge is not going to be easy." The image seems to find my eyes and deliver its side message to me alone: "But if this is the path you turn away from, I think you know what happens then."

My eyes close, trying to shut out the truth, but he's right. I know what happens next—I've been thinking about it for a long time. The thing is, we're running out of options. Discipline workers are getting smarter, warehouses are getting tighter, people've been snooping around our residency… Altogether, we can't keep going like this. We're drowning in a tide of hopelessness, and the wave of the end is bearing down on us. This lifeline Vastate's throwing us is probably barbed wire, but I realize with a surge of dread that it may be our only option.

It is a cue back on stage.

"Now, we will disappear from this beacon in a matter of seconds, and the display unit will turn into a button. If you get rid of this beacon or ignore this message for one hour, you walk away from this path anyway, and I can only hope that discipline operatives will find you and mow you down for your cowardice. When you press the button, however, the Adamantration will know where you are. They will not try to kill you, lure you from your hiding place, destroy your hiding place, etcetera. Instead, a rapture operative will arrive at your hiding place at midnight to give you a letter. If you do not qualify to partake in this challenge, then the letter will inform you that there are discipline operatives waiting out of sight to shoot you, and then they will shoot you. However, if you do qualify, then this letter will relay instructions on how to participate. All letters arrive at the same time, so *you* are the only source of your advantages and disadvantages. Take care, offender. I hope to see you soon."

With that hanging over our heads, the image disappears, and the screen goes dark again, popping up slightly. Almost as soon as it comes up, I press it down.

Vici jumps. "Rat, didn't you hear them? We're two teenage girls—well, you're older and technically a woman, but still young and not very str—well, you know." She's twisting her braid. "What makes you think we can survive this? We don't know anything about this thing! I've scoured the Plexus, looked as deep as I can into the Adamantration system, but there's not a word about it. And what about the Godfathers? I don't want to leave them, and I don't want to die," she adds quietly.

"Listen, Vici, we're both gonna die either way. How do you want to die, exactly? Do you want to get capped by a discipline op when we get unlucky one day? Starve to death as an old lady when you can't steal anything anymore? As for me, I'd rather die trying."

"Trying what? Rat, weren't you paying attention at all? It's meant to make us change our mind about being thieves!"

"I know that. That's the thing. If we get through this, then we can take their thousand vanilla and their days, and we can show them that they can't change us, either, because we'll go right back to being thieves afterward. This'll be nothing worse than a really elaborate swoop, and we're stealing it right from the Adamantration. If one of us wins, then with a million v—sorry, primes—they won't be able to touch us."

"Hardly anyone survives slighting Vastate, Rat," she reminds me shakily. I do my best not to laugh. Oh, if only she knew.

"Hardly anyone survives *anything* anymore, Vici!" I argue instead of explaining. "Aren't you tired of *surviving* all the time? Because I am. I'm sick of it. I'm sick of holding on to nothing and pretending that the Adamantration will ever be afraid of us, pretending that it'll be okay when it won't. That's why we got extracted, was to stop pretending all the time, and that's why we went sour, was to be better than okay."

Vici winces as that memory gets dumped into the light, and I'm right there with her. Whoever you are, I'll be honest with you: we cutouts don't have it easy at extraction. When Vici turned to me and the Godfathers for help, I hesitated, cuz I didn't want another mouth to feed, let alone three, but it was obvious she wasn't looking for handouts. She didn't want to be part of another family. It didn't take a psychologist to see that she was still hurt since when her last group rejected her, because that's what they do. The people that didn't get to pick you can never really understand or (heaven forbid) love you. So I wasn't sure what to do even after letting her crash at my resi, but then she took me out on a swoop and showed me her skill, explaining sheepishly that she'd learned how to hack through the Plexus, which she still had some limited access to.

This occurrence was nothing short of divine, even though she further explained, shamefaced, that it made her have seizures sometimes—not usually when she was in the Plexus, but at random. That was the price she paid for her freedom, and that humiliation reflects in her eyes every day, especially now that I've brought up the extractions. "Vici," I say so she looks up at me. "Everyone has a sacrifice they have to make to have a chance to get ahead, to keep fighting. But not everybody makes it, because whether or not that sacrifice overwhelms you depends on how far you're willing to take it. We take risks every day not to just get by but to be better than 'good enough.' This might be our last chance. Aren't you willing to take it?"

Vici purses her lips. Either she's thinking or she's frustrated with me for pretending to have an encouraging speech and throwing in "take" everywhere I can because I take everything, literally. Then she pushes the button so quietly I almost don't notice her do it until she nods at me. "Let's see how far we can get it to go."

There it is. I knew that under all that dignity and calculation, there's greed and pride and a sense of adventure strong enough to manipulate. Teenage melodrama. It's a beautiful thing.

Sneaking past the Godfathers, we both run into the bedroom, pulling our long LPGs (lightweight penetration guns) out from underneath the bed and climbing up the ladder into the attic. I kick the ladder away and pull the panel closed before joining Vici at the small hole in the front of the attic, where the drafty air comes in, chilling me so I remember to pull my jacket back on and ditch the stupid hat. "Rat?" Vici hisses softly, maybe afraid to wake some ghosts up here. "I know we practiced these things many times and all, but I-I've never shot a *person* before."

"And odds are, you never will. This is just a precaution. Vastate told us the rapture man wouldn't kill us, but I trust him about as far as I could throw him with my eyeballs, upside-down, underwater, if I didn't have any eyeballs. This is only in case those beacons told every discipline worker in a twenty-kilometer radius where we are. Remember, shoot for the arms so that they can't shoot us."

As if our aim is anywhere near that good.

She's quiet for a bit longer.

"And what if we're not bad enough to participate?"

At least that's what you hear it as. Me, however, I know Vici. I know what she means is, what if she's not bad enough to participate. A worried glance tells me I'm right.

But I roll my eyes and play it cool. "Vici, we stole a ball of energy from one of the most important men on earth. Knowing that, they have no choice but to qualify us, unless they want us to kill Vastate or something, which I half wouldn't mind, anyway. Listen. I think the Porcupine might've known what he was talking about, after all. We didn't know it, but I guess we really were 'aiming for the bay' when we tried stealing from him—it wasn't just for the gangs' protection, it was to qualify for this race, which is probably taking place in that bay."

"But what if they didn't enter it into the system that we did that? What if they send out the rapture men early so they can get to everyone at the right time, and we're too late, they don't know, and they come out to kill us?"

I check my watch. Illegally imported Rolex, by the way. Solar powered. Extra compartment on the bottom so you could hide a bracelet or a secret message or something else that's more important than some stupid bracelet. "It's only eleven, and they get here at twelve, anyway. What's going to happen is, they're gonna leave our letters in front of the door and leave. When they go, you stay here where it's safe, and I'll go down and get the envelopes. If you hear gunshots, you know what to do. Lockdown procedure. Now, put your gun down, we've got some time before they get here. Whatever happens, we have to do what that letter says and get to wherever this race is taking place, and fast. There's a loophole here—there's raptures out, and they won't try to kill us when they drop off the letters, but nobody said anything about what they'll do when we leave. Look at me. They have no definite way of identifying us cutouts, so I could be Victoria Oile or even Doug-Hurts-Less for all they know. If only one of us qualifies, you pick who's going, kid." (That's my loving way of saying that I've got a bigger reputation, so if I get picked without Vici, she can still go if she really wants to.)

"Rat—"

"Not now. I'm in charge here, and I'm going to ensure your survival even if I get left behind, because I'm just that wonderful, capiche? Now, after we get the letter, I'll call up to you if it's safe, and we'll get into the car and go. We'll turn off the MechTeamster and find our own way through traffic. We've got flashlights? Multitools? Lighters? Okay, good. Want to go over our probable rivals?"

"Rat," Vici repeats, more serious. She reaches through the darkness until she finds my shoulder with her shaking hand. My stomach drops, but I try not to let it show. I understand and scoot next to her, pulling off my jacket and putting it on the floor, which I lower her to, using the jacket as a pillow.

"It's okay, it's okay. Sorry I didn't get you the first time. I mean, uh, shut up, you, you're gonna be fine," I tell her as she starts shaking harder. I gently help her get onto her side and back away, keeping on talking to her even though I know she can't hear me, feeling helpless and terrified at the same time even though it's happened before. Because this is all I can do when this happens, as she forces deep breaths and locks her limbs close to her. That's the best she can do, while all I can do is sit here uselessly, trying to talk her back, wondering when it's going to end or *if* it'll end. And I won't talk about it anymore because one of the only things we cutouts can have is our pride, and Vici is too important to me, so I can't bear to shame her. Just don't tell her I said that.

Five minutes later, she's back to sitting up again next to me, silent. We don't talk about it, either. We sit in silence as we wait for our judgment to come.

⇹

At some point, deep in our worry about this messenger guy, I get up and grab a box of crackers and a bottle of water, raspberry flavored. The attic isn't heated, so of course the water's nice and cold, but so are we. My breath fogs in the dim light coming in from the hole, streaming from the shining city. Farsia is one more city out of the many I've seen. Before Vici, I've also been to North Bering Island, Zenith, San Angeles, Nagasaki, Macabreak-Frère Jacques, Joanndu, Nouvelle Paris, Kiev, Duchess City, and more. I get around. I hear things. I know people. I've been rolling since day one, and I plan on only getting bigger.

"Probable rival numbers one and two," Vici starts quietly, breaking my reverie. "The Magic Hands Bros, or Les Malins, Mac and Jacques. Tagged after the twin cities they grew up in, Macabreak and Frère Jacques, thought to be the most powerful pair in city history. There's rumors of Mac having opticorrection, but it's not likely. Duos are especially strong, and I know for a fact that Jacques won't go anywhere without his little brother. Mac isn't quite as sharp, and he's younger than us, but he's incredible with his hands, so he's also tagged Mr. Fixit, and he has one heck of a bodyguard. Jacques is the mastermind, cunning, cold, deceptive, ruthless, and rumored to be responsible for several disasters that people simply can't find evidence to blame him for. Thus, he is also tagged Dr. Storm for his inability to be resisted, comprehended, or stopped. However, such a title also comes with the inability to make many friends, which I'm sure will be necessary wherever we're going."

"He'd better not be there," I say, even though the Adamantration'd have to be insane not to qualify the duo. They're so Next it's not even funny. Together, they have very few weaknesses, and it's said there's hardly anyone worse than them, but those worse people are the anomalies that wouldn't need to come to the challenge to survive, so Mac and Jacques stay at the top of the list. "Probable rival numbers three and four: the Dollhouse Girls, also Puppet Girls, Wicked Sisters Lily and Ivy. Their tags come from merchandise: there's something called lily stimulant that temporarily cuts off all connection to mainframes so an electrode can pretend to be a cutout, and the IVY, a weapon that nobody knows what the letters stand for, but it can shoot through five meters of solid rock." Vic nods, storing the information away. "They shouldn't be that much of a problem, at least Ivy won't be. Lily might be tougher, but she's a cold-hearted dog. Acts all smart and stuff, but she's really not. They don't get along, so she's willing to leave her sister behind."

"That's rule number one. Never leave your partner behind," Vici points out, and I nod. "Probable rival number five: Muscle, also tagged Gunshow and Warbunker because he uses steroids and other homespun and pawned drugs to make himself nearly superhuman, plus he has the advantage of age." She thinks a second about the age thing. "Rat, do you think Steele would qualify?"

I shiver. "I don't know, but I hope not. Then again, this is the guy who takes the last number of pi and divides it by zero to defy physics and destroy matter," I joke. "Honestly, seeing him alone was scary. I know you probably think he's pretty cool and all, but you know I can't like him, cuz he's the Tech Adaman, and I hope I never have to see him in person again. Once was enough for me. Twice was pushing it."

"You've seen him before?" Vici gasps.

I shrug. "You know, out on the street. I get around. But I can't think of any crimes he's done, so we should be safe." That's not the entire truth—some vague memory fuzzes around the edges of my mind, something that put the Adamantration in uproar, but I can't get a hold of it. It was a long time ago, anyway, and it must've been pardoned if he's Adaman. Maybe he was a victim of it. I don't know.

"How about the Kill Switch?" Vici whispers. You only talk about the Kill Switch in whispers. It's an urban legend, like Bigfoot or whatever, but people pay more attention to this unnamed felon that tried the biggest swoop ever thought up, and nobody but the Kill Switch even knows what they tried to seize (people called the famous swoop the Seizure, much to Vici's dismay). They failed but only mostly. "Do you think he's coming out of hiding for this?"

As a woman who'd want to be front-page news every day if the news had pages, I'm offended she thinks the Kill Switch is a guy. "Vici, nobody's even seen the Kill Switch before. There's rumors *they* died halfway through the Seizure, and *they* probably don't exist, anyway. What makes you think—"

"Shh!" Vici suddenly hisses, and I tense. "Do you hear that?"

I peek my head out the gap in the wall. There's a man with a fancy badge and retinas that flicker faster than a bad VDU. He's got a DC-5 gun in one hand. Shoving Vici out of view of the hole, I stick the tip of my own LPG out of it, training it on the rapture man's gun arm despite knowing that with my aim, I should probably aim at my own foot if I want a shot (heh) at hitting him. "He's got something in his other hand," I mumble under my breath when a fresh gust of cold air from the traffic blows in through the window, carrying my voice away from the ears of the rapture man. My watch clicks midnight the second he sets the thing down right in front of our door. "We wait until he's way gone."

"Rat, don't you think we need the advantage over the others? You could take him. He's only one man, and I know what you can do to people."

"Vic, those are vicious rumors spread to ruin my good name and slander my persona of grace and humbleness," I whine.

"With all due respect, you may stuff it. Go downstairs and open the door a little, reach out, and take the letter. He probably won't even notice you, let alone try to hurt you. Don't deny that you're sneaky, or I shall slap you."

"It's probably a trap, and I don't trust it," I growl, watching the retreating figure for a few seconds. Vici crosses her arms and opens her mouth to begin the trial with the point that I accepted this whole extermination thing, yet I'm too scared of one operative I've faced down before. I know she's really alright with being left alone, so I put my hands up and sigh. "Alright, by the time I get down there, he'll be out of sight, anyway," I reason as I back up, moving slowly toward the panel, jumping downstairs without a sound. Vici pulls the panel shut behind me, and I make my way toward the front door, opening it carefully and reaching out onto the ground like the outside air is contaminated. My fingers reach the pieces of paper without incident and swipe them inside.

Without even looking at them, I run back to the bedroom and leap up through the panel hole, which Vici opened for me again.

She flicks on the flashlight, and we sit cross-legged, facing each other. The envelopes are real paper, faintly golden. I rip mine open to find another small folded piece of paper, sealed with the corona of Justice Incorporated, which is the dramatically named Criminal Resolution company responsible for making discipline weapons and chartering rehab facilities and those awful discipline men armories on wheels with the sirens. Tearing the corona down the middle—it's some kind of crosshairs inside the Criminal Resolution halo—I open the paper. Vici does the same, and we read together.

CONGRATULATIONS.

YOU HAVE HEREBY QUALIFIED TO TAKE PLACE IN AN EVENT HOSTED TO REGULATE CRIMINAL ACTIVITY. IF YOU WISH TO ENTER, THEN MAKE YOUR WAY TO ZENITH IMMEDIATELY AND GET TO THE CASTAWAY POINT. ARRIVE BEFORE SUNRISE AT SIX IN THE MORNING OR ELSE YOU WILL BE DISQUALIFIED. A CERTAIN NUMBER OF YOU WILL BE CHOSEN TO BE CAST AWAY FIRST, DEPENDING ON HOW MUCH SOCIETY WOULD BENEFIT FROM HAVING YOU REMOVED SOONER. AFTER THESE ARE CHOSEN AND SEPARATED FROM THE REMAINDER, THE WEEK TO COME WILL BE EXPLAINED SEPARATELY TO EACH GROUP. A MEAL WILL BE SERVED BEFORE QUALIFIERS ARE CAST AWAY, AT WHICH POINT THE ADAMANTRATION WILL HAVE LIMITED TO NO CONTROL OF WHAT HAPPENS, AND EVERYTHING THEREAFTER IS LEFT IN THE HANDS OF THE COMPETITORS.
TAKE YOUR BEACONS.
GET TO ZENITH.
STAND BY FOR DAY ONE OF YOUR EXTERMINATION.

My head snaps up. "Get to the car."

It all makes sense now! I think as I scramble to my feet. *That's where the Next and Remainder terms came from, from this crazy extermination thing! And—* my trail of thought stops with my feet when I notice Vici hasn't moved. "Vici?"

She winces, a look between panic and pain on her face. "Shouldn't we ask the Godfathers first?" she asks, but I know her good enough to see she's scared because this suddenly got real. We can go, and our lives will change for good no matter what happens, and that scares the heck out of Vici.

I sigh and grab her shoulders. *One more speech*, I tell myself and think, and I put some meaning into it and say, "Look, kid. Here's something funny I've figured out about Fate: all the big stuff it throws at you, it usually comes with a question that's something along the lines of 'what if?' What if I decide not to be a piece of the perfect picture anymore—does that make me criminal or heroic? What if I pick freedom over happiness—does that make me fickle or determined? What if I join forces with this kid I hardly know? What if I let this rookie tag along with me tonight, what happens then, huh? And the funny thing about it all is, there's no way for you to know until you make the choice. The only part you *do* know before that is the answer to the question you ask yourself: 'why not?'" I let go of Vici's shoulders. "So what if we hauled ourselves over to Zenith to enter in this crazy competition that's meant for killing the Next?"

"The Godfathers would kill us if the extermination didn't, that's what."

"And what if you're wrong? What if we win?"

"Oh, that'll never happen!"

I give her a wink. "Why not?"

Vici gives me a look that tells me she can think of a bunch of reasons why not then bites her lip. "Well, we've got to get halfway across the country in less than six hours first." She leaps out the gap in the wall, and I jump after her, pleasantly surprised. "Still, this isn't fair. We're so far away from Zenith!" she yells as she busts open the door to the garage and jumps into the passenger's seat of the car. The thing's a fricking Paramount Jonquil (read: piece of junk), but at least she can open it with whatever Plexus she's got left. "It's north, and we're in one of the farthest south cities there is. Our qualifications all depend on how far we are from Zenith!"

"No, our qualifications depend on us and how quick on our feet we are. Every discipline op in sight is already gonna be trying to shoot us down. There's no way we could get into any more trouble, so we can do whatever it takes to get to Zenith faster. North, you said?" Vici nods as I turn the car on, gritting my teeth as the buzz kicks in. A screen asks me if I want manual mode. "Oh, yes, I do." I hit the button and slam the car into reverse, the pressure pads on the floor causing the sliding panel to shoot up as I swing out of the hangar, turning onto our front yard.

"Rat, what're you doing?"

"Getting us qualified!" I floor it, spinning the wheel hard so we skid into the tight area between our residency and the one to our left then speed out onto someone else's front lawn until we get into an alley and peel off onto the street instead of waiting at the end of our drive for traffic to break for us. Other mobiles sense our presence and swerve in mechanical panic as I fly forward, gaining speed and diving for the faster inner lane, using any gap there is to get us one more mobile ahead.

"YOU'RE INSANE!" Vici screams, and I smile dangerously, howling with laughter. The whole flying-car-of-the-future joke occurs to me, and I start laughing even more as we soar.

All around us, none of the pedestrians have any idea this is going on.

As we scrape between more mobiles and settle into traffic again, sweeping around to get onto the right roads, I remember how the image of Vastate told us that the public wasn't supposed to know about this whole race thing, and I hope that they don't catch on. In their own little worlds, even if they look up, they might not even know what's happening. Either they'll be so enveloped in whatever they're doing, they won't notice, or the Adamantration will feed them some bullsticks lie. *This is an examination of how well mobiles handle and how durable they are. The mobile is being driven by a professional driver with your safety on their mind. There is no way you will be harmed.*

And once again, the worst thing is it's technically true.

I shake my head, gritting my teeth. Not a *second* has ever passed me by where I've missed that life in the slightest, where I've regretted giving a salute to the people of my house and running out the door before they could stop me. Even though I never saw any of them again.

The buildings run out, and the glass walls stop, and I jump back to reality. "We're out of the city. Now we avoid roads to get away from traffic and go full speed to Zenith," I explain, swerving again to bumble right off the road and onto the ground, where there is no suggested traffic speed, and I can go as fast as I want. "We can merge back into the traffic if we come up to roads and the ice rivers when we have to. Thanks to you working on this thing, we're going a good ten times faster than anything legal. Fifteen times faster than anything Paramount Mobile-Auto could spit out, anyway." It's been an ongoing joke that the only Tersatellan company geared solely toward mobiles makes the worst. "At our speed, it should be a piece of cake to get there by dawn. You tell me if we need to turn or anything. Once we leave a city, I'm lost."

Vici takes a few minutes of quiet to try and settle herself down. We have to merge at one point, but nobody notices, and I add endangerment to my list of crimes. "Aim us slightly to the right," she finally manages, and I do. "We'll have to pass through Hiro and Laketown if we want to go straight."

"Then we don't want to go straight. We can't keep hopping through cities that crazy way, or the Adamantration might call an air strike on us," I kid. "We'll go around. It'll be faster that way."

"In that case, at our current speed, it'll take us five hours. And forty-eight minutes. Give or take thirty-two seconds." She seems calmer after that. I think she still finds comfort in the Plexus, especially with the calculator, which calculates nearly anything. Even though it's really smart, it's simple compared to most things in the Plexus, so she hardly has to go anywhere to get to it, making it almost like another limb that she can command subconsciously. She's also got street maps she accesses a lot. That's okay with me. They can't control her thoughts or anything, so whatever she has to do is probably safe. Besides, no matter where you get them from, spewing facts is something all of us do to calm down. Facts don't have emotions, so they're the best way you can pretend you don't feel anything, either.

Minutes pass without incident as we fly through kilometers of nowhere. Giant, abandoned solar panels glitter the landscape more and more the farther we get from the city. I crank up the heating in the car as we get out of reach of Farsia's air-control particles, which keep the oxygen levels stable and keep the air above the freezing point for the most part even though it's close to the North Pole. In the cities, it's easy to pretend that everything's normal, but out here in forsaken land, things get cold, and the sky fades into colors other than blue above us; tiny pinpricks of light poke through its deep violet canvas, and ribbons of otherworldly colors dance above the crusty ground. It spits up as dust behind us as we speed across it, dust the color of rust, so I make sure all the windows are tight and the car's air monitoring niche works all right. In some places out here, the air isn't filtered, so breathing it is bad enough without all the dust destroying your lungs.

That dust threatens the lives of anything it touches, and it all comes from the huge scrapyards littered around—in the darkness, I can almost imagine the one by us as sick farms from some other dimension. Piles of metals and shells and junk are heaped into the sky, making towers of their own, along with metal boxes for houses, so I imagine it as a city instead. It's all covered in orange rust, which works so fast I can watch as a pile collapses in on itself, the rust eating away at the last of its support. The rust eats everything out here. It's almost alive, they say, because it's not just in the metal; it's in the dirt, it's in the air, and if you so much as get a papercut, it'll fester and leave a great scar if you survive the pain.

The Adamantration doesn't see any point in sending out the air-control particles this far out of the cities, and besides, we needed somewhere to dump our garbage. With the Public Prosperity Sector ensuring a stable population, there's never been any need to expand any of the cities or anything, so there was all this useless land that was contaminated by the substances left over from blasting the nation flat for building on, plus there was extra building material. Thus, the scrapyards. We throw everything into them. They slowly eat themselves to nothing, and we put another one right on top of its remains. The only problem they create is the rust-dust.

Now the Adamantration has another use for the Divide: it makes it so that there's literally no wind in Tersatellus. They cut off everything from the ocean, and some grid woven into the ground keeps the pressure balanced so no wind comes from the sea and none of it comes from the ground, and the hoppers are NEVER allowed to have any sort of fan over these places—therefore, the only moving air comes out of mouths and mobiles, so if they keep the roads far enough from the scrapyards, the rust-dust doesn't move, and nobody breathes it in, and everything's fine.

And here's us, raising dust and heading for the most important city in Tersatellus.

The discipline ops must be out of their minds right now. They're not much more elite than your common civilian, so them trying to fathom driving a car or any other generic mobile off-road where it can kick up chemicals is probably real difficult for them. Nobody chases us or anything. While we're out of the cities, nobody gives a care what we do. I could blow up this car right here, and would it matter? No, they have all the land they need, and this isn't part of it. We're free to go, and we spend long, quiet stretches of time going and going and going, deeper into dark night until we're nothing but another diamond in the sky.

"Hiro, straight ahead," Vici announces, twirling her fiery braid in a bored way. There's sable streaks in her hair, so she looks tigerish, or maybe uncertain on whether she's us or them, metal or rust, and she has to hide her half-cutout mind behind her half-cutout hair. She got the streaks from a tampered DIY hair kit she nabbed from the general retailer we burgled last week—she's been doing it as long as I've known her, so there's no proof her hair's not black with orange stripes, really. I don't see the point, but when we're walking down the street, it's her that people try and access in the Plexus, not me. She never makes a reply, of course, since she can't go that far into the Plexus, so she smiles and keeps on walking, while I trudge along behind, trying to identify threats. I know I'm not the pretty one here. It never even occurs to me to do anything special to my appearance or give myself "auxiliaries," as Godfather Craig calls them.

Well, almost never, anyway. Three exceptions isn't much.

We go around Hiro. I tell myself it looks the same as Farsia, and everything's all the same and boring in Tersatellus, but I know it isn't true. I mean, look at Joanndu. Cielhomme.

I get a thought. "Vici, do you think it's possible to hack into the Adamantration system and figure out where the other beacons are at? Maybe we can see how far they are from this Zenith place."

"I don't have a computer, so I don't think I'd be able to."

Nodding, I launch us through another road. It's almost instinct by now. We keep rolling on, turning around Laketown without anything else to look at, nothing to stop us but the roads. Any hill is gradual, and any lake or river can be avoided. We pass the Nasrin Gulf of the Great Sea, and I can see people there, and they don't even do anything. The whole world's nothing but dirt and sky and ice and roads of people that don't even notice us flying past them. "So stupid," I find myself muttering. My voice has acid in it cuz of this great headache I'm getting. I'm not the best person to road-trip with, by the way. "You're all so blind, I can't stand it."

"Rat?" Something in Vici's voice snaps me back.

"What, what's wrong?" I look around, trying to figure out what the threat is.

"Problem. We're running out of juice." She points to the fuel gauge, which is dangerously close to being zero.

"Oh, beautiful. Where's Zenith?"

"About ten K, straight from here. We might make it," Vici offers hopefully, but I already feel the mobile slowing.

"No, no, no! We were full when we left!" I hit the steering wheel with my fist. The towering city rises up in the distance, shadowed by a mass of darkness farther off. Seeing it makes my heart drop to the soles of my boots, totally distracting me. "Cielhomme," I breathe, "look at that."

Starlight glitters off the glorious buildings of Zenith, the northernmost city in the world. It has the tallest buildings, most averaging out to a few hundred stories, and it is the liquid lightning hotspot because of the harsh storms they get up here. A dozen colossal harvesters hang in the sky, each needing three buildings for support, some more filled than others. The largest one could fit a factory inside of it and needs five buildings to hold it up. Such power flows through those harvesters, the light they produce bathes the entire city in an eerie emerald glow.

It sits nearly on top of the barrier-wall of the enormous Divide, spiking up higher than any of the buildings at a strict four hundred stories high, fifty meters thick, full of stuff to ward off even atomic bombs, and giant MechGuards posted every hundred meters along the top to shoot down anything moving within that gets too close. Okay, some of that might be exaggeration, but it's no joke that the wall encircles the entirety of Tersatellus.

"Look! Zenith, a testimony to our progress! Look how self-sufficient and advanced we are, we can make cars that run out of fuel at the worst point possible! Ugh, if only we could split a mobile while it was moving!" I kick something. We're slowing even more. Maybe we're five kilometers away now, but we might as well be across the country. I stare at the fast-moving traffic for a second then back at the fuel gauge. "Hang on," I warn with that acid bubbling up again. "We're going to abuse this thing a little more. Turn the MechTeamster off all the way."

"Okay. Why?"

"Because that means we're invisible to all the others," I explain, turning sharply toward the rushing traffic. "BRACE FOR IMPACT!"

Another mobile hits our side with the force of a bomb as we shoot into the lane sideways. I nearly fly out the window, but it works—the car starts pushing us. These things were made to last forever, so neither of the cars are badly damaged, but I bet the MechTeamster in the other car is giving itself a MechAneurism trying to figure out why its speed has gone down inexplicably, as if it is pushing something that it cannot see.

"Rat?" Vici asks shakily as we jet into the city and operatives start seeing us again. "How are we supposed to get out of this?"

"Through the windows, I guess, or maybe out the door the way normal people do? Mine's not being barricaded by another car, so we can open mine and…" I stop there, looking out Vici's window into the car that's pushing us. *Oh, dear.*

"And what? Leap into hundred KPH traffic and hope not to get run over somehow? Try and jump ten meters to the top of the glass wall? And how do you suppose we don't get shot by the discipline operatives?"

I finally manage to swallow. "Um, Vici? I don't think it's the discipline men we gotta worry about." Vici turns around to see the guy in the car level a gun at us. "DUCK!" We both dive down to where he can't see us as a bullet goes through his windshield, Vici's window, my window, and the blast shield, until it finally lodges itself in a building. The resulting sonic attack is deafening. "WHAT KIND OF GUN'S HE GOT THAT CAN GO THROUGH FOUR

PANES OF BULLETPROOF GLASS?" I scream over the roar of traffic and the sound of the blast shield still shattering.

A head suddenly pops through Vici's window, and the guy's sitting on the hood of his speeding car, hands planted on the edges, the meter-long gun clamped under one hand. The madman has two lines and a four-pointed star dyed yellow into his hair on one side of his head. His jacket is the inverse, yellow with black stripes in a crazy caution-tape design, and his sunglasses are strictly black. Or I should say, sable. And now you know why I told you.

"HEY, KIDS! SORRY TO BREAK IT TO YOU, BUT YOU'RE NOT ON MY CARPOOLING LIST! GET THE HECK OFF OF MY CAR!" he bellows deeply and plants a foot on the side of our car, leaning back for a better grip. His jacket is nearly blowing off, and I get a brief glimpse of the upper part of his arms, and that's enough to know he's built as tough as a special aforementioned wall. The door starts denting under his foot, and we actually start veering into the other lane of traffic, which is going in the other direction. I don't think that this car could withstand that kind of impact anymore.

Panicking, Vici whips out her multitool and tries to slash his foot, but that boot is solid, so she goes for the ankle when his pant leg lifts in the wind.

I think he chuckles in response to getting stabbed.

"Figures," Vici growls, and I watch the traffic coming up in the lane we're heading closer to. Shaking my head, I grab the shot window and pull myself out and onto the roof, clutching the car for all I'm worth.

"VICI!" I howl, moving in tiny increments down the car to give her some room. "COME ON!"

She's yelling something about insanity being contagious as she pulls herself onto the roof of the car. The guy on the hood of his car watches us like he's got no idea what we're doing but frankly doesn't care.

"Get ready to let go when it hits!" I yell over the wind, hardly getting the last word in before the hood of our car enters the lane on the left. The bus it hits smashes the thing, carrying it along right out from underneath us. Our car didn't get far enough into the lane, though, so the back half of the car hits the front of the pushing car, jerking it to the side and knocking Spike, who I've identified by now, off to the side, leaving us with a landing pad. I hit the hood hard, jarring my shoulder and knee, but manage to roll into a somewhat steady position with my foot fixed onto the frame of the windshield. Ha! I'm amazing!

To my surprise, there's a person driving, her long leaden hair flying around in the wind, her purple eyes squinting at me. The sister sits in the passenger seat, staring at Vici, who's lying against the intact half of the windshield. *Lily and Ivy.*

"HEY!" Spike hollers, and when I look, he's hanging on to the edge of the car right above the wheel, gashes torn on his jacket sleeve and pant leg. He doesn't seem to notice he's been ripped open in various places by my now-missing car or that mobiles are rushing by not centimeters away from where he's hanging. His sunglasses are missing, but his eyes are so dark it almost doesn't matter. "THAT GUN COST ME AN ARM AND A LEG! AND LOOK WHAT YOU DID TO MY CAR!"

I reach over to him. "NEED A HAND, SPIKE?"

He rolls his eyes and grabs my arm. "NO, I THINK I'M GONNA HANG HERE ALL DAY!" Vici's already worked her way into the car by the time I manage to tow Spike onto the hood again. Spike shoves me through the opening of the windshield before following me, the three of us cramming into the back of a mobile that I can only describe as a tank now that I've seen most of its dimensions.

"I wasn't aware that was a new door," Lily sneers. "And I thought you said we'd be your only passengers."

"Well, I figured we're all heading in the same direction, anyway. Aren't we?" Spike grins. He reeks of blood and metal. He's around twenty years old and one of the biggest Next names in the criminal business. Spike is his most common tag, because it used to be his big brother's tag, but he had to take it when the brother was killed in an accident four years ago. Some of the other things they call him are Metal Wasp or Yellowjacket, and he's almost an average nocturnal predator, mugging people for money, except he's gone huge-scale, and he's unstoppable since everything he owns gets woven with metal, and besides, something went wrong during the chip extraction, so he still can't feel pain.

"You know where the Castaway Point is?" I ask, trying to relax. If I were a stranger sitting next to him, he'd probably knock my lights out here and now. Since I'm under his category, though, I know I'm sitting next to a superstar. I guess saving him from a trip of hanging off the side of his car gets me kudos.

He smiles a little more, laughing soft and deep to himself again. "Honestly? No idea. I'm leaving that to the dolls."

I lean forward. "What the heck do *you* want, Mouse?" Lily sneers.

"It's Rat, you retard," I correct her very patiently, and she gives me her "whatever" look. She can be a wicked little brat every now and then. Every beautiful soul's got an ugly side. "I want to know if you know where you're going."

She fingers the wheel for a second. "Well, I was thinking we'd stop somewhere along the way and I'd ask someone where I could find the place." Nobody would deny Lily. The nearby pedestrians would be tripping over themselves to talk to her.

"Let Vici help you."

"Did I ask for help?" Lily snarls, never taking her eyes off the road.

"Look, stupid, you wanna qualify or not?!"

She's trying to decide whether or not to argue for the sake of it when Spike puts in, "She's got a point, Leadhead. And even if *you* don't want to get there as fast as possible, I know that *I* sure do. And if for some reason, your stubbornness makes me too late to qualify, there's gonna be more than one reason for you to be sad."

Lily considers her options. "Okay. Vici, was it? Tell me where to go."

"Turn right as soon as possible. From there you'll ride out to Grand Avenue to East Pierre Street and from there to Zenith Road."

"Whaddup, we get to pass Stillstone," I say, mood brightening. "Oh, and East Pierre's a thoroughfare, but nice try, Vic."

"Ah. I'm sorry, she's right."

Without a word, Lily turns onto the ramp so that we don't go into the tunnel, but merge into the x-road. Then she decides to end the without-a-word thing and comments, "I thought you were younger than Mouse, so how did *you* end up with all the manners?"

I scowl in the backseat. "It's the mobile," Vici explains sheepishly. "She's been on this road trip for too long. Machines give her a headache. Please forgive her."

"I don't need Leadhead's forgiveness," I growl, crossing my arms.

"She's kinda in line to be asking for yours, if you ask me. Whoa," Spike says suddenly. "Think we're the only 'offenders' who got the message?"

I look out the window and my mouth drops. Discipline workers are everywhere, going ballistic, chasing people who, after the drab world of electrodes, seem absolutely crazy. I see two people in the air. Someone's on a strange mobile that's bowling people over on the walkway, making people scream and dive to the side before they speed past. A motorbike settles alongside us, snuggled tightly between the two lanes of traffic. The rider can't even be thirteen years old, but he's not wearing a helmet. He turns to look at us, tinted goggles masking his eyes, and smiles at us all in here, saluting before jetting ahead, handling the thing better than any average pro could.

Across the city, people are racing to the Castaway Point however they can. Some sit in traffic with us. Some dash on foot. Some leap from building to building. A few have figured out ways to take to the sky with machines or suits. Altogether, we are a spread-out swarm of flies, massing into the city until it teems with us, crawls with us, and comes alive again as its ashen skin bristles with sable.

Then the discipline ops open fire until the black-and-white veins are accented with crimson.

One of the fliers lands on top of the car, bouncing off and getting shredded by the traffic. Bullets tear through the air. The poor boy on the bike lifts his foot at the last second, literally dodging bullets, but one rips through the mobile, and I don't see what happens to him next. We run over something with a shudder. "I should've known the Adamantration would pull a stunt on us!

Everyone, heads down," Lily demands, and we obey. "Does anyone have a hat or something so I can blend better? I need to keep driving."

"Blend?" I scoff. "The windshield's shattered. I think they've got a pretty good idea we're not—" the rest of the windshield breaks in a spray of glass. The two up front duck.

"They found us!" Vici yells.

Out of nowhere, a discipline man jumps onto the hood of the car. "HANDS WHERE I CAN SEE THEM!" he yells and sticks the barrel of his DC-5 into the car. Spike leaps forward and yanks the thing out of the discipline man's hands and uses it to knock him off the hood.

"SORRY, NO MORE ROOM!" He swings the gun into position. "Uh, I'd rather a Harsha. Any marksmen in here? Or should I say, markswomen? Geez, I'm the only guy in the car."

As Ivy gently tugs the gun away from Spike, Vici says, "That was senseless! Discipline operatives aren't usually so irrational. He was so . . . I don't know, fearless! They're really desperate for us!"

"If we'da gone through Stillstone, we'd've been fine," I huff and almost start an argument, but then we all go quiet.

Ivy stands up, sticking her upper half out the windshield. We stare. It's said few people have ever heard her talk before. She hardly ever cut her hair before she got extracted, and when she admitted getting rid of her mainframe to her mother, the woman shaved her glorious head bald, so the story goes. Now, she keeps her hair short, but she took back her long locks and made them into a sort of necklace that she wears as a silver cape. It flutters around in the harsh wind as she takes aim and shoots the gun arm of any discipline man she sees, whereas I'd be lucky if I could get a shot within a meter of them. The sight is humbling, and we all go quiet for a minute.

"You're a really good shot," I finally call forward at her, and she gives me a brief smile in reward then keeps firing.

Gunshots echo from every corner of the city, each one making our destination feel farther away until we all start glancing nervously at each other, wondering if we'll be the next ones in the lineup.

But finally, I see a short glowing spire in the distance with hardly any other buildings around it. Vici looks to me for confirmation, and I nod. "This is it," I whisper as we shoot into New Arctic Circle, the northernmost point on the face of the earth.

- III -

The Usual Suspects

The sudden lack of buildings makes it obvious that the place is important, but the few buildings that do ring around the Castaway Point add even more certainty. Empty space stretches between each building, paved in smooth asphalt so the eight buildings seem to be the spikes of a crown coming from a vat of leaden haze, each one more extravagant than the one before it.

"The Sector Headquarters of New Arctic Circle," Vici breathes, and that's the last comment that gets said about the place because the closer we get, the less breath there is available in the car. The plain marble spike of the Castaway Point marks the North Pole; it stands alone inside the ring with the Frontal Belfry dancing its heart out on top, while the seven buildings of the Sectors form a circle rising from the fog, all specially painted and crafted after the point of their Sector. That's what makes them the most mind-blowing buildings in Tersatellus. You don't need a reform or an imagination to tell they're nothing short of incredible.

Right beyond the Castaway Point, the Public Prosperity Sector Headquarters stands, proud and heart-stopping (and freaking short compared to the others), in a stunning alabaster replica of a tree. Above the doors, the giant star of the compass rose with rays shooting out of it is set into the stone. The Criminal Resolution, Transportation, Health & Medical, Hydration & Consumption, and Structure & Architecture Headquarters all have some sort of plus or star to imitate the one on Public Prosperity.

Yes, I can count. I know that only makes six out of the seven Sectors, but no, I wasn't lying to you. The last Headquarters is just a special case—it reminds me of one of those games where they give you a bunch of things and ask you which one doesn't belong, and the special one has to be obvious since you're only five or something when they give you those games. It's too obvious that it belongs in that crown as much as an olive belongs in a gumball machine.

First of all, the metal is the most absolute black in the world—one could call it sable. The second thing that makes it different is the clear tubes of glowing green liquid that snake in and out and up the whole thing straight to the top, where they split into a million jagged lines that flicker patiently in the sky, waiting to take the lightning from the heavens and spread it to the rest of the world, and it really does seem to reach all the way to heaven, considering the Technology Sector HQ is four hundred and one stories high.

Again, possibly an exaggeration, but I'll never know.

Partway up the Pylon, as it's been nicknamed, the harvest tubes thicken and cross at one point, marking the final thing that makes the other Headquarters shun this one: the great symbol. It causes such a cluster of energy, fissures of white electricity crack impossibly slow against the black canvas. There's only one problem. That symbol is sideways. It's not a plus, it's an X; it's not a compass rose, it's a crossroads; it's not a direction, it's a decision. And even though nobody talks about it, it doesn't take much to guess that this is a problem.

Spike whistles. "Hmm, I wonder if it's true that every new Adaman redecorates their Headquarters. You girls're really missing something. The Porcupine's got some great taste in color."

I'm glad that I'm not driving too. Lily's concentrated on the Castaway Point, while all I can look at is the Pylon and its outright defiance. The last time I was here, it wasn't that big or dark. It gives me a feeling that makes my stomach turn at the sight of it, a feeling that I can't figure out whether it's fear or awe or a mixture of both.

I don't get any more time to think about it. We streak into the circle of the crown and screech to a halt right in front of the doors of the Castaway Point. Mobiles of all kinds litter the parking lot. Operatives aren't surrounding the place the way I thought they'd be. "Pearls before swine," Spike laughs before launching out the windshield ahead of us. The rest of us get out the doors the way normal people did the last time I checked and run for the building, pushing and shoving and warring to get into the folding chairs scattered away from the center of the room, already rivals under the keening of that belfry.

Everyone's dashing for a seat in the place before even so much as looking around at the glowing interior of the chamber, which is the size of a church sanctuary with a vaulted ceiling, a giant gold analog on the wall, a perfect column in every corner, a grand chandelier throwing manufactured sunlight on the wheat-colored chamber. There's a great white marble stage in the center swirls and stuff imprinted into the stone. A bunch of chairs (read: thrones) surround the stage, each marble and gold and too big for people—the whole place seems too big for people, too big for us dolls who have stumbled into human territory, or too big for humans who have stumbled into Olympus. The whole chamber has a sort of gravity to it. It suffocates me slowly, and I do not like it at all.

I look at the giant clock and then my Rolex, which is a few minutes behind. It's almost six. The drive here took a while, and I'm still calming down from the ride. Biting my lip, I tap my foot and watch the front doors swing closed. More shooting goes on outside of this gilded heaven, then it fades away, leaving fifty or so of us in the guilty silence of survivorship.

Fifty of us all together in the same Adamantration room. And we're all blackhearts.

Not just cutouts. Not just criminals. Not just your average desperadoes. Something more. Something… worse.

Even though there's the obvious flavor of suspicion of the Adamantration and of each other, there's this connection between us too. I'm stink-eyeing Spade because I left his gang, and I'm showing off my multi to Hai because she lost me my old one, but I start realizing that that's just who we are. We're woven up in our own kind of Plexus of rebellion, and as I get that, something close to an understanding dawns in me about something said to me a while back that I didn't grasp at the time: we really are all comrades. We're our own breed of people because we're the last ones that're free in the ugly way anarchy is free, and we fight for that freedom, bound together by a common enemy. No, I don't know half the people in this room, but I acknowledge them as my own motley crew with a slow smile as it comes to me that every single one of us here's wearing something sable.

Suddenly, the back doors burst open, making us all jump when our trains of thought get derailed. Four figures walk into the room, down the aisle in between chairs, and head for the stage. We watch them, silent and incredulous and wondering if this is it; it's really just happening. All of them are Adamans.

There's Isic Wheel, the Adaman of the Transportation Sector, dressed for the role in a snazzy blazer so he looks professional even though we all know he's a skink, even him. Gridley Nocturnum is the Adaman of the Criminal Resolution Sector, and boy, if looks could kill, she could be a butcher with her hands tied behind her back.

Then my eyes fall on *him*.

The Adaman of the Public Prosperity Sector is the third one in the room. The doors slide closed as our Hades strides out into us, and while we're tense, he couldn't look more comfortable. He's had a few centuries to get a handle on things, including being hated. We all go still and silent, hardly daring to breathe. Maybe he's breathtaking. Maybe we don't even want to share the same air as him. Even I can't tell for sure.

His steps are smooth and even as he walks over and climbs the three stairs onto the stage with the others so all of us can see him. He's draped in white and gold from his boots to his cape. His skin is rich and glowing with health, and his hair seriously looks like it's dark gold. He is everything his people want him to be.

He looks around the room, taking us all in. His face is fierce to me, especially because even his *eyes* are gold, but that doesn't surprise me. What *should* surprise me is that his left eye doesn't have a pupil. No kidding. If you squint, you could see a faint pink line that comes from behind his ear and cuts across his face a bit before swiping back down halfway down his neck. Somehow he knows I'm looking, so his eyes flash over to me, and let me tell you, eyeballs should not be able to jump that fast without any sort of warning. I force myself back in my seat, heartbeat doubling, sweat erupting on the back of my neck.

Yep. There's no doubting it; he's the Gilded Guardian and the Razor, the protector of citizens, and the bane of all things illegal.

Then the gilded man *smiles.*

Absolon Vastate's smile is one that promises me nothing but the best of ill intentions.

Well, well, well, look who decided to show up after all, he seems to tell me, and both of us look away at the same time. I wish I'd burned the note. I wish I'd eaten it.

The smile disappears when the last Adaman comes up onto the stage. Ignoring the stairs, he sets one foot on the stage and lifts himself up, using height to his advantage. His arrival makes the whole atmosphere suddenly change; the rumor passes around, and the room explodes in shocked murmurs and outcries as the man makes his first ever public appearance.

Steele comes to a slow stop next to Vastate, clasping his spidery hands behind his back. Even though he's not as dressed up as the others, he's risen to his full height and jacked up his bristly hair that won him his nickname, and Vastate only comes up to Steele's ear. Some sort of rivalry, a warring animosity presses between the two of them, but you can't find it in one's eyes or his poise or anything, so for a second, I think I'm wrong, that they're really as calm as they're trying to seem. Then I notice how Steele's tense hands are one shade short of Death, and for the second time, he kinda makes me fear for my life, and not just mine.

The Public Prosperity and Technology Sectors've always had tension, of course. All the other Sectors have to get approval of Public Prosperity before making any changes since it presents the best interests of the people, but the Tech Sector has the extra responsibility of suggesting such changes since it represents innovation and progress, not just machines. And if the Tech Sector suggests it, and the receiving Sector okays it, then Public Prosperity doesn't have any say. That's supposed to account for the fact that the public sometimes opposes change even when it's good for them, but it has created honest hatred between the Sectors, and even though these two Adamans are apparently wonderful people, according to rumor, and Vastate was the one who fought to put the first cutout Adaman in place, they get along about as well as salt and vinegar.

What helps this occur to me is the wave of whispers that runs through the crowd as they notice the Porcupine still has on that cloak that seems to be woven not of cloth but solely of the color that defines us in the room as free in the worst kind of way, and I know the sucker does it on purpose because that coat changes colors. It was white when I saw him a few years ago on the street. He's being spiteful. Or maybe he's just showing to us where his allegiances lie.

Vastate clears his throat to silence us and takes another step forward. There's no smiling now. "Morning, offenders." His rich voice stretches out to every corner of the room, but I don't miss how he doesn't specify what *kind* of morning he wants us to have, and there's a layer of venom in his second word, which he obviously means as an insult. "Let's get this show on the road, shall we? I'm sure you are all curious as to which ones of you will be heading first into the challenge we have prepared for you." I make sure I'm not looking at him so I don't see if he's looking at me. "Mizz Adaman Nocturnum will announce the Next, who will then settle into the qualifiers' chairs, and the Remainder will leave for the Holding Center across town. Then, things will be explained... more or less."

The same stillness that comes before thunderstorms snakes in a haze around the chamber, making us all feel as though we are preparing to wage war, as the woman saunters up to center stage to tell us who will be on the front lines. Streaks of gray are prominent in her hair and have been prominent all her life. It might be where her daughters got their hair color from. That's right, the dolls descend from the elite—not even the Adamans want to keep their children once they decide to break away and break some rules. I glance over at Lily and Ivy, but neither seem to care, and their mother won't look at them. Then again, she doesn't look at any of us for the first five seconds, since she's too busy making sure her DC-5 is ready to blow before she looks up and flashes a crocodile smile at us. The sense of drama is strong here.

"What's up, cutouts and convicts?" The woman throws her arms out to each side so the people to her right flinch away from the gun even though we know it's a show, a blank, which could go bang but won't make blood. She must know how bad we hate that. "I'd be Mizz Adaman Nocturnum, and it's my pleasure to present to you all who's going into Hudson Bay first." I frown when I realize Vastate didn't even give a self-introduction. Even though he thinks we're all stupid, he's conceited enough to assume we all know who he is, I bet. Then I register that bay thing again, and I frown even more.

"This is how it works: you all sit and listen to me read this list that our analyst Larry made so I can't be held accountable for the butchering of names, ages, or who gets in first, so don't come crying to me when you don't get your way. We here at Criminal Resolution figured out which ones of you are the worst, and you probably need to take a back exit as fast as possible—the first ones to get shoved into the unknown the fastest're the most likely to die, and everyone else gets whatever fun's left, and sure, maybe there's a chance for some of you to change," she adds when she sees Vastate shift. She rolls her eyes and gets away with it because she's standing to his left, and I'm pretty sure he can't see out of that eye. "So after I'm done calling names of the Next, the rest of you scram, and I'll follow right behind you and tell you what's in store. You know, if any of you live through getting from here to there." Mizz Adaman Nocturnum smiles as the ringing of gunfire fills the silences she chomped into the room, then she clears her throat to get our attention back. "And now, in no particular order, the Next into the bay are as follows."

⇹

"Convicted of Hacking in the forms of unauthorized access to government niches and private niches and Extortion in the form of blackmail: Marceline Sere, age twenty-one."

One. I wince, realizing they're going to go by our real names and that they identify us by our offenses first, as if *that's* more important. Then my stomach drops when the name registers. The woman pops out of her seat, walking confidently over to her throne thing, looking too happy and nice to be smug the way the rest of us might be, but she's not relieved, either. She knew she would qualify, which makes sense. Voxel, as she's tagged by us, is a genius when it comes to anything technical. She's Vici's absolute heroine, since she can crack and manipulate almost any system or niche, usually within seconds. Not even most Adamans are safe from her. Sir Adaman Wheel blanches when she gives him a small wave. She's kind of on the crazy side, by the way—her hair's dyed white with blue at the bottom, which is fine, I guess, but most visible sections of her body are labeled by the black marker in her fist. Thick designs by her eyes hint the veiling of finer, more permanent lines. I don't notice, but Vastate refuses to look at her, though he can't resist touching the fine, permanent line by his own eye.

When the room stops chattering, Mizz Adaman Nocturnum continues, "Convicted of Falsification in the forms of using a false identity, plagiarism, using a false permit, and Theft in the forms of fraud and identity theft: Pierre J. Devine, age sixteen."

Two. The lanky teen jumps to his feet, quietly cheering, which is strange because when we think of this guy, "quiet" is the last thing that comes to mind. Craw was born and bred for what he does. He's got one of those faces and a million of those voices that make him flexible enough to pass off as almost anyone, getting him away with hearts and/or money before anyone usually knows what happened. He is everybody and nobody at the same time. It's uncanny, because nobody's ever actually *seen* that magic throat he was tagged for, since he wears a black scarf around his neck, so that feeds the fire about him being unreal, imagined, the Nobody that exists in some other reality but some of him's here for some reason—probably the flings, the parties and such. If he's anything, he's a player, that's for sure.

"Convicted of Falsification in the form of providing false services, scamming, counterfeiting, selling false reproductions, plagiarism, and Illegal trade and/or possession for firearms and black-marketing to the first and second degree: Thomas Hans, age fifteen."

Three. The guy in question explodes from his seat, pumping his fists in the air and laughing and cheering, nowhere near quiet, WOO-ing and YAHAHA-ing with every breath. His short rusty hair manages to bounce all over the place due to his sheer energy as he cartwheels and jumps into his seat, reclining sideways with his legs dangling over the edge. "D'we gets free drinks? Ya knows, I runned all the whole way here," he lets everyone know, stretching out his muscular limbs that prove he was more than capable of the job. Despite that sinewy build that is the envy of every boy in Tersatellus, my nerves spike at the sight of Mac, the Mr. Fixit who is living proof of three things: what's broken can be fixed; nothing built in history is unchangeable; and where there's smoke, there's sure to be fire.

"Convicted of Falsification in the form of providing false services, scamming, counterfeiting, selling false reproductions, plagiarism, and Illegal trade and/or possession for firearms and black-marketing to the first and second degree—don't you just love the law? So creative and original. Anyway. Timothy Hans, age eighteen."

Four. The big brother silently rises and glides over to a chair, expressionless. The only difference between the two brothers is their age and their roles. Mac does the social snooping to figure out who wants what, Jacques makes the plans, Mac puts stuff together, and Jacques executes the transaction. Still, everyone knows that there are a few things he does on the side that he never gets caught for, things that would make your hair stand up. That plus their age difference makes you think they'd at least disagree *some*times, but you never see one brother without the other, the same way it's impossible to separate Macabreak from Frère Jacques because they're kinda the same city, and Jacques would never let Mac fall behind him on anything. That's the way siblings should be.

Speaking of siblings. "Alright, I don't think Larry'll mind if I lump the next two together the way I should've done for the two before this. Both convicted of Falsification in the forms of providing false services, scamming, and Illegal trade and/or possession for firearms, drugs, alcohol, black-marketing to the first and second degree, gambling, and Homicide in the form of first degree murder: Alice and Alice Nocturnum, ages sixteen."

Five and six. My brow furrows as Lily and Ivy stand up, Lily smiling and waving, Ivy looking plastic. Mizz Adaman Nocturnum and her husband named both their daughters Alice? They kind of look alike, so you can tell they're sisters, but they're not twins. Ivy looks more like she's a carefully crafted doll, while Lily is the sassy manifestation of wildfire. At least they have matching bracelets, and by bracelets, I mean they're each wearing one half of a black pair of handcuffs that mask the chaffs on their wrists made from the same pieces of jewelry, which is probably the point. Their mother must appreciate the message.

"Charged with Assault in the forms of aggravated assault, personal battery, assault with weapon or firearm, participation in mobbing, participation in public combat, and Extortion in the form of property, network, personal, and Misconduct in the forms of endangerment, harassment, and trespassing, Bargain Jericho, now sans homicide—I mean, Douglas Hertz, age nineteen."

Seven. Wearing a smirk of victory, Spike stands up and walks over to a chair, settling into the thing so easily you'd think it was made for him. His brother was Jericho, by the way. Now that you know his name, you can probably figure out why people sometimes call this guy Doug-Hurts-Less. His ankle and arm haven't stopped bleeding yet, and he doesn't even notice. "My car better still be there when I get back," he rumbles. "If you could fix the scratches while I'm out, that'd be great. Take it from the million-mark bill for me."

"Hold it, hotshot, it's not Saturday yet," Mizz Adaman Nocturnum replies, which only makes Spike's smile bigger, which is scary when you can't see his eyes behind those sunglasses (he's got new ones). He could be plotting your doom behind those things for all you can tell. "Alright, here we go. Convicted of Assault in the forms of aggravated assault, vandalism, damage of property, and Extortion in the forms of personal, property, and Misconduct in the form of trespassing, as well as failing to reach standard IQ for the average bacteria and exceeding legal limit of shoe size: Xavier Kael, age seventeen."

Eight. Everyone groans as the albino stands up, his hands deep into his hoodie pockets, his beady rose eyes twitching everywhere as he carefully walks over to a chair. It's hard for him not to trip over his big feet as he slumps along, his snowy dreadlocks swinging back and forth in time with the black club hanging on his waist. People aren't inclined to like Rex, which has, as a result, made him less inclined to like people in return—that's obvious enough from Mizz Adaman Nocturnum's last comments, which don't even faze him. He mutters something about getting insulted. But behind that defensive red front, if you watch hard enough, you can sometimes see another one of the corner kids, the outsiders looking in who want to be anywhere but out. He's pretty down-to-earth, if you ask me, and he looks like he belongs anywhere but that big golden chair.

"Oh, boy. Charged with Theft in the form of grand theft auto about fifty freaking times—now, I'd like to make a special note that Larry left me a pronunciation cue for this name—Reuel M. Motor, age … twelve."

"YEAH!" We all sit up straighter, eyebrows shooting up as the name and age registers, and the kid jumps out of his seat and runs all the way to one of the thrones, which he refuses to sit *in*. That's too mainstream. Instead, he gracefully climbs to the top and sits *on* it, perching with a broad and mischievous smile. I recognize him as the kid from the motorbike. Motor, tagged with his appropriate surname, has been big into sharing for the few months he's had stolen stuff to share, so already the crowd is whispering among themselves, staking claims to whatever prize he gets, certain of his generosity as much as his survival. He's nothing short of a child prodigy. *Nine.*

"Charged with Hacking in the forms of—LARRY!" We all jump when Mizz Adaman Nocturnum snaps then scowls. "Wait, false alarm. I thought he entered Voxel twice." She doesn't seem to notice that she slipped up and referred to the woman by her tag, since the two get along ironically well; the Adawoman, as she calls herself, doesn't hide anything for Voxel to expose. There's nothing concealed about the firearms of her malice. "Anywho. Where was I? Oh, yeah, Victoria Oile, age seventeen, c'mon up here, darling, the water's fine." I pat Vici on the back as she jumps up and makes her way over to chair number ten. She's almost exploding with pride about being confused for Voxel. People're congratulating her on the way, whooping about the swoop last night.

"And now, ladies and gentlemen, convicted of Theft—can I just say Theft?" Mizz Adaman Nocturnum takes a deep breath. "Alright, here goes: grand larceny, burglary, raiding, shoplifting, petty theft, embezzlement, unlawful requisition, abduction, active, inactive, and technical piracy, fraud, identity theft, and refusal to pay, and that's all I get to say because they don't have laws for some of her heists, and they never proved the grand theft auto, assaults, falsifications, misdemeanors, or illegal trade or possessing a Monday-morning attitude every day of the week *and* claiming my personal favorite name of the bunch—you get another name cue, *thank* you, Larry!—is the one and only Erratica T. Race, age seventeen!"

Okay, when I said I was a crook…

I stand up in a wave of euphoria and grin, "Guilty as charged, Your Honor!" Mizz Adaman Nocturnum grins right back at me as I walk over to one of the chairs, nearly fifty other sets of eyes watching me as I take the eleventh spot, sitting down next to Vici. They reach out to touch me when I pass; they've got to make sure I'm real, that I'm not some spirit that can float through walls or something, even though that's exactly how I feel. I feel too lightheaded to think of anything, except that I am going into a competition made to kill people like me.

Suddenly inside the circle, I don't see the people out there anymore that might die when they leave. I only see ten other people giving me smiles and thumbs-ups. Some of them are whispering to each other, Motor is cheering again, and Spike is clapping slowly, smiling in a way that I can't really tell if he's on my side or not. "Her surname's Race? What, was she born for this?" I hear one of them say to the person next to them. Shows what they know.

It's all so amazing, but at the same time, some part of me knew I would make it on that list. That's the same part of me that knew I would be able to split something from one of the tightest residencies in the nation. When the Adaman starts talking again, I scowl, thinking I should've been the last name called cuz that's more dramatic, but it disappears by the time she's done.

"Convicted of Misconduct in the forms of interrupting public order, endangerment, harassment, and Treason in the form of unauthorized attempt to communicate with the outside with intent to harm nation: Layla Kael, age fifty-seven."

Twelve. This time, I don't watch the new contestant as she slinks up. I don't know much about Gypsy, as we call her, except she's Rex's aunt, and if the boy loves conspiracies, the witch lives off them. The Adamantration hates her for being such an upstart, trying to get all the electrodes to feel something or go get extracted. Some of the Adamans mutter amongst themselves about her, which probably makes her happy, because gossip runs in her veins.

Mizz Adaman Waves to get our attention. "Yoohoo, not done yet here. Charged with Misconduct in the form of trespassing, interruption of public order, and Theft in the form of refusal to pay, plus not meeting standard requirements for weight or common sense: Gabriel Story, age seventeen."

Thirteen. Murmuring erupts, and I stand up again in surprise as the skinny boy works his way to his feet, his eyes gone wide with shock. I'm not kidding you, he hardly weighs forty kilograms. He was a faulty citizen for the first seven years of his life, the chip doing all sorts of junk, so he didn't mature properly, and then he got extracted, but it hasn't gotten any better. Now, he floats between gangs, entertaining them in trade for a place to stay and get food and stuff—what he does is he breaks the rules, climbs up buildings, and falls on people or anything crazy a gang feels like telling him to do. Basically he's a fetch, a gang servant, and they call him Shatter and Fracture and stuff because he's so fragile he always ends up breaking something besides rules. There's no way he'll last two seconds out there if someone wants him dead. All they have to do is shove him over, and he'll break a hip or something. He's so weak he can hardly get over here in a straight line, this look of humbleness and horror all over his face.

Fracture wouldn't hurt a fly, I know that. The only reason I can think of why Adamantration's picking him is to show us that nobody's too high to die, and nobody's too low, either—they'll get all of us. But we are not part of the powerless, *no*, when we picked our freedom, we picked the freedom to be defiant, and that look on the Adamans' faces gives me the feeling that defiance is exactly what the situation calls for. So I start clapping.

Everyone watches me for a second, wondering what the heck I think I'm doing, but then Fracture picks his head up with something that kinda resembles hope on his face, and when everyone sees how the corner of Vastate's lip turns down, they start clapping too. The message is clear: *You want Fracture dead? Have fun trying to get through all of us to get there. Because we're not a bunch of random people, we're united. Together, we've defied your perfection, and we can defy your death too.*

Fracture finally smiles and sits down, and we start cheering louder, chanting his tag, dancing, patting him on the back and everything. He gives me a wink of thanks, and my skin goes hot. I might as well explain why something about him still leaves me hanging—we cutouts have strange hearts. What you might call romance is a mutual need to recharge the human spirit to us, and Craw could testify that the source of that spark isn't as important to us—we don't keep them, just go wherever we need to go to get that next spark. Our "love" is only brotherhood, because your real, romantic love takes time, and we're all dynamite pretending to be candles—we don't *have* time. We have a blast. So whenever we go farther than that brotherhood line, we might not go too far, but we go fast, and that doesn't disappear; it leaves afterimages burned into us, so a little wave's enough to light the sparks up again, dancing under my skin. I've rarely had that. But for some reason, I look at Fracture, and I know there was something along those lines before our extractions, before I can remember, something different and non-cutout that I don't understand. We talked about it once a few years ago, and he was sort of upset with me for turning into what I am, but I see him here now and realize there must be a reason, realize there's such a thing as second chances.

The room settles down again, but nobody else is paying attention. They're all talking to each other even though it's not over yet. I notice there's only one seat left open, one name left on the list. Mizz Adaman Nocturnum seems hesitant to even read it or confused or afraid that it's going to hurt coming out or something. "And... our fourteenth and final competitor... is, uh... Elijah Steele?"

No age. No crime. Nothing but a name. A handsome forename with a very important surname that slaps me with the backlash. My eyes fly up to Jaden Steele, who hasn't moved a muscle. Voices start up everywhere, people wondering the same thing I am.

"It's Eli," the final competitor corrects in a quiet voice that cuts across the entire room.

The noise in the room dies, and every head turns as he stands up. He's probably as tall as Vici, who's a bit taller than me, and he looks about our age. His pitch-black hair's still kinda spikey, but it's short, and it doesn't know which direction to go. He's got on the same normal clothes the rest of us do, jeans and a T-shirt, so if you don't look at him directly, he does look almost normal, even more normal than mutated Fracture, who's not so gung-ho on crime as the rest of us. He could even pass as one of us. But there is a strange, strange, strange aura about him that tells the story. Maybe it's the eyes. It's a dead giveaway. It's not a rapture man's artificial fluxing light, but there's something way larger than life in that glowing shade that no eye should be, that vividness of nature incarnate, the exact look of untamed, undiluted liquid lightning.

Whatever he is, I don't think he's human.

Nobody complains or questions it as he makes his way to the last seat. He glances at me, and I jump, feeling electrocuted, and I stare very hard at the floor then train my eyes on the stage.

Vastate pats Mizz Adaman Nocturnum's back and quietly murmurs, "You know, delaying the agony does nothing to lessen it." Then, in a louder voice, "Thank you, Mizz Adaman Nocturnum. The rest of you may now leave." Nobody moves for a second, then they start getting up, slowly.

Mizz Adaman Nocturnum checks the clock, looking composed again. "We got finished a little early. The discipline ops shouldn't be here yet..." The pace instantly picks up tenfold—everyone left behind floods out the doors, some of them taking the chairs with them as shields, and the Adaman skips waiting and walks out among them, spinning her DC-5 and shark-grinning again. "See you all never!"

When the last person leaves, the doors slam shut. I look around at the big-name stars surrounding me (careful not to look directly to my right, since I don't want to get electrocuted again). I'm actually in the same room as the largest criminals in the business, actually watching as Mac starts messing with a cubic machine, and Voxel remarkers her left hand, and Spike chips blood off his face. And there's not one but *two* Steeles under the same ceiling. I am surrounded by legends.

No. I am one of them.

The sly recognition of renown crawls into my mind. I'm one of the greats. I belong here. I've prequalified and then really qualified for some sort of competition made only for the most elite lawbreakers in Tersatellus.

It's about damn time.

But we Tersatellans aren't supposed to think like that (or know those words), so I shuffle the thought aside.

Vastate clears his throat to get our attention again. It feels too big and empty in this chamber now. "Well, now that that's cleared up, those of you still here may be wondering exactly what you've signed up for. What you are about to embark on is a six-day-long race of epic proportions, and of no rules. You're wondering what the object of this race is going to be? Continue wondering, for only one of you is going to know. One of you in this room will be deigned with not only the goal of your excursion but also other details that are crucial to your survival. Then you are all going to be sent into a vast area we call the Hudson Bay. You may be wondering why you have never heard of this place, so I will tell you: it is outside of the Divide."

Sharp gasps and murmurs of disbelief stab through the chamber. Even though I got tipped off, the thought of leaving Tersatellus still slaps me in the face and makes me sink back in my chair, away from Vastate's smile.

"We are gathered here today because of your desire of a freedom that seeks to imitate that of the outside world. You seem to have forgotten that we left that freedom behind for a reason. It is ugly, selfish, destructive, uncaring, and will mean the end of the world. Their freedom to do certain things has led to acts of terrorism, war, climate failure, mass genocide, corruption and worldwide disease, debt, starvation, and death, yet this is the freedom you want. So we are going to let you have it. There will be no rules where you are going, and you will see exactly what your liberty does to people. Freedoms will be abused, and people will die. That is the sacrifice that must be made to help the rest of you learn the truth. I am sending you to the Hudson Bay because it does not obey any laws on the inside of our Divide but is nearly surrounded by it, therefore making it safer from the rest of the world while still giving you a taste of what you are after. Since defense is so tight, you will be let in via transporter. Once inside, you will find your mobiles, courtesy of the Transportation Sector."

Sir Adaman Wheel waves, and I think, *So that's why he's here*, as he takes the center of the stage. "Greetings, and well done on your qualifications. My name is Sir Adaman Isic Wheel, and I'm here to explain how my mobiles play into the event you've qualified for. You will choose one and only one to be your mobile for the duration of the race. None of you can pirate another's mobile—well, you can, but it won't be in your benefit, since your beacons register your mobile as yours, so they'll reject you if you try to use your beacon on someone else's mobile, and if you use someone else's car and beacon, then it gives that person credit for everything you do. This still doesn't mean that your mobile won't be pirated, however."

We look at each other, wondering if he's making himself sound really stupid (*cough cough*, wouldn't be surprised) or if there's something really bad he's got up his sleeve.

"You see, this extermination is meant to 'kill' as many people as possible so that more people have the chance to come back as reborn citizens or don't come back at all. If you fourteen were the only ones to enter the bay and race, it would mean that you would be the only possible criminals to be reformed. In order to keep that number up in the air, we decided that it would be best if the Remainder competitors would be let into the bay and be allowed to pirate your mobiles, which will be your source of victory if you can keep them. If you lose your mobile, as in you are unable to contact it for over three days due to it being destroyed, lost, or pirated, you receive no prize. Now that I know who's Next, I have much to go over before the party begins, but I wish to leave you with a hint of my own: if you are meant to die, then do not believe that these mobiles will be without gifts for you to help ensure that this happens." He gives us one last seemingly innocent smile before heading off the stage.

Vastate steps forward again. "Alright, everyone, only a few minutes more," he reassures us, implying that he thinks we've got the attention span of rodents (irony intended). "There's even more about these pirates than what Sir Adaman Wheel described—when one is confirmed dead, the new one will be sent in, until either the occasion or the supply of Remainder has reached their end. These pirates are going to be extremely important to you. Each day, one of these pirates will possess a clue for you. A clue on what? That is *also* a secret, which none of you will know except the chosen Outlier: the rest of you will have to figure it out, as you will have to figure out the clues you may receive from a pirate, because their clues are riddles.

"Now, because of this, you may think the Remainder will want to share these riddles with you so everyone can work together as if you were friends and figure out what the riddle means. In a perfect world, this would happen. However, you may not feel inclined to work together because of something called greed." He smiles at us, which isn't a good sign. "You see, in order to make sure that only the most wholesome competitors return, we have added an incentive to pressure you against one another while simultaneously rewarding those of you of strong enough integrity to work together to make it to Saturday.

"For every criminal that dies, all the survivors will get an additional day and thousand primes to their prize. If one of the Remainder keeps their riddle to themselves and manages to survive the week, then their prize doubles. If the Remainder dies, you will all receive their clue via your beacon. If the Outlier dies, however, the objectives will not be revealed. The secrets of this race are not written in any niche nor on any paper nor will anyone know it except for myself and the one I choose to give the secret to. If you do not know this secret, then even if you meet the requirements to win the race, you will not be crowned Champion. You can only win if you know how, and the only way the rest of you could ever hope to learn the objective is by this person telling you the secret. But don't believe they will. If the Outlier refuses to share the secrets, their prize triples."

Me and Vici slowly turn to look at each other with a promise that doesn't have to be said out loud. If one of us turns out to be the Outlier, we'll tell each other that much, but that secret will be kept.

Gypsy stands up with her hands on her hips. "I call bullsticks!" she scoffs. "There's no way you'd ever hand over three million primes to any one of us. This whole thing's screwy. If you wanted us dead, why wouldn't you kill us all now?"

"I don't want you all dead. In fact, it would be best if none of you died, if I could somehow get all of you to see sense." Vastate takes a look around the room, and I tell myself I do not see any trace of earnestness in him, and I don't see him force it away. "Then again, I don't see potential citizens in any of you in this room. You're all cutout and criminal, through and through."

"Then why don't you kill us, you coward?" Gypsy demands again.

"Do you really want to know?" Vastate asks slowly, and we all mutter our assent. The muttering gets louder as he reaches into his jacket and starts pulling his hand out.

I don't even register the glint before I'm behind the chair.

Even before the gun's in sight, half of us are using the chairs as shields, and the other half stand with weapons of our own pointed at Vastate. In the case of Spike and Jacques, some have a gun in each hand. We're armed to the teeth and ready for anything, that's clear, but that's not the most amazing thing that happens. A split second after the mass reaction, I hear the gun CLACK three times when something hits it, then it hits the wall, and then it hits the floor. Confused, me and the other hiders peek out from behind the chairs and join the collective gasp in shock.

Vastate lowers his empty hand calmly, and even though it's us he's addressing, it's Steele he glares at. "I'm not going to kill you all right now simply because I can't. As you can see, you have all grown so used to suspecting every ambiguity you face that if I were to attempt to destroy you personally, it would turn out the other way around. You would rather that I, one of the most crucial components to the system that keeps this nation pure, was brutally slaughtered than run the risk of you being harmed in the slightest. By the way, I figured you'd ask. The gun was a prop."

Even though I didn't see what happened, I've got enough hesitant dislike that I step out from behind the chair, annoyed. "Hey, that's not fair! None of the rest of us fired or anything! Yeah, we might be smart enough to keep our guards up all the time, but not all of us are nuts enough to attack! I don't remember voting *him* king of the cutouts, so you can't lump us all together just because of whatever *he* did!"

Vastate puts up a hand to stop me, and for some reason, I stop. "R—Ms. Race, please stop trying to salvage any positive opinion of your kind from me. Nothing could ever make me think any higher of you. Neither could anything make me think any less of you, no matter what the Lord of Flies does," he adds to himself in an undertone. "However, it is still our greatest hope that, during your time there, you see what your wicked ways do to people, and you lose all of your criminal appetite for destruction and come back to us as a renewed citizen that is ready to call themselves Tersatellan again. For those of you this happens to, we will be waiting for you with open arms."

I don't know why, but that part disturbs me most of all.

"Now then, you all have a little less than six hours until noon, when you will come back here to be transported into the bay. The door to my right leads to a dining room, and the door to my left leads to resting rooms. You may not find it advisable to exit the building unless you surrender, but please feel free to explore and introduce yourselves to one another. It's never too early to get to know the competition." With his parting gaze aimed at Steele, Vastate turns and leaves, the last Adaman following behind him with his hands deep in his pockets, the ends of his cloak of shadows dancing in the breeze of his stride. The last thing we see is those shadows waving us all good-bye.

Then the doors slide shut with an ominous boom behind them, certain and final as Fate itself.

We all look at one another, silent for a minute, before Motor leaps off his chair. "Food," he says and runs for the dining room, the past few minutes blowing right over his head.

"I'm with Shortstop," Spike decides and goes after him.

I stand up and go over to Vici. "Cielhomme, that was the most words used to describe the most *nothing* I've ever heard before. Hey, you alright?" I ask. "You look kinda shaken."

She shrugs. "Understandably so. Did you see what happened?" I shake my head, and she glances over to where the prop gun's sitting on the ground. It's in about a million pieces. "It was so fast. He whipped this baton out of his sleeve, knocked the gun flying and went back to normal position in approximately point seven seconds. If he had hit Vastate's head with that, I'm afraid it would have gone flying too."

"That's a sight I'd pay to see." I smirk. "I'm gonna try and get some sleep before this thing starts. If I wake up early enough, I'll get something to eat before we go. Maybe I'll eat everything. I skipped second dinner for that swoop last night, ugh. Anyway, care to join me?" Vici nods nervously.

Both of us keep glancing at that Eli. He's closed his eyes and hasn't moved.

"I want to talk to him at some point," I whisper as I walk away. What I really want more than talking or sleeping is eating, since Tersatellans eat a lot because we're apparently more durable and stronger and heal faster than other people, so we burn energy really fast. But Vastate's probably trying to buy our complacency with food, so I'll skip the eating for now and go straight for the sleeping. Or at least I try.

"Pardon me," a smooth parody of a somewhat familiar voice slides into my ears, and I spin around to see Jacques standing right behind me. A hint of a smile settles on his face, and he sticks out his hand with the grace of a professional gentleman, if there was such a profession. Heck, if gentleman was a Sector, he'd be the Adaman. Criminals never shake on anything conventional, though, and sure enough, when I pull my hand back, there's a sarcastic business card promising the highest quality bewilderment that stolen money can buy, and I shrug, showing him the wallet I grabbed with a look that says *as long as it's not my money*. It gets him to smile even more, and I know we've reached an understanding as he bows his head in greeting. "It is an honor and pleasure to meet you. Tim Hans, locally known as Jacques, at your service. I wish to kindle neither animosity nor suspicion but rather an understanding. My dark reputation applies only to whosoever neglects or abuses their liberty, though I'm afraid it sounds as though I am kind to none."

"Hey there, howdy does and all that's good stuff!" the clone pipes, shaking Vici's hand with his right and waving at me with his left, both vigorously. "Name're Tom, butcha knows they'd tagging me Mac. We's here for buds, not blood, and we gonna haves us a hulluva times or busta back trying! I'd practically drag him here while I hearing there's gonna be a races with *mobiles* and stuffs. I'ma deck that Nuvitadi decor as up as up can am, man, I's be goes hundred of KPH!" He seems to have forgotten his inside voice (and all rules of grammar, though it doesn't sound as stupid as it might look) at home. Speaking of the Nuvitadi, though, his eyes are a startling mixture of red and green, like a pile of emeralds with some rubies tossed in, all glittering together in the sun—identical piles lie in his brother's eyes, charming and haunting as a snake-song so I can't stop staring. Both boys stop shaking our hands at the same exact time, no joke. "Now, who's you? Y'know, I know, but I dunno til I *know*, you know?" I shake my head because I don't know.

"She's Rat, and I'm Vici. As in veni vidi vici," Vici says for me. The Latin is lost on Mac, but Jacques nods. Or should I call them Tim and Tom? Who knows what they really want. It's overwhelming, seeing them together. They look *exactly* the same, same tan, same smile, same nose, same eyes and ears and hair that parts the same way. I'm glad they don't wear the same clothes—my head would explode, I swear. Jacques's in cagey white/camo for satire against the Adamantration with a black bandana around his neck while Mac's in red and black that's too showy for the Arctic, with black fingerless gloves covering his palms, cut from the same cloth as the bandana. The way he slips his hands behind his back when he sees me looking makes me frown in discovery—we're all kinda using our sable to hide.

Then again, he's got that black muscle shirt on, and that somehow seems weird to me, weird that he's also *wearing* it, brandishing it instead of hiding something with it, so the sheer defiance of the color radiates boldly on my skin. And yeah, I know I wear basically the same thing under this hoodie too, but you'd better believe I'm hiding something too. This is different. It's obvious; it's shameless; it's a slap in the face to the Plexus and everything it's meant to be. It almost reminds me of something or someone else, but before I can pin it down, the trail of thoughts gets interrupted.

"Well, are we gonna hit the sack or what?" A voice that pretty much *is* mine makes half of us jump, and I'm very much included in that half. Craw laughs as he walks up, dismissing everything ever thought and said and done up til this point. "Sorry, I had to. Twinning's fun! Is this where all the cool cats hang their skins and call it a night?" We all nod at the same time, which makes him laugh again. His laugh is easy and careless, the kind of laugh you don't need to search for because it'll always find you first. "Aw, you guys crack me up already. Craw, by the way. You can guess why," he says, picking a different voice for every word of the last sentence.

I shake my head, stunned. You wouldn't believe it until you heard it. "That's amazing."

"Ha! You know what I find amazing? Breaking into a Steele residency and making off with a ball of energy. It was all over the Plexus! And that's just the latest thing, probably no skin off your back. They're gonna start calling you the Kill Switches if you keep this up." This guy seems to be the only one that's able to talk about the Seizure so openly. Still, he seems to get our silent message that we're not supposed to talk about it out loud in public. "Anyway, I heard about it from a friend of mine—having a big mouth and all, I'm known for knowing everything gossip. 'I came, I saw, I conquered,' by the way, Tom. Pretty nice swoop, ladies." He turns around and looks into the rest of the room, which most people have evacuated. "Yeah, as for me, I'm here for the thousand dollars and a day and the glory, but not the citizenship. Everyone surviving and going right back to business would be the best thing to me, to rub that in the

Adamantration's face. Hope nobody dies. But I'm not sure if everyone's in that boat with me, if you know what I mean."

The odd one out in point is the only person left sitting now, still oblivious to the rest of us or ignoring us. While the guys're distracted with doing everything they can to not look at him, I glance over and catch his gaze. He looks… nervous. And Craw thinks he's a threat? The guy didn't even have a crime. I realize there's more than one Steele in Tersatellus, and it's probably a coincidence, and he was supposed to be another Fracture, another poor sap thrown in here just to throw us off, and you know what, I resent that. He stares at me, and we try to figure each other out across the distance before I give him a cocky smile and a salute before I walk out of the chamber into the hallway.

Craw's the first one to follow me. Even though we're pretty much the same age, he's taller than I am and looks way older. He's got that tired look of an older person, of someone who grew up too fast and stays hungry too much. It's that cold kind of hunger that gnaws deep in your chest, though, the cutout hunger called loneliness that drives his dance-a-night scheme, that inspires the need to play with fire to feel something besides the cold. Those jaded eyes of his light up around other people, though, as if to hint that fire feels hottest on the most frigid nights of our loneliness, so even though the concept of personal space seems to slip his mind, I can't make myself mind too much.

"Yo, darling," he says, walking up close so he can lower his voice. "You wouldn't happen to be related to anyone named Lashia Horne, would you?"

Lashia Horne, one of my fake names who met this guy last year and became the only person to leave him in the dust and take his beacon to steal his identity since he can be anybody so anybody can be him. "I might be," I say slyly. "Why, is she rich? Did she die and leave something in her will? It's a she, right?"

The answer satisfies him as a "no," and he doesn't know it's me. "Never mind, it's a long story. Listen, I'll wake you guys all up before it's time to go and we can get something to eat together, yeah?"

I blink, looking up at that infectious smile of his. It's suddenly easier to believe the rumors we cutout girls share about the impulse to kiss the Nobody just to see if spontaneous human combustion really exits. But I resisted it once, and it's not that hard after that, so I shrug. "Yeah, sounds good. Thanks," I'm saying before I know it.

"Cool. See you later!" He skates into a room, closing it behind him, and I stand in the hallway, fazed. A few more people find rooms for themselves. Spike gives me a little salute, and Fracture waves, reminding me of times when I used to chase the flames. Now I don't dare follow.

Tom, who's a ways down the hall, pretty much sums up what I'm thinking and feeling, punching his brother on the shoulder. "Dude, ya go *Craw* to talk to us!" I smile to myself, walking into a room. "And we get to shake hands with the Shadows! *Runneding* here's already worth it, man." I watch the clones pass my cracked doorway.

"Yes, it seems that we are idols as well now."

Vici brings up the back, popping into my dimly lit room. Her eyes are glittering little suns. She looks like a little girl getting back from her first fling, and she squeals like one too. "Oh, Rat, we actually *made* it! What would the Godfathers say? What will they say when they find us missing? Wait, they will probably know what's going on. I feel as though they would know more about what is going on than we do! Transporters, Rat, and mobiles and—I mean—it's so—can you believe—"

She stops when a blue head suddenly pokes into our room. "What is vertically above? I'm not meaning to fall from the sky into the words that were being had between you, but were you two aware that human beings are considered pack animals and that sleeping in the company of others actually improves their joy?"

For the first time in a long time, I find a solid reason to laugh. "No, Voxel, I wasn't aware. Wanna bunk with us to improve our joy?"

"Oh, absolutely!" she cries and slips the rest of the way into the room, her hair getting caught in the door for a second. "Oops. Look, there's the correct amount of sleeping mats!" The woman strides across the room and sits against the wall between the two beds, smiling contently. FOREHEAD is labeled backward on her forehead, so it makes sense in the mirror, but nothing else on her face is labeled. Her palms, upper arms, elbows, and the back of her neck and hands are also labeled. She spins the marker in her hand for a second then gets up and writes DOOR on the door before sitting down again. "And now I'm a vandal as Rex is in the state of being, also." She sighs. "I'm sorrowful. I have a few of the marbles on the outside of my cranium, as it is spoken, and this is comforting. Other people are too—comforting, I mean."

I turn and look at Voxel as I crawl into bed. She turns and looks at me too, and if I look hard enough, I can see past the legend, past the crazy, and see another cutout. *It seems we are idols as well now*, I remember Tim saying, and I think I get it now. These are people too, people that have at least two things in common: one, we have our freedom, and two, we're all Next. The Adamantration, or at least Vastate, is trying to kill us, and by the way, the whole world wouldn't mind too much if he succeeded.

We're all on the same level now, and all we've got is each other. I try for a convincing smile. "Hey, whatever works. I'm gonna sleep with the blanket all bunched up because up til now, I've slept with stuffed animals. There's something nice about being able to hold something, to me, that is."

Vici looks at me all amazed, since the whole stuffed animal thing is one of those things I swore I'd never really tell anybody but her because it's so embarrassing—and I never even let her see these stuffed animals, because they do not really exist, and it is an elaborate lie to make me seem more approachable. Sure enough, Voxel giggles and puts her hand on my arm. "Thanks, Rat. I enjoy you." She turns to Vici. "I enjoy you as well, Vici."

We tell Voxel that we enjoy her too then shut out the light, listening to people walk past as we drift off to sleep, wondering what we're heading into. It's still unreal enough that I can fall asleep easily, which happened to me the first night I had my mainframe removed. As I go, I sort of lose track of what's happening to me, thought ceasing, and since my eyes are closed and nothing's really happening, I can't see, smell, taste, or even feel anything. But subconsciously I learn two things before I drift off—these walls are extremely thin, and we criminal type are superstitious.

In the other rooms and even in this one, I pick up faint sounds. The combination lock on my watch clicks as I open it up and indulge myself in my own presleep ritual. Spike is counting sit-ups. Voxel is quietly going over her labels. Vici is listing cities. Across the hallway, Craw is singing something. And someone next door whose voice I hardly recognize at all is saying their prayers.

When I fall asleep, I have a dream. By the time I wake up, I won't remember it, but I'll tell you how it goes: I'm running from something, something humanoid, but wrong in so many ways. Fear courses through me more than anything I've ever felt as the monster chases me, but I'm being dragged down somehow. "RUN!" someone's shouting, maybe lots of someones, but I can't tell.

The world is melting around me until the floor somehow disappears from underneath me. I start falling through darkness, when suddenly this flash of lightning, green lightning, flares all around. Then, in the way dreams do, everything changes, and I'm standing on the edge of a building, each hand holding someone else's hand so there's three of us on the edge. We're nothing but three black cutouts of people looking down at masses of dead bodies in the streets, all the mobiles stopped, nothing moving, nothing alive but us, but somehow, in this dream, I know that what we're seeing down there is only an image, not real, and that I can't trust it. The other thing that I know is that I care about these two people on either side of me very much. Maybe they're my relatives or something because I think I might even love them. But my heart is tearing down the middle because the other thing I know in this dream is that one person is trying to lead me away from the edge, while one person is trying to push me over. It ends there with the three of us on the roof. In the dream, I'm not entirely sure if I'm even me, if I even know anybody in that dream. My dreams are all sort of riddles. To me, they've never been clear, but what I don't know is that they've never been wrong. One thing I will not be able to remember and will not be able to deny is that subtly, silently, irrevocably, my world is beginning to change.

- IV -

The New Gangs

"Wakey, wakey!" Craw's voice jolts me half-awake. "You guys wanna get something to eat now?" *Food.* I'm fully awake now.

I sit up, rubbing my eyes and yawning. "Gimme a minute," I mumble and run my fingers through my hair. It's rat hair, really, with the same coarseness that makes it so bad, fingers work about as good as a salon would, and the same colors—it's gray, it's brown, it's black, it's blond, I swear I even saw some orange in there once. So I don't bother trying too hard. "Okay. Where's the dining room again?"

"Two doors down, across the throne chamber. See you ladies there," he grins, bobbing his eyebrows comically before leaving the room.

"I will exit quickly to secure myself a bagel!" Voxel declares and flies out of the room, instantly awake at the promise of food too. When I roll on to my side, I see Vici not an arm's length away, and I jump.

"Rat. Get to the washroom, now," she says very seriously, grabbing my arm and hauling me out of bed.

"Someone's chipper," I grumble. How does she all of a sudden know more about my bladder than I do?

"Woke up an hour ago. Couldn't fall back asleep. Had, uh, a bad dream." That makes my brow furrow. Didn't I have a dream last night? I can't remember, so I let it pass—I get that feeling a lot. Vici leads the way down the hallway and into the bathroom, which has tile floors and stalls and automatic sinks you'd find in any other public restroom.

"Man, I love rich people. I wonder which room the most money went into?" I say, sarcastic, thinking of the amazing lobby. The rest of this building seems detached and doesn't fit. Too plain. Too real. I wonder what's upstairs. I think I woke up at some point and snooped around the first floor out of habit, and there was nothing even worth taking.

Vici checks the halls to make sure nobody's listening and drops her voice. "Rat, I'm sorry for freaking out on you. This is the only sort of room in the whole building that isn't wired. Voxel and I used her computer to worm our way into the building's niche. Between the two of us, it took twenty whole minutes." My eyebrows hit the ceiling. Food *and* conspiracy. I'm beyond full awake now.

"They're hiding something, then?" I guess. Nobody locks stuff up that tight without something to hide.

Vici nods. "I don't think we're being watched every second, but they want to make sure they can monitor us if they need to. We cut the camera out of the room we were in, making it look as if it were an accident, so they couldn't see us getting into the system. From there, we figured out a few things through the niche alone. First of all, they've already anticipated that sometimes, the criminals will all work together and try to survive for the thousand euros and a day without the citizenship, as Craw said. That's what happened the very first time they hosted this extermination thing, it seems, and all eleven contestants survived, coming back richer and no less criminal than when they embarked.

"Obviously, the Adamantration couldn't have that again. So what they did was, they altered this place, this bay, supplied it, possibly so that it would be more likely to kill us." She shakes her head, trying to clear it. "We're not going to be alone in there. There are things they called leeches, dozens of them, maybe hundreds, that seem to be a threat of some sort. I don't think they're out all the time, but know that we're going to have some friends waiting in there with us. Furthermore, we gathered from markings on the maps of Hudson Bay that we are not the only people being thrown into the balance—this place is highly populated with societies of its own, so we must be meant to kill and be killed by the natives within the bay as well, and it works. Ever since the first time, this has happened more times, and in those times, many natives have died, many cutouts have died, and three Next have survived—all three of them came from the last batch, about twelve years ago."

Three. The number knocks the air out of my lungs. That three among untold deaths means that Vastate was lying. The Adamantration isn't really interested in getting us home as new people anymore. We're only worth anything to them if we're dead.

I shake my head, feeling hollow. "These things really *are* exterminations."

"Exactly. There have been fourteen survivors, Rat, and we have no idea who they are—there were things even Voxel and I couldn't access—but according to the statuses next to their entries in the system, *two* are still alive today. We're betting our life Threads here, and our position isn't looking well."

"Beautiful. Now, what's the good news?"

"That was the good news. At least the better news, anyway. Here's a kicker: only twelve of us are even going *into* the bay today, Rat. Gypsy's dead. We heard a commotion outside and watched people wheel her away. We're not sure if someone decided to make the competition that much easier, or…"

I go pale. "Cielhomme. Wasn't she a faulty citizen, not a cutout? She still had Plexus. Couldn't it've just been her codes messing up once and for all or something?"

"She didn't seem wounded, so I think that's exactly what it was. And we're thinking Vastate caused it. He has the Plexus and its programming, so he could've twisted or cut something for her to seal the deal, and while he can't do that to any of the rest of us because we have no Plexus for him to prey on, it's obviously meant to be some display of power, because even though she wasn't a cutout, she was a circuit breaker." Those are people that still have chips but use the lily or just shut the Plexus down as much as they can and break some rules. I remember all Gypsy's tries to get electrodes to get cut out. She was a rebel, alright. "It's clear from last night's display that Vastate enjoys using people as symbols. Let's hope his suggestions don't prove true."

"Oh, I'm hoping," I assure her, thinking about more than one symbol Vastate was using last night. "Why's there only twelve of us going into the bay, though? Did someone else die?"

"No. Vastate's plan worked. Fracture figured out what happened to Gypsy and he bailed." My shoulders slump, but I try not to let it show. "That was something else we figured out from the cameras. But most of all, we listened to Vastate and Steele fighting over our final competitor."

My eyes get even wider. It doesn't take a rat to know we're at the meat of the matter now. "What . . . what were they saying?"

"Oh, it was terrifying, Rat. You've never heard such anger between two people. Obvious reasons aside, it also seems this Eli isn't exactly registered legally." That hits me as funny—he's illegally registered in a competition for criminals? "The thing is, he's not all human."

"I thought so," I whisper before thinking about it, and Vici gives me her I-don't-know-about-you-sometimes look. "But, er, not really. I mean. What is he, then?"

"He's half Mech."

No thoughts form. No reactions. I can't do anything but stare at her, blank.

"Look, Rat, I don't know what to tell you. It's exactly what they were arguing about. Maybe he's not human at all. He's got the skin, and his structure sounds virtually the same, and there's still some real tissue left, but most bones are metal, and joints are mechanical, and though his brain still carries out tasks of the human brain, with analysis and sensation and control the same as you or me, it somehow knows how to operate all the machinery in his body. It's our skin, but not our flesh and bones, and while it's close, it's certainly not our brain. But is that how you define a human? Skin, flesh, bones, brain? Or are we defined by some sort of soul, the will to live and have our own free thoughts? Then he is human. And the scary thing is, he'd be more human than almost anyone in Tersatellus."

"Wait, what? Free thought? I thought you said he was half Mech!"

"I know, I know, but we think Steele said that this . . . *person* . . . doesn't run on the Mech niche. No orders. No anything. He's totally free. And we couldn't figure out how on earth that was possible, until we invited the Nobody to our party. You're a heavy sleeper, and we couldn't wake you up until recently," Vici admits sheepishly, mouthing, "Craw is *such* a flirt," which relaxes the tension a little. "We wound our way through gossip and hearsay until we reached the topic of Steele's controversial extraction. There are rumors—only rumors, even in the Adamantration, that's as close as you can come to this man—about some sort of genetic brain mutation that made the mainframe absolutely useless to Steele at some point in his life, which was why he was cut out. This gene was also picked up much sooner by his little brother. However . . . do you know how the mainframe raises children, how it's packed with all the signals to make sure they keep breathing right and such so the parents have to do almost nothing?"

"It didn't work with the brother?" I guess.

"Exactly what we believe. We gather he died within twenty-four hours. The thing is, that happened seventeen years ago. How old does Eli look to you?"

I try to breathe, but I suddenly forget how. "Vici, that's glitching insane."

She swats me for the curse. Our language doesn't really use swears, only the mollified versions with "glitch" and "sticks." "It was the best explanation we could come up with. We can't figure out how Steele did it, but don't you remember that sheet that seemed to hide a human figure on the table at his residency?" I pale, remembering. "Yes. This is Anti-Impossible we're talking about here. If anyone could pull this sort of thing off, it's the Porcupine."

"Okay," I whisper, trying to wrap my mind around this. "Okay." I lean against the wall, drawing on it with my finger to help me think. "So . . . I guess what I'm wondering now is . . . what's Eli doing *here*?"

Vici purses her lips. "I've been thinking about that too. And I have no idea. Steele doesn't need the money, plus he's an Adaman, so Adamantration immunity would get him nowhere, but then again, we don't know anything for sure, especially not about any Steele. You know what?" She smiles darkly. "Why don't you go ask him yourself, since you're so interested?"

I think the temperature in the room drops ten degrees. "That, dear, is a wonderful idea." We (read: Vici gawks as I) start for the door. "Oh, do you know how he got here, by the way?"

"What do you mean, how he got here? He ran, fast as a mobile. Or how he got qualified? He used his brother's beacon, I hear, after he murdered a rapture man."

I stop in my tracks. "*That's* his crime?"

Vici nods slowly. "I guess he was pressed for time."

Secret races without any explanations, spying on the most important folks in Tersatellus, mechanically assisted rebirth, and now murder. What a morning.

Voxel and Craw are waiting for us in the hallway, not in the dining room. I nod at them to let them know I know. For the first time, they both look serious. Craw comes closer as we walk to the dining room and whispers, "We're feeding loops to all the cameras, and we've told everybody else already. Very plainly, and with as much detail that we've got. So far, we've got no confirmation or denial."

"Well, have you even talked to him?" I ask, and Craw shakes his head. "Then there's your problem," I say, walking into the dining room.

It's a stuffy room with a long buffet table in the back and small circular tables hosting small clusters of people. You'll never guess who's sitting alone, nervously toying with a cup of water. His hands are above the table, and his expression couldn't be more readable if it was written down. For some reason, these are the things that strike me.

Vici, Craw, and Voxel chicken out and hang back as I walk over and sit down. At first, everything I know swims in my head, making me wary enough to win a contest, but then I remember what Tom said: you don't know until you know.

What if I tried to get to know *the truth before I* pretend *I know it?*

I don't expect him to look up at me, but when I sit down across from him, his green eyes shoot up to look at me. You'd half expect him to be able to animate nonliving objects with that look. He looks surprised that I'm here and has no idea what to do now. "Hello?" he questions, not sure I knew he was here, or not sure I knew he was real.

"Salut. Are you gonna have breakfast?" I question back. I don't think he's so much as had any water.

"I don't eat," he says flat out, and I can tell he's watching my reaction even as he pretends to take a drink. He makes it real obvious that he doesn't swallow. I'm not sure what he wants me to think, but I hold up under the scrutiny.

"Sure you don't. So, Eli—I can call you Eli, right?"

The first sense of conviction finally meets him, and he sits up straighter without noticing. "That's all I want to be called. Everyone else here seems to have about fifty names, but I'm fine with one." It's the most I've heard him say at once. He sounds and looks totally human. In fact, it's almost easy to believe—you know, except for the fact he's pretty much *trying* to come off as inhuman. *Why?*

"Okay, so, Eli. I understand if you don't want to answer this, but was that you in Steele's basement that I tried looking at?" Behind me, I think I hear Vici slap her forehead.

Eli smiles a little bit, though. "Yes, that was me under the sheet. It's cold down there, and the T-shirt wasn't exactly helping, as you can guess." *Yeah, I've been doing a lot of guessing lately.* He glances around the room at all the looks we're getting. "So you're wondering why I'm here."

My eyebrows knit. "How'd you know?"

"It seems to be a common theme around here. And since I don't exactly have guts, I decided against standing on a table and announcing it to the whole room, so I was just wondering how I would let someone know when you came along. Race, was it?" Formality is established by use of surname.

"We use tags, so it's Rat, no Race necessary. Capiche?" I try not to let it sound exacting.

Most people either panic because they've heard of me before or give me this incredulous that's-really-what-you're-going-with look, but Eli coughs and I think he's trying not to laugh. "Rat, then. I'll tell you. It's clear that Vastate is determined to have the heads of everyone in this room. I'm here to make sure that doesn't happen."

"You mean, protect us or whatever?"

I nearly hit Craw (whose face appeared above my shoulder at some point during the conversation) as he decides to add his own voice in. The others have been gravitating over by us, *real* subtle, thinking we won't notice the room getting smaller even though the near-silence of the enclosure gets suffocating.

"Exactly," Eli says, oblivious or uncaring of them.

"Look, boss," I start.

"It's Eli," he says before he can stop himself, then blushes. "Um, I—"

"No, it's okay." I smile, waving him off. He said "Um." This is great. "Hold on to that. Don't let anyone tell you otherwise if you and your free will don't want, Eli. But listen, we're a bunch of hardened criminals here, facing some of the craziest things you could imagine every day. Feel free to tag along, but I don't think we'll need a lot of saving."

"Don't be so sure," Eli tells me, earnest in not a threat but a warning. "Things don't turn out as planned. That place is dangerous. I wanted to remind you that you don't have to go. You're criminals, you don't have to stick with going, and if you change your mind about this, I was thinking I could be of some use in your escape if you needed it."

I stare him down a second, drumming my fingers on the table. "I flew across the country for this, for one slim chance to take the Adamantration's bullsticks and shove it where the sun don't shine. All I ever do is bail. I wanna know how it feels not to. I'm gonna get paid to hang out and explore the world, and I intend to have the time of my life, not run for it."

He purses his lips. "I hope you're right, but if you're not, I want to help."

"Oh, great, I feel so much safer now that the *robot* who *killed* someone to get here now promises to protect us," Lily sniffs as she swaggers into the room. "I've officially lost hope in lasting six seconds out there."

"Ignore her. Why are you trying to protect us, what from?" I demand now that this is getting serious.

"Everything. The locals. The leeches. Vastate. He's put billions of primes into these exterminations, and this one more than ever before. Even the Criminal Resolution Sector can't lay a finger on what he's invested into the destruction of anyone considered dangerous."

"What are you all, senseless? Don't listen! He's just another drone made by Steele to turn you against Vastate!"

Eli ignores Lily, trucking on despite her harassing, though I can tell he's getting annoyed, but he's too desperate to confront her direct right now. "Do you think that twelve or fourteen or even fifty criminals is anything compared to the millions of flawless people? If your criminal records were important enough to invest such money in, then why would he be willing to destroy them and let you have immunity from the Adamantration if you survive?"

I lean in closer, trying to block out Lily. "If he's not after us because of our crimes, then why's he want us dead so bad?"

"He's not after the criminals, he's after the cutouts, especially the strong ones. I've been . . . observing, and I think he's afraid of you and your, um, Plexuslessness. He believes that if you have the immunity, if there are no consequences for your actions, you'll end up getting yourself killed, anyway. That's why there are no rules in this place—it's to get all the liberty-loving cutouts killed by their own hands to prove how dangerous freedom can be. If he can take you from the equation, then he's got the whole rest of Tersatellus under his thumb."

Rex, who's always been under the impression that Vastate will one day use the chips to somehow control people's minds, slams his fist down on the table. "My paranoia's justified!" First it's spoken in the same cheer Layla Kael always had whenever something proved her right, then the smile falls off Rex's face when he realizes what he said, what it means. "My paranoia's justified," he repeats to himself in a murmur, like he's wondering what he's been drinking.

"This is nonsense!" Lily roars. "I thought you were all cunning, hardened criminals who could see through a lie! Someone take a good, long look outside. Those are people out there, and they do have brains, and they are going wherever they want to go and are doing whatever they want to. People nowadays are freer than they have ever been throughout all of history, and here you all are, coming up with some conspiracy about the enslavement of the human race!"

I stand up, because I don't care how much I do or don't agree. I don't like her, and I want to argue. "If that's so, why'd you give up your mainframe, Lily? Why would you walk away from your relatives and your nice, cushy life if you already had everything you wanted, if you still had your freedom?"

Lily tosses her hair in her head-turn to look at me. "Because I was interested in sharp, pointy objects and things that go bang, and the soft voice in the back of my head telling me no was too annoying. Because it would set me apart and make me special. Because every star has to have a backstory. That's what makes them such a character." She lets one pained look slip my way, telling me that's not the whole story, before she redirects her gaze to Eli.

"Thespian," I interrupt her, and she allows herself one last bullet of a look at me, and I put my hands up. Then she goes back to Eli again.

"Look, if you think that it's even possible for Vastate to 'put the nation under his thumb,' then you're wrong. For us humans, the Plexus can balance signals in a brain, but it can't make them feel loyalty. It can give messages but can't force the person to believe them. Even if he tried, it's impossible to manipulate us that way—you can lead a horse to water, but you can't make it drink, not even if it's dying of thirst, because it can think for itself. There are thousands upon thousands of precautionary measures in the Plexus to make sure that no such influence is possible. That's why there are still circuit breakers out there who, despite the Plexus, still find pleasure in having a good, illegal time with guns and drugs sometimes. They're not perfect, and that's what makes them human. You know what is perfect? Machines are perfect. And because they can't think for themselves and do need something else to do that for them, they can be programmed to jump off a cliff without question or, for another random example, programmed to serve its master by tricking a bunch of criminals and murdering them the second the race starts and bring quite a haul of money back in its blood-soaked hands!"

Now Eli stands up, his voice dangerously quiet. "For your information, I have no more programming than you do. I was the one to draw the connections, and coming here was entirely my idea. Jaden had nothing to do with it."

"How'd you know about this, then? I mean, the race and all." Spike doesn't really sound as suspicious as he is passively curious. Then again, nothing ever seems to bother Doug-Hurts-Less. But to the rest of us, the silence is monumental as we wait for an explanation, because the part we really want answered is the mountain of questions implied by that "and all."

For a while, Eli just stares at the table. "Rat got your tongue?" I ask him when it seems he's going to just give up and run away. He looks up desperately, and I give him a wink to tell him I for one am not about to rip him apart the second he says anything. "Stare at the table long enough and you might burn the answer into the cloth if you're shy."

There's some eye rolling and snickering, but Eli returns the smallest of smiles. Then, he starts slowly, "Okay. I know you might not believe this, but you asked, so I'll say it. For seventeen long years, I have waited. It was all that I could do. I've been comatose, trapped inside of a dead shell, hardly capable of bare thought, but I still listened, and I watched when my eyes slipped open, and I have learned. It might not be as complete of an understanding as yours, since my knowledge only expands as far as what I've gathered from conversations I've heard and glimpses I've seen throughout the years, but it's enough that I could learn things about this race, possibly more than you. It's enough that I can still help." He looks back up at all of us, daringly now, passing from person to person as if to personally deliver the message, which couldn't be more clear—he's here for us, and that's all. I know because those eyes tell me so. When you look into them and see what kind of strength prowls under the surface of those seas of liquid lightning, you suddenly want nothing more than to fall back on that strength, and some patient spirit in those eyes tell you that it wants nothing more than for you to do just that.

It hits me that this might be why Eli was showing off how he's not all human—he's sacrificing any chance of us liking him just to look more useful. And that is something I believe a machine would never have the heart to do.

"You claim you've been around for seventeen years, but Steele only made the first Mech fifteen and a half years ago," Vici points out. "How's that possible?"

Eli sighs. Somehow, seeing him breathe is fascinating. "Because originally, I was the son of Renee Aria and Dion Steele, born a legitimate human being seventeen years ago. I've just been through some, ah, modifications lately."

Me and Vici lock eyes. Honestly, I do my best to look calm, but I'm sure my look says *Oh my God, that's so cool!* while Vici is stuck at *Oh my God.*

"That's ridicalus! Look, I know I'm ain't the brighterest box in the bulbs, but I knows ya can't unkill a dead guy!" Tom protests, and Lily's laughing.

"You'll really say anything, won't you?" she sneers at Eli.

"It doesn't matter, anyway. If you don't want my help, then don't take it. As for the rest of you, I'm going to admit that being superhuman does have its advantages. What use do I have for money or time? After seventeen years without movement, one begins to learn the value of freedom, and I respect anyone else who knows that value too." I see that earnestness shining through his careful pieced-together words again. "I'm here to protect you, since you are among the only ones that are left to share that value. But to reuse an old saying, one can lead a horse to water but can't make it drink. I can only give you help if you're willing to take it."

Lily nods for a few seconds with a *watch this* sort of smile.

"We should split up," she says out of nowhere, standing back. "We're all going to try to survive, but some of us want to do it in rather different ways from others. It would make sense to split into two units—one unit for those of us that want to stick to their criminal instincts, and one unit for those of you foolish enough to trust the toaster."

I jump out of my seat and put myself between the two of them when Eli starts toward Lily, who's smiling hotly. "Okay, okay, that's enough. Everybody calm down."

"Calm? She called me a toaster!"

It's interesting and bloodcurdling at the same time to finally see him ticked at something, but I decide to deal with Lily first and resolve the whole situation as a main effect. "You want teams, Lily? Fine, you get teams. But you won't find me on yours. Out of the countless cutouts that've gone into that bay, fourteen've made it back out alive, and from the sound of it, most of them didn't last too much longer. One of us is dead, and nothing's even started yet! I don't know how fond you are of those chances, but as for me, I'm sticking to my criminal instincts of survival, and this is what they're telling me to do. Swallow my pride and take some help. Besides," I add, "you never know, it could be interesting. Who could say no to that face, eh? Listen, I'm sick of all this talk. If you all have these great opinions you're willing to defend all day, let's see you stand for em right here when it counts." Eli stares at me in wonder as I step over to his side of the table. "Who's with me?"

I look around the room to find nobody looking back at me.

Silence settles down onto us. Everyone's frozen, hesitating to make a move. It was easy to be a spectator or throw in a comment every now and then, but getting put on the spot is enough to make anyone nervous. But for every second that passes, me and Lily glare at each other harder, and the line between us grows and grows until it doesn't seem like a preference of where to go and stand anymore. It seems way bigger than that, maybe too big to chew.

But right when I start wondering if I made a huge mistake doing this, the others square their shoulders and start to choose.

"Me." Rex stands up from the table, escaping his slouch for the first time. Without another word, no explanation or reasoning, he walks over and stands by my side without even tripping. Eli looks at the two of us in surprise, and I nod. *Yeah, that's right, we're here, on your side. Why not?*

Lily seems to notice it's three to one, and her smile disappears. "Ivy, get over here!" she snaps, and the girl drifts over to her side of the line. "And what with the rest of you? Oh, and Spike, since I was afraid something such as this would occur, I left behind a gift in your mobile, which I'm sure you wouldn't want to find in a million blazing bits upon your return."

That was his brother's car, and it's about the only thing Spike finds enjoyment in anymore, I've heard from the rumors. "You're such a dog, Lily," he informs her calmly and rolls up his sleeves before thudding in his heavy boots to stand very close behind her, glaring down at the top of her head with a look that says he's thinking about biting it off, but he's too bored to chew that much garbage.

"You can't make the horse drink, but you can shove his head underwater and give him a choice between drinking and drowning," Rex notes in an undertone, and I snort, watching Lily try not to break a sweat.

Something tugs on the bottom of my shirt, and I look down to see Motor there, hardly coming up to the bottom of my ribcage. "I'm with you, Rat," he says, not smiling, but his eyes are shining impishly, and in awe, I wonder if I really did get infamous out there or if I've just acquired some new fans since I've gotten here.

"Me too." Voxel smiles, striding over. She takes off her jacket and sets it on a chair on the way over, tucking her marker safely behind her ear. "We are going into a wasteland too cold for jackets. It is time to try something new."

"No, tanks. I'm takes the devil I'll knew," Tom decides and walks over to Lily's side of the line, but then he subtly shifts and stands next to Ivy, whispering something to her that makes her smile gently and look at the floor. Whatever it is, it really ruffles Lily's feathers, so I can guess. I've been good at that today.

Tim is, at this point, probably farther from his twin than he's ever been before. The joking legend goes that there had to be a warp in time those three years between the brothers' extractions (Tom was a little slow to follow) because they've almost never been separated from each other far enough that they don't share the same air. He looks helplessly between the two sides then sighs and goes over to Lily's side. Still, he gives me a look of apology, and he places himself protectively between Tom and Lily. That's a sight that stabs me in the chest and makes my eyes sting, and when he glances at me again, I hope he can see that he is absolutely 100 percent forgiven and hope he *doesn't* see I'm trying not to cry (that's bound to happen at some point—I'm great at crying, watch). My fists bunch so hard that my nails dig into my palms, and I close my eyes, breathing very calculatedly so the air doesn't shake in and out of my lungs.

Shut up, shut it up, it never happened.

Craw takes his place on my side of the line, patting me on the shoulders. "Who'd pick Lily over you, anyway, Little Miss Epicness?" he jokes, and if steam could come out of people's ears, Lily would turn the place into a sauna, I swear. It's easy to tell by their looks that they've got some history too, so I roll my eyes and smile the way I'm supposed to, but if I'm going to be honest, you should know some part of me finds deep satisfaction at that comment, even though it's nothing but customary Craw talk.

His decision left Vici with nobody to hide behind anymore. When I open my eyes, I don't understand why she looks so torn. My mouth moves without a sound for a second. "Vici..."

She shrugs weakly. "I mean, it makes sense, you know. That way, the teams would be equal. You wouldn't want the teams to be lopsided, do you?"

"They're going to be lopsided already when people start dying," I explain, trying not to growl. *What's going on? What's she doing?*

Vici shakes her head. "We're not inside Hudson Bay yet, Rat. It's not too late. You don't have to do this. We can make our own team, as we had already planned it!"

I shake my head. "What about the leeches? We don't know anything about them or the locals or anything! Vici, this isn't about some controversy about what defines us as humans or whatever, this is about *survival.* There's strength in numbers, and strength in strength, period! I know it seems weird, but... listen, he's not a machine, Vic. I'd know, wouldn't I? You know me. I don't even like computers, and I have a nasty habit of wrecking mobiles, and I broke a MechCounter last year by looking at it, remember?" That's been our joke for months, especially since that's the only explanation for why the thing suddenly stopped working when we were 'shopping' once. Anything that runs on electricity's got grudges against me for some reason. "And now I'm not even getting snippy, see? Vici, I promised I'd protect you when you became my partner in crime. Come on over, and let's keep it that way."

But she crosses her arms and raises her voice. "Where's the Rat that I know? The Rat that never trusted a word anyone said, the Rat that never needed anyone's help, the Rat that laughed at any group with anyone more than two people? I want that Rat back, where'd she go?"

I sigh, subconsciously calling on that whimsical spirit she seems to think I have sometimes. "Sorry, Vici, but I think that Rat might be gone. Sometimes, we've gotta leave behind who we used to be and everything we've ever known so we can get to everything we can be." I step toward her. "It's the same thing I said before. We take chances, we make decisions, we make our own lives out of an existence by doing it, even when it's crazy! Think about it. Do you wanna be 'good enough' out there to survive, or are you willing to try something crazy to see if we can't get a little more, or even win? You made that choice, crossed that line the second you got extracted from the Plexus and when you stepped over the threshold of my residency. We both picked this, and now trouble is the only certainty we've got the luxury of keeping. Now you get to make that choice again. Come with me, Vici," I plead, "And let's see how much farther we can get these chances to go."

Vici looks at me. She looks at Eli.

Then at Lily. Then the ground.

And she says, "No."

She gives me one more long, hard look. "I won't stand for this insanity. Resurrection? The extinction of cutouts? A matter of liberty? Excellent, if that's what we were really dealing with here. But I'm a hacker to my core, and there's no way I'm letting a machine keep me safe. As for you, I don't know who you are or what you've done to my friend, but let her know when you find her, there's always room for her by me." With that, she walks over to Lily's side of the line.

I watch her. I watch her and I think, *I gave you everything you have. I could have never spoken to you. I could have walked away. If not for me, you wouldn't be here right now. You once trembled at the thought of me, and now you think you're so high and mighty for leaving and using me as a springboard, you ungrateful little—*

But you learn to expect it after a while.

I shrug again before saying blankly, "Well, look at that, equilibrium. Nice. Why don't we go to the lobby and see if Vastate's ready for us?"

Everyone starts going for the doors at once, eager to move on past that awkwardness. "Hang on," Eli pauses me and runs across the room and back again. In about half a second. No kidding. He hands me a bagel, along with Voxel, who got here late too (so much for exiting quickly). "Um. You should have breakfast."

Voxel instantly digs in. "Oh, this is on the road to being such fun! We'll be advancing within this as a type of family!"

My heart clenches. "No, no, absolutely not. Don't say that word. Please," I add, trying to lighten my tone. "Families always end up breaking apart because you can't pick the people. Families are flawed because they try to force you all to like each other when you don't have a choice. We picked this, so we'll be fine," I explain, still sneaking confused glances at Tim and Tom, wondering what they've got that I didn't.

Lily's team goes out ahead of us. Vici doesn't even look back at me, and I sigh. Sometimes, you need to let go of everything and everyone you've known to move on.

When I try to shake the thought off, I notice that Eli's still hovering by me, watching me stare at my ex-friend. His scrutiny makes me feel invisible and turns all my thoughts into items on display, so even when I avert my eyes in a poker face, he gathers enough from me to ask, "Is there anything you want me to do about her?"

The question strikes me as odd. Nobody's really ever asked me what I wanted before, so it surprises me into lifting my gaze back up into Eli's. People aren't inclined to keep my gaze—Mizz Adaman Nocturnum was right about my attitude; people always think I hate whatever it is I'm looking at—but Eli proves himself different in that case too, so I end up staring, wondering what's so different about this stranger that he can see right into me and still offer help . . . and wondering what makes me want to take it. But that's not the way I roll.

"No, thanks," I tell him. "It was her choice, and there's nothing that any force on Earth can do to change it—she's a cutout, after all." There's still some pride I have left in her, but when she steps into the chamber ahead of me without looking back, the pride gets a little darker.

"Are you sure?" Eli asks me, and for a second, I'm not sure. I don't know anything for sure anymore. It's all so twisted, so different. Everything changed, and I don't even remember turning my back on it. It all crumbled before my eyes, and now it makes me want to fall apart, so I have to ask myself how I wind up getting bailed on so much and why I thought this might be different. Then something about the way Eli watches me—not waiting for an answer or for me to do some other stupid thing, but maybe waiting to catch me if I really do fall apart—helps me take a deep breath and get some thoughts together.

Good courage, Rat. Are you ready to take this chance? Are you sure?

"Yeah, I'm sure. Just . . . leave her be," I say then hold a breath and stride for the chamber with such outward sureness, you'd think I was chasing after some great destiny into that room. But if you want honesty, I didn't have any idea which of us I was telling to let Vici go.

Vastate is already waiting for us onstage when we walk in, sulking to our seats, guilty as cats back from a walk too late. "Have a bit of trouble telling time, my friends? There's no need to add truancy to your list." He sounds annoyed. *Good, it's an honor to annoy you*, I think, wondering about Gypsy and Fracture and the argument about the guy had with Steele about Eli. Even though I never liked Steele and I don't know about this Eli guy yet, I'll use anything for fodder, and I manage to like Vastate even less. "Shall we begin the transport?"

"Wait, aren't you gonna give somebody the secrets?" Craw asks.

Vastate gives us his toxic smile. "I already have."

Every member of our motley crew suddenly gives their fellow thespians an observation. Vici has her eyebrows bunched, and she starts messing with her braid. Tom's giving the chandelier a thorough absent stare as he fiddles with his gloves. Tim's watching Vastate very closely, revealing nothing. Craw coughs, putting his head down. Motor's looking at everyone with big eyes. Lily's doing something similar, but her eyes're getting smaller and more suspicious of us with every passing second. Ivy stares blankly at Vastate's feet, hands in her pockets, her eyes flitting up nervously every few seconds. Rex is concentrating on the floor, and he's probably wondering if that's *really* his shoe size. Voxel's finishing off her bagel, looking unfazed. A smile is slowly creeping onto Spike's face under his shades. And Eli's looking anywhere but at Vastate, who's giving him the electric stare because I know he's trying as hard as possible not to look at me.

Analysis: it could be anybody. Anybody but me.

I swore it would be me, but once again, I am disappointed.

Craw's giving me a "do something!" look I recognize from Vici doing that to me all the time, so they must've figured out I'm not too good at leaving good enough alone. I take a step forward. "Hey, don't shoot me down for daring to speak to you again, but how're we supposed to know if you didn't give the secrets to someone and then have them killed?"

Vastate sighs. "The secrets have been disclosed to one of you in this room, and quite recently—they are always disclosed shortly before the competitors depart to avoid giving them the ability to think about it or giving them the time to run away."

"First of all, Gypsy didn't run, she was killed," I growl, crossing my arms. Rex shoots me a look that might actually be grateful for sticking up for his aunt, but that's probably a trick of the light. "Second of all, where's the other Adamans that were here last night?" Being in a room where he's the only authority makes my skin crawl, and besides, it feels suspicious.

"Though I have no idea why this concerns you, I'll tell you if it alleviates your obvious terror, my friend. Alleviate means to lessen, in case you weren't aware. Mizz Adaman Nocturnum is currently giving the Remainder this speech, and Sir Adaman Wheel is making the final touches on your mobiles."

"First off again!" I start counting with an unorthodox finger. "I am not your friend, and I never will be, so you can quit that charade any time you like." Another finger goes up. "Second off! I *know* what alleviate means." A third finger goes up. "And third, in case you weren't aware, there were three other Adamans here with you last night, and you've mentioned two so far. Three minus two leaves one more. Keep talking, genius."

Everyone gapes at me, wondering how I don't burst into flames on the spot. Vastate stands still and watches me for a second before he shows off his favorite gift: ignoring people. "Now that there are no more questions and your fears have been soothed, we shall begin. I'd prefer to start the race as soon as possible, for it is nearly noon. Follow me." He turns and walks offstage, and some part of me still wonders why he's alone now, but then I decide it's not worth wasting breath over. We follow him toward the door, where two rapture men on either side stop us, making my blood pressure go way up. "Please relinquish your weapons to the rapture men at the doors. Justice Incorporated needs restocking, and being Next, you have a tendency to possess more weapons than you actually need, even in Hudson Bay." Relinquish our weapons? Sure we will.

Slowly we start going through the doors, giving up our arms to the men on either side. As in, we fork over anything we had visible to show off how armed we were and keep a bunch of stuff hidden. "I know you've got a multi," the rapture man to the left snarls when I try to pass him.

"Yeah, well, that's a tool, so I don't think I'll be letting you have it, Craig." I slip through the door before he can stop me.

Behind me, I hear someone ask, "Do you want me to remove my arms and legs as well?"

"Uh, no, I think the Harsha is enough," the rapture man allows shakily, and I look back to see him examining a firearm as long as I am tall.

"Okay. I sort of have heat vision too, so…"

"I knew it," I whisper to myself, equally sarcastic, and Motor giggles beside me.

"He's pretty cool. Hey, can I sit on your shoulders? I'm postmaturely short," the kid admits.

"Go for it." With insane grace, he climbs up onto my shoulders, weighing almost nothing. "Hey, you're a lightweight too. How's the view up there?"

"Not much better," Motor tells me, squinting. The room is dark, and it only gets darker when the last person steps into the room and the doors shut behind us. Motor puts his hands on my head. "Don't be scared, Rat," he says confidently. "I learned how to fight in the dark a long time ago. Blind Fighter was one of the only games I was good at on the Plexus."

"Did you ever play Take the Wheel?" I ask, ignoring Vastate as he reminds us of the only rules we know and tells us that if we try and climb the wall and get back into Tersatellus, the MechGuards'll shoot us.

"All the time! It was my favorite." He seems relieved to talk about something normal.

"I'd always crash," I admit then start paying attention to Vastate when Craw asks why the heck the room's so dark.

"Relax. The process simply works better in low light—less distractions. These machines are hundreds of years old, and constant light would eat away at them as it would at a fine painting." Boy, *that* sure helps me relax. "If you search, there are small lights by each machine. Stay by them, and if you need assistance, Shepard Addanc here would be glad to help you."

There's the sound of a mass shuffling of feet, and I lose my bearings of the room in the rush, not sure where any individual person is or even where the door's at. Swallowing, I set down Motor and head over to a faint green light. Transporters. These are pretty much the only ones in existence. Don't ask me how they work—I don't know, and I don't want to know. The mechanicalness of the thing makes my head ache, and when the light flickers at my presence, I know I'm in trouble. But despite the rapture men's best efforts, there's no way I'm going into this Hudson Bay place without some tricks. There's all sorts of trade secrets hidden in the inner pockets of my pants, including some powders that do some pretty useful stuff when you mix them with water (or spit) and some "snacks" that help me calm down around machinery. The taste of acid it leaves in my mouth is far from pleasant, but the headache fades, and the light stops flickering.

I'm probably the only one that's able to relax at this point. I figure the whole situation's so obviously sketchy it can only be meant to get us to cop out before we start, but I decide to let the others stew. Someone laughs so tensely that it takes me a second to realize it's Voxel. "You must be applying downward pressure on my chain. You expect us to climb *within* these?"

"I'm also rather incredulous," Lily admits. Her voice sounds stupid, like someone trying to have an accent.

"Relax, this has worked for years, centuries. My systems are perfect." It freaks me out how much Vastate's telling us to relax.

"Do you need my help?" a voice says next to me, and I jump. It slides through my ears and seems to seep into my brain.

"No, thanks," I reply right away, turning around and running my hands along the machine thing. My stomach goes cold. It feels—

"Akin to a coffin, does it not?" I hear the crackling of the man's lips as he must smile, but in the darkness, I can't tell if he's word-nudging me as a friend or if he's really trying to scare me as an enemy. "Quite so. You open it up and lay down inside, and we do the rest."

I hesitate. But there's nothing else to do. There's no way to leave, and I wouldn't if I could. It's time to go.

Are you sure?

My hands find the edge of the machine, and the melodrama of my moment is broken by a shaky voice going, "Uh, are there enough? I can't find one..."

It's Eli. Some hunch goes through me, and I start grinning because nobody can see me. Oh, no. Here's the rest of us freaks going oh, yes, la, the dark, how we love it so! And meanwhile, I'll bet it's freaking Mr. Superhuman out. And he had his hands on the table, not hidden. This guy. I like this guy.

"Over here," I say, because I don't want the Shepard guy to help, and step over to where his voice is and give him a push. "You can have mine."

"Oh, thank you," he says. He jumped when I touched him. As I go and find another transporter, I only find it somewhat interesting that he was warm.

"That's my only charity for the week. Savor it," I tell him as I lift up the lid of my new transporter in the back of the room, revealing a softly glowing inside that resembles a tanning bed if you're an optimist, but all I can see it as is a casket.

The man steps closer to me, so he catches the faint glow. "Since I'm nearest to you, you'll go first." Oh, joy. "Lie down and close the top. There's no oxygen in there, but you won't need it soon enough, and that's all part of the transport. It'll be best if you close your eyes and relax and pretend you're falling asleep." Carefully, I lay down inside the machine, crossing my arms over my chest, corpse-style for effect. My heart pounds in my ears as I stare blankly at the ceiling. This is crazy. I'm putting my life in the hands of Vastate and this loon. *Run for it,* some part of me says. *There's a one-in-four chance that you'll guess the right wall with the door.* It could work. I could catch them by surprise, and I know I'd be able to get outside. Get lost in the traffic. Snag someone's jacket and slip it over myself, sneak in one direction until—

Until what? Breathing already gets complicated when I realize that I can run, but I can't hide. There's nowhere to go. And even so, then I'd be leaving everyone behind, and that is something that's lower on my list than handing my life over to my enemies. I swore long ago I'd never have a gang again, but I made this team. And I'm sticking with it. So I take a breath while I still can and hold on to it.

"The tech workers will make sure everything else is working properly, making the channel for you to travel, and I shall be guarding over your essence, as well as working this launching vessel. All I ask in return is that you unwind yourself." His voice becomes muffled as he lowers the lid over me, but I think he keeps it cracked a moment. "Let all your memories be erased. Let the past fade away."

If only he knew.

It gets even harder to hear him as he shuts the lid completely on me, and the longer he talks, the harder it gets, and my mind starts to panic when it realizes that sound does not travel in a vacuum because there is no mode for it to travel by—not even air. When I try to take a breath, I might as well try to breathe lead. Already, colors are erupting in my eyes, and my chest feels impossibly heavy, my thoughts getting thick as mud. It's all happening so fast. Life is so fast, sooooo short, is there even a point?

I squeeze my eyes shut tight. What if something's wrong? What if there's a malfunction and I suffocate in here and die? What'll happen to the others? Will they follow Eli? Will any of them survive? What if this is it, this is Vastate's plan instead, is to pretend there was a mass accident and kill us all? Would Eli live through this? What if he's the only one that goes into Hudson Bay? What iiiiffffff—...(%\@#) aoiwerh>uuh...=?

Should I be seeing these colors in this life?

What life am I in, anyway?

A voice floats into my brain from far away.

"Your transport is taking place. Blink if you can." It's impossible. You know how you sometimes become aware of your breathing or blinking and then you can't stop controlling it? I'm beyond that by now. Forget blinking, I'm consciously telling my heart to beat, fighting the big black unknown. Trying to blink would be harder than trying to make my body suddenly start floating. It's not in my control. "Good." Good?! "Now, stop all struggle. Let all thoughts of resistance fall away. Your history now ceases to exist. You are no longer Ms. Race. There has never been one of her in all of history, and there never will be." More colors swirl rapidly around my vision as I slowly let go of my heartbeat, stop trying so hard to breathe. My fingers slowly unclench beside me, and my body shifts slightly, easing into the soft metal bars beneath me. What a way to go. Trippy as untied shoes. And this stupid voice... "Let the person you used to be fade into nothingness. She is meaningless now. All that matters is what lies ahead. What matters is you letting go of the person inside of this machine so you can become someone greater..."

So beautiful...

My last breath comes out of my body as a long sigh, and my whole body feels warm and numb as my heart goes so soft and slow I forget when it beats, eternities drawing out between each drum. The colors fade to blackness, and I'm faintly aware of a sound that might be singing, not aware as in I'm actually listening to it, but remembering it.

The darkness pulses, growing slightly brighter, almost unnoticeable, until it flares in an explosion of white light that splits into colors, shapes, people.

I'm easing myself into the machine, laying my Thread in the hands of those who want to cut it, or so my dying history has led me to believe.

I'm watching my best, no, my only friend left pick a side I'm not on.

I'm listening to a loud voice list off my name, accepting me into a secret competition meant to make sure that I die even sooner than anticipated. But that is not my name. No. That's not me.

She's sitting by her friend as the girl shakes and shivers, recovering from convulsions, telling her it will be okay, putting a warm blanket around the girl's shoulders. She wonders why she always says that it will be okay when she knows better.

She's waiting at the station—

She's nosing someone she doesn't know and stealing their beacon while they're distracted—

She's flying across the rooftop—

She's at the extraction site, holding the mainframe in her hand for a second, staring at it in all its corroded glory before a thought eats its way into her head, and she smiles slowly in a way that could only be described as broken. That's what the man told her. Broken. But when you're broken, when they break you, you break them right back. That's the name of the name, love, just the way it goes. Tag, you're it.

She's trying to look at the very special man that's come to pay her a visit at the hospital. They figured out something's wrong with her, but she heard the man say something to Padre about fixing her. When he walks in, she can't see him, but she asks him if they're really going to fix her, and at first, she thinks he's going to ignore her, but then he says in a murmur only she can hear, "My friend, there is nothing to fix. You are broken beyond repair because you were simply built incorrectly to begin with. Do you understand? You are a malfunction, a failure, a *mistake*. And you can never be anything more."

She's wondering what everybody's talking about. They finally found her crying, and she told them about this thing called hurt, and now you won't stop holding her and saying crazy things. The hospital? She doesn't feel sick or anything. She hates the hospital. What's wrong with her? Why won't anybody tell her what's wrong with her? Why are you holding her so tight and crying, Statice?

She's walking down the street, holding hands with the brother you used to be. He's three years older than her, which means he's a supergenius and knows everything, and he's where she learns everything from, everything about the what-ifs and why-nots and how memories are music boxes because you can shut them away or open them up and look through all the pretty pieces of paper on the inside, and a bunch of other cool-sounding stuff that's proof he's a supergenius who knows everything. So she asks him, "Statice? Why is that guy dead?" But before he can see, the nice rapture man picks up the dead guy and drags him away, and something tells her that *everything is going to be okay.*

Then she trips on the sidewalk and stings her hands, and she remembers that it'll never be okay.

This girl that I used to be holds tightly to me, pulling me away from a ledge, while the girl that I can be pulls me toward it, promising that I can fly if I try hard enough.

And then I am gone.

- V -

No Rules to Break

This might not make much sense, but my eyes are afraid to open.

My mouth, lips, and throat are dry, and even though I haven't moved yet, I can tell by the tension that everything is going to be stiff and sore when I do. Underneath me, there's no bed. It's soft, but it's not even a carpet, and some of it seems to crumble right beneath my fingertips. Every bit of me feels warm, suffused in some glow, and a strange light beats down against my eyelids the way a huge crowd knocks on the gates of a kingdom, a crowd I have no idea where it's from or if they're here to attack or make peace, so it's safer to keep my eyes shut. They roar in my ears too. Best to wait til they go away. Bound to get bored at some point.

When the first tiny speck of color starts flitting across my vision, I feel a harsh surge in my chest, harder than anything I've never felt before, and inhale sharply so hard I cough.

The coughing brought me to a kind of sitting position, leaning on my elbow, so despite how sore everything feels—I was right about being rigid as a rod—I stretch one arm and then use it to run my fingers through my hair. But something's wrong with that alone. Because it's moving. There's this rushing sound and this really faint force against my skin that's comparable to a really weak version of being in open traffic. *Wind?*

My eyes flicker open out of shock.

The world around me starts turning as vertigo takes over, pushing me down onto my back again. Breath shakes in and out of my lungs twice as fast as before, but I force my eyes to stay open and press my knuckles to my temples to try and demand some order up there. Slowly the world stops spinning so fast, and I press my hands on the weird ground to either side of me and push myself to my feet at the speed of pencils, squinting up the whole time. Above me is unending sky, and in front of me is a vast pit of blackness with a strange, grainy floor angling down into it. I back away, my feet sinking a little into the powdery stuff, but eventually, I hit something cold and hard, making me turn around.

The Divide, I realize, a feeling of dread settling inside me as I stand next to the monstrous thing. It rises up so tall it's tempting to believe it could touch the sun. The dark mass stretches all the way off to my right, curving slightly, and I guess it's wrapping around Hudson Bay. But the curve is on the inside, which means that I am also on the inside of the bowl.

To my left, the wall arcs much sharper, coming to a corner and peeling off behind me, and off in the distance, I see a similar sharp corner. So this bowl has an opening here, connected by a thin stretch of the powdery stuff.

Scattered across this strip are the other contestants. "Ah, sunlight and persons!" Voxel yawns as she stretches into a sitting position. "What's vertically above?" She doesn't get a response since she's the only other one awake, so I take a minute to step around the corner of the wall and look out.

Underneath the vast expanse of unending sky is a parallel expanse of darker blue, shifting and moving slightly, whiteness peaking on it sometimes. I've never seen anything close to this before, and I have no explanation for what it could possibly be. Even the sky seems small in comparison. Suddenly, I feel smaller than a tiny speck of dirt in one of the huge stretches of no-man's-land between the roads crossing the country. Bending down, I reach and touch it. It's cold, and my fingers go right through it. Water! But why is it this color? I press my face down close, and it smells salty, and tiny things float around in there, so it can't be water because there aren't *things* in water. But what *is* it then? Everything I know is a lie! I didn't know there was a sky underneath the sky! Panicking, I stand up, searching the horizon for some end to the enigma. What is this?

"The ocean." I whip around to see Eli walking up, hands in his pockets. He stops at an arm's distance away from me, looking out at the thing. "It's water and actually covers most of the earth. The ocean's one of the many things the Adamantration left out of the common knowledge after Tersatellus shut itself out from the rest of the world. There are other islands, bigger ones, continents out there full of nations. Tersatellus was the only one to choose such a walled isolation."

"How could they lock us away from this?" I breathe. "They could've at least left some pictures in the Plexus or something!"

"They probably didn't want to create desire for something they couldn't allow."

I dip my hand in again, marveling at the floating things. There are no floating things in the cups and bowls we drink from or in the ice gaps that melt sometimes. "What else haven't they told us?"

"They leave out anything that has to do with the outside world. Not even the Adamans know, except for the ones that were alive when it happened hundreds of years ago." I watch him as he breathes deeply, a salty gust of wind blowing our hair around our faces. It occurs to me that we could get away from here through this space in the bowl's edge. If we could somehow get to one of the nations, we'd be home free since they don't have walls to stop us. The twelve of us could rewrite our own new lives out there, could grow up together doing whatever we want in a big red house in the outskirts of a city. And I could learn everything about the world, and none of us would ever tell anyone that we were from Tersatellus, and we'd keep the truth about Eli a secret and live normal lives as free as the sky.

Right. And after that we'd move to the moon. I shudder. There's a reason there's a Divide. To keep certain things... yonder.

Then something else occurs to me.

"Eli, do those nations out there have Plexuses too?" I ask before realizing that he doesn't have any way of knowing.

He shakes his head, though. "Tersatellus was by far the most advanced nation technology-wise, and it never shared with the other nations. Even if they had the technology, they're all so competitive and close together I'm not sure a Plexused nation would be allowed to go on before the others would intervene."

"You mean it's all kind of like a big clan of relatives where they're vying to be the most advanced while kind of looking out for each other at the same time?"

"Yes, a... clan of relatives." I go back to looking out at the ocean and take a deep breath of the crisp air for myself.

"We're free," I say plainly then laugh once at it. It's nearly impossible to fathom. Yesterday, there was no such thing as Hudson Bay, and nobody ever left Tersatellus before. Now I am in a world with oceans and wind and no rules. "We're freer than ever before, maybe freer than we'll ever be. And we're about to die."

Eli purses his lips. "Not if I can help it."

"Yo, guys!" Craw yells behind us, and we turn. "You might want to see this."

Eyes widening, I walk back among the others. "What's going on?" I demand, watching the water as a hum rises up from the pit, grating in my head, and the darkness seems to solidify. Bright green lines shoot across the black floor from both sides, forming a grid pattern where the lines, no thicker than my finger, are about a meter apart. Curious, I take a tentative step onto it, but this freak sensation goes through me as I start sinking, so I jump back onto the shifting land. My head pounds, and I groan, holding it, then almost fall on the not-so-solid ground when it slides out from under me.

"What *is* this stuff?" Motor asks, kicking some of the ground into the air, which is shocking to watch. This is going to be quite an interesting new factor in footing during, say, self-defense. What kind of ground slips around under you and bursts to pieces when you kick it?

"Sand," Eli explains, picking some up. It runs back through his fingers.

"Oh, of course *you'd* know," Lily retorts, trying to shake little bits of the sand out of her hair as she works her way to her feet.

"Don't you start," Eli warns, and I have a feeling Lily still isn't forgiven for the whole toaster thing. She rolls her eyes but keeps her mouth shut. Wise.

"And this? What is this? Some sort of force field?" Voxel taps on the blackness. "It's in a solid state in this second, Rat." I step onto it again, and this time, it holds me. But I jump off again since it still makes my head hurt.

"This, my friends, is your race track," the voice of Vastate announces. At first, I can't figure out where it's coming from, but then I pull out my beacon, and his ugly golden face is on it.

"I thought we left you inside the walls," I snarl. "There's no way I'm having you sit in my pocket, telling me what to do all the time."

"I WOULDN'T DO THAT, if I were you, Thomas," he yells as Tom rears to throw the thing, sounding panicked like he's actually inside of everyone's beacons. How's he even know what's happening to it? "And I'll be leaving you entirely alone soon, so don't worry about it."

"Yeah, don't get your panties in a bunch, Ms. Race," Craw says, mimicking the guy's voice.

"Boxers, actually," I declare boldly, since he crossed that line first. (I honestly don't have a clue—the thing about stealing clothes is that it's usually too dark to see the words on the packages in the warehouses you're stealing from, and when it comes to clothing fashion, I'm about as useful as a snake. Dwell on this prospect.)

There's five seconds of silence before we decide to ignore that.

Vastate goes on, "I'm here to inform you all that once your track is done loading, it's laissez-faire for us from there, and there will be absolutely nothing we can do to alter your actions, therefore showing you what your freedom really is. You won't even be watched, so scream all you wish, but there will be nobody to hear you. Hopefully, this will teach you the value of having a nation to rely on."

"Wait, y'had to bug us to tell us that you're not gonna bug us?" Rex interrupts. It's the second intelligent comment I've heard him say, and it makes me laugh again.

More ignoring on Vastate's part. "Additionally, if you are not at the extraction point by noon on Saturday, you will be presumed dead and abandoned no matter what your fellow competitors say upon their arrivals. You're not important enough to go scouring Hudson Bay for. That will be all. So long—I hope that you all return on Saturday as changed human beings, and for those of you that have managed to remain exactly the same, then there is nothing that can be done for you. May God spare no mercy for your black hearts. Adieu."

Vastate's face clicks off the screen for good. "Wait!" Lily screams as if it'll make a difference. "How're we supposed to get food? Or clean water? Where's our mobiles? Where's the extraction point?"

For once, Leadhead's got a point. If we don't know where the extraction point is, then we'll be left for dead, and if we don't know any of the other questions, then we'll *be* dead shortly. As if in answer, the mobiles have appeared behind us when we weren't looking, probably the same mysterious way we were. Ah, science. "Okay, well that takes care of that, but what about everything else?"

"Maybe it're a one of them rule," Tom offers.

Lily stands poised for a second, thinking that over, and her fists clench slowly before she whips a Warbunker pistol out of nowhere and starts aiming it in turn at us. "Look, I want to get it out on the table right here, right now, who has that secret. Speak up! Where's your peppy we're-all-in-this-together attitude now, hmm?"

"You were the one to suggest teams," Craw points out. "So if you want to blame people for breaking us apart, you can start with yourself."

"That's it, I'm going to go down the line, shooting people until someone coughs up the rules. Starting with the loudmouth here," she finishes, aiming the pistol at Craw's forehead. He goes about ten shades paler.

Acting on instinct, I leap over and put myself between his and that gun, even though I have to stand on my toes to do it. "You'll do no such thing!" I seethe, pulling out my multi to show she's not the only one who can smuggle weapons. "You put that thing down right now or things are gonna get ugly."

"Things got ugly the moment Spike shoved you into the car, Mouse," she spits back. "What do you propose to do to me? Haven't you ever heard that one is not supposed to bring a knife to a gunfight?"

Oh, boy, if she knew what I knew. But I play my cards and tell her, "Hey, this knife has done fifty things a gun never could, and it's gotten me away from countless discipline ops with guns before. I once accidentally found a flick in the Plexus some sicko made demonstrating how to flay a frog with a pocket-knife. I'm sure you couldn't be that much different."

Lily thinks about it a minute then lowers the pistol. "Fine. We'll do it your way, and it won't work. But don't think I'm afraid to shoot if anyone ticks me off or does anything suspicious, and don't think that after years with guns, I won't hit you where I want to." She sits cross-legged on the sand, and the rest of us slowly follow suit, never taking our eyes off her.

Craw taps on my shoulder. "Thanks," he whispers, barely even audible.

"Don't mention it," I mutter, feeling my face get hot. "I'm just wondering why our fearless protector didn't do it."

"The gun's blank," Eli says very plainly.

I can't stop myself from grinning. How'd he know too?

Lily tenses, her face going redder with every passing second. Ivy smiles slightly and nods, a few meters behind her sister so the furious girl can't see. "ARG, GLITCH YOU!" Lily screams, chucking the dead gun into the ocean and sitting hard back down on the sand, her look so fierce I bet she could burst into flames if she tried any harder. Weapon dealers and any criminal who's ever used a gun knows getting caught with a blank is nothing short of a flagrant offence. It shows you've got all bark and no bite. The only thing worse than having a blank gun is firing one, and while half of me is tempted to think of how she's always rattling off her mouth without ever accomplishing anything, the other half of me wonders if there's another side to her story—she's too experienced to bring a blank gun, or *just* a blank gun for that matter. She plays with the cuff on her wrist and throws knives with her eyes between Ivy and Eli. "Stupid glitching computer."

"Oh? I thought I was a toaster."

"Guys, seriously! We don't have time for this. Why don't we admit right here and now at least who *has* the rules?" I demand.

"Isn't it obvious? Who else could it be?" Lily's saving all her knives for Eli now. "Didn't you see how Vastate was staring at him? And besides, what better option would it be aside from the one that we couldn't torture for the information?"

The suggestion is horrifying and everyone near Lily scoots away. So far, she's not making the best leader. "First of all, just because I'm very hard to kill doesn't mean I can't hurt," Eli starts.

"I'm sure," Lily scoffs.

"And second of all, I thought I'd get picked to be the Outlier too. I was counting on it, actually, and I would've told you if I knew it, but I don't. What use would a triple prize be to me when the prize is useless in the first place?"

"He's right," Vici admits, putting her hand on Lily's shoulder. "Even the Porcupine doesn't have any use for the money or the time, as far as we know. Even if he was chosen to make a point, he would have no apparent reason to lie. We can rule him out, at least for now. I don't think we can set anything into stone right now, anyway, until someone comes out and admits it."

For the first time, Lily seems to relax. "I guess you're right. Who else, then?"

"It's not you or Ivy, because if it was you, then you'd be gloating, and if it was your sister, then she'd tell you," I point out. "And it's also not Tom. I watched his reaction, and he wasn't interested in what was going on. If it pertained to him, he'd be interested. Last night, he was fixing something until his name was called, and then he stopped paying attention again after that. That's how I figured him out."

As if to prove my point, the second I said his name, he started paying attention. "Tanks, I'm thinks." I nod.

"And it's not me, because I would've told Rat, so New Rat would also know," Vici sniffs. Lily looks between her and me, knowing full well the reputation of Old Rat as a conniving cretin that put her trust in none, but doesn't say anything.

"So that leaves Craw, Tim, Rex, Voxel, Spike, and Motor," she wraps up. "And honestly, I think Rex is too stupid to keep a secret that big—he'd have spilled it to the first person he saw because he wouldn't even know it was the clue." Rex shrugs, taking the insult with a grain of salt. "Spike, I hate to say this, but your reaction was pretty suspicious."

"That's the ticket, pardon the other team and suspect your own team members." Spike chuckles to himself. I watched a flick once where someone chuckled that way, and then they had a knife against someone's throat two seconds later. "Sorry, I bunked with the clones, and we had a watch thing going on, and nobody did anything *suspicious*, and besides, if I knew the rules, I'd leave you all in the dust by know." Nobody argues with that.

"Speaking of doing that, where's Tim?" Motor asks, and we all jump when we notice the guy's missing. "Not in sight" is the last place you want Dr. Storm to be.

"Don't fret, I'm nigh. I merely opted to retire from your repartee, as it fails to regard me," Tim calls from by the mobiles. "This one shall be mine."

"If the twins act as close as they look, then we can rule out Tim too." Lily rolls her eyes. "I thought at least the older one would pay attention. Did either of you ever mature?"

Tom keeps messing with the gadget he's holding until he notices it's him that was addressed. "Huh?"

"My point exactly."

Lily tries to continue, but Tom, who's still confused, puts in, "Jim and Jon was matured." Only I notice how Tim slams a mobile door harder than necessary.

"Irrelevant. Whoever they are, they're not here. We're left with Craw, Voxel, and Motor. Rat, they're all on your team," Lily smiles sweetly, lacing her fingers and resting her head on her hands. The three of them turn to look at me. None of them're exactly million-prime-secret-keeper material. "Why don't we start with the girl who digs up lies and information for a living?"

"Secrets are the exact reason I turned my face to such a path for a living and why I was extracted," Voxel says darkly. "It's part of my problem—I can't lie, and I. Hate. Secrets. Truth is very important to me, so I am telling it when I say that I don't know the secret."

"Oh? If you're so big on truth and so down on secrets, tell us all a little more about this problem of yours," Lily urges, honey and venom dripping from her voice. "Tell us everything. What was the big push for you to resort to your life of crime?"

It's another irrelevant point, except maybe to prove Voxel hates secrets, but it's a dirty trick. Maybe that was the whole point. Maybe Lily's trying to word-torture someone so the Outlier speaks up to spare the victim. Voxel frowns. "I'm of the faulty persuasion, and standing at a distance from sympathy, perhaps only giving it a wave every now and then, my father used it against me, keeping my medicine vertically beyond my reach or hit me unless I would learn the art of hacking and perform it in his name to retrieve for him various illegal substances without any suspicion being drawn to him. I had my chip extracted from my skull in order to untangle myself from the spaghetti knots of his influence and ratted him out. He wound up paying me not to tell people, and I didn't. I just let the information leak out so that they would put him behind a wall without a door he could open. Unveiling and telling the truth is what gives me power. I am too powerful to require deception. I do not need this clue. Neither do I need your attitude."

There's quiet for a minute. "Voxel is excused," Lily decides, staring into the sand. "That leaves the boys. How about it, kid? Do you have something to share with us?"

Motor shakes his head vigorously. "Me and Craw spent the six hours playing poker. Neither of us saw the other ever change. I can vouch it's not him, and he can vouch it's not me." Craw nods, still finding words difficult.

Lily decides to skip further examination. "Oh! Well, that leaves Rat, now doesn't it? Don't think we forgot about you," she sings as my heart sinks. "The way you kept looking around the room? Pretty suspicious, darling. And your willingness to have a bodyguard is also strange, don't you think? And I'm sure we need not mention the reputation."

"It would be better if we knew how Vastate relayed this message." Voxel sighs. "If Vastate had to be physically present, then it wasn't Rat. We were in the same cube of walls all night, and when I wasn't present with her, Vici was. But what if he relayed it through dream or something?"

My eyes widen as I remember I had a dream during my sleep. What if it *is* me?

Lily leaps to her feet. "Look at her eyes! She's guilty!"

"Hold on a sec!" My hurried backpedaling betrays something about my true level of courage. "I had a dream last night, but I can't remember anything about it!"

She grabs me by the arms and starts shaking me so hard I think my eyes'll fall out of my head. "Well, then *remember*! Or we all might *die*!"

"Loo-oo-ook, I don't remember what it was about, but I know it wasn't anything to do with the race! I think... I think the ground was disappearing, and there was a lot of dead people and screaming. But no rules or anything," I insist, getting frustrated.

"It's okay, Rat. Just admit it now, and tell us more when the time comes," Vici says lightly.

"What'd I say? It's not me, I swear! It was something totally different!"

"Maybe it is you, but you can't interpret it. Whenever you remember, share with us, and we'll figure it out together."

Oh, now she wants to be diplomatic! "It's not—"

"Stop denying it! It is you! Remember! *Remember*! AAAH!" Lily suddenly stops shaking me when she's lifted into the air.

"Okay, I think you've had enough shaking," Eli says, planting the hysterical flower into the sand.

"Don't TOUCH me!" she shrieks.

"Do you need a nap, little girl?" he snaps, and Spike starts laughing. Lily gets to her feet and tries to get more sand out of her hair, stomping off, hoping to at least resemble a hot mess.

"Alright, even though I still think it has *nothing* to do with the race, I'll work on remembering, though I'll have you know my memory sucks. Until then, we should probably pick mobiles," I suggest, standing up again only to nearly fall back over, balance gone out the window after all that shaking. *She's stronger than she looks.*

"You can lean on me if you want," Motor offers, working his way under my arm.

"Thanks," I mutter, watching the others as they walk over to the mobiles. Eli stops and watches the two of us with a complicated look, and I beckon him over, deciding that, despite Mo's touching gesture, it'll take more than a twelve-year-old to keep me balanced. "Hey, Eli, you want a hug too? I'm having a sale." With a shrug of response, he walks over and puts his arm across my back, leaving his hand by my side, supporting me so that, leaning on him, I hardly have to do anything more than move my legs. The contact seems foreign but not entirely unknown, just a distant memory, and it makes my eyes burn, and I almost shove him away but force the impulse down with a clench of my fists. That's usually my prevention for crying. It makes me look stupid because I'm always grabbing air and letting it go, but it's better than feeling three years old all the time.

Tim's all settled into a sleek white-metal car that looks like it might be part of a jet. The aerodynamics are sweet, not to mention it looks pretty darn cool. As if it was meant to be, Tom hops in one that looks nearly the same except it's black and instantly starts ripping stuff up, muttering excitedly to himself. Lily slides into a roofless car with a purple paintjob, probably because she saw me looking at it. When Ivy starts to get in the passenger side, Lily reaches over and shuts the door. "Sorry, but this seat is not available for you. Your idea to bring a blank gun failed, and your worth has been disproved. Why don't you try and do something for yourself for a change?" It was probably meant as a slight, but Ivy backs away slowly, emotionlessly, and you could argue she's trying not to smile. *The blank was Ivy's idea?* I think, wondering what the girl's up to. Now she's the one to twirl her freak bracelet, which doesn't seem as tight as her sister's. Lily doesn't notice. "Hey, Vici! Care to ride with me? I'll let you drive."

Vici is instantly at the door. "Wait, you're really letting me drive a Carnegie Z-97 Shiva? I hardly ever got to drive before! Move aside!" Smiling, Lily moves to the next seat. I watch, my fists clenching slowly.

"Are you kidding me? *These* are our mobiles? Are they nuts or something?" Spike shouts as he shoves Craw away from a mobile that looks suspiciously close to a tank, complete with camouflage. "Mm! It could use some black-and-yellow, but it'll work."

"Cool! You think they brought in these mobiles with us in mind?" Motor wonders as he runs over and leaps onto a motorbike that seems rather small for an adult or even a teen, but it's the right size for him.

"If they did, then I think I'm gettin' insulted," Rex complains, observing a sad mobile that only consists of a large platform and ten wheels.

"MINE!" Voxel yells, hopping onto the thing. It instantly hums to life, rolling forward a little when she puts a foot forward. She laughs in that way only someone who's off-kilter can and takes out her marker, writing her name on the mobile in big black letters.

When Spike jerks his tank forward, Rex notices what's behind it and rubs his hands together and starts walking over. "Ohohoho, come to papa," he coos to the black-and-white monster truck.

"Aren't you going to pick one?" I ask Eli.

He shakes his head. "Vastate said that these vehicles are going to be a source of victory. So to prove it to you that I'm not going for a win, I won't have a vehicle."

"What, are you going to run with us?" He shrugs. I look back when I hear a maniacal sound like a flute from the underworld and see Ivy climbing into a monstrosity from a soldier's worst nightmare—someone took a helicopter, put six wheels with treads on it, and dipped it in liquid scary. It's covered in barbed wire, the glass is reinforced, the eight copter blades are probably a sort of defense meant to chop people to pieces in record time, and the tail is the barrel of a gun the size of a cannon, along with two smaller guns on the sides. Real subtle. I don't even want to know if that thing's loaded, let alone able to fly. "Yep, Sir Adaman Wheel is well and truly off his rocker," I decide.

"They get more ridiculous down the line," Eli says, watching Craw enter some weird motorbike with an arched roof and wheels thick enough that it stays upright without a kickstand. "Look, there's a safe-looking pickup truck there. That'd probably be best."

I nod, knowing I don't want anything to do with the two remaining mobiles, one of which has no wheels and is clearly meant to be flown. The other one looks too complicated to be comfortable. This truck, however, has a pragmatic bed in the back and tinted windows, with an unassuming gray exterior. It's the only one I can look at without my head hurting just from the sight of it. I open the door and pull myself inside, settling down in the chair. Unlike most mobiles I get into, I hardly feel a buzz in my brain, so I relax. There's no steering wheel, though, or even any pedals. All there is is a screen that lights up, telling me to put my beacon in a circular holder that's to the right of the screen. When I do, a keyboard appears under a line with the word NAME at the beginning. Not a cutout-friendly mobile, then. Incredulous, I type out RAT (there's no option for lowercase). Then it gives me these three options in the form of boxes: water, sky, or land.

"Uh, Eli? You know how you said this would be safe?"

He pops up next to me, looking into the truck. "Oh, just hit land." I do so, and the screen shrinks and moves to the left. A steering wheel pops out in its place, and pedals slide out of the floor. The seat and everything shift, fitting me in, and the boxes on the screen go down to the bottom, and a speedometer replaces it, with additional options for a map and clock on the side. All this, and still no headache. "In this case, I think we're going to get along fine." I smile and pat the wheel. "Alright, Eli. You're on my team, and I'm not going to make you run. You get shotgun." He's about to protest, but I interrupt, "Look, I might have more issues with this thing, so I'm probably going to need your help, anyway."

"I'll run alongside, then. Don't argue. You haven't had to sit still for seventeen years. Go on, I'll hop in when I've had my fun—I've waited way too long for this."

Almost forgot about that one. I finger the steering wheel. "Alright, then. Fun it is," I say and floor it.

The roar fills my ears, rising up even beyond the sound of all the traffic of Farsia, and it feels as fast as taking off in a jet. It's probably nowhere near as fast as the mobile back home could go, but we could never shoot out of the barrel this fast back home. I'm pressed into the back of my seat, the tires gripping hard onto the track, so not a rotation is missed. I fly right past the others, bringing myself to a stop like we're playing leap-frog before leaning my head out the window, laughing. "You guys might want the seat belts on! I've got a feeling this's gonna get fast!" I yell back at them, buckle up, and zoom off again.

No roads. No tight traffic. No blast shields.

There's no rules to break if you're playing the whole game out of bounds.

And oh, what fun it is.

⇹

For the heck of it, I wrench the steering wheel around, the momentum carrying me meters sideways before I stop, tipping to the side for a bit before slamming back down on all fours, and I make a few adjustments on the screen and start doing donuts. With the sound of a swarm of angry hornets, Motor rips past, pulling a wheelie, then managing to lift off ground and backflip so tight his hair brushes against the track, making my donuts feel highly inferior. Craw's using his feet to turn, probably shouting something along the lines of, "Look, Ma, no hands!" Which is small beans to Voxel, who hasn't had to use her hands once yet, which is apparently the point of her strange vehicle. She goes tearing past, her flag of sky-colored hair streaming out behind her. I break my donuts and hurry over to Rex, whose monster truck is part roll-cage, as demonstrated by the fact that he's flipped it 360 degrees twice already, more by accident than design. "FREEDOM!" I howl as I roll right underneath him.

"What the devil, Rat!" he yells, and I jump because his voice's right in here with me. I slam on the breaks and lean out the window again.

"Hey, Rex! D'you throw your voice or something?"

"No, used this thing." Again, his voice comes from inside my car, and I look around for some sort of speaker or something then look back up at him in his truck. He's waving something at me, and when I wave back, he slaps his forehead.

Eli—who decides that going *under* things is too amateur and he leaps over Rex's mobile—runs over to me, eyes glinting, not breaking a sweat (can he?). "The beacon," he explains. "That's what he's trying to show you. It seems they make for a way of communication." Curious, he pulls out his own as I poke at mine.

"Hello? Can you guys hear me?" This time, it's Vici's voice that comes from the beacon.

"Yeah, loud 'n' clear. It's the switch, chaps. If you press it down like a button, you can talk, and I guess everyone hears you. Don't actually switch it off, though. That turns it off." How ingenious.

I press the switch, and it goes down. "How'd you figure this out, Rex?"

"I was holding it when you slid under me back there, so I accidently pushed it down when I yelled, 'n' I figured the rest out from there."

Lily has words with Rex about his discovery being an accident, and they start bantering, but I notice a helicopter sneakily rolling along and remember that this is a race, no matter how hard that is to get into my head. I bob my head forward and start going again, slower so I'm not loud this time. "How's about we head for the first island thing? Maybe we can find out if that's where the extraction point is," I tell Eli, who's keeping pace with the truck.

"Sounds good to me. The others don't seem to notice us leaving."

"Yeah, well, I'm good at not getting noticed. I'm not fast or smart or strong or even charismatic or pretty or some other generic BS, but I make excellent background material, and so far, that's about all I need."

Gradually we approach the island, or what at least suggests itself to be an island. It's not all that big, especially if I zoom out on the map. It's a wide crescent shape from above.

This's so cool. Aside from street maps, there are no maps for Tersatellus. We've even got this secret society that doesn't exist called the Custos. A Custo will destroy a map of Tersatellus the second you turn your back on it, plus they're the reason you're always missing a sock and why you can walk into a room and forget why and . . . you get the idea.

At some point, someone notices me bailing—there's really not that many options for hiding in these wide open spaces of the track with only distant bumps of islands for cover—and they all zoom over at once, maybe kinda scared of being left behind. I don't think anyone's seeing this as a competition. Not yet, anyway.

"And what the heck do we have here?" Craw wonders, taking the words right out of my mouth. Thin towers dot the little island, about six of them, all made out of wood reinforced slightly with metal poles. It's the first thing visible from this distance, and even vague, it's already imposing.

"Guys, slow down," I warn. "We're outside of the walls now, remember. These islands could be inhabited by people."

"Thanks for the tip, rival. Rat, you're terrible at making enemies," Spike snickers. "Here's how you do it—"

"No, thanks, Spike, I'm plenty good at making enemies without your help. Does anyone know if we can rewire these things so they only communicate to certain people?" I'm done with communicating with Lily's team.

"I does. But I'm ain't do it for your or ya team. And *that're* how ya makes a enemies," Tom says, and I can see all the cars on Lily's team stopping and gathering.

Well, great, if they're just rewiring them for their team, then they can hear us, but we can't hear them.

"Don't despair, all! I can also adjust these things, and I can do it while I'm in motion as well!" Voxel pipes over the beacon system, and I see her rolling over to Craw, who was closest to her. "Oh, and if none of you others were capable of doing so, I would do it for your team."

"Well, aren't we all touchy-feely today?" Spike says from the beacon, and I can hear people yelling in the background. I twist my head back to look and Vici's throwing some box out of her car with Tom's help, looking steamed—only I can tell from this distance. Her eyes get big when she's just angry. What she could possibly be doing, even I don't know.

A while passes before Voxel rolls up. "You two are the last ones in the line that does not exist. This is a fix that only takes small amounts of sand-seconds from eternity. Too easy. Who's first before the next?"

"I think I'll keep mine the way it is, so do Rat's, please," Eli says and gets out of the way so Voxel can roll up next to me, and we're both driving at the same time and pace. Her mobile's a thin, flexible black board with four wheels on either side, one in front and one in back. There's a small gray square in the middle that she has one foot in, and faint blue light radiates from under her other foot, which is in front of the box. It's a very simple-looking design, but I imagine it's real touchy to direct, and there's this eerie quality about it that comes from everything that looks simple when it's probably not.

"The Caterpillar," Voxel states proudly as she takes my beacon. "I once took me and myself to a bizarre car rally and slipped my way inside to attend and be there and share my presence. This was one of my favorites, but as you can imagine in your brain, it's not safe to be perched upon and advancing forward or backward or sideways on a street, or legal, if that matters. I believe Motor was right—they brought these in with our personalities rattling around in their craniums. This is a good mobile for you, Rat. It looks relatively normal on the outside, but on the inside?" She glances up from her work at my truck. "I've never seen anything so *this* before."

My own insides turn, and the taste of battery acid wells up in my mouth as I try and force myself to laugh. "Well, there were two other mobiles available, you know. This thing's cool, but I'm really nothing but your average bandit."

Voxel shrugs. "If you're certain. But that chance is itty-bitty. None of us are ever similar to the people we were before, not after it happens."

My heart skips a beat. "After what happens?"

She looks up at me with hard blue eyes. "The extraction. Nobody stays the same person, you know. They put that mainframe in your own bodily Center-Control when you're born. You grow with that thing, and you're meant to die with it. It becomes a piece in the jigsaw of your brain. There's no way you can simply lose such a staple of importantness without receiving consequences thrust upon the top side of your head. The only way to live through something in that vein is if your thinking organ has grown independent from it, if it doesn't need it. For everyone that happens to, nearly all of them get it removed because their brain has already decided it's useless banana-peel garbage. This has happened to enough people in history that they could all fit in a cardboard box together." I shuffle at that image. We all know one independent cutout who could poke air holes in that box with his hair, at least.

She stares at me for a while even while her hands keep moving. "Faulty citizens," she adds.

"Oh," I say to dissociate myself from the term and make sure to look awkward as everyone else is about the subject. "Didn't know that their mainframes were, er . . . looser."

She looks away then. "The words are questionable. I have heard other questionable words that those people are the most likely to punt the pail in extraction because the mainframe will attempt to become useful, lodging deeper than most, so more thought-goo will come out with it. No matter how special your mind is, something's bound to undergo morphing when they poke and prod and pluck it alfresco."

"I guess you're right. Getting extracted really does change everything," I admit, having no idea how we got onto this subject. "Even physically. What about you?"

She shrugs, digging deeper into my beacon. "Something of the mechanism was left behind, which is a common conundrum, and has a variety of possible effects. Mine only adds to my little problem—now, if I focus my viewing orbs, I can see in my sight things that I couldn't start the process of explaining until we were in a minute a little before this one. Has Vici ever done the demonstrating to you what happens if you put liquid lightning nearby a display unit that is displaying? How the pixels and the image and whatnot go all grainy? That's what I behold in certain places. Lightbulbs, exposed machinery and technology, liquid lightning, and now the racing track. All of it's got this kind of grainy field swarming it in my vision that I can't give details to that your brain could wrap itself around, but I think my brain has wrapped itself into that shape now—it's energy, at least perhaps electrical energy. That's what I see, the patterns, how these things work. If I focus hard enough, I can, in some minutes, see it through things, such as the mobiles are full of it, circulating it, emitting it. A bit of Opticorrection helped me, however."

"What, you can't see that stuff anymore?"

"No. I see it in better quality." Voxel hands me my beacon with a smile. "And what of you?"

I hesitate. There's no reason for me to tell her anything, and my "conundrum" has no use, anyway. "I don't know yet," I lie, looking sheepish, like I don't know what she's getting at because I have no experience with being weird. She keeps looking at me, though, her hair streaking out behind her as she stands sideways against the wind. I turn back forward, putting the beacon in the holder and going back to the wheel. "Thanks, Voxel."

But she doesn't leave. "Did Vici know?"

Ooh, right in the loyalty. For some reason, now is when it becomes horrifyingly real for me that Vici has left my side after long years of being more or less partners in crime. Maybe it's the use of past tense that really brings it home. Maybe it's the fact that she does not know. She was the closest anyone ever got to me after the extraction, and that's saying a lot. And all she knows about me is my real name, which she only learned from the qualifier's list, and that I am famously good at stealing things and being nobody in particular.

"There's nothing to know," I tell Voxel quietly as I think that I could fill papers of all the things I know about Vici and databases with all the things she doesn't know about me. Normal things. Favorite color, favorite foods, past gangsters. And things . . . less normal.

Voxel might be about to press, but suddenly all ten of her wheels stop turning, and she goes flying forward. Wanna know how bad I am? I'd laugh. However, this chance to prove my kindness is taken from me because at the same time, all four of my wheels stop too, and if I hadn't been gripping the steering wheel so hard and had my arms locked, my head would be through the windshield, or at least the steering wheel. The seat belt bites into my skin until the halt completes itself, and I slam back against the seat. Even though it's soft, I'm so rattled I swear my head must've found something way harder to hit, and my ribcage feels assaulted from all sides, so I have to force down breaths.

I look around, not even registering my surroundings, just registering that I'm not moving when ten seconds ago, I *was* moving, which means that there is a serious problem. Frantic, I slam on the accelerator, the break, throw it in reverse, but nothing's working. The wheels won't do anything even though the screen is still on, silently asking, *What on earth are you freaking out about?*

I grit my teeth and sit in silent fury for a few seconds as every swear known to man flies through my aching head. *Fine, be that way! I never really liked mobiles anyway! You machines're all the same, and you can all fall apart and rust to pieces!*

For the second time in twelve hours, I reach out and start to pull myself onto the top of the mobile, except this one isn't moving. "WHERE'S—oh," I interrupt when I see that Eli's already up here, letting go of one of the braces they have on the tops of some mobiles so you can tie stuff down on top, which I don't see what kind of person would do that if they had a bed to put stuff in. Anyway, he must've been taking a ride on top while Voxel was next to me when the stop happened. He looks as confused as I am but doesn't have as many capital letters or curses in his "What's going on?" look.

"Why'd you stop so fast?" he asks, helping me up.

"I didn't! The car's locked itself up or something. Where are we?" I take a look around, and that shuts me up.

We're at the very edge of the island we saw, right where the track meets the sand, which doesn't really rise up more than a few inches out of the track, more of a high patch of ocean floor than an island.

This stretch of the beach is part of the inside of the crescent shape, but the place is hardly more than a long beach with some strange establishments in the middle made entirely of plastic, thick and light gray, with no visible entrances or anything. There are eight of these scattered about, each no larger than a residency. Pestering these little boxes are thin trees with nearly black bark and giant feathery leaves coming out from everywhere, not just the top, without branches or anything. Now, I'm a city girl, so I scramble helplessly with my knowledge of this rural phenomenon and come up with the term *pine tree.* Sort of like the Public Prosperity Sector HQ but really small and not the same color and without all the people. Something tells me that this is not a pine tree, but I cling to the assumption anyway with metropolitan pride.

And soaring above everything are four towers, each with four legs and a ladder made of the same dark wood as the trees with poles of metal pressed into most of the wood to help with support. On top are small cabins with wrap-around porches and shiny dark roofs.

The sign off to the left reads TIDE ISLAND with the metal letters pushed into the dark wood. Interested, I jump off the truck. "Maybe someone here will know what's going on," I say as I walk over to the sign, hoping for some fine print or a map (the scandalous things!). Some of the others start coming along, Motor, Craw, and Rex coming to a sudden stop the second their mobiles touch the sand as well.

"Hey, hey! What's with this thing?" Rex yells, his voice kinda messed up, which means he probably hit his face on something during the stop. Craw crawls out of his mobile, which is now sideways, and Motor got flung off his motorbike and into the sand. He scrambles over to Voxel, who hasn't gotten up yet, and helps her to her feet.

"Ih muft have somesing puo do wif vuh beash," Voxel's trying to say even as she coughs and brushes sand out of her mouth. "Ahem. Perhaps they have a requirement to stay on the top of the track."

This is immediately disproved when Vici and Lily's mobile come flying onto the sand, spraying the stuff everywhere. Seeing that fills me with hate. Valiant with indignation, I drift behind the sign to hide with my fists clenched at my sides. "Watch it!" Craw yells at the purple car, stumbling away from them as it comes to a controlled stop.

I think Vici apologizes, but Lily's laughing as the others from their team roll up and onto the sand. "Why, hello, again! Having a bit of car troubles, friends?" She stands up in the car, leaning against the door and seat in a pose.

Rex leaps down out of his mobile and stomps over, his crazy red eyes gone stormy, sleeves rolled up on his hoodie. "Okay, fess up. Whadya do to my truck? And don't think you can dance circles around me 'n' everything'll be good for you, chumpette, cuz I ain't as dumb as you look, and I got some weapons of my own that don't exactly come without ammo."

The model laughs again and jumps out of the car, standing face-to-face with Rex as he comes to a stop, crossing his arms, one of them holding his blackjack. "Oh, I'm so terrified! I'm sorry, but you're not exactly a bodybuilder, freak. Trust me, I've already got three of those on my side. I know how that looks. You don't make that cut."

"Yeah, well, I get better when I'm angry, and if I don't make that cut, then nobody does. Now, whadya do to my truck?"

Everyone's watching this legendary interaction between the superstar and what might, on a good day, be considered the dregs of society. Even I slyly peek out from behind the sign. "Rex, what are you doing?" Vici asks the way a mother would if they found their kid trying to dig under the Divide.

"Somebody's gotta stand up to her already! She can't just walk all over everyone all the time, messing with their stuff 'n' everything!" He seems pretty protective of the truck already, but it's obvious he's also sick of Lily, maybe more than everyone else, and his fists are bunched in a way that says he's not only ready to deck her but he's been ready for a long, long time. Ivy steps out of her mobile to get a better look, a stunned and hungry look on her face.

"Well, you can keep on crying, then, because I'm not going to tell you what I've done with the mobiles." Lily smiles. "But I had to teach you a lesson about not seeing sense."

"Oh, give it up already!" Tom gets out of his car and glares at her. "Look, I'm wanted a advantage, but I never saying ya could took credit. This are stupid, you's stupid, and I doesn't like it. Here's the truth, guys—the cars're plant with these thing." He pulls a box with all sorts of wires coming from it out of the backseat of his car. "It're a programming, it tolds a cars to stick the tires if any bits leaves the track. They're gonna keep stucking til the boxes coming out."

Voxel shoots an acidic look at Lily and crawls under her mobile. "He's correct! There's no way the gray-haired female could've done this deed. I wouldn't have even noticed it if my eyes didn't know what to look for. It's really in there with the stuck manner of a mainframe in a brain. This would take hours to fit, and I can view where it connects to the wheels. Hats off in your direction, Isic Wheel, you have achieved a higher level of my hatred." In about a minute, she pops back out, adjusting her ponytail with one hand, holding another one of the boxes with the other hand.

Lily sighs. "*Thank* you, Tom. *What* was the point of revealing that?" she shoots at Tom. "This was a tactical move. If they believe I know what's wrong with their mobiles when they don't know, and they think I'm the one to cause it, then it gives them the notion that I'm capable of things they don't know about. Knowledge is going to be our greatest weapon, and in that case, I'm afraid I've discovered our weak link."

I shrink back behind the sign. When that girl's in her *mode*, it's the force, the power of her that turns her into some ascended creature who could crush you in the bat of an eye, the power that makes her seem to glow as it radiates from her crossed arms and frown and disdainful purple eyes, the power that suddenly seems ready to swallow something whole. Ivy leaps back into her mobile at that look, and everyone else averts their eyes nervously, with even Spike retreating down into his tank. Tom shuts his eyes and tries to form words, none of which come. It doesn't take a genius to know you've been called a fool.

He looks away, and I hear him whisper, "Because this was never supposed to be a war."

Only three of us seem to be totally unaffected by the sudden wave of power. There's me, watching it all unfold, and there's Eli, standing unfazed as a statue in a storm. Scorn and shame settle in the sand before a car door slams hard, breaking the tension and somehow drawing all my attention at once to the third unaffected figure.

Okay, I shouldn't say he's unaffected.

Tim glides, quiet as a spiteful ghost, to where his brother stands, and he drills his eyes into Lily, whose reign suddenly fades from her surprise. "I'm afraid that you have officially abused your freedom, and I will not allow this to continue. If you ever wish to insult my brother again, you are going to have to do it over my unconscious body. You won't *speak* to him unless you have something productive to say, you won't *touch* him unless you have remedial intentions, you won't *look* at him unless your eyes are clear of all derogatory attitudes, and you won't *think* about him unless it is to make a constructive analysis, lest we shall have a problem. He's done nothing to deserve your contempt, and you will not give it to him unless you wish to earn mine as well, and I believe I have made quite a reputation for dealing with those I find distasteful. Do I make myself absolutely clear?"

Lily's the one to look away now. "Sure. Crystal."

I just stare, paralyzed, like me seeing Tom openly embrace his older brother in thanks and Tim returning it awkwardly but willingly is some sort of sin, like I shouldn't be seeing it. I already failed, and I don't understand, and I'm not worthy to even watch, but I can't stop even though the feeling that something is trying to rip itself out of me is far from comfortable. Almost everyone's watching, though, so I'm not alone. We don't notice as Ivy rotates the car of her copter, and Eli, who had decided to take it upon himself to take the programming boxes out of the rest of the mobiles, finishes the last one and climbs up onto my truck again for a better look at the world. Both of their gazes are directed to the right.

Something a bit more interesting than the first case of teenage melodrama is happening not too far down the beach.

As I watch, a hole slowly opens in the track, and a circular replacement comes up from the depths of Hudson Bay to replace it, but this replacement has a passenger, which was the intention. The man is made of muscle, wearing only shorts and a tank top to show it, and the hair that's left on his head is faded and sticks out everywhere unnaturally in ugly patches. His pupils are dilated to pinpricks, and his mouth is set in a frown that cracks open one side of his mouth, revealing rotting yellow teeth beneath. He stands up from his crouch, flicking his fingers, his heavy muscles rippling but also quivering slightly, looking ready to explode.

Oblivious, the rest of us start wandering back to our mobiles, caught between the desire to see if they work again and the uncertainty of what other surprises are hidden there. "That's not good," Eli mutters to himself, making me jump, because I didn't know he was up there.

The man starts looking around, blinking in this light. He's dripping wet, which makes sense, I guess. He takes one tentative step onto the beach, then, deciding he's safe now, he casually pulls something out from behind his back.

"Get down," Eli demands, getting off the truck, and I duck before he even says anything. He's so calm about it I don't even really get a sense of fear until I hear Ivy scream.

My head whips around in time to see her somehow already over by Tom, flying into the only person who ever even cared before an explosion rocks the beach, blowing flames and sand ten stories high right next to her copter.

Ah. I really get down now, falling onto my hands and knees, peeking out from behind the front of the truck to watch the man walk through the haze of smoke and flame, a giant tube thing on one shoulder with an eyepiece and a trigger and a barrel big enough to shoot small missiles, which is probably what just happened.

The echoes are still spreading out when he opens his mouth and thunders, "GOOD AFTERNOON, EVERYONE! MY NAME IS SIRIDEAN STILE, AND I HAVE COME FOR TWO MILLION PRIMES AND PLAN TO ADD AS MUCH TO THAT SUM AS HUMANLY POSSIBLE!"

My hand flies over my mouth in disbelief. "The first Remainder pirate?"

Eli, who's to my left, looking beyond me, nods. "And I don't think he's in on the let's-keep-everyone-alive plan. Also, if you look closely…"

Spike rips open the door on his tank thing, looking furious, and bellows, "GIMME THAT GUN, YOU SON OF A DOG, OR I'LL GIVE YOU TEN PERDITIONS TO PAY!"

Subtle, I think.

"You'll find he has claimed all the weapons the rapture men took from us," Eli concludes as the man swings the gun around to aim at Spike, and that's when it hits me that this stage has turned a whole new shade of deadly.

This was never supposed to be a war.

Sorry, Tom.

- VI -

Aggravated Assault

Before I know what's happening, I'm being pulled back toward the shore by the collar, and something unfriendly gets fired out of a small cannon with a FJOOoooo—BOOOOM!

Everyone screams this time as the explosion barely misses the tank, which sped backward at the last second, and sand and bits of tree fly everywhere. The force of the blast pushes me backward, and a flaming piece of wood flies over my head. I end up falling on top of Eli, bunching myself up against the flare of heat as the explosion envelops several mobiles, including mine. He pulls me back some more as the flames billow outward, singing the edges of my jeans. When it starts fading, I scramble to my feet on the track, eyes huge. The mobiles look unfazed, but there's another giant crater in the sand, and flaming grains and pieces of wood start raining down. One catches me on the back of the hand, but it doesn't even break skin, just stings a bit, and the next piece that tries to hit me gets flicked out of the sky.

"Stay behind me," Eli says, and I have no intention of disobeying at the moment as we slowly start working our way back toward the truck. The others seem to be okay—their mobiles were far enough away that they didn't get the full brunt of the blast, so hiding inside of their vehicles kept them safe, if shaken. Craw, Motor, and Lily have all taken refuge in someone else's mobiles, leaving their own in range of the pirate. Even though he didn't hit Spike, Siridean seems to accept the outcome and starts striding over to the nearest mobile, turning, so I can see he's carrying so many weapons it's not funny. It wouldn't even be funny to someone who thinks puns and the chicken-crossing-the-road joke is funny. They hang from his waist and off his back, some clipped to his legs. Meanwhile his little finger is probably enough to kill someone, and the look on his face says he wouldn't mind getting a head start.

His problem is, he picks the wrong mobile. Curious about the size, he bends over and puts the small motorbike upright, causing a small shriek of fury to rise up from a streak of color that hurdles over his back and onto the bike, which roars to life, throwing sand into Siridean's face and tearing away. The man whips the launcher back into position and fires it again, causing him to stagger back. The smallest missile yet explodes in front of the bike to the left, and Motor launches himself onto a nearby plastic building, pulling on some gloves and putting his goggles over his eyes as he runs along the gutter before jumping off when the flames subside, shoving his still-rolling bike back straight before hopping on again, making a signal for us to get ourselves in motion before disappearing behind another building.

We stare in awe for a second, even Siridean, wondering if a twelve-year-old really might have more guts than us. *What's Motor thinking? Is he crazy?*

Then Siridean turns, shrugging. "Seeing that you're all rather protective, I guess it's easier to kill you first before I can get the car," he sighs and picks a different gun, one similar to the one Spike had way back this morning when his mobile was pushing ours, and he aims it at the nearest car with people in it.

My heart clenches at that, and I start to flinch away, half-forming the thought that someone's about to die.

Then the color registers—purple—and I know that the scream that's finally reaching my ears is Vici's.

You, sir, have now picked the wrong mobile twice is my first thought as the intention to disobey commands makes me leap onto my truck without help from the window or anything and yell, "HEY! WHAT KIND OF A NAME IS SIRIDEAN, ANYWAY?"

The second thought is *What're you thinking? Are you crazy?*

But the distraction works. The others start to get their mobiles ready to move as the man slowly turns to look at me, and I look him dead in those little eyes of his and take a deep breath. "Siridean! I've really never heard *that* one before! I though you said 'Sir Idiot' for a second there! I'm going to assume it's another sign of disappointment—I've seen it happen a billion times. You carry a weird name, which means when your parents looked down at you when you were born, they saw someone that was about to turn out pretty unique, you know. It either means that they knew you were destined for great things, or that, man, they thought you were gonna turn into some *mess* not even worth naming right, let alone raising. Now, don't get me wrong, Siridean could be a great name, but listen, there's only room enough here for one of us to have Mizz Adaman Nocturnum's favorite name, and considering you flail yours around right before you blast the bits out of foreign places, I think yours's destined for a headstone real quick, though from what you've done to it, I think even the dear mommy who gave it to you agrees it only belongs in the trash now with the rest of you!"

His nostrils flare, and he doesn't even notice the others starting to peel off. As he starts trying to yell something at me, I ignore him and quietly tell Eli to drive and brace myself on the top of the truck.

"—IF YOU DON'T TAKE THAT BACK!"

"If I don't take what back?" I fire, picking up the conversation. "The truth? What, you think your folks *wanted* a junky son?" He straightens up. "Yeah, I noticed, and so has the rest of the world, Muscle." I snicker. "Sticks, this pasty waste of a cutout hardly recognizes his own tag when he hears it. The weird part is, it's almost better than Siridean. Look, I'm sure I'm not the first one to tell you this, but I'll kick a dead dog. You're such an addict, if you personally rescued every single person on the face of this earth, there'd still be no one to love you." Not much reaction. Hmm. "Nobody would be willing to give you another chance." Better, but not it. "And there would still be no room in heaven for such a sick user." Ah, here we go—an atypical reaction. Instead of looking bored or shooting me or blowing up at me, he steps back uncertainly. *So we've got a layman here. Beautiful.*

The truck slowly starts moving, and everyone's off the island by now—the carpoolers decide to leave their own mobiles behind in order to get away from the psychopath. I love how nobody even suggests killing him yet; they all just watch me tell him off.

"It shouldn't be an issue, though," I drive on to keep his attention while we move. "Word's already gotten out you use for pleasure now, not just strength." I don't actually know this much. All anyone knows is he's got tons of stuff, pills, injections, all to get him stronger than your average group of a hundred men, but his eyes flash, and I know that even if he hasn't been adding things to his lineup, he's been thinking about it. I grin. "So maybe if you enjoy this keyed-up life while you got it, all the fire and brimstone won't even seem so bad. When the devil comes back from his daily routine of making chaos or whatever it is he does, you two can be buddies and soak up the fiery nirvana you'll find yourself in. Or maybe you'll hit a high so hard someday that you'll shoot straight through heaven anyway. When you come back, tell me how hard Saint Peter hits you back down. I want to know exactly what angels have to say about scum like you."

"SHUT UP! YOU SHUT UP RIGHT NOW!"

"Hey, don't shoot the messenger! You know I'm only saying what everyone else is thinking about you, Siridean. Even what you're thinking about you. And you're too weak and useless to do anything about it. You're a wretched little addict, and that's all you're ever gonna be. But don't mind me. Just go ride another high and forget about it."

With a cry of rage, he takes aim, and I think he has full intention of shooting the messenger.

Heart pounding against my ribcage, I leap through the air as bullets tear through the sky, and I hit the ground running. Five years of dodging bullets has prepared me for this, slowing everything down and speeding me up, and he's not even trying to hit me so it's not that hard to make it over to the closest tower and make my way up. The bullets can't get into the cabin despite how I hear them thudding against it, and I sigh with relief, smug for a second before I realize that the truck might've been enough to protect me. Genius. Then again, there must've been some reason that was what he threatened Vici and her car with (it was converted so the roof was back up, by the way, so his gun must've been mobile-penetrating).

My fists clench up when I think about him doing that. Vici may have left my side, but there's something in me that I still feel for her, as if a few years is enough for a bond between criminals to actually grow into *friendship* or something.

I'm still high-strung, so I nearly jump out of my skin when Eli jumps into the room, scowling. "CIELHOMME! Did you get up here from the ground?"

"No, I came from a cloud." He rolls his eyes. "What exactly were you thinking back there? Don't you realize the goal is to *not* die here?"

"I couldn't let him shoot Vici," I say through gritted teeth. "There's no way I'd let that happen."

He sighs. "But I thought—well, alright. Now we just need to figure out how to get you back to the rest of them without getting you killed."

"No problem. They're coming to us," I point out before thinking about what this means, looking out the open door of the little cabin. Eli's brows go up, and he turns to look out with me. The mobiles are speeding back to the island with haste. "Hang on." I pull out my beacon from my pocket. "Guys? What's going on?"

"The ocean! I can see it coming up, and I don't think it's coming to a stop," Craw tells me frantically. I squint through the track and try and see the ocean, but it's impossible.

"It must be the tide," Eli says. "Tide Island…"

One of the bullets lodges itself deep enough into the cabin that it pokes through the wall. I put my hands on my head, trying to keep my brains in. "They can't come here! That psycho's still down there!"

"If they stay out there and the tide is too high, then they'll drown." Eli walks over to where the bullet pierced the wall and pulls it out. "Hang on a second." He steps outside onto the porch without so much as flinching, targets Siridean, and hurls the bullet at him. The shooting stops. "You stay up here. I'm going to see if he's dead."

I snort. "If you killed him by chucking a bullet at him from this far away…" But he's gone before I can think of how to finish the sentence. I can tell by the way he sounded so confident about it that the guy's not dead, but the shooting's stopped, so something happened, meaning Eli at least hit him from here. Man, this day gets better and better. I walk out onto the porch to watch him hit the ground as easy as jumping off the roof of a residency and walk over to the collapsed figure of Siridean. It's a sobering reminder that he's not as human as he seems, as I try to believe. I just wish he'd done that before I went on that stupid tirade.

"Everyone, get up the towers," Eli says via beacon so that the message goes out to Lily's team too. Motor is the first one back onto the island. The others start hitting the beach after him, and I watch them scramble for the towers, all ants running from a magnifying glass ray. It's a funny sight.

That is, until the tide swells up over the island.

I gape as a wave swooshes over the sand, instantly covering the place and knocking a few people to the ground. Another bigger wave two or three meters tall smothers the place, and I get a glimpse of Siridean floating away before he's gone. Screams come from the ground as people grab on to whatever they can find, desperately trying not to get carried away.

Fun fact: what with the low temps leading to lack of bodies of water, Tersatellans don't really learn how to swim.

"COME ON, GUYS!" I yell uselessly, trying to take roll of them with my eyes, but it's not possible. "COME ON!" Another wave pummels the place, covering the buildings. Now I know why they're made out of plastic. The worst of the waves stop then, but the water level keeps rising, and the higher it gets, the harder it is to breathe from the panic. What if it reaches all the way up to the top of these towers? When does it stop? It's rising about a half meter every five seconds. It's gonna flood the stupid bay, and we're all gonna die, and it's been, what, an hour? "Come on, come on." I usually only feel this way when Vici's having a, well, you know—I'm powerless to do anything but hope everything turns out okay, and it makes me sick.

I hear coughing and run over to the edge of the porch. Eli's using the ladder this time now that he's got nothing to jump from down there, and he's got Rex under one arm. Both of them are soaking wet but look okay. I'm nearly laughing with relief and stretch to help them up onto the porch. "O-okay, that was kinda the last thing I expected to bo-bother me out th-there," Rex sputters, wringing out his dreadlocks. "What happened?"

"The tide is rising. But this is unnatural. I think it's stopped now, but the whole island is completely submerged," Eli says, looking over the edge. "If the other islands weren't experiencing this, I wouldn't be surprised. The sign said this place was Tide Island, so this is probably the only one with the weird tides. How, I'm not sure, but it may have something to do with those trees—they're akr trees, a kind that doesn't use sunlight but nutrients from saltwater and moonlight to grow, and tides are related to the moon, and besides, the moon isn't quite as sane as it's always been, so this island might just be in the wrong place to feel its wrath. Jaden told me," he adds when he sees me staring. It takes me a second to figure out who "Jaden" is because I've never heard anyone call him just by his forename before.

"Oh. Well, that's great. We have no idea how long we're gonna be stuck here!" Sighing, I sit on the edge of the porch, looking down and around, trying to see if there's anyone in the water. The current is moving and surging about ten meters below us, maybe another ten meters above the ground. Trees bend and sway slightly under the surface, their leaves spreading out in the water. Flashes of silver dance below the waves, and I frown. "Eli, do you know anything about the leeches?"

He tenses slightly. "Not much. They're large things that have some way of hunting nearly anything living that enters Hudson Bay. They were put here after the Adamantration bombed the place bigger for more room for the competitors, and they come out at night. I think they have to do something with the Hudson Bay communication systems, but I don't see how."

Large. So that's not what these silver things are.

"Those are probably fish," he adds helpfully, following my gaze.

Rex comes over and squints. "Think they're waves, mate." I roll my eyes. Eli chuckles a little, probably assuming the guy's kidding.

Wondering if everyone's beacons still work, I pull out mine and press the button. "Hey, is everyone okay out there?"

"Craw and I are in the northeasternmost tower in the presence that is Spike's. All of us are faring satisfactorily," Voxel calls in, though I hear passive-aggressive complaining in the background.

"And I'm with the twins. We're okay, we're all secretly ninja acrobats and didn't even need the ladder. How about you?" Motor asks. Hearing his voice calms me down.

"Yeah, we're okay. Rex and Eli are here with me, by the way. So we can only hope that Vici and Ivy are safe in the last tower."

There's a second of pause. "Lily can be in there with them, but she doesn't have to be as okay," Motor decides, and I can nearly hear the smile on his face. Someone laughs in the background before he clicks off.

I get up, pocketing the beacon. "You know what this means, gents? Everyone important has survived our first misadventure here so far. What?" I ask Eli when he gets a look.

"Everyone's important," he says. "I just wish I know for sure about the others."

Lily called him a toaster and he's worried about her. And he killed a rapture man to get here? "Alright, but they're sided against us, and they're old enough to handle themselves, been doing it for years, so don't get too antsy. I'm sure they're fine. While we're stuck here, though, we might as well see what this thing's got to offer," I say and step inside. It's a simple little room, square, no windows or tables or chairs, but there are wires coming down vine-style from the ceiling, connecting to a board angling off the wall with a bunch of mechanical-looking things stuck to it, which makes me hesitate. My head starts pounding just looking at it. "What *is* that junk?"

"Looks like a machine," Rex says with confidence. And I called him a gent. For Cielhomme's sake, I've met *milk* more cultured.

Eli walks over curiously and starts messing with stuff. An on switch isn't too hard to find. A screen lights up with green grid lines on it, and a large white shape sits in the middle—the island from above, an image that rotates when Eli moves it, 3D images of the structures on it. Vague red shapes light up where our mobiles must be, and in the towers are smaller vague yellow shapes, three in each tower. I move, and sure enough, one of the shapes move, and I stop and stare at it. That's me, in the eyes of some unseen computer. Suddenly I feel small and transparent.

"Interesting. I don't see Siridean," Eli says, but I don't care about Siridean, I just stare, wondering what else these computers are capable of. It sees all of us. We're so undefined compared to the rest of the layout of the island it makes all us shapes seem so fragile or vulnerable. Even though it's crude, it feels too close to spying, eavesdropping, like we're playing God, watching someone pace, someone else work on these machines as well, someone move their arms around, someone frantically running in circles on the wraparound porch, someone probably picking their nose, someone doing pushups, someone sitting on the floor with their head in their hands, dreaming or crying. The computer can't see any of that. It doesn't know any of that. It only knows things are positioned or moving in certain ways. It sees shapes, not people.

I don't mean to, I really don't, but I can't help glancing at Eli and wondering how he sees us.

"Judging that these are people, I think we've got everybody," he says, relieved, before he moves on to the other machines on the board.

Rex fascinates himself with the 3D image. "Ha, look, I can tell who's who! This chap here's Motor, cuz he's so small 'n' calm. And this's oviously Tom cuz he's messing with the machinery, so the last guy in there's Tim." He points to the figures of the closest tower to the southeast of us, where one is working with the machinery; the small one is in the doorway, and the last one is at the corner of the porch. "He's looking out the binoculars, I guess. What…" Rex looks confused as Motor climbs onto Tim's shoulders. Smiling, I step outside, where I can hardly see them from here, and wave. I think both of them wave back. "Spike's obviously the one doin' pumps since that's what he does when he gets buggy, but I can't tell which one's Voxel and which one's Craw. One of em's running around all crazy, 'n' the other one—oh, it's Craw, he stomped, he does that sometimes when he's ticked—he's tryin' to cool her off. And then in this other tower, Lily's the one that's yellin', 'cuz she likes to talk with her hands. Ivy's gotta be the one outside leaning against the wall, cuz Vici likes to pace 'n' touch her hair."

"It helps her think," the both of us say at the same time and look at each other. "You asked about her when I split those shoes for you. How do you know her?" I ask, trying to sound demanding, but it comes out soft.

He drops his head and looks around for a second before nodding. "We were part of the same gang for couple days after her extraction. Y'know, gangsters or chumps or whatever. She left after the couple days cuz they kicked me out. I think she didn't wanna be a part of anything that could get rid of people they didn't want so easy. It was nothin' really to do with me."

"Wait, how were you already part of a gang when you're younger than us?"

He seems surprised that I want to know anything about him. "I'm only a few months younger. Got extracted sooner cuz it wasn't working for me. The Plexus, I mean. I got into a fight with someone. Broke their nose, got two of their teeth. From there, it wasn't my choice. Just 'get outta my society.' But I lived through it. That's all I've ever done, is lived through stuff. You fight through another day, break another face, feel a lil' bad, pretend you don't. That's all any of us's ever done."

For a few seconds, I watch him, and he watches the floor. "What happened to you after the gang kicked you out?"

Rex looks me up and down again, probably wondering if I'm real or at least if I really care or if I'm trying to mess with him. "Same as you, I s'pose. I didn't do gangs no more. Never asked em for help or nothing. All those other guys, they're so much better than me cuz they ask for help sometimes—I know Voxel needed help affording her computer, so she worked with a lot of people, including Craw, and Spike, well, he was more of a helper, gave his stuff to gangs when he wasn't even in em, but everyone was involved with other people. The clones, the sisters, and you and Vici had each other. I don't know how to do that."

I sigh, ending it with a curt laugh. "Honestly? Me either." Rex frowns at that, but either he forgot what he just said about me and Vici or he's smarter than I think, because he doesn't press for details, and we just stand and watch the world from the outside together in lonely silence.

A few minutes pass as Eli waits to make sure the conversation's finished before coming over and pretending he wasn't listening. "What's the news?" I ask him, because he doesn't seem sure how to start.

"One of the systems takes a bunch of different variables into view to try and predict the tide changes. There are apparently six levels of tide—three is about normal. We're in a five. It predicts we're going to go back down to a three in a few minutes and stay there for a while. This tide seems to have a radius of a few kilometers from the island, so we'll have to be that far from this place by the next tide change," he informs us very factually. There's nothing upset in his tone, but something about it makes me think he's upset about something. I guess I will now forever associate the formal sharing of surface-level knowledge with someone trying to calm themselves about something because of Vici. "Now all we have to do is—"

He stops when there's an unnerving rumble in the distance. Rex turns to his dear people-radar and says, "Hey, there's someone new on here."

"Siridean!" Eli hisses. You'd think he's got a personal grudge against the guy. "Where'd he come from?"

Suddenly, our beacons crackle to life. "GUYSGUYSGUYS, hey, are we tipping?! GUYSWEFALLINGOVER. Rat, help, WEGOINGDOWN. Rat, he nuked the thing, and we're falling over!" two voices are yelling at the same time, one too close to the beacon and one farther away, so it's nearly indecipherable, but I get the basic message, and my heart skips a beat.

"Why me?" I ask the world as I fly out onto the porch and look to the tower south of us. Smoke billows up from the remains of an explosion, leaving a gaping nothing where half of one of the legs used to be. On three legs, the whole thing is tipping to the weakened side.

There's a crackling sound, real loud on our beacons, that must be someone grabbing Motor's beacon, which clicks off for a second. Then, "This is Tim" comes from our beacons, with a weird echo in the background that must mean he's using Motor's along with his own, so Tom's picking up Tim's voice on his own beacon. "Siridean has bombed the leg of our tower with the compact missile launcher. If we maintain this position for much longer or if he hits another leg, we shall anon collapse."

"THAT GUY'S STILL GOT MY GUN!" Spike butts in. I hear it from one of the other beacons.

"—Pete's sake! Rat? Spike's abandoned ship for the gun!" Craw tells me, and I smack my forehead.

"Does anything ELSE want to go wrong?" I growl and get answered by another boom that makes my blood turn into ice. *Oh, sticks.* Now another tower only has three legs, the tower only occupied by Craw and Voxel. I turn to the other two in my cabin. "You guys get everyone into Lily's tower. It's the only one he doesn't know if anyone's in. You'll have to do it while he's not looking—I'll distract him again and take care of Spike. Eli, you provide the safety while I serve up the trouble."

They nod, Eli peeling off instantly and diving straight for the water and Rex looking nervous as a dragon with an itchy throat in a paper factory. He walks over to the edge anyway.

"I wouldn't suggest leaping off. He's kinda crazy," I smile, and he nods at me as he mounts the ladder, but the adrenaline makes what he's doing feel way too long. "You know what? It's catching!" With that, I jump over him, going airborne, angling myself into a dive that isn't straight, so I won't go right to the bottom. The bottom will be sand, anyway, and I gotta remind myself of that and promise myself I won't get hurt before I go. Wind roars in my ears, and my hair scratches at my face before I slice into the water the way I did back when I had a pool party for my twelfth birthday.

The icy water engulfs me, salt stinging my eyes worse than the chlorine, and I crumple into a ball as the memory flickers at the backs of my eyelids, feeling two worlds of cold collapse my lungs and skin me alive. Then I float to the top and force myself to move, making it even colder as I splash to the surface, gasping for air, my hair sticking to my face in my eyes and nose and mouth. Spitting, I swim closer to where Siridean is standing on a post on the corner of a building, a handgun in one hand, the explosion thing in the other hand. He's swinging them around, looking for better targets.

Spike must not've gotten the message about Tersatellans not being able to swim cuz he's cutting through the water toward Siridean in his best impression of a (rather dark) shark. He hasn't been spotted. Yet.

Despite the cold, I gulp down a lungful of air through chattering teeth and plant my feet on top of one of the submerged trees. The leaves are swaying around down there, and the water level goes from my chin to my shoulders in a couple of seconds, which means the tide is going back down. "HEY!" I shout at Siridean, who has memorized the degrading sound of my voice and turns on the spot to look at me. "Yeah, I'm talking to you! Surprising, isn't it?"

"Don't you dare start giving me lip again!"

"Or what? You gonna throw pills at me? I know why you need to win this race, by the way! You know that you won't always be able to get those drugs the same way that you always do—I know because that's why I'm here, is because I need money for food, and I plan on being an old lady someday. The difference between you and me is that I need food to keep me alive, the same as other normal things on earth, but what you need in order to survive is slowly killing you more every time you indulge in it!"

"I don't need it to live!"

I laugh hard. It's one of the most derogatory laughs I've ever had. "Oh, really? Try and imagine going one month, starting right now, without even touching or looking at your steroids and paraphernalia." He goes pale, and I laugh again, pointing. "Withdrawal! You'd waste away! You haven't even been away from them more than a few hours, now, I bet, and you know how wasted you already look? You know what else on this earth that needs poison in order to survive, Siridean? Because I don't! Addicts are a demonic breed of their own, living off of toxins, so sick you would break one of the few principles the rest of us scoundrels have left and KILL SOMEONE FOR MONEY TO ENSURE YOUR NEXT STUPID HIT! It's DISGUSTING!"

Siridean's gone even paler, and he's having a hard time breathing, and I can see him shaking from here. He doesn't even deny it, just stares at me, and he doesn't know who he hates more—me or himself. Too easy.

Out of the corner of my eye, I can see Eli assisting (read: carrying) two more people who never learned how to swim over to the last tower, where Rex is already on top, helping people up. A flare of hope goes through my mind before I see Spike rise up out of the water, menacing as Death.

"GIMME THAT GUN!" he bellows and tries to tackle Siridean, but the man moves out of the way at the last second. Their leg movements are sluggish because of the water, but Siridean's upper body is out of the water, and he has no problem whipping the handgun forward and firing. Water flies up, some of it tainted pinkish, and I jump. Spike stands up, clutching his shoulder, blood seeping from between his fingers, but he just looks even more angry now, doesn't even care he's been hit or anything.

Siridean sees the blood, and that's when the rest of his color goes out the window. He backpedals, a look of fear plastered onto his face. A scream I've never heard come out of a grown man streams out of his mouth, scratchy and loud, and he turns and dives under a wave, disappearing.

"Hey, Spike!" I yell and beckon when he turns to look at me. The water level's gone down to my waist by now. "Come on, he's gone! We can deal with him later!" He looks between me and the spot Siridean disappeared then nods and starts swimming over with his powerful, even strokes that make me feel inferior as I start paddling over to my tower, grabbing the ladder and lifting myself out of the water.

"You can swim," he notes right behind me. "Where'd you learn that?"

I almost tell him about the birthday party, but somehow even that one small sentence seems too revealing, too personal. "Oh, you know, couple years ago at a pool. There's really no lakes or anything to learn at in Tersatellus," I say, climbing faster to evade conversation. "Come on, let's get into the cabin. Maybe he won't notice us come up here. Is your shoulder okay?"

"Of course it is." The bullet only clipped him, shearing off the skin on his shoulder. The wound reddens his clothes as he climbs. If it were me, I wouldn't be moving, let alone climbing ladders. I slip into the cabin and sit in a corner, focusing on breathing for a few seconds before wringing out my hair, shaking from the cold—that's saying something, since Tersatellans don't usually notice the cold unless it's *real* cold. I mean, welcome to the North Pole.

Spike, who's probably immune to the temperature too, sits down about a meter away. "Where's your jacket?" I ask instead of questioning his ability to feel anything.

"In the tank. Didn't need it." He sighs, glaring at the opposite wall with his gaze of Death. "It would've been useful, though. Probably woulda stopped the glitching bullet. It was dumb of me."

"Yeah, well, we all do dumb things. My watch's waterlogged now, but I think it'll still work," I grumble as I take off my jacket and toss it to him. "Staunch the bleeding. It'll heal quick enough, but until then, the last thing we need is for you to pass out from a hemorrhage."

"You know it doesn't happen for something this small." He presses the jacket against his shoulder anyway, and I pretend not to notice him staring at me. "You know, I was wrong about you. You're great at making enemies without my help. Better off without me."

I snort, smiling at the center of the floor. "Thanks, maybe."

"Really, though. You knew exactly what to say to that guy to rattle his cage. You're this enigma, you see? You've always got this glaring look in your eyes like you hate the world and everything in it, and then people talk to you, and you're this totally different person, this martyr that goes yelling at freaks to distract them from other people, sacrificing yourself for people, and then you flip, and everything you're telling this guy is tearing him to pieces. To quote a psycho, I've never seen anything so *this* before."

"Mm, yep, that's just me, the thissest of em all. Anyway, I've never seen someone so afraid of a little blood. That was the weird thing for me." I search for a different subject to turn to. "Why do you want your gun back so bad?"

Spike flicks blood off his shoulder, not looking at me on purpose. "Cuz it's not mine," he admits gruffly after a few seconds. "Jerry left me three things—the tag, the car and the gun. And at this point, in this whack place, I've gone from three to one in less than an hour." He glances sideways at me. "What? You expect some teary backstory? Sorry, Voxel's already got that covered for the day, and you can guess I never been a heartfelt kinda guy." His tone is defensive, and he gets up harshly, letting my reddened jacket fall to the floor as he thuds out to the porch. "The tide's almost gone. We gotta go down there and get our mobiles back."

A thought occurs to me. "Hey, where'd *you* learn to swim, Spike?"

"What'd I say about the teary backstories?" he snaps. "I don't hear you explaining yours."

"Mine's only teary for other people. The essence of being a thief is having fun at others' expense."

He shoots me a look, and Larry's crime list for him flashes through my head real quick, and I jam my hands into my pockets, a universal sign of non-hostility (except from this one guy I knew once with brass knuckles). "Just stop asking questions and get ready to haul out," he says and leaves it there, pulling out his beacon. "Hey, does this piece of junk still work?"

"It sounds as though it does," Lily's voice comes out of the beacon, but it must be broken because I can't hear the sneer in her voice anymore. "You know... that was brave of you, Spike. Going after Siridean like that. He didn't look at us once while we were getting everyone over here." She hesitates for a second. "I guess you were brave too, Rat. Before, too. You helped me and Vici out of a tight spot, so from the both of us, thank you."

Me and Spike stare at the beacon for a second. "It's busted," he rumbles, a smile splitting across his face.

"I can't imagine the damage that must've happened to that thing to make it make that bizarre noise," I agree, trying not to laugh.

"Oh, yeah, especially with the salt and all. And maybe Siridean shot it while I wasn't looking too, while he was busy hitting everything but people."

"There's no way she'd ever say anything that nice. Maybe some of the ocean thingummies, fish, worked its way into the thing. What do you think she really said?"

"Something closer to, 'that was crazy of you, Spike, going after Siridean like that.' I think she meant that he didn't look at them because he was too busy wondering how stupid I was gonna get. Maybe she's gonna call me a weak link now, and Jerry's gonna drop out of the sky and rip her face off, big brothers for the win and all that BS. And you? 'I guess you need to be saved too, Rat. Before you say anything to me and Vici, both of us have to spank you.'" I almost fall over laughing.

"Are you still there?" Vici asks, and the laughter fades.

"Yeah, I'm here. Recovering from mild shock," Spike adds without the button so they can't hear. "We'd better get to our mobiles before that junkie comes back and takes them again. Then we ditch the island and figure out how to kill this guy and get the hint."

"He's not on the radar," I say, looking at the 3D screen again in this tower. I feel a little smug about pretending to know how it works and move some things around to examine it the way Eli did, nodding to myself. "I have no idea where this guy keeps disappearing to so fast, but he's gone."

"Great. Let's get to the mobiles, already. Maybe I can figure out how to get my tank to fire." Spike stuffs his beacon into his pocket and starts climbing down the ladder. "Every time you get up one of these things to avoid this guy, he runs away. What a baby."

We get back down on the sodden ground, and I almost kiss the sand. The mobiles are all sitting where they were left scattered around the island. I run over to my truck, examining it. When I open the door, it's totally dry cuz I always close the windows before I leave a mobile. I tap a screen to make sure and it responds to my touch, zooming out on the map, so I climb in and put the beacon back in place, making the truck hum to life. "Everyone's mobiles okay?" I ask from the beacon, and they respond positively, if shortly.

Eli appears by the side of the truck, coming to a hard stop out of a run too fast for any human, but there's concern on his face. "Hey, are you alright?" he asks, looking me up and down.

"I'm fine," I say, rubbing my head as I glare at the stupid truck. "Why do you pick *me* to bother?"

He shrugs, turning to look back at the island. "We should all leave as fast as possible. The tide's going up to a six in a matter of minutes. I'm going to go see if Ivy's strange mobile can move fast enough. We're going to have to average sixty or seventy kilometers an hour if we want to make it out of here before the water comes back up again." I watch him leaving, thumbing the steering wheel. Some part of me wonders why I do that. Push everyone away, I mean. Then I remind myself that nobody ever gets close to you unless they want to stab you in the back, anyway. Learned that myself, and that was a backstory that was teary for other people, lemme tell ya.

Vici slides the hood down on her convertible and rolls out, as Eli walks over to Ivy and talks to her, gesturing to her mobile, which doesn't look suitable to go an average of sixty or seventy kilometers an hour. She nervously shakes her head, and Tom comes over and joins the conversation, jerking his head toward his car, probably offering her a ride. Her eyes go all wide, and he nods, smiling weakly under her overwhelming influence. Something she says makes him laugh, and I try to imagine her voice. He ruffles her short hair, and I realize they must know one another from before now, that they could be anything more than acquaintances. Eli walks off to find someone else to help, as Ivy laughs her fluty laugh in joy and throws her arms around Tom's neck and kisses him.

Then they get in the car and roll away.

Somewhere deep down, I still recognize that something very ancient and very beautiful and very cutout just happened, something as glorious as it is dangerous, like a bolt of lightning illuminating heaven and earth as it sears across a night's inky sky, where it's threatened to disappear into the darkness forever. But that recognition is buried so deep within me that when I feel it and search for it out of confusion, I cannot find it.

⇹

As I bring up the rear of the cluster of mobiles that seem to be more hesitant to split up, Eli faces the dilemma of who to "bother" now. He thinks about it for a bit then realizes he's got nothing to talk about with anyone and stays inside the middle of the group. The twins' normalish cars (they strengthen the resemblance of a jet when they're together) are to his left, with the tank rumbling along behind him with unnerving speed, and Motor, Craw, and Voxel are off to his right, with Vici and Lily ahead.

I sit in my truck and watch his back, the way his legs fly gracefully beneath him, and he tucks his arms tightly behind his back the way speed skaters do or swing them sometimes, trying to figure out what works. It makes me wonder how he'd be if he were born normal. Would he end up a cutout but with bones and organs, a bona fide human being, same as the rest of us? Would he follow in his brother's footsteps? Or would he end up in the trap his parents must've fallen into, fine with being content for the rest of his days? What if he had that choice? I remember what he said before, that just because he's hard to kill doesn't mean he can't hurt. He said it as if he knew from experience. If he could take away that hurt, would he, or does he value his "freedom" he loves talking about even more?

It's confusing to think that maybe someone who can keep up with a pack of mobiles would ever want to be as normal and boring as the rest of us, and of course, it's odd enough to think of him wanting anything. It's always been easy to pretend he's human, but it's easy in the way that pretending you know how to swim is easy—with minimal effort, you can convince yourself as much as you have to, but never all the way.

Then there's that stupid nagging question that won't really leave me alone, what makes someone human, even? My logic convinces me that there's no way that a machine could turn into a man, no matter how free, but then I don't know what it becomes.

But Eli doesn't even fit into that, I realize. He died seventeen years ago, and that's the bottom line. His life ended. That's it. Then the machine part comes in out of nowhere, and we're supposed to believe he's alive, but I'm not convinced that something that died and something that never lived could ever be combined to create life. Two wrongs can't make a right.

But still, he's right there, free willed as far as we know, moving, breathing and seemingly alive. It makes my brain hurt, and the questions run through my head, going in circles, burning into my brain, digging ruts that I might not be able to get my way out of, making my hands get tighter and tighter around the wheel the longer I think.

If I was actually paying attention, I'd notice how Eli glances back at me every now and then to see if I'm okay. And if I could somehow read minds, I'd know he wishes he didn't have such great vision and maybe I'd dial back my I-hate-the-world-and-especially-whatever-I-see-of-it look.

Minutes tick past, and in the rearview mirror, I see the tide rising up behind us. Somehow, it only bulges up around the island, defying the general trait that states that water should settle and take the shape of its container and not billow up in living hills. Still, it's good that we're clear, except for one problem. Time continues to pass, and we cruise along aimlessly, but nobody says what we're all thinking. Nobody's willing to admit we have no idea what to do now.

It's about two in the afternoon when I notice something in my mirror that makes me reach over and grab my beacon. The screen tells me that if I don't put it back in five minutes, the truck'll turn itself off, but I ignore it. "Guys? Am I crazy, or is anyone else seeing those waves?"

"What waves?" Craw laughs, probably about to make the point that we've left Tide Island far behind us. That point never gets made.

Suddenly, anyone not in a car almost falls onto the track due to a random splash of seawater. All around, waves are poking up through the track, making me wonder how water can get through it but our mobiles can't. An especially large breaker slams against my car, and I notice everyone's slowing and hit the brakes before I hit a person.

Some sort of tension hangs in the air as if a storm's brewing overhead, settling down on me and the whole world, but I don't see it as any reason to stop. Annoyed and especially nervous because of this weird feeling coming from the waves, I jump out of my truck, slamming the door shut. "Hey! Why'd you stop?" I demand, looking around for the source of the problem. Vici's sitting down on her mobile, and Voxel and Craw have left their mobiles entirely, while Spike, Tim and Tom are watching from rolled-down windows or else from the safe distance of the hatch in a tank, in Spike's case.

"I'm seeing some strange fluctuations in the energy around our presences," Voxel says nervously, playing with her hair. I notice Motor turn off his bike, stepping away from it. It's on its side with the wheels spinning randomly. The light flickers on it, and the horn even makes a feeble attempt to honk sometimes. You'd think it was being tortured or possessed. There's another flashing light in his pocket that I'm assuming is his beacon. His face is bent in an anxious wince.

"What, are we getting sabotaged again? Why's it only happening to Mo?" I ask, walking over to the kid.

"Stay back," he says, hard, and I stop in my tracks. He blinks and swallows. "Sorry. It kinda… happens sometimes. Usually when I'm nervous, I make stuff mess up. It'll go away, and the stuff'll be okay, but it doesn't work good for a while. I-I'm sorry."

A huge wave rises up and crashes into some of the mobiles, knocking Voxel off hers. "Yeah, nobody can position blame on the top of your head," she grunts, getting back up. "I'd say something sneaky is vertically above at this point. What's making all these waves? This can't be normal, can it?"

I shrug and start, "I don't think—" and that's as far as I get before the scariest sound I have ever heard interrupts me.

Baa-WAAAAAAAAA! Baa-WAAAAAAAAAAAAAA! BWAAAAA*AA-AAAAAAAA!*

Everyone covers their ears, hitting the ground. The sound's like some foghorn that someone's stuck so far into my ear it's in my brain, swarming all my thoughts and crowding them out, making it scream for relief. This siren, which seems to come from the Divide, crushes me from every side and makes me feel smaller and smaller with every blast, so that if I screamed, it'd be drowned as easily as a bug in an ocean. It's so loud, so deep, it sets the whole world on vibrate. It stops after the third time, leaving the world in an eerie silence that leaves such an ill feeling in the air that it could break me open at any second.

Why did they do that? They could probably hear that all the way throughout Tersatellus! I believed I yelled this, but when I listen, my voice is hardly louder than thought. I try to think. We do have the National Early Warning System, but I've memorized all the warning sirens, and I don't recognize that one. What, is Death coming in from Its valley for a spot of tea?

Either my hearing fades back in or the sound was so pervasive that it wasn't really deafening, because I can hear it when Spike wraps up what I was thinking quite eloquently: "What the glitch was that for?"

Everyone's looking around for the source of alarm. It's Ivy who spots it first. Silent, she points to the south, and we all follow her finger, squinting to see them.

Ships.

Big black ships speeding across Hudson Bay.

- VII -

Persona Non Grata

It takes me a few seconds to realize what they must be. Glaciers aren't that dark or sleek or fast, and some sort of intuition tells me they're not fish.

Waves continue to swell up over the track, nearly knocking everyone over. "Maybe us shoulda guessing we'll got a coupla pals, since the places ain't exactly our," Tom admits, watching the ships in the distance. The strange monstrosities streak forward at such speed that I can tell there's three of them by now. "Uh, anyone else's think everybody all might wanna be get back in the cars?"

Voxel scrambles back onto her Caterpillar, and the others follow suit, trying to escape, but these things are so big, going so fast that their wakes're tidal waves. They don't seem to have any sort of set path. Large cabins litter their tops, probably leading below the decks—it reminds me of this boat tour I took once as a kid. These things are each twice the size of those boats in the museum, though, and these have giant guns scattered on them that mean business, looking closer to cannons someone supersized and mounted on a ship than anything else. The turrets spin on them with an ominous clanking choir, three guns on each ship taking aim, and all nine of them fire at the nearest wall. A sonic platoon of BOOM rocks the track. If the sound of them *launching* their explosives makes the world shake, then the actual explosives are bound to be worse. I slam on the pedal, joining the others in tearing away from these ships.

Who are these crazy people? What are they doing here? Why the heck are they firing at the walls?

Great timing, Vastate! You sent us into the Hudson Bay at the beginning of a war!

High up on the thick walls of Tersatellus, every MechGuard in a kilometer radius pivots silently. They already gave their warning. They lock on and fire at the incoming explosives, which consequently go boom. And by boom, of course, I mean an earth-shaking, ear-pummeling, heart-stopping kind of boom. It's just supposed to stop the bombs from getting to Tersatellus, but it feels so much more condemning. In the distance, shrapnel and fire falls out of the sky, an apocalyptic scene that makes my insides squirm.

Then they return fire.

The green lines of the grid around each of the ships brighten, and suddenly, the selectively permeable barrier selects to not be permeable to the ships anymore, and the bottom halves of them are cut away in an awful shriek of steel tearing, fire erupting from the bottoms of the boats that grind to an ugly stop when their momentum runs out, the bottom halves of the ships coming to a burning, quaking rest on the bottom of the bay before extinguishing. I can see people jumping out and running from the things as a swarm of little black dots rain down onto the ships.

"We've got PAC8s! Cover your ears!" Eli yells over the beacon system, and we all have just enough time to wrap our heads in whatever we have at hand before a series of small thuds echo outward. Confused, I start letting my hands off my ears. "Wait for it," he says in an annoyed tone that tells me he knows we all disobeyed. And then the other thuds come.

You know how in fireworks they always have a grand finale where they light off everything they can find? This can hold its own against that finale, but it's even worse than if you were standing right underneath it. It'd be closer if you were flying through it; that's how loud it would be. With the windows rolled up and my hands over my ears, though, I don't go deaf. It lasts about sixty-three seconds—somehow the Rolex still works—and the echoing stops after another ten, at least what I can hear of it. When it finally subsides and I look out at where the ships once stood, there's nothing left but smoking hunks of dark torn metal. I watch it for a couple of seconds. It settles in that if the Adamantration ever really wanted us dead, they'd probably have no problem pulling it off.

It's disgusting, horrifying, humbling, and some part of me finds it kind of... interesting.

Don't you dare.

But there's stuff there. Y'know. Maybe something useful. Could be a nice shelter. Food if we're lucky.

No, now is the time to run! Move at speed in the opposite direction of the place that was just blown to bits!

But stuff.

I tap on the pedal and start to go over.

I don't know why I bother trying, my better sense tells me and takes a break.

At the touch of a button, the window cracks, and I hear the real last echoes bouncing away. "Now that is some pretty powerful paraphernalia," Voxel comments. I hear Spike laughing in the background, so I guess she decided to take cover in a more secure vehicle and hope that others decided to do the same. "The Adamantration and their explosives. They'll blow up anything. What were those things?"

"Post-Atomization Concussion bombs. Packet bombs, as some call them, er, 'some' being my brother. They're clusters of eight bombs that have an initial explosion to separate them all into a broader spectrum, and then they all blow up at random after an amount of time under five seconds for maximum damage to the area, not really flamey so it doesn't do even more to hurt any survivors," Eli says. "Now—Rat, what exactly are you doing?"

"Recon. I want to check these things out. There could be some, uh, useful stuff in there."

Somewhere, Vici slaps her forehead in the face of my greed.

"Hey!" I look out my window, rolling it down. Motor's rolling alongside me, coming out of nowhere, the wind ripping at his clothes and hair. He grins at me. "I wanna come! Your ears okay?"

"Yeah, the truck's kinda soundproof! How about you?"

"I've got earplugs on my goggle straps! They're out now, don't worry!" He looks behind us. "Hey, I think you're more of a leader than you think, by the way!" I look back and see everyone following along, and I groan. "What? Strength in numbers! Everyone wants to stick together, whether they say it or not!"

"Yeah, but why do they have to follow *me*?"

"Because you're the only one that really has any idea what to do here." He looks serious. "Lily thinks she does, but really, she's just dumb. That's why she's letting Vici drive. She's got demands and tries to be a leader, but she doesn't know how to get anyone to listen to her, and whatever she does, it's just what she wants done, or what she thinks should be done. Remember splitting into teams, or when she was telling us to give up the secret? She thinks we're going to do whatever she asks without getting any explanation cuz she doesn't have one. You've got some sort of purpose for everything, or at least you do it, and it always ends up having a purpose."

I look at him then at the road, thinking a bit before I ask. "What about Eli?"

Motor shakes his head. "He's got a purpose, but they can't see it, and they don't like him. And that's bigger than anything. There's nothing really cool about dealing illegal stuff or beating people up or vandalizing stuff, but there's something about thieves that the rest of us think is cool. They admire you, and that's really the end of it. And they follow you cuz you're bold. Cuz you were the first one to step up and make teams and side with the mystery guy, you're the one who's always the first to go off and see the ocean or drive off to the island without waiting for someone to tell you to do anything. You're not a follower, so like it or not, they think you're a leader." He shrugs. "Maybe you should get used to it. Not, you know, *try* or anything. Just keep doing whatever you've been doing, but don't question why everyone's following along. That's another thing. You don't have Lily's bossiness, and I think they respect that."

Since when was this kid appointed to temporary Vici? I sit back in the chair, kneading the wheel. Great. First I was a martyr, and now I've got everyone following me. Now my actions could get everyone killed or at least get their lives threatened, which I've got a habit of doing almost every night for years now. That's not bold; that's me getting what I want.

I close my eyes, half wishing that we never made the cut to get here, that I snatched the letter from the doorway and it said that we weren't qualified because they thought we weren't a big enough deal, so unimportant, in fact, that there weren't even discipline ops waiting for us, and we could resume our lives as normal. I would go on under the impression that nothing in the world could separate me from my partner in crime and that I would always be there, be her human shield, the hero to keep her out of any trouble that would ever come our way. Now I know none of that's true, and we're out away from Tersatellus, and now everything's trying to kill us, and it's not just Vici that I have to watch over; it's everyone.

I take a deep breath and let it go. Motor's right. Half of these people are my age or older. They don't really need me to lead them, all they need is some direction, and I need to treat them appropriately or else I risk becoming another Lily. I'm not really a leader, just someone that's not a follower, and everyone's looking for suggestions, that's all. And I'm nobody's hero. I'm getting on their good sides to use them later if I have to, that's what. All part of the plan. I'm a thief, and I do what I want.

It's a comforting thought.

I arrive at the huge scraps of metal, which are much larger than I thought they were. The thing doesn't really look all that burned, and when I hop out and touch the closest corpse-ship, it's warm but not unbearable. This ship shell is the most intact out of all the three. It's fallen over so the, um, the top is facing me, and I'm right by the front of it, the prow, I think. Twisted metal makes up the top, mostly obliterated, leaving gaping holes that remind me of the yawning mouths of caves.

Something in the corner of my eye makes me turn and look, and there's a few way smaller boats roaring in the other direction. "Hey!" I shout, running over to where they'd be able to see me, but they're half-hidden by the track anyway, going through it, and they seem to be in a great hurry to disappear over the horizon. At least there's survivors.

With a shrug, I go back to looking at the ship and the gaps in the side torn by the blasts. I pull out my flashlight and am pleased to find it still works.

"Oh, boy, we get to see the legend in action," Spike says as he pops out of his tank. He's got his normal vague smile on, but his hands are tense, and I know he's been recently annoyed by something that probably has to do with the black marker smear on his forehead. I ignore him and step into the hull (right?) of the ship—what's left of it after the bottom's been destroyed, anyway, which makes the thing closer to a giant bridge with a bunch of chambers than a real ship.

"Hello?" I shout into the place, swinging the flashlight around. A scrambling sound starts coming close, and I bring my multi into one hand to be safe.

A middle-aged man in strange thick clothes stumbles into view. When he sees me, a painful cry escapes his lips, and he starts pulling himself closer, using the walls as support as he tries to hop on one leg, sputtering gibberish rapidly, and I back away. He's missing half his left leg and his left arm and the left side of his face, which has the very un-face-ish look, and the arm's obviously broken. The sight wrenches my insides, and I back away faster as he starts forming words when he sees we're not getting his nonsense. "Tersatellans," he breathes, which should be a hint that this guy is about to have as much of a proper command on our language as Tom does. His eye rolls all over the place, and he staggers forward again, moaning. "It's no me. I-I-I is follow orders, I swear! I SWEAR! It's top! You understand me? Top, head of ship man?"

"Uh..." is all I can get out. Motor's face reflects the terror that's probably on mine. We've never met anybody outside of Tersatellus before. I had this image that everybody everywhere would be the same, but this man couldn't be any more different. He doesn't talk right, and he doesn't look right—electrodes all wear white, they're all the same patients in their grand ward of unreality, and cutouts all wear colors and black. He's wearing mostly brown, and it's too thick, and his face is wrong, but the thing that's most wrong is the pain, the clarity that would tag him as a cutout if it wasn't lacking our hunger. I've only known cutout wounds, inside and out, but his is a whole other breed of hurt, certainly not an electrode's kind and not ours because (I'm just now getting this) he never had to get extracted.

I stagger back some more, and I swear my heart stops for a second.

The people here... were all born Plexusless.

But without the perks of being a Tersatellan, the guy's unsavable. The only thing he can do is try and push the blame for that onto someone besides himself, and boy, does he try. "Head of ship problem made!" he practically screams.

"The captain?" I guess. Anything to make the poor man's life easier. I've watched *Gone Astray*; I know something about roles on a ship. "It's the captain's fault?"

"Captain!" he crows, nearly losing his balance, raking in huge breaths. "Yes. He tell us, move ship this way. Move in close these dark... dark big, understand?" He makes this motion with his hand all over the place before leaning against the wall again, which gives me the idea.

"He told you to go into the Divide—the wall?"

The man nods fast. "He tell us he gets a talk, air talk from back the wall, go inside, it say, 'Go yes, go, do burn when you get.' Burn? Fire? Do fire walls!"

"The air-talk told your captain to fire at the walls, what, like a signal?"

Another nod. His breathing's gotten to a fever pitch, on the verge of a heart attack, and I know he's dying. "'It's safety,' it say. 'Nobody hurt you. Go.' We go. I push and pull, and we move. I just go what he tell me, understand? I no mean to be crew kill. I swear." With a sharp cry, he jerks forward and tries to run and gets out into the sunlight. There's a splash as he goes right through the track.

For a few seconds, my brain refuses to accept the fact that he's dead, tries to convince me that he can swim out to meet the others or something. Then the seconds pass, and I take a deep breath and do what everyone does when they see another corpse blooding the gutters—move on. As if that'll deny the reality that nobody is invincible, deny what being Next really means.

"Cielhomme. Let's get out of here." The beam of my flashlight suddenly gets allergic to the bloody floor and only swings around in the darkness of the walls and ruined doorways. Its illumination must turn into a physical force, because the whole structure groans, settling on the track. "Anyone else alive in here? If you don't panic, we can drive you somewhere if you want—we've got nothing better to do!" I yell then listen. There's a noise, but it's distant, and it could just be part of the occasional moan of the ship cooling and settling in its grave. Even so, I start to follow it.

"Hang on a second," a quiet voice says behind me, and I turn to see Motor kneeling by the exit where the man disappeared. The kid puts his palm to his lips then puffs on it before standing up to look at me. "That's blowing someone a kiss good-bye. Momma taught me how. She says you should blow a kiss to the dead so they can leave peacefully, knowing someone loved them." Solemn, he adjusts his goggles and starts marching deeper into the hull.

⇹

"Hello?" I keep calling as we delve deeper into the ship, and Motor eventually adds his voice to mine. I crawl deftly through sideways doorways, walking on the twisted walls that now seem to make up floors, dodging fallen stuff, all as subconsciously as breathing so I have to remind myself to stop every now and then to let the kid catch up, though he's not bad. He is a ninja acrobat, after all.

These waiting periods give me time to search the cupboards and other things for anything useful, but there's nothing good left. After crawling through an especially twisted mess where a spiderweb of boards is fallen in, we walk into a crater where multiple explosives must've detonated at once. "Whoa," I say, craning my neck back as bits of the ceiling hang down, threatening to fall, and the whole ship groans, a watery sound rushing around through its pipes or whatever as it settles even more. "This place's pretty huge, huh?"

"Yo!" I jump as a voice off to my left shouts. "You know, there's an easier way to get in." Craw crawls in through a hole in the wall then joins us in looking around. "Unless you found something along the way. Hey, if we got some chairs, we could have our own sick version of that chamber thing from the Castaway Point. The place's big enough, and besides, look, it's already got the stage thing."

I turn my attention to the stage thing in question, which looks to be a giant holding tank coming out of the wall (which is currently serving as the floor) for missiles. It looks closed, but only mostly, which doesn't make sense since it should be closed all the way if they were launching missiles at the walls. Suspicious, I walk over, feet making no sound as they cross the crunchy, broken ground littered with a bed of ashes that float over the whole place. The sick fairy dust catches the light of my flashlight, which I tap on the top of the missile tank. There's a shifting sound that comes from inside, and everyone jumps.

"Here," Craw says, walking over and bracing his hands in the crack of the tank with me. Motor holds the flashlight while we slowly wrench the thing open. A bloody arm drops from where I didn't know its fingers were still lazily gripping the edge, and a scream lodges in my throat until I see the arm's still attached to something. Horrified, I bend over and look inside.

"There's someone in there," I whisper, gaping at the top of the head I can barely see. It's connected to a person who's lodged themselves into the shooting tube. "Hey, you in there. Can you hear me?" The person stirs, but not much. "Help me out, guys," I tell them as searching for something to grab.

There's a whirring sound that makes all three of us step back, and the machine grinds into uncertain movement. A few meters away, Eli's pretty much sitting on some sort of mechanism near the missile tank, pushing buttons.

"Careful, you might shoot him out," I warn. "You don't automatically know how all stuff works, do you?"

"No." He shrugs. "But considering I've been alive for less than a day now, I have to be a very good guesser."

"Does that control the missile-spitting thingy?" Voxel asks from the hole in the wall that Craw came from. Apparently, it's the new hip trend.

"Looks like it." Craw watches with wide eyes as the insides of the tube start to push its stowaway gently back toward the open. "I didn't know this thing still had any juice left in it to run the controls."

"It doesn't," Voxel breathes reverently, and I wonder how she knows for a second before remembering she can see energy. She's staring with a positively astounded look at where Eli is concentrated on the complicated control panel, so she must know something about what he's doing that I don't. "You all get more incredible by the minute, I swear."

The three of us over here look at one another in a way that tells me that none of us believes we're anyone incredible, while Eli keeps focused, and Rex snorts somewhere behind her.

"You wanna get in the ship now?" he asks peevishly. "I wanna see what's going on."

The two of them enter the makeshift room as the person in the missile tank slides slowly into view. It's a young man, maybe about Spike's age, with crazy hair and frozen, distant eyes, a look of shock painted on his face. Seeing another freeborn makes a ripple of shock run through me.

"Is he dead?" Rex wonders, ever sympathetic.

"His arm's the only thing that's hurt," I point out. The guy's arm is charred up to the shoulder, but the rest of him is good. "He must've jumped in here to escape the bombs but couldn't close the door thing all the way. Pretty smart, though."

"It's a bomb shelter!" Craw jokes, half-smiling at his double meaning. Then he waves his hand in front of the face of the victim. "Yoo-hoo, wakey wakey! Any conscience in there?"

The dark eyes come into startled focus, and the guy gasps for a breath, trying to sit up before letting out a choked little scream, looking at his useless arm, his surprise turning into alarm as his eyes go up and down the thing before he starts sputtering the same gibberish as the last freeborn.

Craw puts his hands out to stop him and responds in kind.

We all look at him with raised brows, all except the person in the bomb shelter. He sits up, and the two have some kind of conversation while the rest of us watch. Not only can he make any voice he wants to make, but he knows other languages too? I stare in awe, not even looking away when Motor hands me back the flashlight and goes rummaging around the room, probably bored.

"Okay," Craw says, stepping back. "He says they're from a place called Dagur's Island. The captains of some of the ships got a message from Tersatellus telling them to come on over, they don't bite or anything, and to send some sort of signal once they got here—that's why they fired at the walls. Sure enough, it was a trap."

"What, some ships just happened to be passing by for the Adamantration to sadistically lure in here and destroy for no reason?" I ask, crossing my arms. *Would they do something so horrible just because they felt like it?* Craw goes back to his conversation with the anguished young man to find out.

"He says that yes, some ships sometimes come near Tersatellus, but everyone knows now not to get in spitting distance of the Divide. Everyone does want to get in, though, and have a serious talk with the Adamantration, it seems. They've been after that chance for years, chasing after every hope of safe contact, so any sort of message is nothing short of a miracle." Tersatellus prides itself on how well it keeps away outsiders. "This isn't the first time anyone inside's been attacked by the MechGuards, it seems."

"So somebody obviously wanted to blow something up. Maybe *one* of the Adamans felt a little hostile." That's another draw: the Tech Sector's in charge of defense, but Public Prosperity can make demands, and it can sure as heck make communications to ships. "Somehow, I don't think nuking boats for entertainment is beneath our good friend Vastate the Razor," I growl. The Razor is one of the kinder things cutouts've called Vastate. He's an angel to anyone wrapped in his Plexus, but he's responsible for countless evils against my kind. But I've got enough hesitant dislike that I don't mind splitting the blame between two Adamans for this fiasco. Dropping the thought, I turn my attention to the survivor. "Are you okay?" I ask, doing the thing where you talk loud and slow so the other person learns your language.

He shrugs then winces hard at the pain. When his eyes open up again, they look puzzled, and I turn to see Motor walking over, Eli following behind. Full of pride, Motor sets a half-melted first aid kit on the missile-launching thing and pops it open. "Gimme your arm," he says, pulling out some stuff. "Don't worry, this's good stuff. It won't hurt. No pain," he says, making a hurt face and then shaking his head. "I swear." Hesitantly the survivor offers his arm to the boy, who takes it gently and starts dabbing stuff on cotton balls and tapping his arm with it. "What's your name? I'm Motor."

"I is Baldur," the guy replies, seeming to get less tense as his arm gets all medicated and then bandaged. The rest of us introduce ourselves in a similar fashion in the meantime, and Baldur steps out of his shelter. "I is from Dagur's Island, east in here. We no understand. Why they do hurt us now?" he asks, sounding personally offended by the attack.

"I think they're trying to scare us," Motor offers.

"Sounds 'bout right," Rex agrees, which is one of the larger surprises of the day. Then again, you put down any anti-Adamantration conspiracy, and he'll be on that bandwagon faster than you can spit. "That's why they put Fracture on the list. That's why they killed Layla, and y'know it." He meets all our eyes challengingly as he dares to say what we've all been thinking. "They're showing us that nobody that don't have Plexus's safe. That we ain't even nobody to em, and nowhere in the world's safe from em."

"Then why bother leaving us alive at all?" I wonder out loud. "Why doesn't the Adamantration nuke us all if they want us dead so bad?"

Rex shrugs dramatically. "Maybe this's more fun for em, I dunno. We—us? Us is in big trouble," he explains to Baldur. "You is in the middle of it. 'Pologies, mate."

Baldur hangs his head in exasperation. "I want be go home. I want everything be normal. I want be live."

Rex sighs. "Yeah, I want be live too."

I step forward. "Look, maybe we could help each other. You is from here, so you be know here, yeah?" Baldur nods slowly. "Okay, so you can tell us about this Hudson Bay, and we'll protect you in return, you understand? Protect? I give up. Craw?"

Craw translates, and Baldur lights up. "Oh! Yes, yes! A swear," he says gratefully.

"Yes, a swear," I agree, sticking out my left hand for him to shake. "A promise," I explain to the others so they don't think we're about to get a lesson on the magical properties of the word *damn*. They nod. "I think we've got ourselves a guide."

"Are you sure?" Rex looks at Baldur critically. "We dunno nothing 'bout this guy except he happened to be here. He could be a plant from the Adamantration, and besides, it'd be kinda mean to put him at risk, doncha think?"

"He'll be at equal risk without any other sort of crew out here in the Adamantration's crosshairs, and we don't really know anything about each other, either. Odds are, one of us has the secret to getting us all out of here alive, and they're not saying it, so who can we really even trust? I know it's not me, no matter what the rest of you think."

Rex looks incredulous. "Look, Rat, I know you probly won't, but if you remember anything about that dream of yours—"

"Forget the dream. It's not about to help us," I snap and turn to Baldur. "Was there food on this ship? You know..." I make an eating motion, and he nods and walks over to a doorway, looking around at the place, trying to make sense of its sideways-ness. Along with his wounded arm, it takes him a while to find the place he's looking for, but we eventually get to another decently sized room. This one's mostly untouched by flames but bent up from the impact. Us able-bodied foreigners look around this place for food that survived the attack, except for Voxel and Motor, who work together to get the tables on the wall at a respectable angle. Then Craw and Rex offer to go and get the other team—it's better if we share our resources. I scamper off to one of the adjacent storage rooms, finally finding my element here in this place. Snooping and searching is what I do best, and I find ways into everything nearby, finding the occasional loaf of bread stuff here and can of soup there. All of it gets tucked into an anti-water coat that's tied at one end with the sleeves knotted to make an effective bag. Pawing through the refuge and sniffing around, my spirits are so boosted I laugh. "Well, Vici, it doesn't quite meet the prestige Steele level of organization, but there's some good loot here yet. Ha. Hah..."

My hand trails on an errant can of beef stew as my appetite goes out the window at the drop of my stomach. I have to lean against the wall and, for a second, let myself feel weak and small and lonely. She's gone. She picked Lily over me.

The thought makes my fists bunch up. This is my fault. I should've let her drive more. I shouldn't have been so strict with her going back into the Plexus. I shouldn't have let my pride and fear get in the way and con her into coming here. I should've let the Old Rat stay, should've listened to my friend and joined her on her side of the line no matter who else was there. Tim was strong enough to do that for Tom, who was strong enough to do it for Ivy. I should've been strong enough. Why wasn't I?

Okay, thespian, you've had your fun, now go back to normal, I tell myself but linger anyway.

Soft, crunching footsteps enter the room behind me as their owner climbs into the doorway, raising ashes and dust. I put the can of stew down, looking away, pretending to be interested in something or to have some other reason for not noticing him walking into the room. "You're homesick," Eli says quietly after watching me for a few seconds.

"Homesick?" I scoff. "It's been less than a day. I don't have a home to go back to. I've never even counted the residency I pirated as a real home, and before that, I was a gypsy, just went wherever I could make money. It's a stupid house, not a home, and there's nothing to miss about it."

"You're right. Your home isn't a house, since there's nothing to miss about a house. It's not a somewhere but a someone." He walks over, trying to look at me. "Rat, she's just scared and hurting. She still loves you."

"Oh, please, gimme a break," I reproach.

"You *know* that's not what I meant."

I do know—ours is a tough love that's got nothing to do with holding hands and staring at sunsets and everything to do with the love of the game, not the players. It's the kind of thing where you smile at your friend across a chess board and plot their untimely demise just in case, and I know how much she loved to hate me because I didn't win, but I never let her understand my moves. If this wasn't inevitable, neither is Death and I really will live forever, but I'd bet my life that somewhere in our ugly souls, we're both a little sorry all the same.

But instead of admitting it, I turn on him. "Well, what do you expect me to do, melt in a puddle of tears or something? She's the one that left me, so if anyone's hurting, it should be me. But I'm not, because you know what? Here's a lesson you'll do well to learn quick—it's all fake. Even without the Plexus, people are plastic. They're cheap and weak and fake, and nobody's love means anything, okay? It's a trap. You can give them all your love, and you can pretend that they give it back and that you have a glitching *family* or something, but then they turn you loose the second they don't agree with you and you stop giving them what they want. They don't want your love. They take it and everything you've got without giving it back because they want to use you!" I thunder, throwing the can of stew into the darkness.

"Rat, listen," Eli tries to stop me, but I won't be stopped.

"No, *you* listen. It's a dog-eat-dog world the whole way round, and the electrodes walking around with a steady stream of nonsense pumping into them are better than the rest of us because a person without anything to sieve out all the negativity just wants and takes and hates and does whatever they have to do to take what they want and get rid of anything stopping them. We're all awful people on the inside, selfish little monsters, and everyone's all the same. They tell you what you want to hear to feel good about themselves, feel loved by you, and then they side against you while they're wearing your glitching friendship necklace next to their heart!"

Subconsciously my hand flies up to the chain around my neck, the icon of half a heart with the letters FOREV on it. The other half around someone else's neck says ERMORE. It's my first exception to the no-auxiliaries rule, not only because it's cheesy useless jewelry, but because I took that rule to also mean that I would not have useless adornments called friends. Now I want to rip off the chain and fling the thing across the room and get rid of the exception altogether.

But I don't.

Instead, I stand there, breathing hard, until I force my shaky hand to drop.

"I think it's strange," Eli comments slowly, "how something so sustaining can also be so destructive, how it can bind people to themselves and to each other as easily as ripping them apart. And either way around, they still cling to it. They say if you love something, let it free, but there's some part of it that still belongs to you that you never really let go, do you?"

Sighing, I shake my head. "You know, you're pretty profound for someone reborn yesterday." Something that might be a smile touches his lips, and he stares into the grain of the blackened wood of the cabinet he's leaning on.

"What was it like?" I ask suddenly. "All those years of nothing but listening, I mean."

"Boring," he answers passively, turning his head away, but not before I see something dark and deep and scary flash behind his eyes. His nails dig into the cabinet, leaving little white lines in its sooty surface, and his posture is stiff as a locked gun ready to blow. His other hand mimics mine as if he's got a necklace too, just something to hold on to. "Let's just say that I don't need the lesson—I know it well, but I beg to differ. I've heard of a person's capacity for appalling cruelty, but I have also seen a capability to have overwhelming kindness in the face of that cruelty, and no, I do not think that everyone's all the same."

When he turns again, it's me who looks away, and we stand there until voices rise up in the distance, along with scuffling. We both look at the doorway on the floor as fingers hook around the side, and Motor hoists himself up and scrambles through the darkness and wreckage over to us. "Hi, guys!" he says, all breathless, as he stumbles over, coming to a stop in front of us to put his hands on his hips and grin at each of us in turn. "Look at this, two of my new favorite people standing in a room together! The Lillian Brigade's here, so we can have food now." The kid grabs each of us by the hand and starts pulling us over to the door. Either he thinks we forgot the way, or we're not going to go fast enough for him.

"Lillian Brigade?" I ask as I tug my hand back so I can climb out of the doorway with my food. His bouncy, innocent presence cuts through the last few minutes.

"Yeah! She's really into this whole team thing, so I figured that if there's teams, they've *gotta* have names," he explains like it's the most obvious thing in the world. "So that's what I'm calling them, the Lillian Brigade. What're we gonna be? I've got *lots* of words for groups. They can be clans or clusters or bands or circles—or even squares or triangles. It shouldn't just be circles, or since there's six of us, we'd be a hexamagon! Or a tribe or a clique or a clan or a bunch or a batch or a hodgepodge. Or if we wanna sound powerful, then we could be an army or a posse or a platoon or a crew or a gang. Or if we wanna sound all businessy, then we could be an association or an assembly or an organization or a society or a race! We could be a race!" He looks between the two of us watching him. "But whose race is it?"

Me and Eli look at each other. "It's anybody's race yet," I say. "Nobody owns it, since we all share it, you understand?" It's still Sunday. Nobody's won anything, none of us've died, and we don't know who's the Outlier, so it's fair game still.

"Then I think we should be a band," Motor decides. "None of the sections in a band is really more important than another, so it's kinda nice and equal, cuz everyone gets heard, at least at some point, and we're cool, so duh."

"But a band of what?" I wonder.

"Cutouts," Eli says, and me and Motor both look at him with surprise, so he shrugs. "What else is there to be?"

Either he doesn't understand that Lily's got cutouts too, or he's talking about something more than the Plexus here.

"The Band of Cutouts," I settle, and the four words seem to have their own gravity. Motor smiles again at it then runs off ahead of us, spouting ideas for mottos and colors and thank goodness we all already have tags. I watch him with a strange mixture of emotions, and it dawns on me that his little synonym tirade included two clans and a newly invented shape but not the word *family.*

"Thespians," I mutter under my breath and follow him down into the dark.

- VIII -
Suspicion

The tables are all set up when we step into the room. There's a flashlight stuck into the center table. Unlike in the dining room at the Castaway Point, the tables aren't circular and separate. They're shoved together to make one big multicolored table with benches on either side in a usual cafeteria-style table that we'd see if we stayed in school to learn the things that the Public Prosperity deems okay for us to learn. *They should teach about oceans in schools*, I think as I sit down in the obvious gap between the Lillian Brigade and the Band of Cutouts. *Then again, maybe they do. What do I remember from school?*

Motor's already busied himself telling everyone about the teams, and everyone not listening to him is either waiting for food, eating some of the food we've already brought back, or talking with Baldur. Spike is standing with his hands on the table and a smile on his face, riddling his language with big words and imposingly long sentences spoken too fast. Baldur is at a loss of words with him. Voxel seems fed up with talking with him already, and Lily is getting there, while Ivy seems amazed. Tom translates her silence into all sorts of questions for Baldur, who usually needs translation from Craw, or it's Baldur who needs a translation on what the heck Tom just said, and the four of them establishing a laughter-filled relationship. They never stop talking, not even when the groaning and sloshings of the ship crescendo for a second here and there.

I toss the big coat onto the table, opening it to show off the food inside, since everyone gives me a crazy look for throwing some random coat into their midst. "Make sure it's even," I try as everyone grapples for the packages, and I manage to swipe a bottle of water for myself before everything's gone. It tastes great after all the seawater I swallowed on accident back by Tide Island. When I look next, there's an open can of beef stew sitting in front of me.

"Oh, good, he doubles as a can opener," Lily jokes as Eli claims the vastly untaken seat next to me without so much as giving her a glance of acknowledgement.

Incredulous, I take the can. "Do you really have heat vision?" I have to ask, real subtle, though.

"To be honest, I have no idea," he whispers back, wagging a bright green multitool where I can see it before shoving it into his pocket with a smile. I take out my own and flick out the fork feature, annoyed for the first time that it has a fork but not a can opener. What kind of multi doesn't have a can opener? But one of the knives'd probably suffice, and besides, *I* have a blowtorch to heat up my stew. I focus on it very much, hardly ever looking up from my meal, but it's inevitable—glancing up sometimes, I mean—but if it's too obvious, I can excuse it with a look to the left at Baldur. He seems to have warmed up to everyone. Him and Craw are teaching Tom and Motor how to speak Baldur's strange language. Motor's eyes shine as he gigglingly asks for words someone his age would generally like to know. Ivy looks pretty pleased herself, and I'm pretty sure she's holding on to Tom's hand under the table.

They sit close, not caring how obvious it is. Even though Lily's gotten over having her sibling picking someone else over her, Tim seems a little more affected, watching Tom's turned back and nibbling on some crackers with his head propped up on one hand. This is especially bothering because I've heard these twins could put away a ten-course meal without gaining any weight, they're that fit—that, plus being Tersatellan makes food a huge necessity (even us not-so-fit ones would consider three square meals a day as a starvation diet). Now's not the time to fast, either. He tries to contribute to their conversation every now and then, but Baldur seems intimidated by him even though he really simplifies his language. The contributions usually get him a mixed-emotion glance from Tom at most. But he keeps at it anyway, and at one point, he gets his brother to laugh and respond, which seems to satisfy him.

I watch for a while before glancing forward again at Vici, who's watching the same scene with an absent look on her face. They only get more comical as they all start talking over each other, trying to give or interpret a description of something. I finally work up the nerve to stand up and look at Vici. "Hey, I'm gonna go scrounge around and look for a map for these guys. Wanna come with?" I ask hesitantly. "For old time's sake or something?"

It takes her a good five seconds to even turn her head to look me up and down with unreadable eyes. "We have no old times," she says simply. "And besides, I thought you were all for leaving everything behind."

Lily notices our conversation and looks between us. "Listen, Vici, if the teams or I are what's stopping you, don't feel impeded. I want you to do what makes you happy, alright?"

"No, that's fine, I understand you want to stay, and I'll go look for the map myself," I almost say. It's on the tip of my tongue, but that's where it stays, and I silently look at my partner in crime with hope in my eyes like one guy holding back big gates with menace trying to get in.

She shakes her head, though. "I'm happy right here," she says, picking up her cold can of soup then shoves it away before I can offer to heat it for her.

"Well, if you wanna go spelunking together again, I'll keep my side open," I offer so I can't say I didn't try, then turn and crawl up out of the room and into the dark without bothering with my flashlight since I stop a few meters in, anyway. Standing still, calming down. That needs darkness.

You were supposed to be different, snowflake.

"Yo, wait up!" Craw calls before working his way into the room with me. "I kinda wanted to talk to you, so if you still want company, I'd be willing to oblige—of course, if you'd rather be alone, that'd break my heart, but I'll go away."

"No, that's okay, you can come," I say, pulling out my flashlight and setting it on something so I can search with two hands, my eyes adjusting rapidly to whatever I look at so it all looks almost the same to me. "You wanted to say something?"

The lanky boy walks over to where I'm peering into a drawer of a cupboard that ripped itself from the wall and crouches next to me, his eyes looking as ancient as ever as they search me. "I want to thank you. That stuff on Tide Island you pulled was pretty gutsy, and since you were the one to find him, I think you really saved Baldur. Not to mention what you did for me on the beach with Lily."

"The gun was blank," I dismiss, rising to my feet to search other places of the room. Why is there nothing good?

"I know, but still. Saved me from a heart attack, probably. I dunno if the others would've..." He pauses to look nervously at the doorway. "Wanna check that room over there?" he suggests, pointing to a doorway that'll take us farther from the dining room. I look inside.

"Hmm. Maybe the captain's quarters. This'd be where maps are," I say, dipping through giant jungle-gyms of debris and traps of shrapnel threatening to draw blood at every twist and turn. Craw watches me, so wowed you'd think I started floating. Then he follows me without half as much speed, ease, or success but does manage to find his way in here without breaking too much skin. "If we could get Baldur a map, maybe we could at least learn something more about Hudson Bay. We might even be able to figure out the extraction point, but that's a lot to hope for."

"Yeah," Craw agrees absently. "You know, this is kinda weird, isn't it? Nothing's even explained. Nothing about where we came into, nothing about where we're supposed to be at the end of the sixth day, no guide whatsoever. There's always been rules before, laws, policies, but now... I guess it's supposed to be more likely to get us killed, but still, it'd be nice if they at least explained how someone even got the secrets and stuff. I mean, what if none of us really got them? What if there are no secrets, no race, no prize? It's impossible to tell if a leaf falling in some spectral wind of time and space was supposed to be the whole key to the universe and Hudson Bay, or if maybe he used some device to talk to one of us specifically or anything, so it's not *fair*. That's what I wanted to talk to you about. The secrets, you know. I mean, you're the only one out of all of them that has any compassion about this secrets thing..."

I roll my eyes. Glorification is another form of targeting, and we both know that there's other people in that dining room that've been compassionate, way more compassionate than the one with the reputation of a perpetual eclipse. "Look, I don't remember anything about that stupid dream, okay? It was nonsense, that's all I can tell you for sure, and it doesn't have anything to do with the race. It's just a dream, anyway! There's no way that's how clues are transferred."

"You're totally right," he agrees, nodding his head in the corner of my vision. "It's impossible, right? We don't have mainframes still, and even when we did, they couldn't control what we *dreamed* about. That's ridiculous. There's no way they relayed the secrets through dreams."

I turn to look at his back as he becomes engrossed with an empty cabinet, and my brows furrow. "This isn't about me, is it? This is about you."

He jumps, shutting the doors with a bang. "I never said that!"

"Craw," is all I say, watching as his breaths get bigger and bigger.

Finally, he turns back to look at me, his voice quiet and shaky. "I didn't mean to fall asleep, okay, but I kept losing, so I got bored, and among my other fabulous talents, I can fall asleep with my eyes open, so Motor thought I was taking a while sizing up my odds or whatever, and if he wasn't so patient—it was his fault, okay, he should've said something, should've woken me up, or at least let me win every once in a while! I mean, he's just a kid, and I was the one who taught him how to play! It was degrading!"

"Wait, wait. So you were playing—poker, was it?—you were playing poker, and you fell asleep, and you had this dream?"

He nods nervously, dropping his voice even lower. "It has nothing to do with this, I swear. It was just me sitting in this classroom in the corner of the fifth floor of this weird brick school that had *windows*, not reforms, either, and I kept looking out the window, where I could see another window on the other wall. People at the window were holding this girl's feet while she hung out of it. So I was watching this girl hang out of this window without any sounds at all, and I *knew* it was gonna happen—the window pane slipped up, or they let go or something, and she fell. Everyone in my class rushed over to the window, talking, and I tried to squeeze through them to look at the pavement five stories below, and I only saw one tiny glance of her down there at all bent angles and *twitching* and jerking all over the place, and it was so awful... but that's where it ended, I swear."

I watch him for a second, and he watches me back, this desperate sort of look on his face. "That's got nothing to do with anything."

"Exactly!" he says, sounding relieved. "I'm freaking out, though, cuz what if it's supposed to be an implied meaning or a metaphor or I'm supposed to recognize the girl or the school or something?"

"Well, we'll keep an eye out for brick buildings or windows or crazy chicks, but in the meantime, how's about we look for a map, okay?" Craw nods, swallowing, and I dare to stick my arm out and punch his shoulder. Compassion in its finest form. "Hey. Are you gonna be okay?"

He swallows again. "I think so. But I mean... with this dream and with all this stuff that's happened so fast, I'm confused, I... I'm scared, Rat. Just as scared of what it means to get out alive as what it means not to. Scared the Adamantration's gonna tell us this was all a trap and blow us to pieces. Scared someone's gonna come out of nowhere and kill me just for a thousand dollars and a day, scared that that's all I'm really worth, scared that even *that's* not right, that they made a mistake and I'm not even really supposed to be here, that I made a mistake."

I lapse into silence, watching him again. If you haven't noticed, I do a lot of watching, especially watching people. That's because I'm thinking, wondering why I can listen and watch and think up a thousand ways to break them down, and I can't think of one thing to say to build them up. So I settle for "It's okay, Craw," and I don't even know if that's true or not. Then I grit my teeth and dig deeper, searching for something, anything meaningful to say. "Um . . . I think it's okay, to be scared, I mean. At this point, everybody's scared. They just don't wanna admit it so we think they're cool. Even me," I admit. "Heck, I'm always scared. I'll admit to that. Anytime something goes wrong and I didn't start it, I bail unless that won't work. So maybe the fact you're going on even though you're scared makes it okay, better, even. I mean, you can't be brave if you aren't scared, can you? And the fact you're admitting it—I mean, before anyone even pried about it—makes it cool."

He shrugs but seems to relax, and I feel a thrill. I said something that actually got some sort of positive response! I'm not such a destructive little monster, after all! Smug, I go back to searching, nosing in and out of things with ease, picking a lock here and there just cuz I can, and there are all sorts of gadgets everywhere. No good ole paper maps like in *Gone Astray*, though. Craw keeps glancing over at me, and I suddenly start worrying that what I said wasn't really good after all, or worse, it raised questions. "Hey, Rat?" he starts, and I try not to wince. "I understand you don't really like the whole relatives thing, and I've heard you never had a thing for gangs, but I was wondering what you thought about having a two-felon pretend-gang with me? Look, I'm not trying to make up for Vici, I swear I'm not, but I was thinking I'd keep her spot warm, like we're, you know, friends or gangsters or something?"

"Uh, okay," I say since I don't know how to respond. Friends? Craw's only known for having informers and one-dance, one-kiss flames to beat away the loneliness, and you can guess how wonderful I've been with friendships. "But why me?"

Craw shrugs. "You're cool to me. Thieves're elite. Who gives a care about an impersonator? I mean, look at you go. And you're nice, plus it pays to be on the good side of one of the most notorious people on the street. It freaked me out a little at first, but it's cool to me. Plus, you know me." He gives a very special kind of smile and wink. "I gotta try and worm in as close to people as possible. And furthermore, I've never had a gang myself so I don't know the first thing about treason. So, gangsters?" he asks, suddenly in front of me, offering a hand to shake, his left one, assuming I'm left-handed from my shake with Baldur. Whether his perceptivity is suspicious or useful, I can't decide, but I shake without bothering to correct anything.

"Sure. Gangsters."

Then, my suspicions are confirmed—you see, criminals never shake on anything conventional. Craw takes my hand and puts it up to his lips with a wink before I can react. "Glad to have ya, Little Miss Epicness."

I pause a second, taking my hand back, thinking. "Hey, Craw? Want me to teach you how to pick a lock?"

And thus, the two-felon pretend-gang is born.

Minutes later, we're looking at a digital map on one of the many display units I left behind, which Craw gets a kick out of. "You don't like electronics much, huh, Rat?" he asks. "That's okay, a lot of cutouts don't. It's hard to trust machines after *it* happens."

The memories of sitting on the curb after the "it" in question happened and all the awful sensations of when it was happening are similar to both of us—it's an experience that all of us cutouts share, and it makes any of us shudder just to bring it up or think about it.

He works with the touch screen a bit, trying to figure it out, and while he couldn't hold a candle to Voxel, he's not clueless, either. Better than me, anyway, who's a safe distance away. "What about you?" I ask him.

"Me? I don't have much of a choice." He frowns, and it makes him look even older and more tired. "When they pulled the mainframe out, I was a basket case. Something wrong got pulled or whatever. It wasn't too serious, but it killed all my lung function, and I had to have major surgery. A snip shop isn't the best place to have that done, so it wasn't the best job, really," he confesses, unzipping his high-collared jacket and moving away the black scarf so I can see a jagged scar running from the middle of his neck down under his shirt. "My lungs aren't natural, and that's how I can do all that crazy stuff with my voice and all. So if I didn't trust technology, I'd be kinda dead right now."

I nod, trying to look cool and collected on the outside, but inside, anxiety of a hundred levels shoots through me, so I grind my heels into the dirt against myself, resisting the urge to step away, wishing I could say something. But I can't. I can just ball my fists up so that my nails bite into my skin and try to think of a way of walking out of this without getting either of us hurt, keeping the damage to an absolute minimum.

Minimum damage? You're only good for destruction. Why don't you eat another battery?

"Maybe that's why it felt so easy to come to the dark side," Craw says lightly, brightening up again as he returns to the digital map that I won't come near. "You know, with Eli and all? I can accept it and find it so easy to believe cuz I know what technology and people who know what they're doing are capable of. So as a purebred, technologically-suspicious cutout, what made *you* the first one to go over and side with him? Or is the mystery better left unperturbed?"

He gives it a dramatic flair and throws me another one of those smiles, and I think, *He's just like him. Stiletto. The last real gangster I ever had. The reason I swore not to have another.*

I stare at him for a second, trying to think of what to say besides what I'm about to because I'm scared to say it, but maybe I can prove to myself I'm something brave, after all, that I don't really run from everything. So I tell myself it's okay, I'm just talking to Stiletto, and I start with, "I hate cinnamon. When I was young, I swallowed a cinnamon candy the wrong way, and I thought I was going to die, and ever since then, I could smell the stuff from a kilometer away. Machines are the same way, except it's been that way as long as I can remember. I hate them because they hate me back, and I can feel it all around, suffocating me."

Slowly, when I'm not sure if he's looking at it, I put my hand out at the little screen, and when my finger touches it, it's hard to tell, impossible if you're not looking hard enough, really, so maybe it doesn't even happen, probably doesn't, you know, um, but it goes fuzzy around my finger, making my head spin, so I take my hand back.

"I sided with Eli because he doesn't suffocate me."

I stare at the screen, thinking, *You knew that. And you still wonder if he's human when you of all people know he is.*

Craw nods, switching the screen off. "Well, I think we should probably get Baldur the map," he decides and starts leading the way back to the dining room, and I hope that the young friendship was not just brutally murdered by my stupid decision. Taking a second to collect myself, I follow behind. But not too close.

"*There* you two are! What were you doing all this time, nosing out in there?" Vici attacks when we walk into the room, and I take a step back, shocked. Then I remember: she's hurting, supposedly. And seeing me with a new friend probably doesn't help any, so I pretend to laugh—and if it was a joke, it wouldn't be hard to laugh at, considering I was with the biggest flirt in Tersatellus—and make my way over to Baldur, who's sitting at the head of the table with his game face on, surrounded by everyone as they wait to have the secrets of Hudson Bay revealed. It's got a lawless feel, one we all know well, as if getting info in a way that doesn't include beacons and killing or torturing people isn't supposed to happen, but hey, that wasn't mentioned. There's no rule against consulting the natives. The idea excites me, speeding me forward, so I don't notice Craw observing me, not offended in the slightest about Vici's remark—he actually wouldn't mind too much if the assumption were true. Then the fancy ends, and he shows Baldur how to work the map display unit, and we all crowd around the cripple.

There's lots of dots scattered about the blue void marked Hudson Bay with thinner outlines showing how small the place used to be before they nuked the place bigger to make more room for ships and stuff to live here. Apparently, this was supposed to be a sort of in-between meeting point, a place where Tersatellus could interact with the rest of the world, but then the Adamantration decided to be totally independent, so Hudson Bay turned into a world between the heaven of Tersatellus and the reality of the rest of the world. Most of the dots, Baldur explains, are really large areas of bare rock sticking out of the ocean, totally uninhabited. He points out many major islands that sustain life, admitting that his people never really contacted others beyond their ports because the rest of Hudson Bay has turned into something of a freak show.

Baldur's only been a ship guy for a year, so he doesn't know that much about the Bay except for Dagur's Island, one of the northernmost islands, though it's still east of here—we were inserted into the Bay at its north point. Dagur's Island was taking Tersatellus's influence, and it erected walls around itself and didn't associate itself much with the other islands, but there was a nature of fear about their avoidance. Baldur says that there were rules on the island that were stupid to him, such as everyone was demanded to give up silverware or anything made of metal so their leaders could throw it in the water for some sort of sacrifice, and nobody was allowed to get a suntan on Tuesdays. All these rules were upheld so fervently Baldur and his shipmates've had an easy time getting suspicious about it all. Now he's wondering what other things the powers that be are hiding.

(Ain't we all?)

He pauses his speech to adjust the map and let the crashing of something in a distant area of the ship fade. "Hey, Baldur? What's the most best technology island? Technology, smart, this map is technology? That's probably the place with the equipment to extract us," I explain to the others with a great transition from baby-talk to professional speech. "If they needed those casket things to get us into here, they'll probably need something to take us out."

"Ah... me is think. I have know that none islands have any best technology at night. All lights is out, everywhere, and shadow is rise when sun is fall. That is what they is say to me. But..." Baldur thinks about it, playing with the map. "Yes. Little tall place, go up-down, big ships, big, big town, um... Parl, pearly place... where? Ugh..." He tries to remember where the pearly place is at.

I stand up, feeling too energized to sit down. I'm anxious and excited, and I don't think it's about Baldur anymore. As if there's cinnamon in the air, I sniff it, and there's nothing to smell but the ocean and fire and destruction, but it's not so much as something I'm smelling than something I'm feeling. "Guys..."

"I feel it too," Rex says, standing up as well, fists clenching and unclenching. Some of the others look at one another. Everyone's got an odd, tense look on their face, and the energy keeps growing until we're all standing.

"Something'm up," Tom growls, rubbing the back of his neck.

"Get out," Voxel says with a shake of her head. "Everyone get out of this area, right now. This place gives my insides the ants of anxiety that tell my brain it is about to jump down onto our heads."

"Why?" Motor asks even as we get going, fast.

"There's something wrong about this, this place. I don't like it, and I don't trust it," Spike says but pauses on the way out to snag a loose pair of rugged sunglasses off the floor and perches them on his nose.

The feeling of suspicion deepens as we go. We're running by the time we're nearly out, so I almost don't notice the little surprised and angry huff behind me—it takes the close-following sound of impact to get me to turn around. Motor's on the floor, looking pretty ticked. "It's my shoelace," he grumbles, twisting back to get the thing untangled from a splintery piece of wood that's stuck in a rut that looks *made* to trap kids with loose laces. Cursing, I hurry over, flicking out my knife. "I can do it," the kid protests.

"No time. Sit still," I say as I start cutting of the little white lace with gusto.

I really can't explain this feeling to you, but it's the same kind I get when I'm in a house right before someone turns the corner, someone that ends up unable to see me because this feeling let me duck behind some furniture. Sixth sense for danger. The saying goes that some of us know trouble so well by now that we know our way to and from it par cœur, our minds are guilty enough to already know what sort of things could be after us so when we would be after us if we were trouble, then it would be now. It's confusing but makes me edgy, so I almost nick Motor with the knife.

"What's with the rush, anyway?" he complains, waving off my apology. "What on earth are we running from?"

Without any explanation, I flip the knife back and grab his arm, towing him behind me until we've cleared the ship, catching up with the others as we all run toward our mobiles with unspoken urgency. Baldur can't step on the track, it turns out; he's not part of the ship it's now reacting to, so he sits on a chair from the ship and gets dragged along by Tom. Motor's about to demand what the heck we think we're doing when the explosion happens.

Everyone stops and turns around in surprise as the ship we were in goes up in smoke. This explosion is much more quiet and small and seems to concentrate more on flames than impact, which doesn't matter much since the ship was buckling, anyway. They would've collapsed on their own. The Adamantration just gave them this kiss of Death, and this one little blast's all it takes for the whole fleet to start to collapse into a flaming, groaning heap of scrap metal and buried history. Somehow, the scene doesn't catch me off guard like it should.

"Well, what was *that* for?" Eli wants to know.

"It's a sign!" our paranoid conspiracy-addict Rex says, his face lighting up. Lily gives him a look, but before she can release her verbal arsenal, he rapidly continues, "Look, normal people there woulda been sittin' ducks in there, and now they'd be peking duck in there, but we all knew to run outta there, right? It's our suspicion, that's what it is, our criminal natures and criminal minds! That's why the discipline ops never stopped us, and it's why the Adamantration don't kill us off so easy—they can't, cuz we're too good for em!" He's almost dancing, only stopped by his unwieldy feet, but the scary thing is, he's right, just kinda weird about it. I'm the next to break out into a smile, and some of the others start to follow suit.

"So we're too smart for the Adamantration of adults, eh?"

"Too right!"

"So much for nobody's safe! They can't touch us!"

"Criminal natures for the win!"

"We'll be dodging bullets next! And flying!"

"The Adamantration doesn't have a chance of stopping us!"

"Guys?" Eli interrupts. "Not to rain on your parade or anything, but I don't think that bomb was from the Adamantration. It's too small, and they said they wouldn't be watching us. Even if they went back on their word, the flames are all on this side here, meaning that they came from over there," he says, pointing north, beyond where our mobiles are sitting on the track. I'm sure he's about to explain how stupid the angling would have to be or something that would prove the Adamantration couldn't've done this, but then the proof presents itself. A familiar-looking gun hoists itself over the roof of my car and fires before anyone can so much as think.

Baldur slumps in his chair. Someone has to stop him from falling over because he doesn't have any control of his body anymore.

Corpses normally don't.

Siridean leaps out over my truck and lands in front of the mobile, one knee pressed into the ground. "You know, that bed makes a great hiding spot," he comments conversationally as we all back up, the lot of us making that high susurration of unidentifiable origins that always springs up out of a frightened group of people.

My mind connects the dots—that's how his figure kept disappearing on the radar on Tide Island, he'd merge it with the image of the mobiles by being near them! He's probably been hiding in the back of my truck this whole time, a thought that makes me sick to my stomach. And now our guide and an innocent man is dead, a condition Siridean seems intent on putting someone else in, pronto.

He stands to his full height, a gun in each hand, one trained on Spike, the other on me. Fear shoots through me, and I freeze. "Hey, you on the ground, get up," Siridean demands, and Craw, who dropped to Baldur's side the second he fell, gets up slowly, putting his shaky hands up, Voxel whimpering as he abandons the body—she and Motor screamed when it happened. "That's right, everyone with their hands where I can see em. Nobody make a sound, especially you, and nobody move, especially you." The man wags the guns at me and Spike in turn. I open my mouth to protest or ask what he wants from us or some other stupid thing, and he steps forward, his crazy eyes locking on me as he presses the barrel to my forehead. "You think I'm playing, little girl?"

A shudder runs through me with a mix of cold and hot fear and fury, and I force my eyes to stay open because I don't want to know what I'll remember if I so much as blink. This is not a new position for me.

Maybe if I move fast enough I can get a gun away from me but then he'll have time to shoot Spike, who will kill me if I leave him to that, so I sort of just freeze, staring.

Off to his left, Eli observes me for a second before adopting my tactic of becoming background noise and slowly starts sinking down to the track.

"What're you doing, Siridean?" Lily suddenly starts, turning the man's attention to his right. "It's twelve to one at the moment, and as your dealer, I'm well aware that your strength ebbs every moment you're awake."

His eyes flash. "It is not!" he shouts, but his voice cracks under the sudden wave of Lily's influencing power.

She smiles hypnotically. "You aren't? That's amazing. Superhuman, even. Being someone strong as that would make you quite the formidable opponent, but still, I'll wager you'll only get a few of us down before you're overwhelmed. United, however, that's another story. With our numbers and your strength and clue, there's no way you'll die this week. Even without your clue, our combined forces would be unstoppable, despite all the lesser, weaker pirates that are to follow you. Besides ... depending on your answer, I may or may not have a treat in my pocket for you." Siridean's so intoxicated by her smile and its implications it's all he can focus on. In fact, after a second, he trains his left gun on that smile, which disappears, taking the owner's ability to breathe with it.

"I think you'll go first, you little siren," he says shakily, and he starts thinking about pulling the trigger back a little to see how we react, but then he notices Rex to Lily's right is staring with huge eyes at something behind him.

Without even looking, as if the whole thing was reflected in Rex's eyes, Siridean spins around with incredible speed and fires at will, blowing off three rounds, two at Eli and one at the oncoming shoe (you read that right), which was coming at approximately the same speed as the bullet, so the two speeds cancel out, and the thing falls to the ground in a smoking, holey heap as Eli falls back on his hands, narrowly avoiding the same fate as his shoe. What Siridean doesn't expect is a second volley, and this shoe catches him full in the face, some mechanism in the footwear registering the impact and letting off the force a concussion grenade. Eli goes and retrieves his shoes and shoves them back onto his feet before going to check for sure if Siridean's really out. When he nods, we all relax into a state as close to normal as our pounding hearts will allow, which, for most of us, is about as close to normal as it would be if we just ran a marathon up stairs.

Of course, Spike is excluded from this. "Where can I get me a pair of those things?" he snickers.

"You'll never live to find out if we keep getting ambushed," Lily snaps, trying to steady her shaking. "Great, now our guide's gone, we lost our source of food, and we have to figure out what to do with *this* guy."

"It's pretty obvious, isn't it?" Spike says with a grin that isn't helped by his shades. "We kill him."

The whole time this was happening, Motor's been standing apart from the rest of us, and in a circle around him, the green grid lines have sputtered and faded away. At Spike's last words, the circle gets wide enough to include some people, which the poor kid was trying to avoid. Voxel's eyes cross, and she squeezes them shut, pressing her hands to her face. The map lets out a mechanical screech as it goes crazy colors before falling to the ground, where Craw (who used it as a makeshift shield when Siridean started firing) drops it as he starts coughing uncontrollably. The thing falls through the track and disappears.

Motor takes a step forward to help, but the coughing gets worse, turning into big, painful hacks that hardly allow for any breath in between. Craw drops to his knees, holding the sides of his chest as his eyes water and he shakes all over. Rex starts forward next, but when he enters Motor's circle of darkness, he gags and staggers back, shuddering. By now, everyone's trying to ask what's wrong with mixed levels of intensity. Spike enters the circle with a no-funny-business expression that suddenly fills with pain, real pain, and he clutches his wounded shoulder, spewing profanities as he takes an exit. Everyone's stepping away now with unnerved looks on their faces, but nobody looks more upset than Motor, who has no idea what's going on.

"It's the black circle thing," Lily decides over our shouting as she takes a tiny cautious step in, only to quickly step back out again. Ivy takes a strange swoon against Tom's shoulder as it happens.

Nervous, I walk without drama into the circle, where I gently pull Motor away. The void of darkness in the grid follows him, lights springing back to life where we leave, and everyone stares at us in shock. Craw rakes in huge gasps of air as the coughing finally stops. "Motor?" I start, and he looks up into me with his big innocent eyes. "You know how you said you, uh, make stuff mess up?"

"It's th-this thing that hap-ha-ha-ho, *happens* when I g-get nervous," he says in a rush, tripping over his words in his twitches and hiccups. "I make stuff close t-to me go hay-haywire, but it's just mechanical-al stu-uff like main-fr-frames and screens and th-th-the tr-track! Not people, I, I think I just ma-ake electrical cu-urrants go weird, not, not people!"

"Yes, people!" Lily huffs. "Clearly, you're affecting the rest of us, and last time I checked, we weren't *all* cyborgs."

"I thought I was a can opener," Eli says.

"Whatever! The thing is, all people have electric currents in their brains, signals that tell everything what it must do—that's how most drugs work, by blocking or heightening some of those signals. So if that's what you're 'haywiring,' that makes you a mobile glitch machine."

"Watch your language, he's only twelve!" I scold for an excuse to cover the boy's ears as horror grows on his face.

"No, he's not," Voxel says gravely, and we all look at her instead of the growth of Motor's circle. "He really just aged to seven in the month of the Squirrel. In my many hackings of the niches of the Plexus system, I uncovered the truth that Mizz Adaman Nocturnum misprojected the age purposely to decrease our sobbing and pitying. He's a so-called faulty citizen, got his mainframe removed much earlier than thirteen—it actually got gone months behind us. Otherwise, it'd keep beginning to kill him whenever he got antsy, since the whole predicament was the thing's inability to function up to par, anyway."

"I th-thought getting ex-tract-ed would make it s-st-stop," Motor whimpers, putting his hands to his face as everyone jumps back from the advancing circumference of his void. Moved by the explanation—so this is why he's twitching out too—I go and be me and pat his shoulder.

"It's okay, you can't help it," I tell him, but my voice gets muffled by the top of his head as he jumps closer and presses himself against me. He feels so small and fragile in my arms I'm scared to touch him because he might break into a million pieces. Because of the trembling of his little body, I know he's crying or trying not to. I've never held a crying kid before, but somehow Motor folds up in my arms like everything about the situation's okay just because I said it is.

"Excuse me," Lily says with an odd tone, "I think *he's* rousing."

We turn and look at Siridean, who couldn't escape the circle and is now wiggling on the ground like a sleepy fish out of water. His eyes fly open, and his mouth makes an O before he drops back out of consciousness, which makes Spike do his ugly, condescending "ha ha ha."

"The reason he's always stoned and such was to get rid of the interference of the Plexus coming through the half-mainframe they left behind in his head. Hold him steady!" Lily commands when Motor gets to his feet and starts trying to get out of range of the man, and a bad, bad smile stretches on her face. "I've got an idea."

"I don't wanna hurt anyone," the boy mews.

"Well, tough luck. It's about time we get some structure around here. We're going to get this clue if we must pull his Thread in half and get the clue on our beacons."

"I *really* don't wanna *kill* anyone!" Motor cries.

"Don't do this to him, Leadhead," I snap, protective of the kid all of a sudden. *Seven. He's only seven!*

"Considering how even you must run out of offences at some point, you can't antagonize the man forever, so I don't think you can produce a better idea."

"We still shouldn't turn to torture," I say, but she's already getting as close to Siridean as she can without touching the circle.

When his eyes open again, his back arching, Lily pounces right into it, turning up her power meter again. "Listen to me, Siridean. You're going into withdrawal shock right now."

"I was listening, you idiot," he sputters as he clenches and unclenches his fists. "I'm not talking."

"Fine. Get everyone's weapons back from him, Mouse." Scowling, I get up and pull the weapons off Siridean's slightly vibrating body and put them in in a pile outside the circle.

"You little dog. DON'T SPEAK TO ME!" he roars when I open my mouth to respond, earning him a swift kick to the ribs to add to his blessings. In the meantime, Spike happily takes his rocket launcher and other accessories back. Ivy and Lily each take two guns, Lily getting the bigger ones, and they might snag a few more when I'm not looking, plus there's lots of ammo for them. Tim and Tom grab a small army's worth of worrying gadgets, and from their faces, I can tell they're not getting everything back in the state it was in a few hours ago. Rex gets out his club and waves it around with exaggerated glee before he clips it back onto his belt just to join the party. Vici slyly steals a knife I don't think is hers. Even Eli takes a bag of tricks that Siridean either didn't bother with opening or was too discouraged by the contents to use. After seeing the display of violent footwear, I don't really underestimate anything he owns.

"Okay, Siridean. Now we're all armed, and you're not," Lily says, hovering over the shivering figure. "And you're stuck powerless, writhing on the ground." Writhing. Nice. I bite my lip, trying to look nowhere, especially not at Vici. Behind me, Motor groans, holding his head and shaking as sweat pours down his body, sticking his hair to the sides of his head. This is who Vici decides to watch with a frown on her face.

"Maybe we should do something to try and help the situation at hand first?" I snap at Lily, but she ignores me and keeps talking to Siridean.

"Stop being so irrational!" she insists. "This can all end if you just agree to help us!"

"I won't hurt nobody, but I'm not giving you no clue!" Siridean replies.

"It's a start," I say. "We should quit now."

"Not until he complies!" Lily crosses her arms, fire in her eyes as she looks down at Siridean. The look alone'd be half enough to persuade me.

Motor can hardly keep himself sitting up at this point. It's all he can do to force shaky, random breaths in and out with horrible but near-silent squeaks as tears run down his face. Vici looks on in empathy. "He must have a remnant of the mainframe left, so he's hurting himself," she mutters softly and starts over.

Oh, sticks.

"No, st-st-ay-ay b-back," he gasps, and I turn around just as Vici enters the circle. She instantly starts falling and lightning shoots through me, so I catch her faster than I can think, lowering her to the ground and stuffing my jacket under her head. It's the scariest reaction out of all of them, at least to me with its awful familiarity. It doesn't stop when she's out of the circle! No, no, no!

"What's going on?" Lily demands, her voice high with half-buried worry.

"Nothing. Stop staring," I growl, guarding Vici with my body. "Why don't you be useful and figure out something for them to do?"

"Distraction, eh?" She smiles to herself then turns to Eli. "So, speedy, why don't you run and get Motor before he gets himself injured?" She gestures to Motor's fast-retreating figure, managing to make her suggestion sound more demanding than a suggestion should be. Knowing full well what's really up, Eli shoots her a look before dashing off (now that there's no walls and we're all standing still, his quickness is really freaky). "And now, everyone, please redirect their attention to the toaster as it attempts to capture the shrimpy glitch on legs." Crossing her arms, she flashes me a grin, careful not to look at the figure by my feet. "There, all problems solved. You're quite welcome."

There's a tense few minutes of silence, unbroken by the people watching either who's in front of me or who's behind me (most choose the second option rather than be on the receiving end of my famous smoldering glare). Wait, I stand corrected—most of them suddenly break the silence by trying not to laugh at something, but I don't bother to look around.

Slowly Vici relaxes, and her eyes flicker open, confused at first before her defeated, it-happened-again-didn't-it look makes her eyes close back up. "How long?" she whispers.

"No time at all, snowflake," I reply, which is what I always say, and she smiles because it's familiar and comforting.

"Vici, I'm sorry!" Motor howls as he gets led by the hand back over to us. He still looks really upset, but all the green lines around him are back. In his other hand is his untied shoe, and his goggles are dislodged on his head, so I can guess everyone laughed when he became a glitch on less than two legs. "I'm so, so sorry! I *really* didn't mean to!"

"It's okay," Vici says, sitting up with a bit of my help. "I guess it's my fault, anyway. Are you alright?"

Motor shrugs, rolling his eyes like he can't understand why anyone would care about something so unimportant as how *he's* feeling. "Are *you* alright?" His voice is back down to normal volume but still scratchy.

"Yes, I'll be okay. Let's just not talk about it, please." She nods to Siridean, who doesn't seem to feel like getting up anytime soon. "What about him?"

The man's head snaps up in attention. "I'll be good!" he barks before letting his head back down, then, forming another thought, lifts it again. "But I'm not telling you nothing. Don't think I'll just forget this. Especially you, kid. You're looking a lot less important than a thousand primes and a day at this point, so consider yourself at the top of the hit list." Motor doesn't even blink at that, but Siridean wouldn't know because he lays his head back down with his eyes closed. We all watch him for a quiet, awkward minute.

"If we're gonna kill him for the clue, I'll do it," Spike volunteers. "He wasted all my ammo, and I don't really think he's more important than half the wax in my ear, let alone the ink for a name on a hit list, if you want my humble opinion."

"That won't be necessary," I say.

"Seriously, though. I don't got a lotta wax. Or ink, neither. We should skip the list and jump the gun if you're sniffing what I'm putting out."

"*Thank* you, Spike, but he's got a purpose to fulfill." Even Siridean looks at Lily for that. "He's going to hold our late guide steady while we deliver him back where he came from. Siridean, back in the pickup truck with your victim, and don't drop him."

"What! I didn't sign up for this!" Siridean protests, and I'm right there with him.

"Uh, excuse me, but I don't remember my truck turning into a hearse!"

"Considering it was a hidden bunker on wheels for the last odd hour or so, it must be magical! Siridean, go! The rest of you, we're leaving. Someone guard him, and let's rid ourselves of this place." With a toss of her hair, Lily stalks toward her mobile. Everyone else follows her example, while Eli hops into the back of my pickup.

"Oh, you gonna throw another shoe at me if I misbehave?" Siridean asks edgily, dragging Baldur very carefully by the chair as I hop into my truck, sliding the beacon into place.

"Pipe down and respect the dead, would you? The less you know about me and my capabilities, the better."

"Better for who?" the man grunts as he hoists his victim into the mobile, their faces the same shade of Death. When he gets his ambiguous answer ("Both"), he just sighs and leans against the wall of the bed so he hits his head on the edge when I jerk forward and stop fast to let Motor pass by my side. I know I'm not gonna hit him, but it's instinct.

"Eli," he says quietly as he goes, "did you feel that thing they were talking about earlier, in the ship, before the fire, I mean?"

"No. It's like they developed a sixth sense or something." Motor relaxes at that and carries on.

When he's gotten onto his bike, I start forward fast. *Keep them busy,* I think as everyone scrambles to catch up. *Don't give them too much time to think about Motor or Vici or the fact that someone's dead.* I glance up in my back mirror at the two pale figures, one with fresh blood still streaming down his face, one trying to avoid the blood as much as possible as he slowly slips into the ache of withdrawal, and it's hard to tell who's holding up who.

"Well, *you* look miserable," Siridean somehow finds room to talk. "An open book, y'know, with pictures in."

"I'd rather be running, but I have to watch you instead," Eli says.

"Running? Along with all the mobiles or something? What're you, superhuman?"

Eli perks up a little. "I prefer to think so."

Siridean smirks. "So much for knowing nothing about you. You know you don't gotta respond to everything people say to you, right?"

"Why shouldn't I respond?" Eli frowns, confused.

"Why'd my dealer call you a toaster?"

No response. He's getting the hang of it.

"Yo, guys," Craw starts via beacon, unaware of the conversation I was trying to spy on. "If we're gonna be a band—"

"I'm the drummer boy!" Motor declares, and nobody argues.

"I shall embody the strings," Voxel says. "My vow to candor obligates to me to say that the rest of you haven't the grace for it."

"I call woodwinds," Craw finally gets to finish, with a sudden wave of sound from his mobile that makes everyone jump. "I finally figured out why this thing was meant for me!"

The sonic surprise annoys me enough, but then Rex adds, "Uh, is piano part of the woodwinds?"

"No, Rex, that is a controversial instrument that can't decide whether it's part or the strings or the percussion. No wind is required," Voxel informs him with preschool-teacher sounding patience. "It's sometimes considered its own group, so you can be piano. In a conventional sense, that leaves the brass and the conductor between Rat and Eli."

"No conductors," I say, forcing all the things I could say to put down the horn and the genius piano question. A ton of snide comments spring to mind, just itching to be heard, and for a second, I entertain the notion before I notice the screen on my beacon fuzzing slightly by my fingers, and I jerk my hand away, worried. *It's never been this bad before.* I take a deep breath and put my hand back, trying to make it stop. It's not like I even know what I'm doing, so I have to pull my hand away sometimes or I'll explode from frustration, but once—if I don't imagine it—the fuzziness fades. The beacon freaks out again when I get excited, and a few of the pixels start failing, so I pull my hand away quick, staring guiltily at the little black dots. "Well." I sigh. "You stopped it for a second before making it worse. Maybe Mo'll know something about this? No, no, it's no big deal, no big deal. What if you just have acidic blood, sweat, and tears or something? That'd be cool, right? And saliva! Why don't you eat another battery? I can't believe he said that to you! Eat another battery! Maybe he should get another reform or follow another order or wear another smile while someone else bloods the gutters or—"

A knock on the back window wakes me from my little reverie, and I reach back and swipe the pane open. "Your sudden silence concerns the others," Eli tells me, raising his voice over the wind, which is reinforcing his aerodynamic hairstyle. "Also they'd like me to be the brass section, since it's appropriate, don't you think?"

"Do you have any brass in you?" I ask him with a mixture of curiosity and apprehension. It's a question I never thought I'd ask, and it seems equally awkward to the both of us.

"Honestly, um, I don't know. What'll you be if not conductor?"

I don't miss the change in subject, but I don't mention it, either. Besides, even if we did stay on topic, I have so many questions I wouldn't know which ones to ask or how to ask them or anything, so I just excuse myself from talking altogether with a "Lemme think about it" that doesn't get him to turn his neon gaze somewhere else. "What?"

"They're talking about you. Lily's team. Some of them want to know why Motor didn't affect you the way he did with everyone else, plus they don't like how it was your mobile Siridean hid in all this time. Altogether, Lily is very suspicious. They've begun gathering all the information they can get about you from your friend, and so far, their search has come up short. Would you care to listen?"

"I'll pass. Did you tell the others about the brass section thing?" He shakes his head, so I (carefully) grab my beacon. "Hey, guys. Sorry, I got distracted for a while. Eli's being brass—"

"Hang on, I wanted to be brass," Rex butts in. "I was asking about the stupid piano thing cuz I failed piano lessons on my first shot. I passed my trumpet lessons, though. Eli can be the piano."

"He seems fine with that," I tell Rex without mentioning how bad I wish I could reach through the beacon and strangle him. By the way, fine is an understatement: Eli looks pretty pleased if you ask me, but he's doing a good job hiding it. "Okay, we've got piano, brass, strings, woodwinds, and drums, so any ideas on what that leaves me with? I have an idea, but it doesn't really fit."

"Keyboard?" Rex suggests. "Or is that part of the woodwinds?"

"I'm done," I announce as I toss the beacon into the passenger seat.

"Keyboards and organs and stuff still count for piano, for simplicity's sake. Besides," Craw says carefully, "I'm not sure if she, or we, want something, you know…"

"Electric? Don't worry, I don't get stage fright," Motor saves, pretending to think the hesitation to include machinery has something to do with him. "Plus it wouldn't work cuz Rat isn't black-and-white. She's a hundred shades of gray with silver lining." My head snaps over to the boy on the bike in surprise, and he gives me a salute. "I'm poetical! It's a gift! So what's your idea, Rat?"

"Choir," I admit. "But it doesn't make sense since I couldn't carry a tune to save my life."

"Maybe," Eli says without the beacon. "But you do have a voice. And you know how to use it."

I stare at him in the mirror for a second then shake my head, wondering how everyone got so profound without me. "Choir it is," I proclaim, all noble and stuff, and the team cheers.

The team. The band. The Band of Cutouts. A band that I'm a part of. A smile stretches across my face as I think about it. Finally, despite the crazy situation I'm in and the crazier people that're in it with me, I've found a group of individuals in which—with a little luck—I might even belong.

- IX -

Suppression of the Truth

Either there was another display unit or someone got another one. Then someone had the brilliant idea to give the even more brilliant Xavier Kael the map, so getting to Dagur's Island takes a great deal of patience. I let Voxel do all the explaining that no, the sky is not north; yes, the compass rose words tell you what direction everything's at; no, it can't lie to you, and south doesn't rhyme with tooth; yes, west is to your left, no, your *other* left, Rex, that's not an island, that's Spike's tank. In a way, it gets so ridiculous it's entertaining, so when Voxel gives up ("Left, left, LEFT, Rex, I'M to your left, I'm waving all two of my arms, turn your skull already—not *behind* you!—that's it, have my capitulation!"), I stop being done and pick up the thread.

"I'm sorry, I'm sorry, I just can't follow directions!" Rex says, sounding more exasperated than sorry for anything. "Which way's left?"

"Nine o'clock," I try. "You know, like on an analog clock? No? Okay, what about this: you read left to right, so wherever you'd start at—"

"I can't read," Rex interrupts darkly.

"Oh." That explains the sooth thing. I think hard for a second. "What's your dominant hand, then?"

"I'm ambidextrous."

The phrase strikes me as weird in every way, but I don't give myself time to wonder what corner of his brain it came from because somehow, it goes to a memory to a thought to an idea to a bunch of words: "Your left side is the side of the piano with the low notes, Rex."

There's a moment of silence where Voxel waves excitedly, no doubt shouting some obscure phrase or another that she doesn't share with us because it would run the risk of confusing him—I'll bet it's all he can do to talk and drive at the same time. Then, "Why didn't you say that in the first place?"

"You're welcome. Now, let's figure out where to go."

Seven piano or trumpet references, thirteen wrong turns, three pauses to let people climb back into their mobiles after flying out, trying to avoid collision with a certain unpredictable monster truck, and countless frustrated "'pologies" later, Craw catches sight of the island in question, and we all start going over. I hope it's not just a fourth false alarm.

The bickering stops as we roll over toward the place. It looks like it used to be a great point sticking up out of the bay, a little crooked, maybe, but the top's been sheared off, so only half of it's left, and it's been hollowed out in the middle, so all that's left is a shell, a huge crown of dark granite or some other stone, paled and buffed by years of salty waves beating on its outside. The wall stands an easy thirty meters into the air, which, with the Divide towering in the background, seems almost small, but up close and personal, it's still imposing with glinting solar panels lining the top in a sort of ring of shields, proper and uninviting. Waves crash up against it, their white spray shooting up through the track before slowly falling back down through it, invisible. With some searching, we figure out there's some sort of gate on one side of the wall.

"Whatcha gonna do, roll up and knock on the door and say 'Here's your dead chap' 'n' run?" Rex asks as we approach. The place has "proceed with caution" written all over it, and dropping a corpse on their doorstep is just about the last thing I want to do.

"Why don't we ask Lily? This was her idea," I point out, and a few seconds later, we hear Eli using his beacon to talk to Lily, putting it more eloquently than I would've (he'd like to know what the genius's brilliant plan to deliver our late guide to his home is after we arrive at the impenetrable stone gates if they aren't even allowed to open up during this time).

"She claims to have had a vision of Siridean carrying his victim in his arms and groveling to appeal to the islanders, begging for their forgiveness, and they, under the strict assumption they have security cameras posted everywhere, will promptly fling wide their gates, take the corpse with grace, and kindly advise us to the nearest extraction site." Eli pauses. "It seems she wants a more direct quotation, so here goes: 'Make Siridean carry him over there, and he'll cry a little, and they'll take the body back, and when they do that, we'll demand to know the secrets of the bay, including the island with technology, even if we have to hold them at gunpoint!'" Another pause. "Yes, that *is* how you sound." I watch in the mirror as Siridean laughs at something, even though he's managed to go even paler as the conversation goes on, then, after more listening, both of the living figures roll their eyes at the same time. "She's appealing to a higher power and begging for help now—ah, wants to know whether or not any of us fools have a better idea."

"I might." Everyone probably has a collective inward groan as Rex, of all people, speaks up. "If you zoom in real close on this map thing, you could see people on here if they were out, so this is oviously some governmental spy stuff, and I don't like it, but anyway, if you zoom in, you can see this weird spot on the insides of the gates, like the transition room at the snip shop." When you walked into that place, there was a hallway you had to stand in where weird showers would dust you in some stuff to kill all the germs on you, because the place obviously had to be sterile, but I don't see what this has anything to do with the situation. "So I was thinking, what if it was like that, where they got this area for outsiders so they can come in but without really being *in*, y'know? We go in there, explain what happened, and talk it out like normal human beings. And maybe get info or something and book it," Rex says quickly, trying to abandon the last three words of the sentence before that, but everyone picks up on it, and the tension in the air goes taut. I sink down in my seat, hoping not to get noticed, wishing I were in almost any vehicle but this one—I say almost because the last place I'd want to be right now is in Rex's size-X shoes. The static still goes on, so that means he's still holding the button down, either trying to think of something to say or to stop anyone else from saying anything.

"As if there's a such thing as a *normal* human being," Siridean grumbles, rubbing his temples. "What'd everyone shut up for?"

"Probably deep in thought, that's all," Eli says, trying to find a good load of nothing to look at. Then he goes on to explain to the Brigade what the better plan is, again making it sound better than it did the first time, but he doesn't mention who the plan came from so that it has a chance at not getting shot down by Lily the second she hears it.

After a bit of convincing and editing, the plan is accepted. "Oh, and by the way, I'm no fool—I know that Rex is the one with the map, since only he could be the reason we were taking such idiotic routes, so I know where this plan came from, and I'm only agreeing because it's amusing to watch him dig himself a deeper grave," Lily says, hardly getting in her last word before another voice cuts in: the leery voice of the subject at hand.

"She's insulting me, isn't she?"

I'm too busy driving to notice Eli go all hesitant in my mirror. "Um, not really," he tries.

Lily almost instantly picks up on what Rex must've said on our channel. "Speaking of digging a deeper grave," she snickers, and even Siridean smirks. "Then again, I'm not sure if they bury robots or not when they're deemed malfunctional." Siridean's smile disappears, and Eli turns the beacon off without response.

We finally roll to a stop in front of the gate, which is made of two huge doors made out of the same stone stuff as the wall with wide steel bands reinforcing it. And by huge, I mean *huge*. They go the whole way up the wall, and each door's wide enough to let in twenty of Spike's tanks side by side, and they look like they go even below the track. The sea sprays us with fine mist as we all hop out of our mobiles, wandering over. Knots form in my stomach looking at the place. Lily walks right over, and at first, I think she's going to come over and slap me or something—there's something about her face that says she's always ready to give someone a good crack across the face—but she brushes right past me to Siridean, twirling her gun in her hand. "Okay, Siridean, this is how this is going to work: you are going to carry Baldur nicely over to his people. No careless dragging. Pretend as though he is still alive, as though you didn't murder him, and maybe these people won't think of you as low as you deserve to be thought of."

"But… but I can't get blood on me!" The man's voice starts going higher than it should.

"Oh, so you're afraid of a little blood?"

"Terrified, and with a good reason too!"

"And what reason would that be?" Lily demands, and Siridean bares his ugly teeth at her.

"You're gonna have to wait and see for yourself," he seethes. "I hope they kill you first." For some reason, he glances at the sky, grim satisfaction mingling with his fear.

Anyone not watching the two of them have a conversation seems to be looking at me. When I notice this, I suddenly get self-conscious and step back, ready to jump back into my truck. "What? Did I turn into a new species while you all weren't watching or something?" Even Vici's giving me the weird look!

Someone taps my shoulder, and I whirl around to see Craw standing there, totally absorbed, as he hands me my jacket. "Left this on the ground," he says, and I realize I'm standing in front of everyone with only my black tank top with the not-thick-enough straps, and I grab the jacket fast, pulling it over my back and my bare arms, hoping they just think it's because I'm cold or modest, but I know that some of them must've caught sight of the tattoo. That's the second exception to my no-auxiliaries rule. "Rat…"

"Not now," I snap, walking over to the gate.

Now that I'm close, I can see outlines in the doors, presumably for people to get through, along with a tiny little one for a sliding-door spyhole that seems laughable compared to the size of the rest of the doors. The doors are raised off the ground, like they were only guessing where to put them, and I remember that the track isn't here year-round or even decade-round, and they probably don't get many visitors on foot here, considering this is over a body of water and all, so how am I supposed to get their attention? With nothing to lose from trying, I start with the obvious: knocking. My fist makes a pretty melodramatic sound against the steel band I knock on, and I'm kinda proud of the sound, even though it makes my knuckles hurt. "Anyone home? Uh, ouvrez-vous or I kick you." Lily slaps her forehead, muttering something about being surrounded by fools, as Rex trips facefirst over his shadow, and Siridean walks up with the cloth covering of the bed of my truck (he must've hidden under that before) wrapped around his victim.

Half of us jump when the slat covering the spyhole slams open, and a pair of beady eyes stares out at us. Muffled gibberish pours forth from the hole, and when I say, "What?" the eyes roll.

"Who is you?" the deep, gruff voice demands. "No, no. I know. What is you here for?"

"Wait, how do you know who we are?" Rex asks back as he tries to get up.

The eyes get even squintier. "I know. You people is come when black bowl is fill. I is see. You people is come, you kill and bleed and is eat when bleed and die when is eat. Monsters! Oh, monsters!" Fear streaks through his features, widening his eyes as they fly all over the place, his mouth trembling.

"No, no, we're not the same!" I insist. "We don't kill! We're good! Well, except for him." The man catches sight of Siridean and the body, and if his eyes were wide before, they're saucers now. "Do you know this man? The dead one, the ugly one's ours, unfortunately. Do you want to, uh, take care of him?" I've heard that people outside of Tersatellus have special ways of caring for their dead. Instead of burning them like most Tersatellans do, some places bury their dead the way only some of us criminals do in special places or lay them in tombs or some other creepy stuff.

The sentry stammers a second before getting a word in, and that word is barked out as the worst curse in the world: "Blood!"

"Yeah, they don't seem to mind it too much," Siridean comments. "The big, scary guy's covered in it too, and the old guy."

"I'm sixteen," Craw huffs, and Siridean seems to really look at him for the first time and gets disturbed, but not as disturbed as the sentry, who's hyperventilating by now.

He utters something that I take is a real curse and slams the slat shut, muttering that there's only one way to go about this. Then the rest of what he shouts at people is lost on me, first because it's all foreign, second because it soon gets totally drowned by a clamorous clanging and clanking, and I stagger back as the doors slowly start to go in forward.

They only end up a couple of meters wide before they stop, and the sentry appears on a wooden platform almost level with the track in the gap. He's shorter than I thought, a stout man with bristly dark hair and a mustache I didn't notice in the shadow of the wall. His clothes look strange to me, like Baldur's did—a deep-green shirt under a thick leather jacket and pants that seem to be made of fur, with boots and gloves, so it's obvious he's not usually in places with heating, but he's not exactly accustomed to the cold air like generations of technology and acclimation and food-burning Plexus-changes have gotten the rest of us.

He observes us grimly. "Come in. Hurry! There is still time," he spurs, and I rush in so he doesn't break his arm gesturing so hard. Inside the wall, I figure out that it curves and splits in two places, so there's this place right here to make a sort of smooth diamond-walled section inside the great circle of the real outer wall. This must be the room thing Rex was talking about. It's huge, probably the size of a city district. Rising up a meter out of the track, a wooden pier shoots back away from me, where it connects with a wide boardwalk that leads to a bunch of other piers, and I realize that this must be some dock or port. The piers are all placed far enough away from each other that one of those three giant ships that were screaming through the bay earlier could fit in snuggly. Two such ships (well, they're a little smaller) are docked at the far left of the wharf, bobbing peacefully.

The boardwalk grows right out of the head of the island, which peaks up above the track just before it hits the inner wall, which has significantly smaller doors. This little patch of land hosts tiny buildings crammed up against the inner wall, spilling onto the boardwalk for the most part. They could all benefit from some safety codes, and a new paintjob wouldn't hurt, either, but they look cool. Pioneery.

A woman, probably in her forties (I think that's how non-Tersatellans look in their forties), runs out of one of the houses, her wispy hair flying behind her as she comes over, face twisted. She takes the pier, not trusting the track, and gets to the end of it, a few meters away from us, just as the gates close on us. I keep my hand on my multitool as she jumps down onto the low, rickety platform and comes to a stop. "Baldur," she gasps, panting, then turns to me, her profoundly deep brown eyes gone wet and wide. "The ships … the sirens … I heard the sirens and then the explosions … What happened?"

"They got a faulty message from Tersatellus that led the ships into an ambush," I explain, hoping she's as good with this language as she sounds. It could use some work, but it's better than Baldur. "The defenses blew all of them up. As far as we know, there were no survivors. We found him with the burnt arm." She reaches for it gingerly, almost deterred by the blood, then touches his arm, shuddering at the cold.

"Many say this." Her voice is bitter. "His dreams were Dagurmen dreams. Misguided, starstruck. They want to see the Great Nation. They want to see yonder. This is not allowed. This is dangerous. They do not listen. The Great Nation, the frostbiters are rude for not talking to us, they do say, but your people are more kind to us than others would be. Many of our men return. But this …" Her hand trails up along the guy's arm to the side of his face where the bullet hit, and her eyes wander up to the man holding Baldur. "And then, after the 'ambush,' what?" she demands. Siridean swallows.

"*Then*, my dear, we saved his sorry, half-charred hide, and we were all pals for all of half an hour, and he was gonna help us, and we were gonna pull a miraculous recovery for the whole lot of us out of a hat when *this* little sucker came out of nowhere, blew everything up a second time, and killed our pal Baldur the rest of the way." Spike smiles, clapping his hand on Siridean's back so hard you'd think he was trying to break his ribs or something. It wouldn't be surprising, and it also wouldn't be surprising if he succeeded, considering how he made headlines last year with Sir Adaman Ivan Carver of the Structure & Architecture Sector at an invitation dinner that was supposed to get the formidable cutout on "the right side." All I can say is, don't choke on your olives or do anything else that may call for CPR when Spike is in spitting distance.

"Well, the Devil take you, then," the woman growls at Siridean, who doesn't so much as flinch. His eyes are distant, and his face is slack except for the random twitch here and there.

"No time for this," the sentry says nervously. Now I can see I thought he looked taller because he was standing on the pier to look through at us. "Hilda! You know is the time." The woman who I take to be Hilda looks up at the sky with worry, and she nods. "Blood."

"Blood," Hilda repeats then turns to us. "You cannot stay here. Yes, we live under the shadow of fear, but our wariness is what has protected us from the dark Fate as yours. Our people must stay protected, no matter what that is meaning to you. I know not what the other islands are thinking of this matter, but for us, no strangers allowed." Her face darkens. "Especially not contenders, especially not bloody, and especially not after sunset."

"What's wrong with the sunset?" Voxel asks, looking up at the sky. It's starting to darken a bit, and I check my watch because the light can get pretty erratic now with the moon's closeness making some nights just like day—it's after five in the afternoon, if the thing isn't broken by now. My shoulders fall. We've only been here five hours.

"No talking about it!" Hilda hisses, beckoning us up onto the pier and leading us to the hut she came from. Everyone here seems to be in some terrible hurry. "These are the places where families wait for their families to come home from sea," she says softly, holding the doorframe and standing at the threshold for a second before she takes a deep breath, squares her shoulders, and breaks down crying.

"Oh, for the love of Pete," one of the men in our assembly mutters.

Motor walks over to the woman and puts an arm around her legs, shushing her quietly. "Hey, don't worry, Ms. Hilda. It'll be okay. Baldur isn't gone, okay? He's just waiting on some other shore right now, waiting for you to come home. So you just have to keep sailing for now, but you'll see him again someday. Life's just the stormy bit of the odyssey, but somehow, all ships make it home no matter where they gotta go on their way to get there. My mommy told me that, and she's always right."

"And now we've got Socrates on the loose," the same guy as before says under his breath, but Hilda doesn't notice, just gulps and nods, Motor trying to help out as she stands up, but he's really just there for emotional support or something.

"You'll have to forgive me," Hilda apologizes, fumbling with the knob before opening the door to her little hut thing. "Baldur was the last family I had left that the sea hadn't taken. But I don't plan on following them just yet, and I do not think you do too, so I am afraid you'll have to step within."

Inside the hut, there's a room made of the same dark clapboard as the outside, with a table and some chairs in the middle of the floor and a couple of pallet beds to the left and a door in the wall ahead. There's tea, still steaming, sitting on the table. Hilda looks at it with a sigh then walks straight into the other door as the rest of us file into the hut—it's a tight fit, but none of us really want to get gestured to again, so we make it work.

When she walks into the room again, she sets a stone plate with burning powder on the table, letting the bitter smoke drift around. It smells tangy and briny, and it's enough to make my eyes water. There's nothing little about Voxel's otherwise similar condition, and worry crosses Craw's face as he starts coughing again (much less bad this time, though), and most of the others put their shirts up over their noses, wincing at the smell. "There. The bathroom's to the right if any of you are needing it. Now, you, you, you, and anyone else with blood on them, follow me," she says solemnly, and Spike, Craw, and Siridean follow the woman into the other room. Lily doesn't have any blood on her, but she idly follows the group, sweetly nudging Siridean with the barrel of a gun every now and then. So that's why he's behaving. Motor takes up the back of the train, so either he got nicked in the ship too, or it has something to do with the way he's walking right next to the man who wants to kill him, holding Baldur's hand.

We start a bathroom rotation, more to let some people escape the nasty odor than anything—you don't get born into the most technologically advanced nation on the planet without getting all sorts of treatments for improved waste treatment, but at this point, I'd prefer selective smell or something. "When did explaining stuff go outta style? I don't like this," Rex complains from beneath his shirt, which is pulled up to his forehead so it looks like his faded red hoodie grew white dreadlocks.

"You do not enjoy anything, Rex," Voxel says, still sore from the whole *left* thing and bats at her eyes, almost knocking the collar off her nose. We look ridiculous, but hey, anything to stop the stench. "What is this substance?"

"*Elijah* likes it," Spike pokes back into the room just to point out (the man's got the edges of his jacket against the bottom half of his face since he's too cool for pulling his shirt up like the rest of us).

"I tolerate it, is all. And it's Eli," Eli corrects for the second time today, and I worry that Spike's found out a new way to bug him. Eli's the only one not covering his face at all, but Tim still looks normal, since he usually wears the hood and bandana (the sentry nodded at him like, "See, here's a smart one, actually wearing a proper jacket in the Arctic"). He pulls off the bandana, though, and hands it to his brother, whose showy muscle shirt is cut too low to be worth any protection. Then Tim pulls his arms into his jacket, turns it around, sticks his arms back out and puts the hood over the bottom half of his face, using the pull strings to tie it in place. I wish I still had a hood or half the brains to do that with.

There's some Lillian-protesting coming from the other room, and Spike ducks back inside. The rest of us look at one another, wondering what to do now that the major enforcer of the separation thing these teams have going on is gone. We tense when Hilda yells something and Lily's gun comes flying into the room, nearly knocking over the dish of powdery grossness. The smell of it mingles with an equally unpleasant smell coming from the other room. I walk around, trying to occupy myself by "looking" at all the knickknacks.

For casualness's sake, I mess with my Rolex as I poke around, turning the hands. It's funny how you get the hands to turn—there's actually a false loop in the metallic band that shifts so you can open the face. If you try turning the little dial on the side, it seems to do nothing, when really, if you keep turning it in the right combination, the tiny lock opens, and you can get into the secret compartment. That's what I end up doing by instinct, since I've done it so many times before, and a little bracelet braided out of steel wool sits against my wrist for a second before I push it back inside and keep wandering.

Keeping her expression blank and neutral, Vici shortens the one meter I've left between us in my meticulous trek over. "What've you got so far?" she asks, and I open my palm to show her the small collection of items I've split by now. "The shells are mere eye candy, but those rocks may be worth something," she appraises before stepping back into her place, where she attempts to have a conversation with Ivy. The poor girl will only whisper near-silently, though, so she whispers everything to Tom, who attempts to translate, but a good half of what he says is lost on Vici, who's always been a proper sort of girl, so despite Tom's obvious eye rolling, Tim translates where he has to. Which isn't such a bad thing because it's obvious Vici quickly becomes fascinated just by his voice and the way he talks. That isn't saying much, don't worry. Even I would happily sit at his feet and listen to him talk for days. It's proper, and sometimes overkill, but it's natural, not the tone of someone trying to impress or persuade anyone, like Lily always sounds, and I realize that if this is his normal voice, then his persuadey voice could probably talk Mizz Adaman Nocturnum into robbing a bank.

Speaking of robbing, the gears in my mind are turning, and I wonder if I could excuse myself for just a second and get away from this little hut and find a way into the rest of the island, the bigger part where the residencies and people and valuables would be, somewhere I can disappear in the crowd and live it out for the week, maybe. Screw the others and get out alive. Just a thought.

"Everyone's ears're busy meltin' over the Brothers Debonair, 'n' Rat's just over here, falling in love with the door," Rex mutters, and I realize I was staring, and everyone gets a laugh out of it.

But the whole conversation and easiness ends all of a sudden when Hilda screams, "*EVERY*THING?" There's a reply then a pause. "Out! OUT! Get out right now!

"Aw, but I wanna see the twit's reaction when you find her other gun!"

"OUT!" both Hilda and Lily shriek at the same time. "Leave the house!" Hilda adds. "Leave the docks! Leave Dagur's Island and never come anywhere close to it again, or else get a whole new wardrobe!"

"She doesn't like how everything I got's got metal in it." Spike grins as he strides back into the room, smelling of chemicals, a white bandage peeking through the hole in the shoulder of his jacket. "That's why she tossed the gun out too. She'd love Elijah." The fact Eli feels compelled to correct him again only makes Spike's smile wider, but he doesn't say anything, just walks out of the house.

Lily stalks into the room next, and Craw after her, covered in minor bandages for all the scrapes he got in the boat. He holds himself stiffly, and the sadness in his eyes makes him look older than ever. "She's gonna send him into the city cuz she thinks he's got a chance." My fists clench and I almost argue, but only almost. He explains.

Siridean walks back into the room, and Lily makes it clear she's got her weapon back where it belongs. "I'm not gonna do anything," he repeats himself, but it's unnecessary because he's so withdrawn, so thirstin' (as they say on the streets) he probably doesn't have the energy to squish a bug, and he's swaying back and forth as it is, too weak to stand straight. The third time's the charm with me—not with the repetitions, sorry, what I mean is that this time, I notice that Siridean's wet and so is Craw and so was Spike. "She hadda scrub us to get the blood off, which'll be *great* in the cold," Siridean says, his voice hoarse and near zero volume.

"You can thank me later, in some other life," Hilda says as she walks into the room. Her intense eyes sweep over all of us. "Now, the rest of you leave."

"Wait, what is this stuff?" Rex asks, taking a step forward to enforce the question, but the effect gets lost when he almost trips again. Lily shakes her head in disgust.

"It's an essence we use here to ward off the wicked, ugly spirits," Hilda says, adding sulfur to the smell as she lights a match to rekindle the little flames in the dish.

Rex crosses his arms. "I think I'm getting insulted again."

"Oh, not *people*. Listen to me, and listen well." We all give the woman our complete attention. It's her voice, the tone of a parent who's just used your full name. "If you know what's best for you, you'll find some place safe tonight and hunker down, hunker down, hunker down." She taps her fingertips on the table to the beat of her suggestion. "You think you're smart. You think you're friends, eh? It's all buddy-buddy? Well, when it comes to survival, and they come for you, that's when you really figure out where your loyalties lie. Because when they find you, you'd better hope you can run, you'd better pray you can hide. Because if you can't? If you can't, well, it doesn't matter how close the lot of you are, how intent you are on a prize—people are going to die. And when it comes to the killers, it's best to be afraid."

"Wait! What are the killers?" I demand, resisting Hilda's sudden shoving. It's about time we get some answers around here! "Why can't they find us? What'll they do? Does it have something to do with the sunset or the whole blood thing?"

Her deep-brown eyes go blank as she shakes her head and breathes. "I . . . I . . . I cannot say. It is too . . . you see . . . to talk about."

Not a word more will ever be heard from her on the subject.

Taking a deep breath, she shakes it off and shoos us back toward the door, but Tom stops her. "Hang on a sec. Here." He hands her a lighter. "This'll make a little spark if you push this with your thumb and then a little flame so you can light your weird candles with it, okay? As a tanks. And a sorry." Hilda takes the gift with a nod of appreciation, not even trying it before shoving it in a pocket.

"And to you, I bid only this: good courage."

Before anyone else can say anything else, she gets us back onto the boardwalk, slamming the door of her hut behind her, and no matter what any of us says or does, she pretends we're gone. The other huts are the same way, if they're inhabited at all.

"Hey!" The sentry from before bobs over. "You all is better get out of here. Now!" he snaps when none of us move.

"Or what, little man?" Spike sneers. The little man in question huffs and holds up a remote.

"They is no stupid. They know you is do this thing, talk with locals, try to stay. They give us ways to is you gone."

"Oh, I'm so scared! Almost as scared as you little freaks are of nothing! No, wait, if I got that scared, I'd probably keel over or something. Go ahead, push a button at me. I wanna see what it does—I is curious."

The sentry shrugs his shoulders and pushes the button.

His vaguely annoyed look that tells us we're gonna need something more than courage out there is the last I see of him.

The track inside the walls suddenly pitches at one end, making a nearly forty-five-degree angle incline that tosses all of us off our feet and toward the slowly opening doors. I tumble wildly, lashing my hands out for any sort of handhold, not to stay, just to stop the stupid rolling, but I come up dry and narrowly dodge a sliding wall of mass as it flies past me. The shells and rocks I forgot to put back scatter out of my hands, and everything's flying out of everyone's hands and pockets. I gasp and duck my head as a bowie knife comes from nowhere and almost cuts my face in half. Finally, we come to a painful heap at the bottom of the incline, right outside the gates, which seal us all out once and for all.

"Spike, why don't you keep your curiosity to yourself from now on?" I groan and stagger to my feet to look for the shells and rocks that dropped out of my hand. That's when I realize that none of the stuff flying past me is landing on the ground, which strikes a nervous chord in me. While everyone else busies themselves with standing or grumbling about a big wave breaking against the wall, I take out one of the rocks I thought to put in my pocket and drop it. Sure enough, it goes straight through the black track, a little splash coming up through before dropping back down. Right, the track goes right through native stuff.

Tim, who's already thought of this (so I would've learned it two seconds sooner if I'd listened to him) is explaining it to his twin, who's panicking about the loss of either something he pronounces *really* weirdly or something I've never heard of. A few of our items are scattered on the track because they're of Tersatellan make, but some of them might've got stuck on the inside of the wall.

"My gun!" Lily yells furiously. "Those fools made me lose my gun!"

"Lost and found," a cold, crazy voice says, and I turn my head to see Siridean backing away, eyes flying all over the place, and it's easy to tell he's finally lost it. There's a gun in one trembling hand, and his other arm is crooked around Motor's throat, his fist clutching a beacon tightly as the kid's feet struggle to find the ground again. "I'm taking the truck and the brat, so if you don't want to die like your last friend did, I suggest you keep back. Consider yourselves pirated."

There's a dark look in his eye as Eli starts walking forward in the same deliberate, I'm-going-to-get-over-there-whether-you-like-it-or-not way you see discipline ops and other killers do in the flicks, and he doesn't even bother trying to move out of the way as Siridean fires. In the flicks, they never fire, but this isn't a flick, and it happens faster than I can gasp.

There's this sharp PIIIING that probably makes my skull and every pane of glass within a kilometer radius crack, and there's a slight black mark on Eli's forehead, but he doesn't even blink, let alone flinch. "Oh, bulletproof," Siridean oozes. "I really shoulda guessed. Okay, then." He presses the gun to Motor's temple, and the prey kicks harder, clutching at Siridean's arm to make him let go, or at least not choke him to death. "Now everyone keep back or the *brat* gets it. And believe you me, I won't hesitate. And kid?" He turns and talks into Motor's ear. "If you try your little circle of Death thing again, you don't get the leisure of dying fast, got it?"

My mind's flying in a million directions at once as I search for something, any hope to hold on to, frantically searching in the man's eyes for anything left to hurt, but something's whittled him down to the most basic form, and I know there's nothing left to abuse but a shell. But you know what? That's enough for me to work with.

Okay, so these boots weren't exactly made to double as concussion grenades, but I love em anyway as I stamp on a lace and pull it loose and kick my own footwear off my foot, and it sails. Kick for the cans, I learned once in my last gang, cans in this case being a euphemism. (*Toldja* I was good for hurting stuff!)

Siridean's eyes cross, and he sinks to his knees, and Eli bounds forward and tackles him, and I run and grab Motor away. The beacon falls to the track, and Tom's trying to get out some sort of explanation about this fish-shaped gadget that's apparently supposed to be able to bind Siridean up or something, but he gets interrupted by the fact that Siridean gets crowded by people trying to get Eli off him.

Siridean can't get a word of protest in edgewise; he only flails as everyone desperately tries to pry off the figure that's suddenly throttling him, spewing such things you'd never expect from, well, anyone. In all the chaos, Siridean decides to have one last word in by pulling the trigger as much as he can, the first and second bullets finding open air, the third one making another PIIIING, and the fourth one almost hits me, but only almost.

There's a short little scream, and the body in my arms shudders.

The world goes about fifty degrees colder.

My head drops in shock, and I can only see the red.

"Motor?"

An earth-shattering bellow of rage erupts a few meters away, and it takes the might of every other person present just to anchor Eli out of reach of Siridean. "LET ME DESTROY HIM!" he thunders, and they pull harder, because it's a promise, a promise that nobody wants to see executed, coming from a source that has suddenly become so terrifying nobody wants to see what it can do.

"Motor," I breathe, ignoring them, my blood roaring in my ears. "Motor!"

He winces and grunts, forcing himself into a sitting position. "N-no, I, look, I'll be okay," he says. "It just got my arm, see?" Blood soaks his sleeve, and I can see that the bullet only went through muscle because even though it's bleeding like crazy, he can obviously move the arm. Tense as all Perdition, I gently roll up his sleeve and look at the ugly gash rent in his forearm then move quick to cut his ruined sleeve off his jacket and use the fabric to staunch the bleeding cuz that's what they do in the flicks; it's all I can think to do. He's gone pale and shaky but takes deep breaths and tries to stay as still as possible for me.

"What've you done?!" I look over as Siridean staggers to his feet, stumbling away from the snarling monster he's created, looking at the blood on his hands with horror before his eyes start scattering again, sometimes separating from each other to look in other directions. He hyperventilates, touching the back of his head, his nose, his mouth, all oozing redness. "WHAT'VE YOU DONE?!"

Eli, who's always had a thing for responding, opens his mouth to shoot something back that *I* probably couldn't think of, but then a wave comes and knocks over half of our ragtag assembly. I scramble up to try and get out of its way, but it's so sudden and big there's no getting away, and it pushes me flat on my back, drenching me instantly. There's no time to react as another one leaps through the barrier and trips us all up again, so even Rex, who triumphantly kept his balance the first time, just misses Voxel in his fall. "What's going on?" he barks, back to being annoyed.

Siridean, who's backing up with his arms thrown out to either side without any regard to the tide, laughs in an insane sort of way. He's snapped. Lost it. "Time and tide wait for no man, ladies and gentlemen." He jerks a thumb upward. The sky's gone amber, and the sun is sunken far below the wall, but a sliver of the moon is visible above it in the opposite direction. "Have fun drowning, kids, and if you all die, then I'd like you to know that there's no way you could've ever figured out the clue, anyway. It's been a pleasure beating you all, but in the end, may the fittest man win." These are his parting words to us—he then pulls a vial out of his pocket, downs the liquid in one gulp, and revitalized, starts running, picking up speed as he goes.

"Don't," Voxel says, her voice a mixture of sternness and consternation as Eli takes a forbidding step forward. "Leave him to fly. We have other problems."

"Hang on. Before we go," Spike grunts, almost under his breath, and doesn't give Lily so much as a sidelong glance as he breaks the unspoken one-meter rule between our teams and hands Voxel her marker. "I grabbed this while we were falling. It hit me in the head, so don't think I was trying to do it, like, outta kindness or whatever."

"Well, you have my thankfulness. Here," Voxel says, uncapping the marker, and displays her thankfulness by helping smudge out the last of whatever was on his forehead.

"Oh," Rex says, remembering something too, and he's the next to cross the meter. There's a big white 13 on the back of his hoodie that I never noticed before. He holds out Vici's multitool to her. She takes it before he can drop it.

"Thanks," she tells him, shocked that he had the capacity to catch a falling thing out of the air in our tumble and the grace to give it back. "I hope it didn't hit you in the head."

"Nah, don't worry, it didn't hit me." Rex smiles, a strange sight on his face that transforms him from some insolent nobody with their hands in their pockets standing in the corner to an uncanny but almost *stable* figure that hints at kindness, which goes against everything the world knows about the albino. "You're welcome." Then the smile falls off, and he coughs, looking down and stepping back, almost embarrassed, his hand shooting back into the pocket of his hoodie. "We really oughta skate, pronto. The nearest island thingy—I dunno if it was just a rock or whatever, but it's better than nothing—it was soothwest of here on the map."

"Do you expect us to go in that direction, coming from you?" Lily asks like she's curious whether or not he's that stupid. "Not all of us are as foolish as you are, Rex."

"I'll take his word." We all look at Vici. Her face is set, and she nods, her expression saying, "Yeah, I said it."

"Me, too," I vouch, and Rex shakes his head, unable to believe his luck. Another big wave surges out of the track (he falls over again and gets right back up, accepting the fate by now). "Besides, it's our best lead! Would you rather drown?"

Lily glances at the ground, probably wondering like me whether the tide can *really* get high enough to drown us, and weighs her options. "Well, a place to spend the night wouldn't hurt," she relents, and nobody needs to be told a second time. Everyone scatters for their mobiles.

Eli fetches Motor's bike and helps the kid on. His hands shake as much as his voice as he keeps trying to apologize. He won't even look at anyone. All he can look at is the gash on Motor's arm.

Oblivious, I run over and leap into my truck, pushing the beacon into place so everything lights up again and slam on the pedal without even buckling in. Maybe it's a thief thing, but I'm already liking the place. With the windows up, it's almost soundproof and almost waterproof, and I feel almost safe. Then I notice something that makes all my comfort fly out the window, uh, even though it's closed.

"No," I breathe, staring at the screen in disbelief, my heart skiving beats all over the place. "No, no, this can't HAPPEN again!"

Unable to believe it, I tap the screen, willing it to change, but even the map won't show up, cruddy and undetailed as it was. Just a circle with dashes and a colored line going around the top half of it and a black little needle that is not in a happy part of the line. And the word WARNING in bright red letters beneath it. That has *never* been a good sign. Now is no exception.

"Hey, I see it already!" Motor cheers over the beacon system thing, and before I make the connection that I must be the only one this is happening to, I mentally deck myself in the face of my brain for not offering the kid a ride. What was I *thinking*? "But I can't get it on my map—oh. Uh-oh."

"Oh, good, I'm not the only one uh-ohing," Craw says, sounding quite concerned.

"What're the problems everyone possesses? The island was merely blocked from our view by Dagur's Island and the great shadow of the Tersatellan defense, but now that we know where to cast our eyes, it seems not too far away! Have faith!" Voxel cheers. I look up from my button mashing to see what she's talking about, and I go pale.

Ahead is a monstrosity of a place surrounded by a tiny beach before the ground turns green and trees start shrouding the entire thing. It's a bit higher off the track than the other islands we've seen, and with good reason—the rising tide crashes against the shore, increasing gusto with each wave, until it's nearly up to a large mechanical tree that I recognize as another solar panel spot, the dying light still glinting off its black mechanical panes that remind me of the leaves of the real trees on Tide Island. Beyond that is a sharp, gigantic shape of a sort of mountain shooting way up into the sky, twirling and formidable, made of the same dark stone as Dagur's Island and its walls. I'm busy gaping at its sheer size and spikeyness when Voxel continues, "Oh, dear. Is the return of our friend giving us these problems?"

"Great, let's add another bat to the belfry!" I growl to myself as I spot Siridean's superhuman form sprinting toward the island ahead of us. No, he wasn't the problem to begin with. "So everyone else's having some mobile trouble too?" This time I use the beacon.

"Keep going, it could be a trick!" Motor tells us, and I push harder on the pedal, hoping he's right. Eli, who has the blessing of not having a stupid mobile to worry about, tells us that the Lillian Brigade is also complaining about their mobiles, especially Vici, and he wants to know why.

"Wait!" Rex suddenly pitches in, and we all tense. "The screen in my car's got a warning thing on it." He seems to be panicking for real, so I don't bang my head against the steering wheel the way I want to and tell him that's happening to everyone. "But why? What's happening?"

"Mobile Basics 101," I say grimly. "Needle in the red is the universal sign for running out of fuel."

There's a tight pause. "Is that bad?"

"Yes, Rex. That is very, very bad. It means that if we don't do something fast, we're all going to drown."

"This's about sixty seconds left of fuel for a three-minute drive," Motor gets a little more technical. His voice suddenly hitches. "And something tells me we're not gonna get the option of coasting!"

"Why? The tide?" I look all around me as the waves get ever more frequent, some of them breaking against my car. There's nowhere to look now without seeing water poking up through the track, slicing through the blackness before dipping back down only to rise up again.

"I can see it," Voxel breathes shakily.

"WHAT, what's the MATTER?" I yell, ready to explode already with anxiety.

"It seems our mobiles aren't the only things running low on power," she says, and my eyes lock on the world ahead of me. In the distance, the solar panels stopped reflecting the glare of the sun, and I have the nerve to be glad the light can't mess with my vision anymore before realizing how dark the sky is. "You don't believe that the Adamantration would be kind enough to allow these panels to be lunar powered as well, do you?"

Brief stretches of sea become visible as parts of the track flicker and fade from existence. The holes shoot across the track like the whole place is a dish with the liquid getting drained so dry patches show up, but the dish is moving so the dry patches never stay in the same place, and on this huge scale, they're moving with unfathomable speeds. I veer away from one such hole at the last second so that I almost miss Siridean leaping over holes and dodging at breakneck pace, but he's just one man, and when the next hole opens up, he jumps, but not far enough.

I watch him drop silently straight into the void. That's it. Gone. With a roaring crash, the sea swallows him whole, and that is the last that I will ever see of Siridean Stile.

"Yeah, Voxel, no such luck," I mutter and buckle up.

- X -

Nocturnal Predator

"Hey, Eli!" Rex yells over the sudden rumble of the ocean. "I saw something like this in a flick once, the *Metal Insurrection*, where these rebels in some revolution were teaming up with some good came-to-life Mechs against the normal ones—don't think that's what I'm saying, I mean, there's this one part where they make this great big war machine, and they had no way to power it up, so all the Mechs got together and..."

"I've heard of the flick a million times," Eli says, his voice sounding off. "You want me to try their energy transfer thing?"

"Is it tryable?" Rex asks, doubtful.

"I might as well make the attempt. Everyone else, do what you have to do to keep rolling!"

"You got it, boss," I mutter and flip the switch for speed-lock, and the pedal sticks to the floor beneath my feet where I left it, so I have my hands free to search the vehicle for some sort of extra fuel reserve or energy-conserving mode or *something* with only the occasional glance up to keep track of Eli's dash over to Rex's slowing vehicle—he's closer to Rex than the rest of us and farthest from me. My heart leaps into my throat as all the gridlines go out at once with a daunting BWOOoooooo.

Come on. I squint in the darkness for Eli. He reaches out for the mobile, but it apparently can't work from any sort of distance, or what if it doesn't work at all? I stop looking around to watch, muttering "Come on, come on, come on!" around the knuckle I'm biting. With a fresh burst of speed, Eli slaps his hand on the slowing vehicle, which kicks forward with sudden revival. "YEAH!" all of us whoop at once, but I'm the only one to go on, "WHAT'RE YOU DOING?"

"Oh, like you didn't already figure this idiot'd be the first to jump ship!" Rex snarls as his monster truck angles hard to the left away from us. "Don't pretend to get upset, and don't pretend to miss me!"

I'm about to use some special words with the boy, but Eli interrupts, "Deal with it later! Keep going! I'll come to you!" So I swallow my words and whip out my multitool and start ripping off the dash, trying to think of anything that Vici taught me about mobiles that might help. If only I'd've listened! As Eli starts over toward Voxel, who's the next closest to him, Rex sets his angle straight for the island and slams down the speed-lock before leaping out the side of his vehicle, falling three or four meters through the air before hitting the ground running, about as unbalanced as a mountain, toward the Lillian Brigade. I waste a second glaring at him as he goes.

And thus, the first betrayal is complete.

Tom's out and pushing his car, which has almost zero fuel left in it, when there's a clatter behind him as the twin car screeches a sudden right with whatever speed it has left, and Tim shoots out the side, landing on the track with his hands and doing a flawless roll before pushing off with his feet into a sprint with one fluid motion. The car flips into the air from the force of the turn and drops into a chasm behind him when the track opens up to show the sea not a meter below. Tim slams his shoulder into the back of Tom's car next to his brother, giving it some momentum. "Go help Spike!" he grunts. "I haven't the knack for it." Despite the panic all over Tom's face, the twins manage to lock eyes, and the elder reaches out and squeezes the younger's shoulder. "We'll be fine! I promise, we'll meet again on the shore!"

Pursing his lips, Tom nods and turns, running over to Spike's tank. The man's hardly keeping the thing moving when the boy leaps onto it, hands flying around the controls, pulling all sorts of things out of his pockets with precious drops of energy to donate to the vehicle before jumping behind it and helping Spike push, and between the two of them, the modifications, and the fuel, they get the thing hauling.

Lily obeys every word as Vici spews information from experience, diving into reserves of the car, which hisses in protest. Their well of knowledge is almost exhausted when they suddenly start rushing forward again. The two look at each other in shock before turning to see behind them, where a familiar albino gives them a hard smile. "KEEP TRYIN' TO KEEP IT GOIN'!" he yells over the wind and the water, and the girls face forward again, improvising. They're sharing everything they can think of with Ivy, who is silently working to keep Tom's car moving, but somehow it ran out of fuel faster than the others or something, or maybe it had something to do with the fact it was the first car to get Sir Adaman Wheel's gift removed. Whatever the reason, the whole thing shuts off, so there's no help whatsoever to keep the wheels moving, and Tim is regretting only having a couple crackers lately and not much breakfast, but for the sake of Ivy and Tom, he keeps pushing.

It's not exactly milk and honey over here, either. In order to have the slightest chance of reaching the island, we have to keep going at full speed, which doesn't make Eli's job any easier. After boosting Voxel's mobile, he goes over to help Motor, who's fallen behind the rest of us, and offers to carry him or something, but Motor shakes his head vigorously. "I'd slow you down! Go help

Craw and Rat!" he shouts and watches as Eli jets off for Craw, who's closer. The kid drives with one arm, the wounded one pressed close to his chest. Breathing hard and shaking, he bows his head so it rests on the cool glass of the screen on his bike.

If I had been watching him closely before, I would see him find room in his young heart to blow a kiss good-bye to Siridean, the man who wanted him dead more than anyone else. If I could watch him closely now, I'd see that under his forehead, the screen starts flashing.

Craw whips his bike to the left then right as the holes in the track flash in front of him. At one point, one flies in front of him so fast half of each wheel rides over the hole, tipping the whole thing to the side so he has to wrench it to the other side so the track coming back doesn't slash his tires. "Flawless timing," he says as Eli comes over, his voice not panicked but amplified.

"Thanks," Eli finds the need to reply breathlessly, his contact giving the mobile a burst of strength. Craw whips his head back to watch as the donor stumbles as a result, his speed halving for a second, but Craw has to look forward again when the gaps in the track get wider and more frequent.

"Get in when you get here, okay?" I call into the beacon, looking back worriedly, but Eli starts picking up speed again, and he still responds, so I know he's okay, and I turn back to my task of putting the last drops of energy from my blowtorch into the emergency fuel pipe (I can find anything these days), trying to steal more seconds before the mobile'll shut off. The screen's off to save energy, and I'm manually keeping the pedal tied down with my jacket, doing everything I can. My hands relax on the wheel as the truck jerks forward, and I check my back mirror to see if Eli's coming to get in.

My gaze freezes on the mirror, and I don't even look away when Eli flings open the passenger door and slips inside, gasping for air.

He presses his head to the back of the seat for a few seconds with his eyes closed, trying to calm down, but when he opens his eyes again, it doesn't take more than another batch of seconds to figure out something's wrong. "What?" is all he manages, and I point to the mirror.

Behind us, the headlight of a motorbike is flashing rapidly.

"Motor!" Voxel cries, the first of us to voice the problem.

"Don't any of you guys stop for me! It's not that bad, I'm keeping it down, so it's mostly the lights and unimportant stuff, anyway. I'll be fine!" Motor insists.

Even I have to shake my head. "If it were me in your whole situation," Craw says, "every mobile within ten kilometers would be dead. You've got more guts than Spike, dude."

"Thanks. Let's see how far that gets me."

When I can tear my eyes away from the mirror, the sight makes me gasp. "We're almost there, guys, c'mon!" I cheer, willing the truck to go faster, then frantically swerve around a gap that gives me a glance of the waves, their white tips getting highlighted by the light of the moon and the fading glow of day.

Long minutes of dodging stretch past, but we make it.

Voxel hits the thin stretch of sand first, leaping off to kiss the ground. Craw gets there next and manages to work his way out of his motorbike right as I rip myself out of the car nearly on top of the other two. Laughing or crying or a mix of the two, the three of us huddle close in an embrace before turning to watch the flickering light in the distance. After a random glance to the left, I run back over by the truck and put myself under Eli's arm, supporting him the way he did for me hours ago on another beach, and help him back to where the other two are standing. We survivors feel privileged to breathe, to feel the waves touching our toes, to watch the track, which looks malevolent and alive now that we're standing still.

Motor tears across its inky expanse, dodging the gaps that the thing throws at him, his expression set and severe behind his goggles. "He's going to make it!" Voxel jumps up and down, pumping her fists into the air, and I laugh with relief.

Then, out of nowhere, *something* rises up out of the sea behind him.

"By God," Craw gasps, and I couldn't put it better myself.

Even from here, I can get a good look at the thing. It's an easy two, maybe three meters tall, humanoid in a nightmarish sort of way, thin enough around the middle to wrap both your hands around. Its legs and chest are in the shape of a wishbone, the legs thinning out to the end to stop in points without any feet, more like tentacles, and they're black, fading to an ugly shade of blue around the middle of its body. Its torso fills out a bit, and its arms shoot right out of its shoulders without going down like normal arms but bending so it must be boneless as gelatin. At the end of its arms are what I assume are fingers, even though each one is as long as my forearm, and they end in an even sharper point than its antifeet. But its most concerning feature is its head.

Connected to its body by a thin neck, the thing's head is twice the size of mine with most of its face taken up by an open mouth big enough to fit a watermelon in. Inside that mouth, there are eight teeth, four in the front row, four a bit farther back, so each tooth in each row is ninety degrees away from each other. Sitting above its mouth are three beady, burning ruby eyes without pupils or anything, just three soulless dots in an arc. Out the back of its head shoots a thick, tail-like thing that's almost as long as it is tall, fading back to black, rounding off before coming to an end. Altogether, that head reminds me of a bigger, exaggerated look at a—

A leech.

"Oooooh, no," I say as dozens, *hundreds* of them start rising out of the abyss. The backs of their heads twitch in the air, enforcing the resemblance of a tail, and I notice some of them have their rows of teeth turning absently, each row going in an opposite direction like some sort of chainsaw. Motor doesn't notice them, especially not the one that came up behind him. But it notices the kid with sudden attention that's almost tangible, and it shoots forward, skating on what's left of the grid. Then the most disturbing thing I've ever seen happens—the thing's head-tail turns itself inside out, which means that it shoots out of the thing's *mouth* instead, this side shiny and blacker than black, and I realize with horror that that's its tongue. It lashes forward and wraps itself around the back of Motor's bike.

Voxel screams as the kid flies forward off the thing, landing on his shoulder and rolling a few meters before skidding to a stop. He curls himself in a ball of pain for a second before pushing himself to his feet with a great deal of effort, putting his goggles back in place as he starts running over to the island.

The leech flings the bike into the sea with a crash before returning its gaze to its intended target.

"We've got to do something!" Voxel cries. Me, I was getting ready to run from these things, but unfortunately, she's right, and something inspires me.

"I'll get him," Eli volunteers and starts forward, but I stop him.

"Wait! We don't have time. The track's disappearing by the second, so there's no way you'd be able to get him over here before it's gone for good." By now, the track's becoming an endangered species, showing up in random patches, and the leeches avoid those patches now and stick to balancing on the surface of the sea. "I'll get him—could you keep the track live?" I ask, pointing to the solar panels.

There's a wince that tells me it won't be fun for him. "I can try," he says anyway, and as he goes over, I turn to the other two.

"Voxel, can you look at the track and figure out where the gaps're going to be?" She shrugs and nods at the same time. "And Craw, can you tell me where the gaps'll be?"

"Sure, but Rat?" He grabs my wrist before I can go, looking into me. "Be careful, okay?"

"Always," I promise with a wink before turning and hitting the track, pumping my legs for all they're worth.

"RIGHT!" Craw already yells from the shore and some dumb part of me wonders what he's agreeing to while the smart part moves me so I dodge as a gap comes at me from the right. Some of the gaps are closing back up.

All around, leeches float up from the heaving tide, dripping water as they look around as if from hibernation. And everything that comes out of hibernation comes out hungry. Their tongues start out real flat when they come up then flick around in the air, tasting it, seeking victims, and one of them comes up with a prize. Suddenly, all the leeches close by surge over, all their tongues launching forward, ripping the figure to pieces in no time. The tongues retract, the pieces stuck to the sticky insides, so there's a bulge in the sacks, but the bulges start diminishing as acidic liquid starts leaking out of their mouths. They snap them shut, so their faces only consist of three eyes as the rows of teeth kick up to thousands of rotations per second, and the tongues pressure the morsels close to the blades so that everything that isn't dissolved gets shredded to scraps instantly. While the teeth slow down, the tongues disappear farther, dipping down into each body, so they look closer to human for a second before the tongues fly back out of their heads, and their mouths open up again, and they turn in search of another meal.

On the shore, the other team crashes into the sand. A horde of leeches turns their attention to the group as they detach themselves from the mobiles, and Lily screams bloody murder at the sight of them. "Go, go!" Rex commands with whatever breath he can spare, and Vici grabs him and helps him toward the building that sits behind the line of trees beyond the beach. Ivy gets a similar warning from her beau when she tries to go over to him and turns and runs after the other three. Spike (who pretty much ended up running instead of doing much pushing) abandons Tom and the tank, not noticing as it starts to roll back on the slight incline of the beach. Tim staggers away from the car he was shoving. He should only be described as dead, but he weakly kicks sand under the wheels of the tank, trying to stop it from coming toward his brother, before he collapses into a defeated heap on the ground.

A sudden close-up view of one of the leeches is enough to inspire a scream from inside the building. "Telling her I's okay!" Tom gasps, throwing something shiny for the leech to chase with one hand and shoving Tim away with the other. The elder takes a breath and half scrambles, half crawls toward the building, which is made out of stone and wood, like a much larger and much more professional version of Hilda's hut—the buildings are also similar in the fact that, oddly, neither of them have any windows, except this ones got thick panes of glass on the doors too thin to fit a fist through.

None of them seem to notice the three figures standing together farther down shore. Voxel squints at the track, veins standing out on her head. "Left," she chokes.

"LEFT!" Craw bellows, his voice echoing long and far, and I've never been more grateful for those boisterous lungs of his as I dodge to the right, a gap scraping past me.

All around me, the sea roars, reaching up for me, and I try to jump over the waves, which works for the first couple of times, but I wasn't built for this. As my strength fades, they start hitting me, so I get knocked on my hands and knees for a second before scrabbling back to my feet, gasping for breath. For the first time, I'm bitterly wishing I could be one of the normal stars out there, be somebody, somebody that maybe they don't have friends or a gang or the Plexus, but they've got a talent other than the stupid ability to be background noise, a talent that could maybe include being fast or being durable. But I'm neither. I'll never be anything more than I am, and it makes me feel so weak, so stupid, that the next time a wave trips me up, I almost let it wash me off the track and into the ocean, but at the last second, I hear a voice in the back of my head, and it makes me grit my teeth and hoist myself back onto my stupid feet, and you'd better believe I keep on running and running and running, ignoring the pain in my legs and chest and everywhere, blood running hot in my veins.

The voice told me, *Go ahead and give up, hero, see what I care! See what anyone cares! You're a MISTAKE, and they left you for a reason. They didn't miss you then, and nobody'll miss you now. Why don't you eat another battery, Erratica?*

WHY DON'T YOU EAT ANOTHER BATTERY?!

"You don't think we let go of one more bandmate than we had to, do you?" Voxel asks nervously.

"They're both gonna make it back," Craw snaps, almost forgetting to lower his volume back down. When quiet, his voice is shaky and fragile.

"Not them. What of Rex? You don't think he was merely testing us, do you? Or maybe threatening to leave without possessing the intention-card of doing so, as in how some people beg for attention?"

Craw watches my retreating form. "No, I think there was something else he wanted," he says. "Maybe . . . maybe someone."

Voxel glances behind her at the building. "Perhaps you're right. Why—right, right!"

"RIGHT!"

She winces, putting a hand to her ear. "Why do you presume the monsters are avoiding our existences?"

"I dunno," Craw replies, watching the swarms. As there's a lull where the coast is clear for me, the leeches redirect their attention and slowly start to edge closer, closer, too close for comfort. A desperate thought occurs to Voxel.

"Um, would you please encourage our friend for us?" she asks, and Craw sighs, drawing in a big breath.

"C'MON, RAT, YOU'RE ALMOST THERE!" he belts out, and the too-close leeches all back up.

"It's your voice!" Voxel grabs the boy's shoulders and thrusts him in front like a human shield, peering over his shoulder with wide and fearful eyes. "Keep yelling! Do it if you wish to live for more seconds!" she demands when he starts protesting, and with a wince, he goes on emptying his lungs.

I don't even bother trying to make sense of the sudden vocalization except to wonder why Craw wasn't choir (not that I could be woodwind, anyway). Another wave knocks me over, and I go spread-eagled onto the track, coughing and sputtering and cursing, but I force myself up right away, now more at a pathetic struggle than a run, but I know I'm seconds away from Mo, and I try to make myself go faster, both in spite of and because of the big ugly leech coming up behind him. It jerks forward, flinging out its tongue and wrapping it around

Motor's middle. "RAT!" he screams as he gets stopped, and I just manage to grab on to one of his legs before the thing can pull him into its mouth, into the teeth.

"MINE! Give him BACK!" I yell, totally psycho by now, and lash out with my free hand at the tongue. To my shock, my hand goes right through the tongue. It has the same consistency as gelatin. My hand's covered in sticky black liquid that tickles when I pull it away, and my whole body shudders as I try not to throw up. The leech stares at me blankly, and I get the impression it's stunned, wondering what on earth I think I'm doing, the same way a discipline op looked at me when I started improvising fake martial arts to get myself out of trouble once.

Needless to say, it didn't work out well.

Furious, I keep punching at the tongue until I crack wise and go farther down, figuring there must be some reason the tip's able to hold on to Motor. Closer to the end, the thing gets solider like I thought it would, and the leech shivers. "Get it, get it!" Motor urges, and I whip out my multi and go to stab the thing's tongue right near the end when the leech suddenly relaxes its grip on the boy so he drops to the ground with a cry of surprise. Its attention is bent on me, its eyes twitching and shimmering, and my heart slams against my chest as it moves forward, a hiss that I really don't like coming out of it.

"Heheh, yeah, no," I say and yank Motor off the ground, throwing him onto my back before turning around and blazing back the way I came, jumping off to the right after a warning from Craw.

"Leave me alone, you stalker!" Motor shouts at the leech as it follows us, flicking its tongue in the air. "Find someone else to eat!" It dips to the side as a wave brings me to my knees, but I don't fall over for Motor's sake. He's light and if anyone knows how best to perch on someone or something, it'd be Motor, but still, I'm tired enough of running without anyone on my shoulders, so I'm exhausted in no time even with panic giving me rocket fuel. And the stupid leech won't stop following me!

In a quiet corner of the shore, another leech watches, almost curious or something. Then the tank nearby overcomes the sand guard and jerks back so the leech hisses and speeds away. The boy fighting off another leech from the ground doesn't notice.

A couple hundred meters down, Craw's yelling comes to an abrupt stop as he gasps for breath. "I can't be doing this," he chokes. "If I run outta steam before they get back, *then* what?"

Voxel shakes Craw's shoulders. "You won't run out of steam, for it is our Threads at risk here! Let that inspire you, please!" She stops, a nervous look on her face. "Speaking of running out of steam…" She looks over to where Eli's barely holding on to the solar panel tree, shivering. "Are you alright?" she calls over.

He doesn't respond.

I hate myself and everything about me because my legs barely manage a walk anymore. Breath scrapes in and out of my lungs so hard it hurts. "What do you WANT?" I scream at the leech. Mocking it and yelling at gives me some small measure of comfort even though it doesn't do a thing—I wouldn't be surprised if it couldn't even hear me. Motor cries out and ducks against me as the thing's tongue lashes out again, but this time, it goes for my hand, which I pull away at the last second. "Oh, you want my multitool, don't you? Well..." I unscrew the blowtorch part, which is useless now, but my hands're shaking, and it's too hard trying to keep Motor in place and do this at the same time, so I end up tearing it off and chucking it as hard as I can. "FETCH!"

It turns its head in the arching path of the piece before diving after it.

I plod on with the grim satisfaction of tricking it, trying to summon some reason to go faster. It's all I can think about, focusing on each step, each breath, so I don't notice the desperate voice in the distance as it cracks out, "RIGHT IN FRONT OF YOU!"

And then my foot finds air.

Shock shoots through my body as gravity takes me and the water starts coming at me, its rush filling my ears, filling my head with panic because I hate falling, oh man, I hate falling, so without thinking, I reach out for anything to hold on to, anything at all. Time seems to stop for an instant as some bleary memory flies through my mind. I'm running... The ground is disappearing... We fall...

Only this isn't a dream, and I have no choice but to see how it ends.

Voxel covers her mouth with her hand. "RAT!" Craw shrieks as I disappear from sight.

The thin piece of track my hands find purchase on cuts into my palms, and I bite down a scream. Motor almost fell off and now hugs my waist tightly as we hang. Water's coming all the way up to my knees, and we're in the trough of a wave. When the crest comes at us, the edge of the track moves anyway, and the sea takes me, but not before I grab Motor and, with a burst of strength (read: not wanting to die), fling him up onto the track and try to follow.

No such luck.

The wave pulls me under into the silence of the ocean, filling my nose and eyes with stinging. I have almost no energy left in my limbs left to fight. Because of my running, my oxygen runs out in about two seconds and my brain *really* goes into crazy mode and my eyes open up so they sting even more and it's dark out so I can't see much but I can somehow make out the hundreds of shapes down here with me and I know I'm history. Whether they're only animals that live in water or leeches, it doesn't matter. They probably want to eat me alive. *Eat!* Shaking my head, I paddle for the surface for air. *Why don't you... learn how to swim, idiot?*

Motor's close enough to the shore that, if Craw yells loud enough, the leeches will leave him alone, and the kid looks between the beach and the place he last saw me, looking torn, and nearly unable to stand from the pain of the salt in his wounds. It's too much stress to bear, and the barrier starts thinning even more underneath him, so he's forced to move, but he adds his voice to Craw's to try and guide me to the surface.

Under their voices, nobody hears the alarmed cry of pain as the tank keeps rolling back. The leech goes away, but now the leech is not the problem.

The voices do help me figure out which way I'm supposed to go for air, and when I hit the surface, I take in huge gasps, trying to keep myself afloat as I look around for some way up onto the track, trying to make myself cry to get the seawater out. But it's too much and I'm not enough.

Why… don't you eat… another… battery?

Gritting my teeth, I reach my hand into my pocket, not caring that I go under the surface of the water again. There's a second of worry where I can't find my "snack," and I think it must've fallen out at some point, but no, it's still there, a reserve of my own. Triple-A. It would've been good for powering the truck another centimeter, because mobiles are stupid and don't know how to use batteries very well. As for me, I'm smarter, and, with a quick prayer that's all I got left, I stick the thing in my mouth and wait.

It takes about two seconds for the sizzling to start, burning my tongue and the roof of my mouth as the casing gets eaten away in places, and acid spills into my mouth. The thing is, the taste isn't totally unpleasant to me, and besides, it disappears fast, along with the rest of the casing. In ten seconds, there's nothing left of it. Nothing but the taste of battery acid.

Do. Not. Ask.

Motor cheers as I surface again, and I flail, trying to stay afloat and searching for a good wave. When I find the kind I'm looking for, I scramble over, get caught up in its thrall, and let it spit me out at the edge of the track, which shifts so my great calculation gets thrown off, and the edge cuts into my stomach. "*Oof*," I wheeze and struggle onto the track with Motor's help.

"Rat, you're okay!" he cries, and once I'm onto the track, I don't care it's unstable. I pull him into me so hard you'd think I'd never dream of letting him go. For a few glorious, painful seconds, we are the only people on the planet, sitting here together, shaking against each other, breathing hard. Then I hold him at an arm's length away.

"If s-something goes wrong, I w-want you to know I'm sorry I didn't of-fer you a ride or an-nything after your arm g-got hurt," I chatter, my breath showing up in the cold as the sky turns darker and the night gets colder.

"N-no, it let me feel n-normal," he stammers back, and I don't think it's entirely to do with the cold he's not talking right. "Besides, n-nothing's g-gonna go wr-wr-wrong, okay? C'mon." He tries getting to his feet but can't quite manage, so I get up first and hoist him up onto my back with my new sliver of strength I got from ten seconds of not sprinting.

"Hold on tight," I tell him, and he adjusts his goggles, and we get going again.

Over on the shore, Eli mutters, "I'm going to die."

"And I'm gonna overheat and break myself," Craw says, his voice so scratchy it's almost unintelligible. The two boys look at each other with odd looks since the phrases seem oddly backward. Voxel looks between them, then at the track, then at the group of curious leeches, and whimpers.

"Okay, okay, allow me to attempt something," she says and pulls something out of her pocket and touches it to the track. The expanse of darkness stirs. "Yes, okay, I'm certain. Friends? I'm going to try and alter where the track is and is not. Eli, this concentration should mean you won't need to give it so much, because it'll be covering less area, and Craw, you can stop giving them directions and focus on keeping those monsters away. Possess it?" Even though nobody replies, she takes a deep breath, and her eyes go distant as the patches of track all fly in front of me and Motor, making a vague but unbroken path from here to the shore with ocean on every other side.

Still, leeches gather off to their right, a safe distance away from Craw's random screaming, their hissing growing to a fever pitch. They're so thick nobody on the shore can see the person or the tank they're pressing in on, but some of them lose interest and glance at my band.

"Well, get BACK already!" Craw yells, ticked that his one use is getting thwarted, and he gets up off the ground, swelling up his chest as he becomes the sole object of the leeches' attention. "Yeah, I'm talking to you! Why don't you beat it already? What do I gotta do, sing it for you? Scram! Get lost!"

But they press forward even more, their tongues flicking at the air as a salty sea wind picks at everyone's hair and clothes and bandages. They perk up, going still at the smell of blood, and the one in front starts spinning its teeth.

"Not good," Craw mutters, yelping as the first tongue launches itself at him. "Uh, GUYS! I'D LIKE IT IF YOU HUSTLED!" he screams as a bunch of the black tongues lash at him, and he answers with slashes of his bowie knife, which one of them takes the liberty of running away with. "Sticks! OKAY, GUYS, GET TO THE PANIC STATIONS!"

"Almost there, almost there!" I'm saying as we come up on the island, down the aisle of darkness that gets thinner every second I'm on it. "Hold on, please hold on!" It feels delirious—my whole body's frigid and aching, but it's moving anyway. My breath streams out in front of me, fogging my vision of the three on the shore. Craw's grabbed a big branch from the forest and is whacking at the leeches with it, screaming the last of his lungs out, his breath so thick in the air it looks like smoke, and Voxel's fingers are flying on the device she's got, and Eli is not moving at all.

As we get close, all the leeches suddenly turn their attention to me and Motor in one big turning of heads, and terror makes me stumble as they all lurch forward at me. Between the fear and another wave, I drop again so that one of the lunging leeches shoots right past me. My impact makes the track go wobbly, and for once, it seems like an actual thin surface, a sheet for instance, sagging and rippling under me. It makes its own waves, one of which touches one of the remaining leeches. It lets out an ear-splitting sound, and all the others back away, which is enough for me.

"Cry some more, thespians!" I shout at them and leap off the track right as the last of it disappears, and my feet hit the wonderful surf and sand.

Woo! Timing!

Craw's finishing off his third splintered branch when his lungs give out. Motor drops off me, and the two of us catch him as he crumples. "Voxel, get Eli!" I shout across the beach, doing my best to bat away all the tongues. Then one gets a grip around Motor's arm, and I figure out fast that these things are hungry, and some girl isn't going to stop them. What the situation calls for is a something similar to one of our versions of Cops and Robbers called Sacrifice.

I'm pretty sure you can gather from the name where I'm going with this.

"Get everyone inside," I say before I let go of Craw, step back, and pull my multitool back out.

Every blue head turns in my direction again. My heart stops at that sight. Good, I'm already dead. I take a deep breath.

"HEY, UGLIES! IF YOU WANT IT, COME AND GET IT!"

And with one last glance at everyone on the beach, I run into the woods.

The leeches ignore everyone else and follow me the way I hoped and dreaded they would. With me, their curiosity is more intense, and they follow faster, a pace I can't match, not even on solid ground, not even after my little snack. After only a fistful of seconds, I know I won't be able to outrun them for my life. But I've ran through enough alleys with angry folks from either side of the law on my tail enough times to learn that if you can't outrun em and you can't outgun em, then you gotta outcon em (okay, I know it's not perfect; it's close enough).

A thought comes to me, and I cling to it, clamping the multi in my teeth so I can use both hands to grab on to the low branch of a tree (pine?), somehow figuring a way to climb up onto it with the aid of other branches, then crawl onto another branch, then onto the roof of the building, where I wobble across the surface until their hands, then even their tongues can't reach me. They stare up with such dumb looks I have to laugh, the rush of survival blowing through my mind.

Then, after hissing among themselves, one of them grabs the end of the roof and starts lifting itself up after me.

The laughter stops there, and with nowhere to go on this roof, I worm forward and stab at the hand. This does nothing. As it pulls itself up, its tongue stretches for me, getting closer and closer, so I do something crazy, something I thought I'd never, ever do in my life.

I throw my multitool.

The leeches scatter after it, and I don't have time to mentally massage away the pit that drops into my stomach at the loss of my favorite tool. I work my way down, minimizing the falling until I'm on the ground, where I sit still, exhausted, and focus on breathing in the smell of dying grass and dirt and sap. I've never been so tired in my life, and I'm thirsty enough to drink the ocean, but for now, the leeches are occupied, and they won't bother me, so I lie here and rest, my eyes closing, a warm feeling filling me up. Yes, everyone is safe.

And everyone else is tired as you are, and I'm sure they'd be smart enough to move if they were in this situation. Get up! Thespian! I push myself to my feet with the help of a tree and look around, feeling alone for the first time in a long time. All around me, strange sounds chitter or hoot or, of course, hiss, and the ocean breeze fills up the thick brown leaves of all the trees, making them whisper and sway, and I turn in a circle, listening to it all, watching as my breath unfolds in front of me and stars dot the sky. In the distance, the moon shines through the trees, not full enough to give the light of day but still enough to give everything an eerie sort of glow. It all seems so peaceful I don't notice the leech until it's in spitting distance.

I sense it more than anything with a surge of disgust that makes me turn around to see it breathing down on me. "Get away!" I shriek, but the thing's tongue reaches out and gently wraps around me before I can escape, squeezing me tighter and tighter, so I start screaming and kicking. The leech's teeth start spinning, slow but loud like it's trying to TALK me to death! "NO!"

Go for the eyes, a savage thought says, and I rear back a fist—

Then there's a sharp hiss off to the left.

The leech turns its head toward it as the wind groans, bringing the sound to us. There's a bunch of leeches doing a freaky dance by Spike's tank, and the leech by me doesn't look back once before going over to join in. Thanking anyone who'll listen, even the trees and the rocks and the grass, I scramble back to the front of the building as fast as my legs will carry me.

Inside is one big room lit by a lantern hanging from the ceiling. In the far left corner, the Brigade is gathered together with Rex staring at the ground, looking about ready to pass out. I think Tim *is* passed out if he's not dead. As for my team, who's in the corner to my right, they look even worse—Voxel's pressing her hands to her temples, Craw's struggling for little sips of air that must be agonizing according to the look on his face, and Motor's curled up on the floor with his arm cradled against his chest. Eli sits in the corner, leaning against it, his eyes closed, looking pale as Death.

I sink down among them, trying to think of something fair to say, but I can guess the answer to "Is everyone okay," and I can't think of anything else. Everyone else gives me some gesture of recognition, so I reason it must be fair to ask, "Eli?"

Slowly his eyes flicker open, the guttering light of the lantern igniting that electric green gaze of his. His lips twitch in a sort of smile. "Come on, it'll take more than that to take down the Band of Cutouts," he says back just as quiet, and I return the smile in full, my eyes fogging up, so I have to gather everyone in a group—no, a *band* embrace to keep them from seeing if I start crying.

And for that one precious moment, we all feel safe at last.

⇹

And far away in the heart of Zenith, Absolon Vastate paces the halls of the castle.

The Criminal Resolution Sector Headquarters isn't really a castle, but from the towering stone walls alone, it does put up a good resemblance of one, the sort that brings to mind lots and lots of dungeons. Even in this normal chamber—er, room—the barred and covered video display units, the table, the two chairs and the lights are all aligned together with such purpose and lack of embellishment, they look precise enough to draw blood at the slightest touch.

The Adaman of the place stares at Vastate from the doorway with the intensity of a hawk. "You've been at this for quite some time," she snaps. "Are you finished yet?"

"Not quite, Mizz Adaman Nocturnum, but it shouldn't be long. Thank you once more for the use of your space," Vastate tells her. "Soon its attributes will prove most helpful to me."

"I don't know what for," Gridley grunts and turns to leave. "These rooms're as good as any of yours or the Castaway Point's for meetings, and I don't see why you need a private conversation with the guy, but I'm not about to ask." The door slides shut in her absence.

Vastate lets her leave without responding—he only has attention for his trademark razes that take place at four Adaman residencies across the nation, all of which have 666 mounted above the doorways.

It's standard operation: the rapture operatives beat down the doors; they demand an audience with the targeted person; the person in question fails to show; after sixty seconds, the operatives destroy everything in sight. Vastate watches them all behind his eyes through various programs of the Plexus as they go about their vicious process, ripping papers off the walls and inventions from their webs on the ceilings. He offers fresh orders here and there, but for the most part, the operatives don't need orders. The procedure is simple. Break in. Break it down. Take anyone alive. This, to eliminate the people that wish to corrupt the order of life. This, to uproot the weeds from their roots and give them to the fire.

But there is nobody inside any of the residencies.

Vastate scowls as he watches the operatives attempt to take the Headquarters nearby to no avail. "Of course," he mutters, "it would be the Pylon where you'd hide from my invitation. But is whether or not you are even *there* is the question, my friend. Why don't you quit this game of hide-and-seek already?"

He's about to send for reinforcements when footsteps echo in from the hallway. His brow shoots up into the air, and he redirects his attention to the door just as it slides open.

The figure in the doorway interrupts his attempted greeting with "Evening, Sir Adaman Vastate."

"Evening, Jaden," Vastate returns without skipping a beat as he calls off the rapture operatives. "I must say that I'm surprised you showed." The door slides shut. "I didn't believe you were fool enough to fall for the invitation."

"Don't think I don't know what this is about," Steele says evenly, putting his hands on the back of the nearby chair.

"Ah! Even better." Vastate smirks. "Might I ask why, if you had such foresight, did you *choose* to come anyway?"

Steele watches him in silence for a few seconds.

"We all have our own purposes for doing strange things sometimes, sir."

"That we do, Jaden, that we do." Vastate walks over to the other side of the table. "Will you sit?" he asks, gesturing to the unwelcoming metal chair that Steele seems to prefer to strangle. The gilded eyes dance as he slowly steps around and lowers himself into the chair anyway.

Nodding with satisfaction, Vastate takes up a cup of some near-white substance that might have been coffee at some point and walks to the other side of the table.

"Whatever your purpose may be, I'm glad that you have chosen to hold another 'conversation' with me," he goes on. "I find you rather interesting to talk to, Jaden. About the results of the last extermination . . . about this one," he says, stirring the drink without any outward intention of drinking any, content to stir it. "If anyone was to manage to throw a monkey wrench into my perfect extermination system, it would be you, Jaden. You and I both know you have a knack for ruining perfect systems."

The man at the other end of the table says nothing. Vastate frowns and pauses as if he forgot what he was going to say. Steele watches.

Vastate looks up again and sets down his cup, lacing his fingers together as he takes a seat. "Ah, pardon—I digress. I invited you here this evening to tell you that the entry that we were *conversing* last night seems to have pasted the competitors together into two teams. Also, if the cameras in the Castaway Point are to be trusted, he claims to plan on getting all of them out alive. You're all onto me now." He winks, leaning back in his seat. "But don't fret. They'll be dead or changed by Saturday, I guarantee it. There are ways, and they work well. A grand total of fourteen competitors have ever made it back from Hudson Bay alive—thirteen of them have either died or accepted my offer back into society, and the sole cutout remaining of those fourteen, I have the honor of sitting in the same room with."

The genius gestures to the room as if there was any question to which one he was talking about.

"You see, I've learned through experience that even the most insolent, base, and foul criminals have *some* measure of affection, and without anything to purify that affection, well, it turns into quite a beast, a beast that can be used against even the most heartless of people who have them, correct? And you learned through the same experience that I do not fear unleashing this beast within to destroy any unfiltered man, woman, or child from the inside out, now isn't that right?"

Steele's lengthy fingers curl around arms of the chair under the table as Vastate leans forward again.

"Tell me, Jaden. Do you miss them, the ones that had to die for the greater good? Does your kind have that kind of capacity? Or is this 'walking away' and 'moving on' everyone talks about regarding to loss easier than you'd like to believe? Do you really let the dead bury the dead without looking back in sorrow on the Hudson Bay and everything that's happened before and since?"

"What's it matter?" Steele demands tightly instead of answering. His hair's risen on end so it stabs into the back of his chair, and his arctic-blue eyes never waver. It is the patient look of someone who is waiting for the chance to do something dangerous, something that the gilded man has come to expect from time to time. It's the quiet ones you have to watch for.

"Oh, it's nothing you have a right to know about. Again, I digress, and I think I'll stay on this path of digression for my own intentions and purposes. This is where we get to the real reason I summoned you here today. Right. The course of the extermination is set, and its outcome is old news, but you know I'm fascinated by what must go on in that sick, twisted head of yours." Vastate eyes the head in question like he could crack it open and spill its contents onto the table at any given moment. It's a look that Steele's come to anticipate, but he doesn't mind. So long as Vastate keeps on digressing as planned, there's no way for him to find reason to go back on his promise and tamper with the bay. After that afternoon, when Public Prosperity commanded a missile strike on some ships, it was clear that the whole Sector needed distracting or else the cutouts wouldn't survive much longer.

It has also been clear that something has been going awry there—more razings, less tolerance for Dagur's Island, and other places from the bay struggling to take a hint—and that something must be done, or at least investigated. After all, Steele has never been one to leave well enough alone. So when that invitation arrived shortly after the missile command, the path of action that had to be taken was clearer than anything else; after all, it doesn't do to deny one's cue back on stage.

Vastate goes on, and the traps sink deeper, tying both Fates around an anchor. "Lately, this fascination has led me to some questions, namely, why cutouts resist the Plexus that binds the rest of us citizens together, and why they feel the need to break any rule they can get their hands on. And the memory I have most scoured for the answer to this question is the offering of the spoils after the last extermination. Yes, in all the history of the exterminations, there have been fourteen survivors, but only one of them has ever been Champion, managing the impossible feat of surviving the whole week of pain, trickery, and prosecution while also uncovering the secrets necessary for victory.

"Now, the late Mr. Luc Aldrich, who was given the secret to begin with, and Miss Adaman Stephanie Crowne also successfully got to the Extraction Point, but it matters not that they were survivors with you because the former has had his funeral and the latter was but a minor player in the much broader scheme of things. A winner, she was, but no Champion—however, she can still serve as an example that to the winner go the spoils. You remember that I gave her and everyone else the chance to have a most precise and personalized reimplementation of the mainframe at the offering of the spoils. This is what I wished to talk to you about this evening. Miss Crowne eventually took that chance, and both of us know she is currently sitting tall and proud as Adaman of the Health & Medical Sector with a clean record and a clean conscience. Yet curiously, you refused. Now, in order to try to answer my question, I would like remind you that the spoils of victory still do belong to the victor, especially the Champion. Will you finally take them?"

Now the two of them stare at each other.

When Steele does speak, he first sighs, and his voice is flat and insolent, and it says, "You really have lost your mind. And the answer is no."

Vastate leans forward again, lacing his fingers. "*Why*?" he demands. "Do you believe that it takes away some freedom, some necessary right that every human possesses? It does not! It gives them the right that everyone deserves, the right to live well. No, I am not the man you seem to see me as, and my goals for my inventions are not what they seem to be. What appears to be razing and control are only essential protections against the forces of darkness in this world. These goals of mine are so much broader and more blithe and superior than mere short-sighted destruction. And one day soon, they will encompass all people, with no exceptions. *None*."

The two of them stare at each other for a solid minute before the man in white stands up, shaking his head. He's looking in the wrong place for information, but information is not what he wanted. His real plan has worked. One way or another, his prey is caught at last.

But why did you walk right into the trap? How do you intend to stop me from doing anything about the cutouts if you . . . Ah, I must focus and forget the cutouts for a moment. There are bigger questions to answer.

Thus the traps are set.

"Turn out the lights before you go. Oh, wait, you can't." Vastate smirks as he shuts the light off then closes the door behind him, sealing the room in complete darkness. The smile no one has seen on him before stays while he walks back to his own Headquarters, thinking to himself that while his place feels much more homely, Criminal Resolution's Headquarters do have some very helpful attributes.

Not once does Steele move throughout the conversation, nor for a long period of time after it's over.

This is because his wrists and ankles are manacled to the arms and legs of his chair.

But it is not often that Jaden R. Steele plays victim for any purpose besides his own.

<Nightfall One>

IF BEING HUMAN IS A CRIME

- I -

Caught at Last

Safe?

Not by a longshot.

I'm running out of praises to splash over my team when I notice a sound going on outside and turn toward the door with a frown. "Those doors don't open for anything, even if it's a man with a million primes out there," Lily commands, her voice hitching, and she shudders. "We're all staying right here and not touching those doors until those *things* go away."

Leeches pass by the doors with energy, oblivious to us in here, but something out there's making noises. I get up to look outside to see if they've got an animal or something when Tim stirs with a long moan that'd make you ache just hearing it. Lily's about to repeat her instruction for him, but he interrupts, "Where's Tom?"

My blood freezes when I realize the boy in question is absent.

Something slams against the doors, and I turn back to them, creeping over as it slams and slams, then jump back when a voice cries, "HEY, LEMME INTO!"

"Let him in right now!" Tim demands, dumping every drop of his best persuasion into the phrase—it's called malice, and it makes my hands move without even thinking, diving forward for the big plastic-brass handles of the doors.

"DON'T YOU DARE!" Lily counters, pouring forth her own power, so I hesitate. Death by Lily? Death by Tim? Death by leech?

But Tom suddenly appears in the window, blood, sweat and fear all over his face, and his pleading eyes beg at me as the leeches advance fast from either side. Pursing my lips, I fling the doors open.

"NO!" Lily screams, but I don't even hear it over the leeches.

Acting on instinct, I reach forward and grab Tom's arm just as one leech wraps its tongue around him, but it nearly knocks me off my feet, pulling harder than I ever imagined, so I have to brace myself with one foot against the wall to the right of the door.

"Mine!" I yell again at the leeches. With a yelp, Tom kicks forward against the ground with his good leg—his other leg is crushed and mangled. Blood makes his arm slick, and I have to hold on as hard as I can, and he frantically grabs my arm twice as hard, crushing my wrist with his strength. "HELP ME!"

I bark back at the others, who're trying to come forward or press themselves away, screaming or clasping hands over their mouths, only a few of them staying still and staring.

It's Eli who gets here first, locking both hands around Tom's other arm and planting his foot into the wall to the left of the door so the two of us are mirrored. Ivy flits over next, nervous as a horse in a pit of snakes, but makes attempts to pull in Tom, who's still kicking and cursing for all he's worth. As the leech yanks back, its teeth spinning, we almost lose our grip, but Tim finally manages to join the party despite his total exhaustion. He's the first to touch the thing, sinking his fingers into the taut end of its tongue and trying to pull it loose for all he's worth. "Let… him… go!" he snarls, his eyes blazing in such fury and desperation, you'd expect him to catch fire at any second.

Ivy follows Tim's aggressive lead and whips out her gun, firing into the thing's head so it lets out a high cry that makes the windows vibrate, but it otherwise doesn't do anything. The bullet gets swallowed by the thing's gelatinous head, and it keeps trying to rip my arms off. "Everyone, on the count of three!" I order, starting the count with "One," and they all get ready to pull. Ivy and Tim each take an arm as another tongue wraps itself around Tom's legs, much to his dismay.

"THREE!" he screams at us, and the walls crack with the force of our pulling. I squeeze my eyes shut, planting my other foot on the wall and going parallel with the floor, tugging even though I can feel my arms getting pulled out of place. Then Tom's arm slips in my grasp, and he jerks back, dragging us all out the door a little. Suddenly, something attacks my back, and I almost let go in panic as Lily claws at me, hauling me backward, and I don't know whether she's trying to help or trying to get me to let go because focusing on her crazy voice is outta my abilities right now. "AGAIN!"

Motor runs up and grabs Tom's good ankle with both of his hands and digs his shoes into the threshold of the door as we all make another exertion with the sick tug-of-war, but we still don't make any ground. Another tongue wraps itself higher up on Tom's chest, squeezing so hard his eyes cross. More leeches gather around, hissing, and they start flicking their tongues forward, at Ivy with the gun, at Motor, but even with the panic they bring to the table, we still can't get Tom into the lodge. He'll get pulled in half if we keep this up.

He drops his head for a second then looks up again, and he's got that look in his eyes that makes my heart stop. "Guys…"

"Don't go there," Tim growls. "Don't you dare even go there."

"No," Tom wheezes, wincing as we get dragged forward even further. "It won't work—uh, I'm going gets creamed in a sec, or they'll gonna get more and yank us all back and everybody dies, or they'll gonna starts pickin' ya off."

"Don't *do* this!" Tim's voice is starting to crack with ferocity, and I can see tears running down Ivy's face. "I've already lost two! I *can't* let it get to three,

I just can't!" I assume he's talking about their parents, because the same pain flashes across both boy's faces—the names Jim and Jon that Tom let slip a few hours ago never enter my mind.

"Tom, you're gonna make it, bud, just hold on," I say as I burn all my strength to pieces.

"I willn't lets this happening to yas," he gasps as the leech tightens its coiled grip. "Eaten by freaks? Whatta ways to goes." He gives a lopsided smile at this then leans his head forward and kisses Ivy softly on the head before looking at us. "Keepin' on sailin', everyones. See yas all on that home shore, or the castaway point, whatever you's call it," he promises.

Then he lets go.

The fingers around my wrist goes slack, and I try to tighten my grip on his arm, but it catches me by surprise, and the blood makes it slip right out of my grasp. We stumble forward as he flies back into the night toward the ocean, and all I see is a flash of gray before the doors slam shut. "No!" Tim flings Lily back and shoves the doors back open, and the rest of us (who all fell over) get to our feet, shaky and slow, staring out at the sea, reflecting the star-spangled heavens in our views without obstruction. No leeches. No Tom. Nothing.

He's gone.

Trembling uncontrollably, Tim staggers out of the lodge, turning in circles. "TOM! *TOM!*" he demands his brother back from the world, not willing to believe the truth. I step out too, looking around, but there's nobody in sight. Tim's whole frame shudders, and he stops and falls to his knees, one hand planted into the ground, trying to support him, the other hand against his heaving chest the way people do when they've been shot. "No! NO! *NO!*"

It's the most sobering, heartbreaking thing ever, him on the beach all alone. I feel leaden and hollow as I trudge over and collapse to my own knees beside him, cautiously putting my hand on his pale and frozen one as he chokes on sobs. It feels so *off*, so wrong, like the world's been cut in half, or there's only half the oxygen left in the world, only half the air in my lungs, half the blood in my veins. This isn't a peanut butter and jelly, right-and-left-shoe relationship. There's no day without night, no right without left, no up without down, and obviously no Frère Jacques without Macabreak, so how could there possibly be Tim without Tom?

At some point, he glances sideways at me and swallows a deep breath before reaching over, and for a second, I think he's going to kill me, but he just weakly pulls me against his chest. "You were with him to the very end," he tells the top of my head, his broken voice whispering against my hair. "You have my infinite, humble gratitude. But please … please, could I move on with the belief, no matter how thick it seems…"

"That he's still out there waiting?" I whisper, and he nods, pulling me tighter to him, and I feel that he's doing that because if he doesn't have something to hold on to, he's going to fly off the wall deep into the black night and never ever come back. I've been there, so I know. There are some dark, scary places your heart falls where it can't come back from if there's nobody there to show it the way. I just say what I'd want to hear. "Of course it's okay, Tim. You loved him—you're never going to let him go. And besides… nothing really makes sense now. Who knows?"

I leave it at that. It's hope, but not the stupid kind, just the asinine kind. Maybe Death's on holiday. Maybe Tom's gonna come stumbling back any minute with one heck of a fishing story. Maybe he meant something about the castaway point. Who knows?

Tim breathes hard, his breath rattling in and out of his lungs against my head, and I feel only one hot tear fall onto the back of my neck before he sets me down, covering his face with his hands.

Motor, who's held back from us a bit before now, steps forward with his hands on his hips and breathes in deep. "Yep, still out there somewhere," he says with such firmness, just hearing it makes you want to believe it. "Still sailing like the rest of us. And we're gonna find him someday."

We stare at the ocean waves as Ivy drifts up behind us, blowing a kiss to the lost boy. "Bon voyage," she breathes, her gentle voice reminiscent of the ocean breeze as it caresses our faces, salty and sweet.

Eli is the last to come up behind us, and I stand up, and we slowly move to support each other as Ivy sets her hand on Tim's back, the big brother setting his hand on Motor's shoulders. "Aye. Bon voyage," Tim murmurs, his burning eyes watching the sea more intently than us all.

Off in the distance, there's a soft hissing sound, and we get Tim to his feet. He does his best not to drag them as we get him back into the lodge. "Seems you owe me a hundred marks, Rex," Spike says. "He's bawling. Toldja so."

"Spike, this isn't the moment or location," Voxel sighs.

"Nobody asked you. All I'm saying is, when Jerry died, I took my inheritance and ran. Mourned for all of two seconds. This idiot's had the waterworks going for minutes now. Tsk, tsk. Hey, Doc, guess what? This is a *war*. People're gonna *die*. That's the *point*. Get that through your head, or you're gonna end up blooding the gutters too."

"Cease your imprudent chatter, lest it be your blood to quench the soil," Tim snarls, pulling a middle finger on the most powerful man in Hudson Bay. (Both me and Vici forget not to take it as code and glance around the room before remembering that that's not exactly a double meaning for everyone.) The truth is, that one bitter tear's all that fell, but he hasn't wiped away the tracks yet, just lets the blame burn against his face, and that tiny glimmer of evidence is enough for Spike to pick on, or at least try—Tim isn't exactly the kind of guy that anyone can pick on, though. "And as for you?" He turns to Lily, who's shut the doors and is looking for something to reinforce them with, pretending nothing just happened, and he takes another step toward this side of the room. "I've figured out where my loyalties lie."

"Well, that's alright, since it's a trade, isn't it?" She pats Rex on the back. "I thought you were the smart one, Tim, but apparently, the foolishness is genetic. What a pity."

"You may consider yourself a worthy recipient of my contempt," Tim seethes. "I would unite your loose verbal cannon with my heel with all due force to render you mute, but my footwear has done no sin to deserve your spit and bloodstains, and moreover, your orifice has done no boon to deserve my footwear's presence, and lastly, I am too kind to remove whatever fantasy you have left about your wretched countenance by removing the daggers of your maw. Therefore, I anticipate you shutting it ere the severity of your impudence may overcome my pity of it."

The room goes silent except for Craw, who starts clapping. Even Spike grins.

But Lily isn't very moved this time (or she just hides it real well), even though there's a five-second gap before she can think of anything good to return. "This, coming from the boy they had to *carry* inside?" she finally scoffs. "I'm terrified. Especially with your metabolism, I'm sure you have enough energy to come at me, but not much more. While you all lose consciousness trying to regain the energy for a rebuttal, I'm going to go to the back room and try to find some food, since not all of us are mice and morons, and we need more than crackers to survive." She turns to leave with a toss of her hair then whips back around before exiting through the open doorway at the back and continues, "Oh, and Ivy? Get over here right now." The girl winces and obeys without a word.

Eli's already gone back to sitting down, and the rest of us who were crazy enough to stand join him on the floor. Lily's right about one thing—we're all done in and ready to pass out. Nobody feels compelled to say anything, so we all just sit here in mournful, tired silence, nobody willing to address the question.

Voxel is the first to voice it. "Now what?" she asks.

"How about nothing?" I return, trying not to sound aggravated or scared or anything else that I am on the inside. "How's about we sit still for a change?"

"That's good for now, but what about later?" she presses. "Think bigger. We have no fuel for our chariots, no food for our own systems, no idea what those things out there are or anything. What movements should we make if they try to enter our cube of walls? What are we to do when the sea spits up the next pirate?"

"I brook the curs no longer," Tim says darkly, whipping his arms forward so thin, curved blades flick out of his sleeves, braced to him by straps around his wrists and forearms. The precision of the design makes them accessible and hidable without any effort. "Perhaps I shan't kill them, but neither shall I find the need to show them mercy henceforth—this is a war, after all."

"Cielhomme, Tim, did you hide those from the rapture men?" I have to ask, staring at the cunning tools. He gets a glint in his eye.

"These, and much more. Especially…" Sliding the blades back into his sleeves, he pulls off a necklace I didn't notice him wearing with a strange, jagged disc hanging from the end. When the disc touches his fingers, it bends and twists, shifting itself into the shape of a creepy sort of pistol, with the chain of the necklace hanging down from it in what I figure out to be a chain of ammunition. Consider my mind blown. "This is my favorite, though I have others. I'm armed to the teeth." He casually licks his fangs, and I'm scared he's telling the truth.

Whoa. We got the walking armory to join our band. (And from the other side of my mind comes the thought that whoa, I got the handsome guy to hold me, and I almost smack myself.)

Motor snaps his fingers and says, "Gun twirler." We all look at him. "What? It's just a suggestion. If he's going to be a part of the band, he could be the gun twirler—or slinger, if you think that sounds cooler."

After seeing Tim's confusion, we all explain the whole band thing to him. "Ah. In this case, I'll accept my suggested role with honor." And with that, our new member becomes a part of the band.

Nobody even mentions Rex and his leaving. We don't know what to make of it.

There's a huge BOOM behind us, and everyone jumps, turning around to see Spike letting down tables with much less care than necessary to make sure they come down gently. "What? You'd rather sit and eat on the floor?" He lets another one fall—they're the long cafeteria kind with benches attached—and plants one boot on the edge, kicking it over toward us without even noticing the screeching it makes as it slides across the floor, leaving glaring white marks on it. "If we get anything to eat at all."

Oops, my mens rea has hoisted me back on my feet before I even think about it. That's the thing about being a thief for this long. Kleptomania. The drug becomes the answer to everything.

Everybody looks at me. "Um, I'm already famous for sniffing out food anyway, so…" Since I don't know how to finish, I leave it there before stiffly walking over to the back of the room, trying to get Vici's attention before I leave, but she's soothing Ivy, so I can't get her to look at me. The silver-haired girl watches me over Vici's shoulders with her angled purple eyes. Her short hair's lighter than Lily's, I notice, and the cape she wears is flat and unbroken and brushed, brushed, brushed. Plus, her face doesn't have the nitty-gritty that all human beings try to hide all the time—she looks too perfect, a doll with porcelain skin, glass eyes, and moonlight-threaded hair, a doll that's always sat on a dark, dusty shelf without ever being touched.

Seeing Lily in comparison when I find her in the back room under the harsh white bulb is a bit of a shock. How could they be related? Her hair isn't as shiny, and it separates, flows around in uneven waves that hang heavily off her head, but her summer skin seems to glow with life. Without the city amenities, she's already starting to look more rugged than refined. She notices me behind her and turns, straightening up from the stove she was looking in to put one hand on her hip. The creases on her brow and the freckles on her nose seem so prominent compared to her blank sister, and for a second, her face is full of hidden thoughts and pains that duck behind the headstrong facade on top of her music box of memories when she notices me looking at her. "What do you want, Mouse?" she huffs, sounding tired. It's obvious she preferred being alone. Is the loss of Tom affecting her more than she's letting on? Ah, these thespians all have an angle. I wonder for a second if I can guilt her into feeling worse, bully her a bit so she knows her place, but I decide against it.

"What're you doing, Leadhead?" I ask, returning insults as I notice the rest of the room. It's some kind of storage area, stuffed with cupboards and boxes and stuff. They seem water-damaged but fresh, no dust.

"What does it appear to be? I'm searching for sustenance." She turns back around, nearly crawling inside of the stove crammed into the corner. At least I think it's a stove, or it was before it turned into a rusty box.

"Okay, first of all, you don't have to talk all high and mighty all the time," I say, frowning at how fake her voice is. "It doesn't fit you. There's something weird about it, and it makes me think you're covering something up." Something *else*, I mean, but I don't say that.

Lily turns back to me just so I can see her eyes roll. "Aw, what's it to ya, anyway?" she simpers, and it's impossible to miss her tough Western-T accent. Its reveal makes me jump and makes Lily's ardent eyes spark with pleasure. She seems to relax, going from a queen-of-the-world confidence to the characteristic smugness of almost everyone who comes from the left side of the nation, and man, do I kick myself for not seeing this coming! Everyone from those parts comes fully equipped with the notion that they're tough stuff. "I gotta act all Cool-McGhoul around the rest of these junkies cuz they ven up to the cats that word big, see? But I don't need your venning, cuz frankly, I don't give two axels about what you think of me, nah. So I can word jack at you, I can."

My head whirls, trying to make out the dialect, and I only manage to pitch my own voice sideways and go, "Well, love, if we hoi polloi scratch you that far then la, I hope I never earn your axels, and you can stick em where the sun don't shine."

Her face falls in horror. "You're a Joanndude?"

"No, just thought I'd fight fire with fire." I shrug.

She rolls her eyes. "Gritting feeb. You couldn't word yourself out a wet paper bag, nah. Anywho, what's second of all?"

"Second of all is, when you're in some abandoned shack, don't look in an oven for food." I pop open a cupboard, and a whole bunch of stuff that's probably food peeks out. Who'da thunk it. Lily scowls a second, not trusting it, then works her way over—it's set behind a bunch of stuff—and pulls out a crinkly bag.

"Crackers." She laughs. "Alright, it's no Seizure, but it's grub." She clears her throat in a sort of half-apology when I tense about how easily she can throw around the whole Kill Switch thing. Maybe people who aren't thieves don't understand the gravity of that story. Or maybe a few years is long enough, and the Adamantration's done a good enough job at burying it that it's gone from defining history to fading into the background. Either way, Lily respects my reverence and drops the subject. "C'mon, let's grab some and boogie. This place creeps me, it does."

"Yeah, I mean, how's the lightbulb on if there's no power, anyway?"

Lily freezes. "I don't know," she says, donning her other voice again before taking her armful of food into the other room. The strange thing is, I look around, and there's no switch or even a pull-chain in sight. And I know that light wasn't on when we got here, so she must've done something. When I step into the big room again, she throws me one last glance that makes one thing clear: neither of us are as normal as we're pretending to be.

Thespians, I think again, then wince, wondering if I do have some Joanndu left in my bloodstream after all.

"Here we are, guys. She tried looking in the *stove* first," I whisper, rolling my eyes as I set the food down on the table. There's a few packages of dried beef, canned vegetables, all homey stuff, but I make sure the Lillian Brigade doesn't see the box of cookies I found in the back of a different cabinet. Everyone's sitting at our table except for Motor, who's sitting cross-legged *on* it.

"What's wrong with food items residing in their heated habitat of old?" Voxel asks as she reaches for a can. The others look just as confused as to why food wouldn't be in a stove. Oh, man. What're they teaching kids these days?

"Stoves weren't used for keeping things hot forever, you know," I explain as I set a package of water bottles on the table. "They do the same thing in places in Tersatellus that use real food. Some of them got it fresh, not dried or canned and processed or synthetic, so people'd stick stuff in the stove. It'd heat up, and then they'd take it back out so it'd be safe to eat, kill the germs, and make it taste good. If you kept it warm all the time, then everything would look and taste jerkyish." I display a piece of the dried stuff before eating. Voxel nods, not even watching as she opens her canned corn with one hand, her marker multitool flicking back and forth around the top. Tim monopolizes one of the meat packages, and the stuff starts disappearing after he examines the ingredients. Craw picks a box of dried fruits and starts eating them carefully.

Motor rips into package of cookies, kid-on-Nuvitadi-Day style. "Oh, Rat, thankyouthankyouthankyou!" He sets a cookie in front of each of us before cramming one into his mouth. Anyone in his shoes might find room to complain about not having milk, but Mo just washes it down with water without letting it hurt his happiness. The sight of his childish joy over something so trivial as cookies is so beautiful it almost hurts.

To his right, Eli's holding his cookie with uncertainty and gives me a timid look, almost asking me for permission. "Um. I know I said I don't eat…"

"You do now." I give him a nod, wishing everyone wasn't pretending not to stare out of the corner of their eyes with bated breath—everyone but Motor, who's oblivious in his happiness. Eli watches the kid as a sort of example before turning back to his own cookie and taking a bite. His eyebrows jump up as he chews and something sad tells me this must be the first thing he's ever tasted, so the not-eating thing wasn't really a lie. Between the seventeen-year wait and the "modifications" and the apparent fasting until now, none of us were sure this moment would ever come.

The corner of my lips twitch. This is the most monumental cookie-eating that's ever taken place.

"Not bad," Eli says when the last of it's gone. The rest of us can't help glancing at one another with amazed eyes.

"How are you enjoying your ability to savor?" Voxel asks, disowning her can of corn for the cookie in front of her. This is why we got sent to the extermination. We're eating cookies before we finish dinner.

"I…I like it," he admits, sounding as surprised as the rest of us look.

"Wanna try something else?" Motor searches the table for more food to victimize until Tim offers a strip of jerky. I try not to react when I realize he's only working on his second pack (Cielhomme, what it must take to power that factory of a body!). Eli takes the offer with a word of thanks, and we watch as this disappears too. He's already looking better now that he's getting energy back. It's interesting to watch, but the thing is, it's hard to look at him for long enough before I start wondering where the monster I saw before went, thinking of what happened between him and Siridean, remembering the brutal look on his face. What reminds me is the way the others aren't sitting quite as close to him as they are to each other, so I know they haven't forgotten, either.

Whether he senses this or he's got some other reason, Eli turns to Motor, a mix of emotions on his face. "So how's your arm?"

"It's feeling better now that it's stopped bleeding," the kid says through a mouthful of crumbs. "If I leave it alone for a while, it should be fine." At least Tersatellans heal fast, or so I hear. Never had a comparison.

"I'm sorry it happened." Eli sighs, putting his head on one fist with his elbow on the table, which he glares at with that look of his, so I keep expecting the table to burst into flames. "I came here to stop things like this from happening, but they still do. I just keep coming up short and letting you all down. To be honest, it's…The longer I go on, the more powerless I feel."

Tim shakes his head, rising out of his withdrawn observation. "We are all powerless more oft than not. One must learn to resign to the fates that are out of their hands if only to better put forth every amount of their effort to change whatever destiny they can let so much as a finger's hold on. In due course, we all must lose control. Thereinafter, the question is whether we allow it to control us in turn or fight to take it back. This is the art of being human."

There's a moment of silence. Then Eli says quietly, "Thank you," to which Tim nods, staring out the door.

And after that, trouble.

Boots march their way over here, and everyone at the table jumps when Spike's hands hit it, a smirk sitting under his shades. "I smell drama," he rumbles. His eyebrows crunch, and he snatches a cookie out of the package, stuffing the whole thing into his mouth before picking up an empty package of beef. "So you've been through three of these things already? And it's been, what, five minutes since it all got here? This, everyone, is what the boys back home would call depressive overeating."

"It's hardly overeating if it's meant to be a full meal, which we have all been sorely lacking today," Tim replies, still not turning around. "Moreover, you would claim it to be undereating if I consumed any less."

"'Consumed,' he says. You're killing me! Whoops, bet you're still touchy with the K-word."

"And why should your word choice concern me?" Tim questions, turning around now, and I catch a dangerous look on his face. Sweat erupts on the back of my neck as I recall a boatload of rumors about him that start with that look. Time to make myself not a part of this picture.

"I dunno, I just kinda assume the weakness runs in the genes, I guess—I see it as this puzzle thing. You're weak on the inside, the socially awkward, mental-emotional loser without any relationships outside blood, and he *was* weak on the outside, couldn't even move out of the way of a tank rolling a kilo per century, which must be what squashed his leg and is the reason he is now *dead*!" Spike snorts as Tim twitches at the word. "Yeah, that's right, dead. As a doorknob. Deceased. Lifeless. KIA. Blooding the gutters. He bought the farm, bit the dust, kicked the bucket, checked out, went to meet the maker, and he's on a bed of lavenders, pushing up daises, however that works. So. Does my word choice *concern* you yet?"

"On the contrary, it's about to concern you," Tim says with deadly serenity as he gets to his feet.

"What're you gonna do, drown me in an ocean of tears?"

"Actually, it is my best intention to strike you repeatedly in that ugly mug of yours with such force and velocity that your nose spears out through the hind of your vacant skull. Alas, this is not quite humanly possible, so I will have to be grateful that I do not appear physically weak in your eyes, for the terminating sight they shall anon behold shall be my fingers eagerly tearing them out of their sockets. At any rate, I am in the mood for dessert." Anyone with food in their hands puts it down as everyone's appetite flies out the door.

"Sounds great. Sure you wouldn't rather have this, though?" Spike picks up the cookie from the table in front of Tim. "Here we go, reason fifty-two to start bawling in one… Aw, sticks, what comes before three?" Then, with a snicker, he eats the cookie.

That's how the fight starts.

Before he can so much as swallow, the man gets a punch in the jaw like a brick out of a cannon, and he stumbles back to the center of the room, crumbs spilling everywhere. When the glasses fall off his face, his eyes look livid, but he calmly brushes off his mouth, somehow getting it to move despite the damage. "Wull, c'mat me, den." Tim leaps over the table, landing with ease manifesting from every part of his existence except his burning eyes. Oh, Cielhomme, oh, Cielhomme, this is the side of the criminal that people usually don't live through witnessing.

"HEY!" Lily yells from across the room, and I let her be the brave (read: crazy) one while I backpedal. Spike returns fire, launching Tim straight into the wall with a sock to the gut. He gets up without so much as a cough, waiting as the big man stalks over, then uses the wall to shoot straight into Spike, nearly knocking him over, but he's too strong and tall. Spike catches the next fist that comes, then the other fist in a classic display of power, then his brow furrows as the fists disappear—his whole competitor's slipped out of sight, the last place you ever want him to be. Hands come up from behind Spike and lock around his shoulders, hands that throw him into the wall harder than I thought imaginable. My heart shudders in fear, and I try not to shrink away. Rubble rains down from the wall and ceiling, but Spike just stands up, undisturbed.

"Stop, stop it right now!" everyone's yelling, but the two are in a world all their own. Each of them is a half of some other equation, belonging to something that is missing, one with old scars and the other with fresh wounds, and while neither of them are showing it, both of them are hurting nonetheless. And I can guess from experience that they're just trying to bury that hurt with anything else they can get, which usually means hurting someone else.

Tim feigns a punch, swiping his arm past Spike's face so he focuses on dodging as Tim flattens his hand in the air. It angles down at breakneck speed, planting itself into the ground as a base so he can flip up and kick Spike in the face with one foot after the other so hard I feel the impacts in the floor (it makes me wonder how Spike's nose doesn't really shoot through the back of his head). Then he deftly lands and twists into a dodge from Spike's fist. The man only seems to have a knack at punching and isn't fast enough to evade as many hits as Tim. His nimbleness is otherworldly and incredible to watch as he lands hit after hit on his target. But the problem is, Tim starts running out of the steam he hardly got back, and Spike gets smarter and gets in a few of his own powerhouse blows, sending the younger guy flying across the room.

It turns into an unfair torment that hurts to watch, to hear the breath hissing in and out of Tim's lungs, but he keeps getting to his feet and fighting his unhurtable foe. Fury and rampant grief provide him what energy can't, which is dangerous because all it does is keep grinding him into the zeroes, and he doesn't even care. When they break you, you have to break them back, and that's all that matters.

"This isn't fair," Voxel comments grimly. We've stopped trying to stop them by now. "He can't feel pain. His blasted analgia has something to do with the mainframe, I believe."

After getting punted across the room for the ninth time, Tim stays down longer than usual, and Spike stomps over and lifts him up by the throat, his eyes dancing. "What, exactly, was your plan here? What were you *possibly* hoping to accomplish against *me*? I've got two years and ten thousand hours of getting blood, sweat, and tears from people on you, and you've got nothing on me. So." Tim's feet tremble and search for the floor as Spike grins. "Give up yet?"

Then, out of nowhere, Tim's feet find the what they were looking for as Spike hits the floor.

"WHAT!" is all he can choke out in a bellow of rage and pain, yes, pain. Behind his fallen figure, Motor stands with his hands on his hips, feet fixed apart for balance, goggles resting on his forehead, so you can see the rugged fortitude and disappointment on his face without any anger or spite or violence, like Justice incarnate. Spike tries to make some remark, but nothing but air comes out.

Motor has no such problem. "Okay, if you're all so big on getting some rules, I can't make any promises, but I can make some suggestions," he huffs. "First of all, if you're gonna take a cookie, *ask* first. I learned that when I was about three, Spike. What's that make you?" The man just groans, shifting on the floor and doing a real good job at mimicking a dying walrus. "And second of all, I don't care whether or not you play nice, but if you're gonna go looking for trouble, then fight fair, or don't fight at all!"

"Fine, *fine*, now quit already!" After a pause, Spike suddenly relaxes, staying limp and motionless on the floor before drifting over and sitting at his table with surprising speed. With a satisfied nod, Motor turns to Tim and does his best to help him to our table, but despite the pummeling, he forces himself over by himself. Once there, Motor unzips his jacket and pulls out the first aid kit from the ship. I stare at it like it's magic. It didn't come out when he got shot in the arm. It didn't come out after he flew off his motorbike or fell in the ocean. But now, here it is.

Still, something he said bothered me, and I think the others picked up on it too. Nobody says a word in the entire room as Motor pulls out the cotton swabs and the medicine, and Craw refuses to look at me or Mo, so I know he's thinking what I'm thinking. At first, I was just reminded that one of us is lying about having the clue, and really, nobody's excused from suspicion (not even me). But now the ugly realization dawns on me that if Craw fell asleep—and left to help Vici and Voxel too—then there was a time when nobody was watching Motor.

As that awful thought develops, the kid lets Tim take care of himself (he refuses to have it any other way) and hops off the table where he was perched. The lantern still sways as Motor walks under its glow and picks up Spike's sunglasses. After pushing a lens back into place, he walks over and hands them to Spike, who could be about ready to punch Mo across the room or scramble into the supply place away from him—his face is impossible to read. But miraculously, he just reaches out and plucks the shades from Motor's hand, setting them on his nose with an even more miraculous "Thanks. And, uh… good show, shortstop." He gets that crude smile I used to give Vici that says, "Eh, yeah, I'm sweet as a sack of knuckles and you'd better believe it, but you and I, we're square." Motor returns fire with a cheery little smile and walks back with a bounce in his step.

"Well," he says when he gets here, "I dunno about you guys, but I'm tired. I'm gonna try and get some sleep while we wait for Tom to come back or something else to happen, okay?" Still nobody says anything, so he hops back up onto the table and curls up without any regard to the fact people don't belong on tables.

The sounds of the night dominate the quiet after that. Wind calls, hollow and lonesome, and the hissing of leeches floats in sometimes. Tim puts his broken face in his hands, and we all try not to watch, try not to think, try not to feel anything at all, as if that'll do anything to change the reality, change us back into the people we were before, but it's hopeless. It's a different hopeless than when Baldur died or when someone we knew but didn't really know was blooding the gutters back in Tersatellus. This is an aching hopeless that's too real, too close, because this time, it was one of us, and it's already turning us into monsters, tearing us apart. This means the Adamantration was right about our love and freedom, that it really is a trap, and we're finally getting caught. This means we're not uncatchable, not indestructible. This means war. And now, we're starting to lose.

It's as if now that someone's died, we've got to feed off the adrenaline not to hurt, got to do all sorts of reckless stuff to keep ourselves going. Vici is the next to cross the room with a strange look in her eye, and I watch her with a brow up, but it's not me she comes for. Motor pops open one eye when she taps him on the side. "Yes, Vici?" he asks, already awake (minus a stifled yawn).

"So you can do that thing on demand? You know … that haywiring thing?"

Motor sits up, first frowning, then brightening. "Oh! Yeah, I guess. Um, why?" Now he's nervous.

"And you can target people without affecting anyone else?"

"I think so, if I try hard enough. If I'm nervous. But why?"

Vici takes a deep breath and holds out her hand. "Then haywire me."

Me and Motor both jump. "What?" he cries. "No, I won't do that to you!"

"Look, I have this theory." Uh-oh, that's one of her I'm-about-to-get-sciency things. "When I walked into your circle, I already knew what was about to happen, and it would occur regardless of you," she tells him uncomfortably, dropping her voice to a whisper.

"Then why didn't you tell me?" I jump in, trying not to sound hurt. She'd always tell me if she knew she was about to have a, a y'know.

Vici glances behind her with a guilty expression. "Well, I thought it wouldn't look so bad if it happened to me the same way everyone else did." My eyebrows shoot up, but Motor doesn't react to learning he's been offhandedly framed, or he doesn't get it. "So it's not going to hurt me. Let me have it, Mo." He hesitates, looking to me (smart kid), and I shake my head with gusto. "I promise, I'll be *fine.* There's still something I need to know, and it won't hurt me, okay?"

My chest goes tight when I realize I have to let her do what she wants or she'll hate me even more, so I nod to Motor. After another hesitation, he chooses to believe me, and an expression of focus that's an endangered species on most people twice his age takes over his face. I feel a change in air pressure, and Vici's eyes go wide.

"I knew it," she breathes then turns to me with her I-need-to-share-this smile. "Rat, I can't access the … you know … no maps or calculator or anything! There's no connection out here, but that's just it, at least the calculator doesn't require any sort of network, I just had it up. Do you know what that means?" She turns back to Motor. "According to this and Spike's reaction, you must stop whatever Plexus function the mainframes still have left for us! You must break the electric currents or something!"

"No, cuz then I'd make stuff shut off, not mess up," Motor points out, embarrassed. Vici thinks about it without really paying him attention.

"Maybe … maybe it's different when you're nervous," she says slowly. "When you're hyper-upset, you make the currents go berserk, but when you focus, they stop. But maybe it's only for machinery or electronics, obviously not nerve signals, otherwise we'd all probably have the same reaction, or else go far more ballistic. That's why Rat wasn't affected—her extraction must've been flawless." Oh, boy. As if I'm not hanging on to every word of this analysis. "Do you know if you have electric reactions with any other conditions, if you're extremely content or joyful, for example?"

"Um . . . I don't know for sure," Motor admits. "Except for one time I heard Santiago tell his friend that he feels high when he's around me and I'm real happy. That means 'uplifted' or something, right?" He smiles about knowing the big word.

"Of course it does," I lie. "Who's Santiago?"

"If it's anyone with a mainframe, then this is wonderful," Vici spills, on a roll now. "It's a distinct possibility that your mainframe's limbic functioning was damaged somehow since it filters sensations by regulating the electric pulses in the synapses in the brain, and it also interprets these pulses as signals to control connections between other mainframes and otherwise act in response to the owner's state of mind and being so that people they're communicating with have a warning if they're highly upset, for example. That connection could be why the limbic functioning affects other people's mainframes or even a machine's internal processing system when severe conditions dominate the limbic functioning, and that's probably how, if your signals are overloading the functioning, it loses control and starts affecting you negatively!"

The Greek is lost on me, and at first I think it's even more lost on Motor, but then he launches a return volley: "Uh, so for that last bit, it's kinda like the eval modem in a standard mobile misreading all the data when there's too much of it cuz the mobile's overworking, so the misreading makes it transmit the wrong status signals to the processor, which makes the whole mobile mess up?"

"Yes! Exactly!" Vici's ecstatic that someone's finally understood something she's said. Motor doesn't look half so enthusiastic. He's gone all pale.

"I saw a mobile do that once," he says quietly. "It did that for about five minutes, and then something popped, and it shut off and didn't work again."

"Okay, I think this conversation's over," I butt in again. "He was trying to go to sleep, anyway."

"Alright," Vici relents with a sigh. "I'd wanted to do some sort of test or two, but . . ."

"Wait, I've got a quick idea, if you want. This should be safe." Motor digs into his left pocket, crosses his eyes, digs into his right pocket, and pulls out his beacon. "We can—" he stops talking when the screen blinks to life in his hand, which doesn't usually happen even when it's on. The occurrence is so familiar I think news is about to start scrolling. Then I see the screen and my eyes bug out and I yank out my own beacon and flick it on. Sure enough, I get the same screen.

Vici backs away fast then turns around and runs for the other side of the room. "Everyone, everyone!" she's yelling, and for a second, I think about telling her to knock it off, not tell them, but that'd be stupid, and besides, they're bound to turn on their beacons at some point, so I get the attention of the rest of my team instead.

"Guys, get your beacons," I say, looming over the table because I'm one of the idiots who thinks better standing up, or at least I think I do.

"What, what's vertically above?" Voxel asks, taking out her beacon. The others already have theirs out and are staring at the words on the screen.

SIRIDEAN STILE HAS BEEN EXTERMINATED.
CONGRATULATIONS. YOU HAVE HEREBY SURVIVED
THE FIRST PIRATE. STAND BY FOR YOUR CLUE.

Craw taps Motor on the shoulder and gives him a thumbs-up and a big smile, and a thought comes to me that almost makes me laugh. "Did you lose your voice, Craw?" He nods sheepishly. "All right, that makes sense. Sorry. Rest for now, okay?" The screens blink again, and we all turn and watch as letters start scrolling:

A RIVER UNDER MUSCLE, THEY SENSE TO HUNT YOU
A RIVER UNDER METAL, THEY SENSE TO HIDE FROM YOU
TO ADVANCE, THE FIRST, YOU MUST CONCEAL,
AND THE OTHER, YOU MUST STEAL
BY MASTERING THE MASTERS THAT HUNT HUNTERS

"Is that *it*?" Spike questions. "Hey, Voxel! You speak nonsense, right? You got a translation?"

"I can offer no hand of help here," Voxel concedes. "Not a word presents itself as intelligible. Siridean's words that exited him directed to the difficulty of this knot were truthful."

There's a murmuring on the other side of the room. I guess they decide Spike needs to be punished because he gets picked as ambassador to come over here, and by the look on his face, he's not too happy about the choice. "So, uh, do any of you geniuses have any idea about any of this? Leadhead seems to think you'll tell us if you do. And that I'll fly off the handle if you don't. She says, 'You're armed, you should do it.' Like that's what she meant. But anyway."

I look at the others at my table, who range from contemplative to baffled. "Sorry, Spike, but I don't think there's anything. It's impossible."

He tenses. "Don't you dare use that word with me," he warns. "Next thing anyone knows, you'll be jumping off a bridge."

"Possibly that's what it is! A bridge, I mean," Voxel explains, "rivers run under bridges, correct? And bridges are made of metal? Oh . . . but not muscle."

"No, but it was a good idea," Spike says to all of our surprise. An actual compliment? What did Motor *do* to him? He senses our change of mood and turns to leave without a word.

"Hold." He stops in his tracks when Tim speaks up, running his nails along his teeth the way I've seen him do before when he was deliberating whether or not to say something with Tom and Ivy.

"'Hold,' he says. Hey, imitation's flattery, isn't it?" Spike puts his hands half-way in the air with his joking smile when Tim shoots him a look. Cielhomme, how's the man not incinerated? "Whacha got, Doc?"

Tim glances at me for affirmation, and I nod to let him know it's okay to share. Keeping the teams separate ain't exactly my first priority when my best friend is on the other side. "You have all most likely come to this conclusion as of now, but nevertheless, I'll put it in the open that the hunters must be the demons without, meaning the river under muscle must be our blood, which they are attracted to. By concealing it, perhaps their senses will diminish, and with their senses will go their ability to hunt us. As for the latter river and the masters, I haven't the foggiest idea."

"Oh, *sure*, I knew that." Spike shakes his head. "Don't underestimate yourself, and *really* don't overestimate the rest of us. It doesn't suit you." With that, he clunks back over to the other side of the room.

"Where'd *that* come from?" I wonder, and Voxel grabs my right wrist and brings it up to her face. "Hey, what're you doing?" I yank my arm back, protectively covering my Rolex.

"Douglas Hertz, date of maturation: six thirteen in the evening on the first day of the Month of the Wolf," she recites from some database of info in her head. "I knew it." Voxel stands up on the bench and cups her hands around her mouth to make an announcement, taking in a deep breath.

"Don't even," Spike grumbles. She sits down. We all stare at her with questioning eyes, but she shrugs us off, smiling to herself.

"I'll catch him *anon*," she whispers with a wink at Jacques for the weird word.

"You do realize it's the Month of the Dragon, right?" I start to ask, but she butts right through.

"In the meantime, let us postpone the unweaving of the meaning lurking behind these evil letters and try to—"

Rest? Again, not by a longshot. There's no rest for the wicked, and if we aren't wicked, then nobody is—after all, thou shalt not steal, and I should know that pirating a building is a form of that. Now it's time we get caught in the act.

The roar of a chainsaw suddenly shatters the peace of the night as the blade appears between the front doors, hacking through the wooden block Lily put up before it slips back out and falls silent. Then, with a BOOM, someone kicks the door in. They're only a dark silhouette against the silver-spangled backdrop of the swollen moon as it floats out of the ocean's waves. The only thing about them that catches the light is the glittering teeth of the saw, still revolving so leech teeth come to mind, and before the wielder even speaks, I know our safety period is over.

"ALRIGHT, GOLDILOCKS, WHO'S IN REV'S LODGE?!"

- II -

Cops and Robbers

I'm not sure who does it, but the table suddenly flips forward, and I grab Motor off it before it goes down with a thud. Voxel slips under it and onto this side away from the door before it touches the ground, and Eli jumps over it to join us. "Get down!" he orders, and we all duck behind the table as the Brigade follows our lead. Keeping Mo tight against me, I peek through the crack between the folds of the table with wide eyes.

A peeved young woman steps into the room with an air of such purpose and domination I'm tempted to believe she's a westerner until I figure she must not come from Tersatellus. Like the people from Dagur's Island, she's wearing different clothes, but hers are entirely camo with her hair pulled into a ponytail under a camo cap, and the nonblade parts of the chainsaw in her hands are also camo. Yes. A camouflaged chainsaw. Real subtle.

"Stowaways," she hisses around the lazily smoking cylinder in her mouth, which she spits into a nearby bin I didn't notice. "Y'all must be the Filler offerings, then. Y'all come when your big dark bowl's too full of the ugly bits nobody wants in their soup, and it's up to us to make sure y'all don't go back."

Lily rises up in the back with her hands in the air. "Listen, ma'am, we apologize for trespassing, but we were hiding for our lives, so I would really appreciate it if you shut the door now." I marvel at her gall, but it makes the lady laugh.

"Y'all're cute, kid. Ma'aming Rev. Aw, Rev, they don't know no better. Alright, y'all kids're lost."

"Yes," Lily says, "yes, we're absolutely lost. We have no idea—"

The woman puts a hand up to stop the words and kicks the door shut behind her. "It's alright, kid. Rev understands. She's been through this before, when she was a kid about knee high. They're always so freaked the first night through to their last." She looks at her wrist, which has nothing on it. "How long y'all been here?"

"A little over six hours."

"Mm-hmm. And how many of y'all're left?"

Lily hesitates. "Eleven," she finally replies quietly.

The woman whistles. "Eleven? Last time, only nine lived over six hours, and about a million pirates were kaput. Y'all're real hotshots."

"Um, excuse me?" Now that I guess she's not gonna kill me on sight, I get to my feet above the shield-table, and the woman fixes her eyes on me. "What exactly is going on? Who're you?"

"This is Revany Remington," she introduces with a bow. "Most people shorten that to Rev for obvious reasons! The chainsaw, if ya'll didn't get that. She talks in third person, if y'all didn't get that, either. Y'all think that's crazy, and y'all're exactly right." Revany throws her arms out to either side, looking around with smug satisfaction. "Welcome to this ugly lil' rock of land the other ugly rocks call Camp Crazy. This used to be an Alcatraz, folks, yessir, this is where they'd stick us when they don't wanna deal with us, but the they in question skeddadled, and new people said we were free to go, but that also meant we were free to stay. Formerly prison, this place. Formally Fort Night. There's a funny story for that name... Anyway, if y'all wanna live, figure this: we've got our turf. Get off it, or we'll have to protect it."

"Get off? You realize this is an *island*, and there's no ice to drive across to get anywhere else, right?" I demand. In the back of my mind, I wonder what'd become of Tersatellus if they dumped us criminals into one certain isolated spit of land and let us do whatever we want without them. Makes me shudder.

"No. There's four of us. There are four of our lodges. There are four turfs. There are only two teams. There are only two claimed turfs. And then there's spaces in between. Get there or get mentally impaired."

"What?" Lily's gone all pale, so she must've understood something of the crazy speech. "But... but what about those things out there?"

"Oh, they're fun enough, and only killed enough of us to make us four. Besides, y'all're Filler kids. Who cares if y'all go from eleven to none?" Revany shrugs. "They'll be more interested in the players, anyway, so y'all should be fine as long as y'all don't interfere with our nightly play."

"What play?" I venture.

The chainsaw woman smiles with all of her teeth. "The only play that's worthy of playing, of course: Tag."

Tag. The word resonates in my soul. The game of chase and be chased. My whole life summed up in one breath.

Lily looks confused, so I have to mouth an explanation at her since in western Tersatellus, they play Cops and Robbers. We're all still confused as to why a child's game is being brought up (or why the word *game* gets replaced with *play*) but as long as her speech isn't as bad as Baldur's, we'll take what we can get.

"So as long as y'all aren't in it, y'all're basically safe. Y'all can't play now, so y'all better run or get run over. Rev doesn't need no Filler kids running around her lodge. Stand up, now, and let ole Rev look at em all." Pressured by a tug of the saw's chain, everyone else gets to their feet, hands up. Revany looks over them with a whole mess of emotions running across her face. "Oh, and we've got a Filler *man*!" she laughs when she lays eyes on Spike.

"And woman," Voxel says crossly, but Revany only looks at "the man" with hungry eyes. He makes an uncomfortable sound.

"Yessir, we've got a much brighter batch this Filler, huh! Last time there was two Filler men, and oneotha sonofa…" She shakes her head, cutting off her thought with a huge grin that's pleased with something that doesn't look particularly nice. "If trouble was solid, some of the last Filler batch'd be *made* of it, especially Lucky. I could do with seeing some of y'all later."

Voxel's fists ball up. "Well, we won't bother your hair for any more seconds, Ms. Remington," she says in a clipped way. "Let's exit quickly, everyone." She swings her legs over the table and stalks out of the lodge. Revany looks at all of us like she's not sure why we're not leaving, revs her chainsaw and stands aside with a smile to let us all start streaming out.

Dread settles in the pit of my stomach as I step outside. Some part of me wants to protest, to ask if we can share the place, beg for some sort of help, but the look on her face tells me everything I need to know. Either she really is a nutcase, or she's way too sane. Hers is the intense focus of a serial killer, and most of them are crazy, and the ones that aren't just don't care. I can't tell with this one. She holds the chainsaw as tight as her jaw, but other than that, there's this ease to her that tells me we don't mean anything to her, that we're nothing but some casual trespassers in some routine that we're not a part of.

Still, I glance back at the comfortable lodge longingly. I *could* ditch the others and sneak back in and hide. But they might *follow* and try to find me and ruin it. So much for that safety, eh?

I step out onto the chilly, damp beach and shiver in the moonlight, looking every which way for leeches to come flying out of nowhere. Somewhere in the distance, I hear them hissing. Sometimes the ones that stayed behind lurch out of the water, but none attack, and it's been a full ten seconds. So far, so good.

On his way out, Spike (he was last) turns to look at Revany, whose eyes manage to settle on his imposing figure again. "So. What's this game of Tag you're so hyped up about?" he rumbles. Voxel pivots on the beach and walks over to where her Caterpillar, my truck, and Craw's bike are crashed, all serene and half drowning in the foamy waves.

"Every night, we play," Revany says through her clamped teeth, energetic, even frenzied just from thinking about this Tag thing. "Our north alliance versus the stupid west alliance. Bloods are worth one point, Bruises are worth two, and y'all lose a point by being tagged by a Blood, and y'all lose a life by being tagged by a Bruise, obviously. Play starts at zero midnight. Winner by oh-six-hundred gets Bruise immunity the next day. Oh, and kill a Blood and get ten points—kill a Bruise and get fifty. But only one Blood's ever been about to do that. He was a Filler, but he coulda been one of us. The only one else that's ever come close was Elyssandra Stroud, and she's dead, or Ripvan Remington, and he always wins with us. That doesn't stop the west alliance from trying, though. Wescotts used to be good, then they all died, and the Vertos took over, and it's all gone to pot."

She pulls out another black cylinder and lights the end on fire with a match, smoke drifting from the end as she takes a drag.

"So y'all can come back before zero midnight if y'all want, and Rip and Rev can see if y'all'll benefit the north alliance here, got it? Don't go to the west alliance, got it?" she adds with heat, and we all nod, backing away slowly. The second Spike's across the threshold, she slams the door shut. He frowns in annoyance when it hits him in the back.

Then he tenses along with the rest of us when he notices the hissing picks up.

"Alright, guys, no use in standing around. Let's find some middle ground to take over," I say and get going, suddenly too nervous to stay in the same place. Maybe it was Revany's crazy-person talk. Maybe it's the leeches.

"Wait, um, please," Eli finally finds his voice. I get the feeling he's got a real don't-speak-unless-spoken-to attitude. "Shouldn't we at least try to defend our position there? We weren't doing her any harm, anyway."

"Oh, please," Voxel scoffs, "that female was even farther from stable mind than yours truly."

"Yeah, she was totally off the handle, and there's no use in trying to reason with unreasonable people," I reason, but my reasoning doesn't seem to satisfy Eli.

"We still could've tried. What would there be to lose?" Motor nods in agreement.

"Well, the door's shut now, so it's a moot point, anyway," I point out, using my Vici-Vocab to sound smarter. Speaking of which, her group's already moved out, so this looks like a good place to split up. I start looking around for any idea of a good place to go when I notice one of them's lagging behind. A thought hits me so I start jogging over. "Hey, Rex, wait up! I gotta talk to you."

Arms swinging around for balance—he hit a rock, probably—Rex turns around to face me. "Great time for a chat, Mouse."

"Good evening to you too, Sasquatch." He flinches. "I meant to ask you before, but I forgot til now, so I'll make it quick. Why'd you leave?"

"What, the lodge? Thought that—"

"The *Band*, Rex."

He looks away. "I dunno why I was ever a part of anything. That ain't how it works. I ain't a part of Lily's stupid team, either. You can all get eaten for all I care, and I don't belong to no one." He starts the process of turning around again.

"I'm not done!" With a huff of annoyance, or maybe it's relief, he stops turning. "Last question, then I'll stop bugging you. How'd you start pushing Lily's car so fast back there?" He starts staring at a tree. "You know, in our crazy rush to get here? It's got something to do with what you told Lily about how you got better when you're mad, doesn't it?"

"Why're you acting like it's such a big deal?" Rex demands. "It's just adrenaline, just your heart dumping all sorts of sugar and energy junk through you. There's nothing special about that."

Half of the people I know with a *normal* IQ don't really know that much about how adrenaline works, that it has to do with the heart, and you don't get bursts of strengths from this passionate desire or some other romantic crud. Okay, I'm part of the unenlightened half of the normal people, so I'm not sure, but still, this coming from someone with barely enough IQ to whack private property with a stick is pretty weird. "How'd you know that?" I ask, and then my brow furrows when another thought comes to me. "This has something to do with your chip, doesn't it?"

"I never said that! I never said anything like that, and you said last question!" he shouts, but I wait, even when he attempts to walk in a circle and pull his hair at the same time. "It happens to half of everybody, okay? They yank out something they weren't s'posed to cuz it's so attached, and they gotta act fast before you die, or else you die, and then you're dead! And I ain't stupid, okay, I know it happened to Craw with his lungs and Voxel with her eye tubes and Tom with his hands and fricking everything with Eli, and everyone else's got some sort of problem with that stupid thing, so you can't call me a freak. If anyone's a freak, it's you!"

My surprise and my need to stay as far under anyone's radar as I can makes me shoot back, "Freak? I'm not the one with a whole new take on bloodshot eyes and no idea how to read, now am I, smart one? Or can you even tell that?"

Again, he flinches. "Boy, Mouse, you really know what to say, don't you? How do you do it, huh, Mouse?"

"Hey, I didn't come here to talk about me, okay? I'm good at reading people, that's all. Their face, the way they talk, what they say, what they don't say, their reactions, their smell, even the way they walk, it all *means* something. Either that or I'm really good at guessing. Don't trust me either way. You survive by being suspicious, and I survive by being enigmatic."

"Awesome. *What* in the name of fire and brimstone is 'enigmatic'?"

"Enigmatic," a dictionary-imitating voice echoes from the darkness ahead as Vici steps out of the woods. "An adjective describing something or someone with qualities of the mystery of the unknown and is worthy of every suspicion that you'll never be able to confirm. Come on, Rex, Lily's waiting for you." She doesn't let me get a word in before she ushers Rex back toward the forest with a meaningful glance back at me. The problem is, I don't understand the meaning. So much for reading people.

"Well, that was weird," Craw croaks, making me jump. The Nobody's good at popping up whenever you don't expect it, and from the look on his face,

I think even he didn't expect himself to make any sound. "Hey, I got my voice back!" When the hisses disappear, so does his smile.

"Don't worry, we won't make you keep yelling at them," I say, and he relaxes, which gives me another secret rush again since usually everything I say rips people up, as you can tell. You have no idea how annoying that gets. I open my mouth and hey, let's *not* have friends for a while! "I wonder how that works, though."

"Rex claimed that your breathing vesicles are in a similar situation as my eyeballs," Voxel says with wonder and curiosity. Craw looks at me in panic, so I rummage for something in my brain to say.

"You know, he was probably just assuming something was different about Craw because of his ... shall we call them advanced vocal talents? He's probably jealous too," I add with a wink, and Craw gives me a gratified nod. "But still, what was that thing he said about Tom, Tim?" It slips out before I think about it, and Tim's dark eyes slide over to me, so I know I made a mistake.

"Nothing. There was nothing wrong with him," he says in a way that doesn't allow for debate. "Now, I refuse to be the only convict trapped in this bay to be hailed by the truth. I'm a felon the same as any of you and deserve to be treated thus. Call me Jacques again."

I nod, remembering how I banished my birth name not because it sounded stupid but because of how painful it got hearing it all the time. It gets to a point where the whole world has names for you, and if you were still the person you used to be, then those names would hurt, but something's changed you into someone you were not, someone the young you wouldn't even recognize, someone that keeps looking for that young innocence of the person you can never be again. So you stick to the tags and accept whatever they want to call you, no matter what it is. Because whatever they say, they're alright. Because you're everyone but you. Because even being called some infected animal every time someone wants your attention is better than hearing the truth. And besides, anything's less painful than the real name. It's not a name anymore. It's another scar, a voice that whispers to you, telling you that you're wrong and broken and hopeless and alone, reminding you of everyone you've lost, and if you listen close enough, then you'll hear yourself on that list.

"Anyone else with any requests?" I ask, burying the thought deep in the music box of my memories, burying it under a million names to the tune of some dying lullaby.

"Can you use magic and poof more time in between now and the time we gotta leave so we can sleep?" Mo inquires, and I shake my head. "Dang. It was worth a shot."

"Did you even get any sleep all morning?" Craw makes sure he's vague so that he doesn't raise any questions about whether or not he himself got any sleep all morning.

"Nope. I woke up real early Saturday to split a bike in case I got prequalified, then I got to Zenith from Greenwater Creek, then after getting entered, having a snack and playing cards, you left to talk to Voxel and Vici, so I explored a lot around the Castaway place so I wouldn't think so much and get nervous. So I didn't sleep since yesterday." The kid yawns to prove it.

"You're from Greenwater Creek?" I ask with reverence. And I try to convince myself I think all cities're the same.

"No, I'm from Saganaki City."

"Prime, mon homme," Jacques says, and they give each other the easterners' salute, and I almost laugh.

"Alright, well, sorry you're tired and all, but we need to get moving, er, course," I say, trying the dialect for myself though the accent is hard. I keep thinking we're about to be ambushed by leeches any second. "Should, um, should I carry you or something? Or am I too much of a fuzz?"

"I think it's trying to communicate," Jacques whispers to Motor, who giggles. "Here, allow me."

Motor favors the guy's taller shoulders right away, admiring the view before putting his goggles over his eyes. Then (with a word of permission) he puts his arms and face on top of Jacques's own head and goes still. He's so small and Jacques is so unaffected that the kid looks closer to a whack accessory than a real person.

"Shall we be off, then?" Jacques asks when they're settled. "Since the natives already have their stakes claimed in the north and west of the isle, as Ms. Remington suggested, then we should find it appropriate to do the opposite. The other team seemed to be heading south, so it seems that down shore due east would be the proper direction to go."

"Sounds good. I like being where I can see what's going on and where I can see all you gorgeous people walking around," Craw remarks as he starts going down shore in the wrong direction, since Voxel was already going that way.

"Guys, east is this way," I tell them, and they both turn around and try to come up with some excuse for not knowing which way's east. Then they go silent. None of us say a word, not as we pass the half-submerged monster truck and the shiny purple convertible, not when we pass the crooked tank, and especially not as we stare at that sleek black car sitting high, dry and lonely on the crown of the beach.

A crisp ocean wind yawns at us, pushing away the hissing sound for a bit, but it makes me shiver. Craw comes up beside me. "Yo, Rat? By the way you're walking, and as promised, I have been watching, I can figure out this much: you're still wet and cold. So don't call me a master at figuring people out or anything cuz that's all I can get, but that much's pretty useful. Here, don't wear that soaked thing." He pulls off his jacket and holds it out to me while we're walking. I hesitate, then the wind gusts again, and I pull off my soaked jacked in a hurry, pulling on Craw's fast so nobody can catch another look at my tattoo they're so interested in.

I mentioned that everyone has this smell to them and that this jacket has a high collar. This collar gets zipped all the way up by both the owner and now by me—Craw zipped it up to cover the tip of the scar on his long throat but I do it so it comes up to my nose, and I can breathe in the smell, a mix of a bunch of things I don't recognize except this sharp, lingering spice of basil. They really need to bottle this stuff or something. It's almost intoxicating.

Likewise, Craw wraps my hoodie (well, it used to be a hoodie) around his neck over the scarf with a wink at me, and we all keep on walking through the night, me up front, Voxel on my left, Craw to my right, Jacques behind him, Motor fast asleep on Jacques, and Eli walking behind us all, watching, listening, waiting.

As we go, I figure out that the strip of sand is much shorter now that the tide's so high. The beach gives way to the same black-gray rock as the cliffs in the middle of the island, with waves breaking strong and hard against the steep rocky shore. The whole place has this cone shape that starts out gentle and escalates fast at some point past the trees to get to a peak at the top of the crooked spire that stands out as a void against the starry sky. I watch the top for a while, enchanted by its strange formation jutting up out of the crowd of trees, until a tall, living-ragdoll figure separates itself from the black outline only to melt back into the darkness. Then I look away and don't look back.

"They hold us in their eyes," Jacques says quietly, and I turn my head to the side again. Sure enough, the ugly forms lurk behind the tree line, their tongues wagging back and forth, whispering by letting small pockets of air out of their tongues, which must be somewhat hollow if they can pull them inside-out the way they do. "It seems that their senses aren't so keen—they see us, but as neutral."

"You're right," Craw agrees. "These bandages are doing the trick, or we've healed over. It looks like we're safe, after all, so… think we should split up? Only pairs or something—nobody goes into the woods alone—but Rev said there's four lodges, so I bet we could find this east one if we split."

"Excellent. I have a need to speak with this one," Voxel says and, without waiting for anyone to agree or disagree, grabs Eli by the arm and trucks into the forest without the slightest pause, even out of fear, so I don't get the chance to ask what her purpose is or what on earth she thinks she's doing. I watch for a second with wide eyes until I can't see them anymore. The leeches sometimes look at them but don't make any moves. Craw and Jacques were right—these things care as much about us as Rev and the rocks do.

"If our party is breaking into pairs, then I believe this one is fairly obvious." Jacques shrugs Motor into a more comfortable position on his shoulders. "We'll reunite here in ten minutes to discuss our findings, be they fruitless or fertile." I don't bother asking how he'll know what time it is.

"Alrighty then, we'll look over here," Craw decides for the two of us and takes the lead, marching ahead. Still freaked out about walking close to the things that're bent on eating me, I hang back, and he turns around to look at me with a lopsided smile, eyes tired as ever. "Don't worry, Rat, I've got your back. Gangsters, remember?"

"Yeah," I falter, "gangsters," and walk after him.

Cool darkness blankets us with only thin shreds of moonlight filtering down through gaps in the trees to see by. The leaf-covered ground is uneven and full of roots and weeds and rocks to trip me up, along with the reaching tree branches to whack me in the face. As a metropolitan, it takes me a while to get used to it, and even then it's nowhere near as good as my normal sneak, but I manage. It's what I do for a living. My eyes are wide, forcing images out of the dark, and my senses are on high alert. I even push down the collar of the jacket just in case. I'm not gonna smell the lodge, I know, but for some reason, it helps.

The glowing red eyes stare out of my darkness here and there, which puts me on edge and makes me jump at the littlest sounds. Craw, on the other hand, is totally calm, even though rocks keep spearing up out of the ground, which starts getting that much steeper with every step. "The tides and explosions must've made all these islands into pretty weird shapes," he comments. His voice makes the red dots disappear around us, and the whispering shushes so I can almost make out Voxel's voice far off to our right. Craw looks back at me nervously.

"Still not gonna make you talk to make them go away," I tell him, glaring at a trio of red eyes as it pops up nearby, but it doesn't leave.

"You don't have to. Make me talk, I mean. Now that there's finally a lull, there's something I wanted to ask you, Rat. You know, as a friend and all." As a friend and all. Oh, for *sure*. He stops, looking around, and I notice agitation in his eyes, his eyebrows turned down to emphasize it. "I've kinda asked or gathered from the others, so I wanted to know from you, you know, when it got clear, when you knew you were gonna get cut out of the Plexus."

"Oh." Biting my lip, I turn and look away, at the moon, at the red dots, anything but Craw and his jaded eyes and my jacket shielding the scar on his neck. "I . . . I always knew, I guess." With a sigh, I turn back to look him in the eyes. "I didn't see myself as having much of a choice." *You are a mistake that can never be anything more, he said, but you showed him. You had to. There was never another choice.*

Craw sighs too, looking at the ground. "Yeah, that's about what the others said. Voxel had to do it to try and get rid of the crazy, Mo had to do it to try and get rid of the haywiring, it never worked for Eli in the first place . . . You all knew right from the get-go. Everyone always knew they were different. I think that's . . . interesting, I guess."

There's something in his voice that makes me wonder. "What about you, Craw?"

He purses his lips and looks up, holding his elbows. "Nope. I was a boring, normal, stupid kid once, and it never even crossed my mind to get extracted until I was about thirteen."

"So the message wasn't what persuaded you?" I guess.

"No," he says after a pause then doesn't continue, so I have to press for an explanation, and he sighs again, harder this time. "Okay, I shut it off sometimes, everyone does. It doesn't mean they're rebels or wannabe-cutouts or anything, not unless they go circuit breaker and start doing crimes. We were only having fun. Me and my little group of friends. We lived in Pike, that little town right by all those funky rock formations, and what we'd do is we'd sneak out of town—we'd only talk about it in person so none of our parents could pick it up in the Plexus—and we'd go out to those rocks and climb around on them. I know, big whoop, but we were all just normal kids looking for some fun, and it wasn't that big of a rule, anyway. Until… until Louis fell off."

Craw swallows. "It was icy, I remember, so everything was easy to slip on. We all got off the rocks really quick when it happened, but then the others stopped freaking out, and I got the messages telling me that it'd be okay, and all I had to do was stand back and wait for the boon ops from the Med Sector to come and help Louis and he'd be fine. But they weren't there *right then*, and he was hurting *right then*, and I couldn't sit around and do nothing, no matter what the stupid bit of metal told me. So I made the choice. Real life happened from there. But I feel so bad cuz I'm the only one I can find that wasted those stupid, stupid thirteen years in total ignorance before that."

"No, you didn't," I say firmly. "Whether we knew we were gonna get extracted or not, we all had to go through those years of being useless and stupid, since it's almost suicide to get extracted until you're thirteen—up to then, there's nothing anyone can do, so you might as well enjoy the oblivion. And it's not really oblivion. I try not to remember, but I don't think it was that bad to the point where people should look down on you for being normal about it. To me, it's almost better if you figure it out yourself. I'm actually kinda jealous. It's supposed to be a choice, a choice for freedom of the hard-knock life or being normal, and you had to make that choice while the rest of us didn't. We had the answer thrust on us. You could've taken the easy road, but you didn't. That's pretty cool."

Craw looks at me in surprise, not even bothering to wonder why I didn't have a choice. "You mean it?" I nod, and he puts on his half smile. "Gosh, Rat, that's… that's one of the best *real* things anyone's ever said to me. Thank you. It's exactly what I needed to hear."

And *that*, my friend, is something that I myself have been waiting so long and with such burning passion and patience to hear that I let him fold me into his arms. *Yes, Rat, you are something more than Death and destruction. You can say something real to someone and mean it and have it mean something to them. You're good for something after all.*

Yeah, I know he probably said it because he just wanted to flatter me because he's smooth, but it worked, okay? I'm not made of steel. It's got me in a daze, gives me that hot, cutout-only rush, and it roars in my ears and hurts my face so I realize I'm smiling too hard. I get that under control before pulling back a little to look at him again to make sure he's real, but I don't pull back far enough. My eyes look at his from such a short gap, our foreheads touch, and we share the same cold, static-y air where the friction of our foggy breaths threaten to set off sparks. Our noses are almost touching, pulled in as if by gravity, and that is, by the way, how Tersatellans kiss, and the sensation of a symphony and the color red goes through me, and I can't help but think that here it is, making up for Lashia Horne; this is redemption.

The feeling doesn't even go away when a certain blue-haired woman pops into sight.

My ears register the crunching footsteps, and I fling my eyelids open, question marks sitting in my pupils as I turn, stepping away. I'm awake but still watching that fading afterimage of a dream, still dizzy and drunk on basil and fiery, metallic breath. Voxel's brow is drawn way down, and I notice Eli slightly behind her wearing the same look I probably did when I first saw Tom and Ivy really together.

Well, it was bound to happen, and you know it.

"Are you two faring satisfactorily?" Voxel asks, sounding pretty confused herself.

Craw just manages to cough and blink in shock as if it's just now dawning on him who he got found with, and I have to be the one to step back, pocketing a jam drive I found in his wallet. "We're fine," I manage, swallowing to make up for why my voice is so choked. "We haven't found anything, though, but it's so hard to see in this darkness and all that. I've bumped into him about five times now."

"Satisfactorily," Craw echoes a little late.

"I see," Voxel says. "Well, you are two fortune-having souls, for the unlikely duo of Jacques and Motor have encountered a sight to be seen rising up from the grounds of this strange place. Follow us, and view the view for yourselves!" She turns to go then hesitates. "Do I dare leave the two of you alone?"

The two of us in question both laugh at the same time. "What? Nothing happened," I insist easily, and Voxel shrugs and moves along, Eli following behind her. Craw gives me a sideways glance and a crooked smile before starting forward. I set off last, waiting for him to prove me wrong, to give me some sign that something happened. Maybe I'm some dreamer instead of a cynic for a second because some part of me wants it to be more than nothing, but I don't get my sign, so I'm left to absorb the shock and move on.

Fricking thespian didn't even kiss me, I smirk inwardly. Redemption for Laisha Horne, indeed. The sucker probably knows. I'll bet.

↮

Fricking thief didn't even find the lodge, I give myself another kick when we get there.

The forest breaks into a ravine a bit ahead, dropping off first into a simple valley filled with pebbles and grass between us and the mountain. Off to the right, it drops into deep crevices where nothing can grow but rock and shadows. Here, the lumpy rock faces've been baked lighter by the sun and have an eerie glow in the moonlight. In the shallow valley, which is speckled with dead, dying, or near-dying trees, scraps of cloth are dotted along a something I think is a path through the grass. One end leads to the crevices, while the other end leads to a stone and log cabin in a circular clearing surrounded by trees so close together if you stepped a few meters into them, you'd never know the clearing was there.

The whole minicliff is so sudden it seems manufactured to me, but so does everything that's perfect. Speaking of which, Jacques stands at the edge off to the right, near the deeper section, staring into the dark abyss. Somewhere back home, a supermodel is dying for his autograph. "There's a gathering of our hunters close at hand," he mutters, kicking a rock down in there before stepping back. An annoyed wave of hissing comes up from the pit, but none of the leeches show their faces. "But what are *those*?"

"They're camping tents," Eli says and points out the little things of cloth (since I didn't get what Jacques was talking about). "People would use them as a nomadic shelter. There must've been people here before, but long ago—they look old and abandoned. Not a good sign."

"Why not?" I ask, wondering why someone would pick such a flimsy scrap to sleep under. Might as well forget about it.

"Because if they are absent now, then where have they gone?" Jacques answers my question with a question. "Ms. Remington claimed there are only four residents remaining on the isle. What has become of the others?"

Another gentle breath of wind whistles through the valley, bringing the sound of the hissing up to me, and I shiver. *There's your answer.*

"I'm in the state of being skeptical," Voxel admits. "There are dozens of these tents of camping. If the leeches hunt by the scentings of gore, how could none of these tent occupants not infer this and save themselves?"

"It doesn't matter. We're not here for a history lesson," I say, starting to the left of the ledge. This place would be a deathtrap for Rex, so at least we're safe from him. "We should get to that lodge. It'll be all neglected, probably, but at least it'll give us a safe place to crash and think. Maybe we can even wait til dawn and get some sleep in the meantime, and the track can come back, and we can figure things out."

That's the second delusion about us ever having safety I've let myself make in so many hours. I'm really on a roll tonight. Maybe I only ate the positive end of the battery, ha! I'm so sorry.

During our hike, I fall back a bit, going over my options before picking Voxel to ask what she wanted to talk with Eli about. She's the least likely of anyone on this island to keep secrets, and honestly, Eli still worries me too much for me to ask him anything. When I ask, Voxel struggles to find an innocent way to put it with her whacked vocab then finally settles with, "As a technician, I had some inquiries to inquire, out of curiosity, of course. It's not every day one in my shoes is given a chance to talk to a…" She hesitates, and at first, I think it's about him being part machine or getting brought back to life, but to my surprise, she finishes, "To a Steele."

Oh, yeah. I look to my other side, where Eli's keeping pace. "So are you as smart as your brother? Is your whole clan of relatives full of geniuses?"

"Not quite," he confesses. "But I know enough about myself to answer most of the questions. I'd be hard-pressed to listen to Jaden's soliloquy without picking up useful things here and there."

"The man monologues," Jacques translates before Craw can ask.

"Cielhomme, how does the Lillian Brigade expect to win anything? We've got all the smart people over here," Craw comments, shaking his head.

Voxel snorts. "That's not truthful to the highest degree. In all my wildest fancies, I would never have the haziest vision of myself having the knowledge-power to gain access to the inside of Jaden's lunchbox, let alone a place of residency." Am I the only one who thinks it's weird to use the guy's forename? "It's been many years since I began to crack into anything of that man's owning, and I've had exactly zero progress. I have found my hero in Vici and have uncovered the conclusion she is in the possession of superpowers. You all must be. I'm immersed in the presence of myths and marvels."

"Yeah, and you're one too, Voxel. We're all pretty cool, aren't we?" I smile, letting the camaraderie wrap around us so we can forget the rest of the world of pain and mystery for a second. Nobody related by blood or pact to desert or to desert us, nobody to be suspicious of, nobody trying to kill us, no past to grieve for, no future to be afraid of, no secrets or lies. Nothing but the Band of Cutouts, us and here and now with our pretend safety and superpowers and fragile fellowship of fugitives.

I'm the first one to the doors of the lodge, which looks the same as the first except it's got some rocks in its structure and the windows on the doors are dark, so I pull on the handles and walk in before the others. Musty darkness sighs over us with the smell of rot and neglect, and the boards try to creak when

I walk on them. Jacques twists the plastic end of the pull-string on his jacket, and a thin stream of light shoots out of the tip, igniting the millions of dust motes that're floating around the room now that the doors are open. Rickety scaffolding's littered on the soft, buggy floor, tables sit with forsaken cups and stuff strewn on them, tools lie around next to boxes and boots, and the whole place reeks with forgotten dreams. It reminds me of something I can't quite put a finger on, but I get that a lot—did I say that already?

"Abandon all hope, ye who enter here," Jacques mutters as he shuts the door behind Voxel and tugs the flashlight / pull-string-tip off his jacket, setting both the tiny contraption and Motor on a table before pulling the rest of his jacket off.

My earlier suspicions about how he looked underneath the jacket are confirmed—he's buff as a Western Warbunker, lean muscles curving gracefully under so many cleverly placed weapons; I didn't know it was possible to be so armed, and with a black tank top, he looks exactly the same as Mac. Not a muscle is different, like they've both only done the same exact things as each other, and now he's the one to radiate defiance that feels as bold against my skin as Mac's. It's so weird to me, since they're three years apart.

"*Cielhomme*, dude, on any other Sunday, you'd've knocked the fudge outta Spike," Craw says, not even pretending not to be jealous.

"Your resemblance to your late brother is even sounder than I first imagined it to be," Voxel finishes the conclusion I told you about, except mine didn't include one of the words she threw in there. That's the word Jacques pays attention to, and it makes him stand up straighter, his eyes flashing over all of us in an instant.

"You ought to know that the Next are not made *late* until midnight takes them," he returns heavily. (There's a saying that you have to wait for midnight before you can even start thinking a fellow in arms is dead, because the famous tend to be dramatic—also it's an even reference point for when your gangster doesn't come back from the soiree, so you know you gotta go get them.)

Then Jacques drapes his jacket over Motor, who's been asleep this whole time. Squinting in the darkness, I can see something gentle cross Jacques's hollow face as he adjusts Motor's goggles. But it might've been my imagination because before I get a better look at it, it disappears.

The rest of us slowly fall back into motion, too jittery to stay still for too long. Voxel finds a seat in a dark corner, slightly hidden by some scaffolding, and starts messing with her beacon. Craw positions himself in front of the doors, staring out and humming to himself, only abandoning the post to wander back over to the tables to look inside the cups, which're as good a place as any to look for the answers to some of the questions raised tonight. I'm glad he doesn't try to corner me about what happened, even though every time I think about it, my heart starts spazzing out the same way it does when I'm under attack.

The shock of it does go away. Besides, he's always been a total flirt, and all of Tersatellus knows it. Nothing that Craw does means anything because he isn't anything or anyone, and when you can be anybody you want to be, you can appeal to anyone you want to appeal to, so nobody's special to the Nobody. People only like him because they want to be fooled, and he can trick them into thinking they feel something. He's not even handsome or brawny like Jacques or anything. I think it's his easiness, like life's nothing but a game that takes two people to play, and that's what makes him a player.

Finally restored to my default state of indifference (read: I'm honestly ticked at him in that smiley version of angry because he got me back without knowing it), I happily scour the wonderland of tools for something to replace my multi. Or you know, threats or anything. Eli paces up and down the room until some fancy takes him over to one of the scaffoldings or something, and after he's done with that, he always goes back to pacing. I've never seen him sitting totally still except when he was half-dead—he's always tapping his foot or wringing his hands or doing other stuff, even though a cookie and some jerky shouldn't make enough energy to sustain constant motion after he dumped all his strength into keeping the track alive for me.

It occurs to me that after seventeen years of not having any ability to move, my biggest fear would be going back to that motionless prison. I stop my search and watch him, trying to imagine even one limp and lifeless day in a body I owned but couldn't control. It makes me shudder.

He strays over here without noticing it (even though he's learned how to be background noise, he's still got a thing or two to learn about picking up on it), so he jumps when I say, "Hey." His eyes darken when he sees me, and I don't mean that as an expression. I hesitate, another question about night-vision adding itself to my huge mountain of other questions. "Um, Eli? There was something I . . . I kinda wanted to ask, but . . ."

A million dust motes fly up into the air as he sets himself down on the floor in front of me, cross-legged. He does his best to look still and prepared for questions, but I don't miss how his foot subtly twitches back and forth, and he taps his fingers on his knees in a rhythm. "Fire away. Now's probably the best time, anyway, and I'm starting get used to it. Just don't ask how *it* happened, because that's not my question to answer, and I have no clue how I was reanimated. Everything else is within bounds, I think."

I decide to ditch the question about whether or not he can see in the dark. "What happened with you and Siridean near the end?" I ask instead.

Eli bites the inside of his cheek. "Look, I'm sorry for blowing up back there. I was hoping I'd be a much calmer person, but, um, seeing the strong prey on the young and vulnerable . . ." His fingers, which are almost as lithe and long as his brother's, dig into his knees now so the nails bite deep, reminding me of when he did the same thing to that cabinet in the ship a while ago.

"Does this have anything to do with what you told me in the ship about witnessing people's cruelties and kindnesses and differences?" I press, trying to sound passive. The same tenseness from before settles in his posture, and he stares at the floor with such intensity I swear I don't understand how the rotten wood doesn't burst into flames.

"It might," he says, vague but acidic, and I know I'm crossing into dangerous territory, so I tread lightly, softening my voice.

"Does it have something to do with your brother?" I can't call him Jaden. The name feels foreign in my mouth, way too intimate for me to use since the guy's so elite and mysterious, and besides, he's older than me. Twelve years older. It's not hard for the idle thought to occur to me that the man was about my age the last time there was an extermination.

"It might," Eli repeats himself, his voice even more deadly quiet.

"And does it have something to do with Vastate?"

After all, I have ways of knowing that a lot of his assumptions about the Adaman at the start of this thing aren't really true, but he believes them, and I could see he had burning reasons to.

Eli's liquid lightning eyes slowly float up to bore into mine so he doesn't have to answer.

I take a deep breath to steady myself, because under his watch, I need all the steadying I can get. "Well, you're not alone, you know. It might not be the same to you, but we all hate his guts. His Sector's in charge of the Plexus, of course, which we all have different reasons for hating, but it's in charge of the rapture men too. They're so wired it's not even funny, and too many good people've died at their hands. Too many fellows in arms've blooded the gutters just because they don't have some Plexus telling them how to work." Jacques buries his face in his arms for some reason, but I don't notice. I'm too busy trying not to remember standing on a street corner, watching a family die, a house burn, a piece of the world razed to the dirt. "We've all seen the strong prey on the innocent. I'd say that's worth blowing up about, or else nothing is."

Eli nods, calming back down, or at least lowering the intensity of that look of his so I don't get crispy-fried in a couple minutes. Since I think my complexion's fine and I don't want to get fake-baked sable by another glare, I keep quiet about the issue but resolve to talk to Voxel later about this argument between Steele and Vastate about the guy, though I have some guesses. Vastate was the one to fight the rest of the Adamantration to get Steele employed. Maybe he's just using him. I'd love to believe that.

Anyway, until I get to Voxel, I let myself ask one more question that got thrown onto the pile during our conversation. "Eli? I know you told everyone you kind of figured it out by listening, but can you tell me where you heard about the race from?" I ask, even though I can guess the answer.

Sure enough, his eyes flash and he replies, "What do you think?"

"Was he in it last time?" Somehow, the answer seems really important.

Eli frowns. "I'm not sure. As one of the four Adamans that plans out the race, he'd talk about it aloud on occasion, and that's how I gleaned the information, but I never thought of that before. Even when Jaden would leave without taking me with, it was never for more than a few days at a time, with the only exception being once quite a while ago where he was suddenly gone for over a week. But I had no way of telling time for sure, so I don't know how long it really was or how far back it was, and besides, he came back and moved on as though nothing ever happened. It could've really been only a day, or he could've left more often than I thought. It's impossible to tell." He seems bugged about it.

"So you couldn't move *or* tell how much time was passing. If that's what dying is, then I'm looking forward to it less every minute," I remark and get to my feet, dusting off my jeans. "But really, thanks for the chat. I know it's hard to be honest, especially when it's personal, and when you get down to it, it always is."

"Right. You, um…" But Eli stops himself.

I throw him a smile. "I'm a thief and a liar. How much more honest can I be?" He can't look away until I do. "Alright, get some rest, I'll find someone else to bother. Hey, has anyone seen Voxel?"

The musky coldness in the room thickens when everyone tenses. Without a word, Jacques points the beam of light around the room, but the blue-haired woman is nowhere to be seen. Craw sets down the mug he was inspecting and walks over to his post at the door, giving it a gentle push. It swings open the way it should if someone slipped out and didn't shut it all the way so it wouldn't make any noise.

No, I think, reliving the memory of Tom slipping away from me. *No, this can't be happening again!*

"Wait!" Craw stops me as I take a step out the door. "What're you doing?"

"I'm gonna go get my multitool back," I snap, rolling my eyes. "I've gotta look for her! We can't leave her behind!"

"So much for criminal instincts and survival of the fittest," he mutters, but Motor's already awake and ready to go.

"I'm coming with," the boy pipes, sounding groggy but determined. He's got his goggles pushing his bedhead hair out of his eyes, shining with the I'm-gonna-have-my-way look only someone his age could pull off.

"Agreed. You're not to go alone," Jacques seconds, readjusting his jacket over all the weapons.

"Alright, you're right, nobody gets abandoned in a band," Craw relents, walking out after us, then looks back in the lodge, confused. "Eli? Is he gone too?"

It turns out that Eli's already outside, shutting the door behind him. "No, I'm right here with you. It's about time I figure out what I can do for you people." His eyes flash (again, not just a phrase) when he steps out of the shadow of the lodge. We follow close behind, leaving the safe place in favor of the moonlit, leech-infected valley, deeper and deeper until we disappear from the light, and the shadows swallow us whole.

⇹

"It appears to have had successfulness," Voxel whispers into her beacon, crouching in a tent in the valley. "I have exited the premises. It was the lodge of rock and wooden building materials, in the easternmost lodging location of the island. Did you have successfulness in your quest for lodging and in your endeavor to escape it?"

"Yeah," a rough voice comes from the beacon. "It was on this weird rocky beach, real close to a river going down the mountain thing. Leadhead was so freaked about hunkering down she didn't even notice me go. They're gonna have a fun time trying to get out of her stupid mess when they figure I bailed. If they'll care. Where're you at?"

"I'm taking residence in the valley within one of the cloth pyramids of camping. My beacon is a void-maker with the ability to move, similar to Motor on nerves—any technologies they, and by they I mean Eli, use to discover my location will not find me. And you?"

"Well, I'm in the valley, at least. You're real specific. There's dozens of those stupid tents. What's this about, anyway?"

"This is about a celebration that I did not have, and you were about to lack. It's already many months after my twenty-one and many more after your twenty. We can't afford to waste it."

"You gotta be joking. You're jumping through all these hoops for some stupid birthday?"

"Downward force is not being applied to your chain. I told you, there are gifts to be bestowed, for this is an act I take rather seriously."

A pause. Then, "Fine. I get it. Sorry about being slow on the uptake. I'm coming with gifts too, I guess. Sit tight, okay?"

With that, Spike shoves his beacon in his pocket and keeps moving without a glance back at the four-person army of the remaining Lillian Brigade bearing down on him from behind, the army that marches, slinks, and stumbles toward ours, unaware that these two storms are about to cross paths once more.

- III -

Until Midnight Takes Them

Craw and Jacques both seem to think slopey rock and gravel is fine for walking on, while to me, it's an ice rink. The stupid rocks slip under my feet down the incline, and I fall sideways for about the fifth time. "Fire and brimstone! If this is what Rex has to deal with all the time, I feel sorry for the sucker!" I growl as I clamber to my feet. Motor has to wave his arms around to keep his balance, and even though he still falls over sometimes, he doesn't do it nearly as often as me. But I've got a pride to keep intact, so I keep my arms down and resolve to falling around on the treacherous terrain. It's slippery to Eli too, but he manages to kinda *skate* around on it, using it to his advantage without struggling the least bit, and if the circumstances were more normal, I'd swear he's having fun. The possible night vision may have something to do with it. He was telling us about not being able to find Voxel's beacon earlier, so I'm thinking he's got radar too. This guy's chock-full of surprises. Or maybe he was just commenting about how she didn't leave her beacon behind. Stupid assumptions. Stupid rocks. What the heck is Voxel thinking? What am *I* thinking, going out after her?

The gaps of the valley get steeper and tighter, so we have to walk through the bottom of them. We were at the highest point of the valley at the lodge, and we couldn't see Voxel from there, so that's why we're looking here, yelling her name when one of us gets the urge to. Craw's the one that gets that urge the most, which helps when the curious leeches press too close for comfort, close enough to see into their glistening mouths, and they keep hissing at one another. They really like to look at me.

"You don't think their senses get stronger when they're hungry, do you?" I wonder nervously, remembering how one of these things grabbed me before running off for the tank. By now I've figured out it was choosing Tom over me. Likewise, they start finding interest in Jacques, who glowers back at them. Their hissing picks up when he starts rolling up his sleeves to get some defenses.

"Stop," I warn. "I got them to let me go by throwing my multi away. They seem to like metal stuff for some reason." Craw laments his lost bowie knife with a sigh.

"Then how does the 'river under metal' thing make any sense?" Motor asks.

"I don't know, but I can prove it. Look, does anyone have anything metal they wanna chuck at those things? For science," I add, imitating Vici. Jacques pulls out a broken-looking piece of machinery the size of my little finger, and every blue head in spitting distance turns as he tosses the thing off to the side. Even his throw is beautiful. Whatever the thing was, it never even hits the ground before the things go into a frenzy of tongues and teeth and hissing at one another, fighting.

"Yeah, I think they like metal!" Craw laughs, making them all back away. "You go, freaks, bruise each other black-and-blue—oh, wait, you're already there!"

My brow furrows at that. *Bruise... what's that supposed to remind me of?*

A cloud moves over the moon, covering us with darkness, and all the leeches turn at once, focusing on something ahead of us. "Hold," Jacques says, and for about five seconds, everything in the valley is still.

Then they all start forward at once, chattering.

"What the...?" I scramble after the horde, watching leeches come from every direction, swarming something up ahead. A mixture of cries swells up beyond the hill, and I run harder, freaking out, and I almost get to the top of the hill to see what's the matter when there's a flash of white and red, and the next thing I know, I'm being tackled, and I'm flying through the air for a second before landing in the gravel with something on top of me. Pain shoots through my hip and knee as they take the brunt of the hit, then we roll down the hill, the rocks stinging everything, and I lash out in return with a punch to the face. My hands find ropes to lock on, and they pull until someone howls, kicking at me as we come to a stop at the bottom of the hill.

"Hey, hey, quit fighting like a girl!" he yells, whacking my hand with something tougher than a fist, so I let go, groaning while I clutch my hand close. It fades fast, but still, OW! I fight into a sitting position, prying one eye open to see Rex towering there above me, holding his club in both hands. Squinting at me, he opens his mouth to say something, but I kick out at his feet and knock him over just as Jacques swoops from the hill and plucks the club out of Rex's hands, pinning him to the ground with it.

"*Dang* it, Rex!" Lily roars from the crest of the hill, stomping down it with the wind inflating her viper hood of hair, giving a sort of menace to her beauty. Ivy and Vici and Spike're gone, so Lily's all alone to demand, "What have you done with him, Mouse?"

"Oh, please, I didn't even get any hair out! He's the one that tackled me!" I protest, picking rocks out of my hands and face.

"Not him! What've you done to Spike?"

"Haven't seen him. Now, where've you put Voxel?"

"She's coming up right behind you," Lily says the same way a teacher points out the obvious answer to an obvious question, and I turn around to see Voxel tearing through the valley toward us, her hair sailing out behind her. "Now, quit your lies and tell me what you've done to Spike!"

"What on earth's wrong with him?" Eli asks from the top of the hill, looking down the other side at something before turning back with a look I don't like.

"How should I know? All I know is they started attacking him for no reason!" Lily huffs, but there's worry in her indignation.

My eyes widen, and I take Eli's place at the top of the hill as he runs down the other side. In the valley below, the swarm of leeches is nearly swallowing Ivy, Eli and Spike, Spike most of all. Voxel flies past me, and I'm the next to go, hating myself because I keep getting into all these situations where if I run, then everyone'll hate me, and I don't want to be in that position. This one isn't much better, screaming and grabbing at the gelatinous bodies. They all have the same mind, the same goal, and lash their tongues at Spike. Something weird happens; they manage to rip his jacket off, and they stop attacking for a second to devour the thing.

"WHAT! ALL THEY WANT IS MY CLOTHES? GLITCHING PERVERTS!" he explodes, swinging a fist at one, who moves back as easily as dodging a fly. "I'M GONNA KILL EM ALL!"

"I believe that your current situation renders such a feat impossible," a calm voice says from the hilltop, and the mass hissing stops as all the leeches turn to face the figure in white with steel glinting in the new moonlight at his arms. I look back between him and Spike, who's scowling about the "impossible" thing, and the next time I look at the figure in white, he's grinning a burned and burning grin. *When they break you* … "Oh, I beg your pardon. Does my word choice concern you?"

When the leeches all slowly start forward, the glinting pieces of steel disappear, and the heads all turn back to Spike. "Of course," I breathe. "It's the metal in your clothes. They're attracted to metal!"

"Well, d'you expect me to strip it all off or something? For Pete's sake, you're *all* perverts!" Spike swallows and shuts up when the leeches start pressing in again, making my mind go fuzzy with panic. I back away from the metal guy. "Alright, what'm I s'posed to do?"

Jacques whips the blades out again, and the heads turn. He's keeping them balanced between us, but it's that same fragile balance that you can barely find when you try steadying a fork on the side of a plate, and it's bound to tip sooner or later. "I'll lead them away. There were construction uniforms at our lodge. You are supposed to leave and get a change of attire if you wish to live."

"Oh, like I want any help from you!" Spike snarls, and the blades disappear, and the leeches turn back around, sounding mighty ticked about getting turned around so much.

"I have a feeling you want my help very much, save if you *prefer* to buy the farm, bite the dust, kick the bucket, check out, go to meet the maker, and lie on a bed of lavenders, pushing up daises. Who am I to judge whether or not your pride prevails over your need to survive?"

Spike hesitates even in the face of Death. I would too, knowing what Jacques has up his sleeves.

"Please, go," Voxel begs him.

He huffs. "Alright, fine. Start running."

With a curt nod, Jacques slides the blades out again and floats down the hill toward the mountain, vanishing from sight before I can stop him. Well, better him than me. All the leeches pick his blades to chase instead of Spike's cloth with nowhere near as much metal in it.

"Whaddaya know? It worked. Your lodge's over there?" Spike asks. I nod, not trusting my voice yet, and he sets off in the direction he pointed. We watch until they disappear.

"It was his clothes?" Lily sneers, coming over the hill as me and Eli get Ivy to her feet. "Why would you curse his clothes?"

"Look, I didn't do anything! The leeches like metal, and Spike's clothes all have metal in them," I explain in as low a voice I can manage.

"Oh? Then why didn't they target him before?" Lily challenges, and it catches me off guard.

"Maybe they're like me!" Arms swinging all over the place, Motor manages to make it to the top of the hill from the other side then comes to a stop within spitting distance of Lily. "When I'm hungry, I can smell food really good, or maybe I can just notice the smell better."

"Well, I've never heard of an external input heightening one's senses, but I don't suppose it's impossible," Vici says, jumping out of a nearby tree. Without even wondering what she was doing up in a tree instead of helping us, I start over.

"Vici! Are you okay?" I have to ask for some reason, looking her up and down.

She looks annoyed. "Clearly. What makes you all think that those things want to eat metal if this mysterious 'river under metal' wards them off somehow?"

"I'd think the way they were so intent with the metal jacket and blades gave it away," Eli says from the top of the hill. He's so busy trying to see Jacques or Spike he jumps a little when a surprisingly well-aimed rock gets kicked up to his feet from mine.

"Don't talk to her like that," I defend, and Vici turns her head to the side in a way I know means she's too refined to roll her eyes. Some part of me's aware that every time I see her, it hurts even worse, but then the rest of me wants the hurt to end that much more. I have this sad attempt to have some sort of conversation with her.

The others align themselves into the customary groups, whispering among themselves in the silence the leeches left behind. "Voxel, where did you go, anyway?" Eli asks without looking away.

"I have affiliations with the same gang that Spike has affiliations with, and I didn't want the invisible lines dividing our teams to deter this, so we continued our exchange of information in quiet, where the ringings of your disapproval could not be listened to," she states. It's not a confession because that requires guilt. I listen out of one ear while I continue to attempt contact with Planet Vici. When the horde of leeches is out of sight, Craw suggests we all go back to our lodges, but I don't want to leave my losing battle.

"Wait. Maybe we should search together for the river the riddle was talking about," I say, desperate to keep Vici where I can see her. The Brigade all exchange looks, then Rex steps forward.

"You got a spy, don't you?" he accuses, and now I'm sure he's lost it.

"We had to go west around the mountain to get to the south end of the island, and we found a river with a metal dam going over and around it," Lily says. "None of us even mentioned it, yet you bring such a thing up now. You get more suspicious by the moment, Mouse. This, along with discovering the leeches' taste for metal? It seems you have some sort of insider knowledge. Do you care to share?"

It takes me a second to figure out what she's talking about. When I do, I almost blow up. "Look, I don't have the secrets, okay? I know as much about the race and winning and the extraction point and the leeches and these crazy people here as you do!"

"Again, the locals weren't mentioned, yet you bring them up! How would you know which secrets to claim you don't know unless you knew them?" Boy, that one makes my head spin. "Why don't you admit it already? We won't pry for your precious million-prime information, I just need to hear you say it so I know you're not entirely the lying scum I perceive you to be."

My fists ball up at that even though I'm used to names by now, used to getting compared to scum and other dirty stuff. "You can't pressure me into lying to you and pretending I'm the Outlier to get you off my back. I'm bigger than that."

Lily reaches some sort of boiling point and snarls, "Oh, you're so sure of your valor? Then why don't you tell us about this honestly innocuous dream you had, Mouse?" and pulls out her real, locked-and-loaded gun, pointing it straight at me so every nerve tenses at once, pouring that tingling heat through me, that heat that comes from the chemical reaction of the bonds between me and my self-control start breaking down. My wiser thoughts get fast and high-pitched, so they're harder to hold on to than the darkness that always runs below them.

"First of all, *jack*, let's just put it on the table that your willingness to sling mud about this whole Outlier thing's nothing if it ain't shifty," I scoff, sharp and slow as a twisting knife. She bristles at the westerner insult and her aim at me falters. "And second, I'm not the only one having dreams!"

This time, I don't even think about it *after* I say it, let alone before, but it's not my fault Craw curses in surprise, and it's not my fault Lily pulls out another gun and points that one at him. This time, in my heightened sense, I do catch the look on his face that tells me that they know each other too. Is it betrayal? Does it go away because there's something on Lily's face that says she doesn't mean it, that she's all bark and no bite no matter how many bullets she's got in those guns? Am I safe or not?

"You put those away right now," Eli demands (for the second time—I was too busy freaking out to notice before), but Lily ignores him, all fired up and ready to start pulling triggers.

"So you still aren't as innocent as you'd prefer to be, eh, Nobody? You were the first to ask about the clue with Vastate, and now you're accused of dreaming?"

"Yeah, about a girl falling out of a building! Hopefully it was you!" Craw spits. "I'm as innocent as I wanna be. The rest of you, I'm not sure about. Cuz guess who *wasn't* there when I woke up?"

So it all comes out in the wash.

Lily's face twitches as she connects the dots and makes a guess then shrugs and points both guns at Motor, who almost falls over in surprise. "I don't care who it is, so long as someone coughs up the truth or a few liters of blood."

Behind her, Ivy straightens up, Rex and Craw scrambling away as the doll takes a huge breath like she's coming up from drowning. Life suddenly dominates her eyes, a single-minded, crude, savage and raging life making her face animate with strength and her lips curl up in a vicious snarl.

Every beautiful soul's got an ugly side.

I have enough time to think this and some half-formed thought about Motor's haywiring and Lily's oh-sticks look before porcelain hands lock around her throat.

No more time to think after that. The gun blows, and I hit my knees, hands over my ears, scrambling with my legs, trying to be a smaller target and make it over the hill. Horror slides through me as I realize that Lily's not on my list of problems anymore. Something hot and sticky's sliding down my face from my right hand, and by the time my brain finally lets me admit what it is and what it means, fear's crippled me into a tiny ball on the ground.

When I notice Eli on my level, motionless, my mind flies into action. The other boys are on their hands and feet, crab-crawling away from Motor. Lily's screaming, shrill and afraid, as Ivy strangles her. Eli's on the ground, and Vici's backing away as fast as she can. They all become a blur as I launch forward into space and pull Motor away from the group. Once we get a certain distance away, Lily and Ivy collapse to the ground, gasping for air until Lily shoves Ivy away and scrambles to her feet, waving her guns all over the place. "That's IT, I'm about to—" but we never get to hear what Lily was about to do because she stops when Eli comes up out of nowhere and rips one gun out of her hand then starts going for the other when she staggers back, aiming it at anyone who isn't bulletproof. "Stop, stop or I'll shoot!"

Eli stuffs the gun into one of his pockets, his lips moving silently over bared teeth for a second before he can compose himself enough to explode, "CIELHOMME, you're so STUPID!"

"Rat," Vici and Motor both whisper at the same time, but I already know. I've already felt that sticky blood on my hands and the side of my face. I'm already standing, staring at my hand, wondering if I'm really that unlucky that Lily's wild shot took off the top of my middle finger.

My *middle* finger too. I could use all that right about now.

Suddenly, our ears start drowning in a wave of hissing so sharp it rips my senses to pieces, and I can only turn in a circle with my mouth open as the sea of leeches starts coming out of nowhere. With a desperate look in her eye, Lily starts firing into the crowd, and my eyes lock on her very metal gun. That thing's going to attract even more leeches and get everyone killed. But hey, I'm already bleeding, anyway.

Before Vici and Motor can stop me, I lurch forward, shooting across the barren landscape toward Lily, not wavering even when she aims the barrel straight for me cuz I know she won't fire now. "What're you doing?" she shrieks, so preoccupied with trying to keep the gun out of Eli's reach that I can grab it in both my bloody hands and tear it out of her grasp.

"Saving your worthless life!" I snarl, looking her full in the eye before sprinting away from them as fast as my feet can carry me as I add under my breath, "Stupidest thing I've ever done."

Deep in my heart, honestly, I'm terrified. The monsters rush at me from every side, and I squeeze my eyes shut tight because this is it. I'm gonna die, and I didn't get to say good-bye to anyone. And what am I dying for? Getting the leeches away from the others like Jacques did for Spike? Am I doing it so Vici's safe? Am I dying for a good reason, some beau geste to say that hey, the last thing Rat did wasn't spill the beans about Craw? But who cares? Dead is dead, and with everything I've learned about what Death might be lately, you'd better believe I'm scared out of my wits. Me and Death, we've got this understanding. We don't talk anymore. I don't think It'll be pleased to see me.

Between that and the genius eye-shutting, I slip on this gravel and roll to a stop on the ground, where the hissing overwhelms me. Well! Time for a hopefully-not-last almost-stand!

I scream bloody murder, pulling the trigger over and over without worrying about how much ammo the thing has, firing at every red dot I see as they bear down on all sides, all teeth and tongues. The first one grabs me, and the ammo comes to an end as it pulls me fast toward its spinning, spinning teeth, and on a whim, I kick the thing's tongue near its mouth so my boot almost touches the teeth, which rip into its tongue. With the sound of nails on a chalkboard, it loosens its grip on me. I struggle to break away, but another one wraps a tongue around one of my legs. I'm very good at this, so I get away again, but there's a lot of them, so one gets me again.

Then the newcomer lets go when it gets a marker to the eye, and the first one's grip gets broken the rest of the way when strong hands lock onto mine and pull me away.

I hit the ground in a sputtering heap, barely moving when one of the monsters licks the gun out of my bloody hand. Where its tongue touches my wound, the numbing adrenaline disappears, and pain makes me want to shrivel up and settle my differences with an old chum, but two hands grab either of my arms, trying to get me away. The furious leeches surge forward after me, and they'd probably make an easy meal out of all three of us, but someone else bounds in front of me as a shield on legs. That still ends up making the leeches even more ticked, so they lash forward with their fingers for the first time at all of us. I figure out quick that they aren't just fingers, they're talons, and they rake a neat row of holes in my jeans and the skin on my leg, which only increases their frenzy. I kick with my other leg, and the talons're solid enough to bend and snap, but there's more where that came from.

"BACK OFF!" a new voice thunders behind me, and the leeches screech, scattering in every direction, not really going away but going ballistic, but the yeller keeps going on loud enough that everyone in Hudson Bay probably hears, and he follows behind me as we scramble away, two people holding me up, the protector dashing about, leaping in front of me whenever a leech jerks forward to try and eat me alive. One of their tongues grabs my leg, and I hit the ground, growling in pain as the acidic liquid on their tongue seeps into my bloodstream, lighting it on fire. The other leg has a kicking spree.

"I beg of you, stay your course, we have to get to the lodge!" one of the voices at my side yells, and I almost come close to recognizing these people, but then I fall back into the delirium of pain when they lift me to my feet again. I try to find the will to move my legs, but no matter how bad I want to, I can't even think through this haze in my mind, smothering me along with the hissing. Instinct's all I've got. There's nothing else I can do for the haze of pain, nothing except breathe, breathe, and hope for a miracle.

"Hang on!" another voice joins in. At first, I think another tongue hits my back, but it's too small, too gentle, and it doesn't stick; it loses its hold the first two times before taking a fistful of jacket so it can keep hanging on, pushing me along, giving me one more anchor to keep me tethered on this side of Death's river. "Go, go, go!" the little helper's yelling as a tongue nearly punches my head off, but the attack gets knocked away at the last second by the protector who's done that a good dozen times already. Another blue hand swipes for me, scraping my cheek, but I hardly even feel that anymore on top of everything else, and grinning in madness, I kick my legs in a way that might be running, I don't know, but it helps us go faster. There's still some of the sting left in my consciousness, but only enough that it drives me forward, forward, for what seems like forever, and the thought hits me that this is all I've ever done is run from these things, and it's all I'll ever do, is keep running through this blurry valley under the blurry night sky along the blurry line between disaster and safety, never falling on either side of the line.

That's my third delusion about safety I make tonight.

The pain suddenly comes back (but not in full, so I know acid's faded from my system) with my awareness when the presence at my back disappears, and I hear the sound of pebbles spraying over each other. Then there's a bigger spray, and the huge booming sound that might be some incredibly loud voice I was getting used to stops, and a crash of hissing falls into my ears.

About ten things grab me at once, grabbing a hold of anything they can touch and pulling in all different directions. Nothing I do stops them, and only their own stupid rivalry keeps them from eating me alive. My head whips around, and I search for some light at the end of the tunnel, but Voxel and Jacques, who I figure were the ones at my sides, get swallowed by a sea of black-and-blue, and Motor's sprawled on the ground, Craw with his legs over him, so he must've tripped over Motor, who tripped because—

This time, without the yelling to cover it, I hear the gunfire, and I have enough time to think that Lily got her gun back before I catch a glance of her through the forest of leeches, Death with lead hair and a pistol. A third bullet bites the ground nearby, sending pebbles everywhere.

"Someone stop her!" Eli commands furiously, trying to work his way over to me. He's making a great effort at it too, getting close enough so I can almost reach his outstretched hand, close enough that I can watch full well as another bullet cuts through the sky and scrapes the side of his head with a horrible grating sound.

You'll never guess what material makes him so bulletproof.

There's this one moment of silence and stillness where I swear, the whole world holds its breath and nothing happens at all. It's one of those "oh, sticks" moments that comes before all the sticks hit the saw.

I drop to the ground painfully as most of the leeches abandon me to direct all their best efforts, tongues and talons and all, to try and rip Eli to pieces. They trample all over me, and I curl up, trying to look for a chance to move, but there's no luck for us sinners, and there's nothing I can do but let their rubbery legs stab into my side, my legs, my face, everything, in their mad dash. Above their hissing, the blood-curdling, window-shattering grating sound of talons on steel starts up again, and I just shake in fear and hopelessness. This is it. Eli's going first, and then we're all going to die.

And then, fzzzPOP.

There's another moment of deadly calm, but this one's only a split-second long, closer to the time it takes you to drop your jaw in shock, before the leeches all start their screaming again. They fly out in every direction, making me curl up even tighter on the ground. When the last one's gone, I hear a thud against the rocks then listen for a very long time to my shaking breaths, my pounding heart, and the retreating hissing until there's none of them left to hear.

Every inhale tastes bloody, and every exhale is singed with curses while I wait for the world to make sense or go away.

When it's all gone, I slowly try sitting up, a crushing fear and despair almost keeping me down, or maybe it's that fear that gets me to a somewhat upright position and pushes my eyelids open. I swallow nothing—my mouth's dry as sandpaper. "Eli?" I croak. Motor and Craw look up from their tangled heap, and Jacques and Voxel stagger over from where the horde pushed them down. Eli's on his back, not moving, and I suck down a deep breath and crawl over on my hands and knees over to him. "Eli?"

This time, he pushes himself halfway into a sitting position, holding the side of his head and twitching. His breathing's ragged, and his eyes are shut tight as he presses his hand harder against the side of his head, one of the many places where there's thin gashes in his skin, thin as papercuts, but they show deep ruts left by the leech talons, ruts that were probably dug even deeper by their acidic tongues, ruts that show silver underneath.

"We didn't die," I gasp in an airy chuckle and yank him closer to me in appreciation of life. The two of us wounded victims lean on each other and sit in silence for a second, grateful just to be alive for these precious seconds, before Eli takes a deep breath and pulls his hand away from the side of his head.

My heart stops, I swear.

His hand's covered with a thin layer of glowing green liquid.

A stampede of questions floods through my mind—namely, *you bleed liquid lightning?*—but I settle for one: "Will it heal?"

"It is already," he replies, equally breathless, and I notice the ooze slowly stopping. Right at the spot where the gash cuts in and the little river starts, the liquid's coming out as red, red as blood lit from the inside, before it turns back to green when it hits the colder open air. Of course, it's red when it's warmer;

that must be how his complexion's like ours, well, some of us. Eli wipes the rest of it away, and it fades to static and green mist in his hand. "When it's exposed to oxygen, liquid lightning separates back into electricity and thunder, which is what Jaden called the gaseous compound they use to make the stuff," Eli explains, watching his hand for a second before turning his gaze over at me. "And what about you? Will you heal?"

Without saying anything, I look at my injured hand. The middle finger has a dark, creepy scab covering up the top, and sure enough, when I check my leg, that's scabbed over too. It must be something in the saliva acid, and the fact that Tersatellans heal so fast might help my cause. "I think I'll be okay," I manage, and the other four watching seem to relax a bit. My eyes float over all of them gratefully, and I hope they get the thank-you through that look, because they aren't about to get it in word form. Those last five words caps my limit, and now I think I'll have a little lie-down and pass out for a day or so. Yeah. Oblivion's nice this time of year.

Before I have the chance, though, the crunching of footsteps comes out of nowhere, and the owner demands, "Why aren't you fools in the lodge? They won't be repelled forever!"

Eli's eyes close peacefully again, and I can almost see the thoughts forming in his head. *I am not going to blow a gasket. I am not going to fly off the handle. I am not going to lose it.*

I think he is simply going to kill Lily in the fastest, calmest way you ever saw.

She doesn't even have time to say anything or throw her hands up before he comes up from nowhere for a second time and yanks the gun out of her hands again, this time knocking her to the ground with it, and doesn't even stop pressing the barrel into her forehead when her skull's flat against the rocks. "You feel this? This is metal. Those leeches are attracted to metal and to blood, and with this metal weapon, you chopped off the top of Rat's finger then kept firing every chance you got. You nearly killed every single one of us here. Give me one good reason not to put a bullet through your head right now or so help me, I'll do it."

"What . . . what made all those leeches disappear?" she stammers through gritted teeth. Her eyes rocket around for a safe place to land, but with the rest of us getting up and the others from her team finding their way over, nowhere's safe because everyone's ticked. I stare at her. What did make all those leeches disappear? It happened after the pop, but I thought that came from—

"Incorrect reply," Eli says. "Try again, with logic included this time."

"What made the leeches disappear?" Lily repeats herself, this time meeting all our eyes daringly. "Are you really naive enough to believe in miracles? Or are you just too stupid to know they left for a reason?" She spits to the side. "You want logic?"

"Yes, I do," Eli says with such a mix of violence and pleasantness, it makes me think of a time I watched Vici dip a flower in poison to see what would happen. It didn't end well. It also reminds me of myself, and it makes me smile. Cielhomme, he's learning from *me*.

"What made the leeches disappear?" Lily repeats for a third time. "I did, that's what."

"Oh, sure," Craw mocks hoarsely, rubbing his throat. "Where'd you figure out how to do that?"

Lily's eyes flash, and she smiles in spite of her situation. "I know a lot of things you don't. A database ton of things you don't know, some of which are vitally important. That's why you can't kill me." She laughs to herself. "I'm the Outlier. I know the secrets."

Eli straightens up, keeping the gun trained on her forehead. "You've got to be kidding me," he seethes. Still smiling, Lily shakes her head. I stare at her in a whole new way than before, with more fear since I can't read her like I thought I could, with more hatred for everything she's done and everything she is, and more wariness because now I know if she dies, then our hope and the truth dies right along with her.

"Don't believe for a moment that this marks you untouchable," Jacques growls. "Everyone exhausts their worth in time. Remember that while you keep your silence and refuse to tell us anything, you're as good as dead." To emphasize the point, Eli sets the gun off to the side of her head and now that smile's gone, along with most of the color in her face. She gives a feeble nod and gets to her feet with the rest of us, turning in a circle to watch our crowd glaring at her, and when she doesn't find a friendly face level with hers, she tries to escape, but where she thought there was a gap in our person-wall, there was actually another person.

Lily nearly turns into the second person to trip over Motor in so many minutes, but he tugs on the edge of her sleeve before she runs him over. "Hey, Lily? I know you're probably not gonna tell us anything about the secrets and stuff, but I wanted to thank you, anyway, cuz now people don't think bad thoughts about me, and we're not all suspicious of each other anymore."

Lily moves her mouth for a second with this torn look on her face, which almost softens, but then she tugs her sleeve back and snaps, "I didn't do it for you, brat."

"I know, but thanks, anyway." He steps aside to let the girl stalk past. We all stay behind for a long minute, absorbing the ugly reality until the hissing sound tickles my ears and everyone rushes (read: does a drunk-looking scramble) for the relative safety of the lodge.

When we get in, a lightbulb I didn't know existed or worked gives the room poor light that's still comforting so that once the door's barred (courtesy of some scaffolding), everyone starts settling down at the table or against the walls like the dust, totally spent and ready to flop.

We made it. That's what counts.

"Well, *you're* all a mess," a voice derides as Spike thunks out of the back room with normal jeans and a thick black construction jacket half-zipped over his chest, showing off some fang or claw strung around his neck I didn't notice before. He probably couldn't find a shirt in his size so he had to settle for the jacket. "What'd I miss?"

"We got attacked," Rex says as he looks for Jacques to take back his bat from. "Lily's the old maid, I mean Outlier."

Spike gasps, and his face lights up with a dodgy smile. "Really? Well, if the boot fits! Do we get to torture her for information now?"

"I'll hold her down," Eli volunteers, wearing the same smile, since he was the one who got the torture-threat first. Lily regrets it by now, and she starts backing up with her hands above her head.

"Stop it, all of you! I couldn't confess if I wanted to," Lily says. "I'm under the impression I'll be exempted from the race—hear that as *killed*, smart ones—if I tell you the secrets." Rex rolls his eyes at that.

"If indeed you hold the dark knowledge you so claim to keep in your heart, then would you be so inclined as to tell us how it was revealed to you?" Jacques asks, smooth as silk licked by cats with buttered tongues.

"Blue Lou, you sound so *natural* at it," Lily sighs, and I can tell she doesn't really come close to thinking about it. Yep, so much for our criminal instincts. We're all about as bad with our mouths today as if they're weapons from outer space. To make things worse for Lily, Blue Lou's obviously western, which is the only type of talk she sounds *natural* in, so it's not hard for me to figure out what she's so amazed about. Her ilk's about as smooth as corrugated sheet metal. If only she knew he was an easterner too.

She shakes her head, coming back from blind admiration at Jacques's glorious speech pattern. "Sorry. It was conveyed in a dream, of course." Rex rolls his eyes again—I don't know why he rolls his eyes around so much if his balance's screwy as it is. "But I will remind you this: there is a certain way to win, something you have to do in order to be Champion, and you have to know what it is, so you need me to have any chance at winning."

"Alrighty, then," Craw says, sitting down at one of the tables. "It's not much different now that we know. It doesn't get us anywhere, and there's no use kicking a dead horse, so we might as well leave it alone if you won't talk. I dunno about you guys, but I'm beat." I swear Lily shoots him a grateful look. The others nod, getting more comfortable wherever they're sitting, and nobody says anything after that. I'm not sure if everyone plans on trying to sleep or something, but suddenly, it seems like a great idea.

I watch Voxel for a bit, wondering whether I should talk to her or not, but my brain's gone numb from all the moving, and every speck of me has that heaviness to it that says that if you keep moving, it's going to knock you out so you can't move anymore, so I close my eyes, sinking against the wall, so tired I couldn't really care about anything unless I really, really tried to. Go ahead, let everyone keep their secrets. Just let me go to sleep. And if they try to pull something on me and awareness or Death interrupts, I'll pretend their face is the glitching snooze button. Adrenaline? Ha! Don't even talk to me about it. I am tired. Good night.

We drop out so fast we don't have time to pry about the meeting that started the whole fiasco. When most of us are out, either sleeping or just hovering in oblivion, Voxel gets up to her feet and drifts across the room and plops herself down next to Spike, who's bored into doing thumb wars with himself and is now so entertained that he hardly looks up at her except to say, "Hey."

"Hey," Voxel echoes carefully. "I've finally come in contact with you to speak of the last morsel of our discussion."

"I can see that. Go ahead and get it over with, already."

Voxel takes a deep breath. "Happy birthday, Spike." The deep breath comes out as she relaxes. "Oh, you have more of my gratitude. Now that this has finally lifted from my lungs, I can sit in a state of increased pleasure."

Spike snorts as he beats himself at his thumb war. "Well, you had *one* okay sentence. Thanks, though." Nodding, Voxel labels the wall with her black marker before snuggling against it with obvious plans to stick around, and Spike almost gets up to move, then just sighs and shoves his shades back over his eyes, puts his hands together on his stomach and kicks his feet out on the floor, knocking out with the rest of us.

Most of us, anyway. Craw, Lily, and Vici are asleep at varying tables, Motor's asleep *on* the table, and Rex, Eli, Jacques, Ivy and I are sitting against the walls with different levels of consciousness. A few meters down my wall, Ivy lifts her head to stare, blank and cold, at her sister, who nervously fingers her cuff bracelet and pretends not to notice. It goes on for some time until the doll's eyes shift, and she notices Jacques staring at her, emotionless, and they nod at each other before Ivy goes back to putting her head on her knees and Jacques sits cross-legged with his eyes closed. Either he isn't asleep or he's dreaming, because he twitches every now and then. But finally, even he slowly relaxes until the only movement is the rise and fall of his chest, and in a miracle that would never happen in real life, the room of thieves and hackers and ne'er-do-wells is almost motionless. Almost.

Eli's fingers tap a steady rhythm against his knee as he watches everything without much blinking involved. Even blinking turns into something daunting when there was an age where you'd wait weeks between each time when your eyes would come open. But eventually, only because everyone needs all the energy they can get, he settles down and folds his hands.

Without the rest of her moving the slightest bit, one of Lily's violet eyes graces the room with its observation, coming to a slow stop on Eli. "You think you got a soul for anyone to take?" she whispers, and purple clashes hard with green.

"What makes you think I don't?" Eli whispers back.

Lily shakes her head slightly. "They can make artificial intelligence, but people can't make life so easy. You. Are. Fake. Faux, false, you're nothing but a machine behind a facade, computerized data in a tin can with a lying label slapped on it, and you won't admit it, and I can't stand it."

"Why don't you tell me more about you and Ivy before judging how human I am?" Eli growls, and the doll girl picks her head up to stare at Lily, who shoots her a complicated look, so she sets her head back down on her knees without a word. They both hold on to their matching bracelets without even noticing.

Lily opens her mouth to say one more thing, but a voice scratchy enough that it's not even recognized says, "Hey, Outlier, stop being a hypocrite and mind your own damn business."

There's a guilty and nervous tension, nervous about the real swear, guilty about getting caught talking. Lily drops the conversation, burying her head in her arms again, leaving Eli alone to finish his prayers and go to sleep, eyes still open and fingers still tapping, patient and relentless. There is a hint of a smile on my face. It is not nice.

As the minutes start passing along, I float in and out of sleep until I give in and unlock my watch and rub the steel wool bracelet against my fingers until the void of blackness comes takes me. This fuzzy thing that might be a dream floats through my mind. In it, I think I'm standing on some sort of raised thing, maybe a stage or the top of a building, and there's this huge crowd around me. I can hear it and feel it more than see it, and for some reason, I'm waving at them, and I get this impression I've been doing it for a while in that distant, dreamy sort of way. Then people start jumping off the roof, people who come out of nowhere and go nowhere, so this crowd starts jeering, harder and louder. They push forward toward me, and I cover my face for some reason as the jeering turns into hissing that smothers my screaming as I get swallowed by a sea of black-and-blue.

I jerk awake, panting, and then sit there for a couple of seconds, still high on the panic, before slamming my hands to the sides of my head against the awful, sharp ringing in my ears I woke up with. It feels like it's coming from my head because something this bad *can't* be real, but it gets muffled by my hands, so it's gotta be coming from outside. It sets my teeth on edge, and I press my hands harder against my ears as the frenzied screech gets louder and louder. *Leeches*. Some of the others're waking up now and looking around with the same what-in-the-name-of-fire-and-brimstone-is-going-on-out-there look I must be wearing, and Rex, annoyed as ever, opens his mouth to get it verbal, but he gets interrupted by a familiar voice:

"Y'ALL GOTTA BE KIDDING US!"

Everyone who wasn't awake flies back into consciousness at the roar of a chainsaw cutting through this pair of doors the same way they did the first, but this time, we're not trespassers, and we stagger together and stand clustered as we wait for the doors to get kicked in, but it doesn't. Instead, the one to the right swings open, and a young man with Revany's same love of camo swaggers in, all decked out in a neat suit, hair gelled down, and a smoking stick hanging out of his mouth. He takes it between two fingers so he can say, "These are they who trespass on North territory, surely?"

Revany slinks out from behind him, looking over us. "Every one of em."

"What's the deal?" I demand, stepping forward. "You said the east and south ends of this place're abandoned! We're not doing anything wrong."

"Oh? You do nothing immoral, but incorrect and unwise, ah, that is another type of wrong that you do so happen to find yourself in," the young man says, pulling in a breath through his cylinder thing. His voice shimmers with an accent I don't recognize.

"Who're you, and what'd we do wrong?" I ask, crossing my arms. "I'll have you know you woke me up by freaking out the leeches, by the way."

The young man smiles a wolf's smile and twirls the stick in his hands. "My apologies, lass. My nom de guerre is Ripvan Remington, according to the state of being that teammates share surnames adopted from those of the keepers who once guarded these lodges when they did belong to prisoners, though the sense of kinship is not fabricated, for we all share the same condition of mind that makes elsewhere places push us away, that states that we are not prisoners here but players. Your wrong lies in not becoming one of us."

"Rev offered y'all a spot on the team!" Revany yells through gnashed teeth. "We coulda worked together against the Crazy Crew, and y'all coulda got the immunity, but now y'all're against us! Well, now Rev hopes that all y'all ignoramuses die off, same as half the last batch."

I store the information about immunity for a second and ask about the last batch. Ripvan angrily crunches the smoking stick in his fist. "They come ashore," he narrates, "afraid and beaten and broken. Half of them wish to convene—others lack trust and go their own way. Some on either side die from their foolishness, which causes them to be eaten, and the others survive from either our assistance or their wit. Our team wins because of them. Not the Remington team. When I first come to this island, my loyalties fell to Elyssandra Stroud, as the Strouds are the true owners of the northern lodge before the Cantrells take over the island only to abandon it, but new lead rises there as Elyssandra, our greatest player, is taken down for ten points. Nobody notices until it is too late that one of the Fillers are missing, and the outcast steals the prize, while others resort to treachery in their hunger to win what he has already taken."

At the second mention of this prize thing, my curiosity reaches a point where I can't ignore it anymore. "What's the prize?" My question makes Ripvan's head tilt up, and he holds out the smoldering remains of his black stick.

"The prize," he says, "is twenty vials of air. But not just any air. This air, when the vial is burned, turns into a solid, and when you light the end of this solid black air on fire, it burns, and the smoke keeps the Bruises at bay."

So the Bruises they're talking about are the leeches! And this stuff makes them go away! That must be what woke me up—they were screaming and running away from the smoke.

Do you know what that means? That means that if we play their stupid Tag thing and we win, we can be totally free of those crazy leeches tomorrow. Which means that playing and winning is now top priority.

And I thought of all that within five minutes of being woken up.

Lily looks at the crumbling remains in his palm for a second before stepping forward. "Let me take a look at that," she orders, flicking up her power meter, so Ripvan doesn't move as she examines the black powder. "Yes, it's the same material. My guns run on gunpowder, and I was running out when I found this powder at our lodge and put it in. I'm under the impression that's why they all fled when I fired."

"Then how come it didn't do that until we almost got back here?" I snap, *so* ready to make her an idiot in some way or another even though I've got no idea how guns work and if some of them really need powder or how she could manage to somehow find a proper substitute when she's the one who went looking for food in a stove.

"Since it was still using the gunpowder instead of this stuff up to that point, smart one. Why don't you think before you talk, Mouse?"

"I've never heard of a gun that works that way," Vici says, frowning.

"Well, our market is vintage and far-fetched, so the general populace being unaware of it is exactly the point. But I used all of it, the black stuff, I mean, so it's all gone." Lily puts on her own frown as the little pile lets out a puff of smoke. She bends closer to it, taking a sniff, and suddenly keels over, gagging. "UGH! It smells as bad as—"

Before she can finish, the lightbulb above our head picks up brightness out of nowhere until it's blinding. I stare up at it, feeling strange. It starts screaming along with the bursting pipes in the walls and the electric tools around us. Screws fly out of their places, pelting us, and outside, the track flares up and goes berserk. My insides all get this one huge itch or something that's so bad it's painful.

"What the heck's going on?!" I yell, diving for cover as all the tools run themselves to pieces, flinging their bolts and stuff at us along with the screws and stuff. Then they start popping and dying one by one until the lightbulb explodes, and I don't mean the popping kind; I mean a full-on explosion. Most of us scream in panic, while a few brave souls leap out and smother the flames until the room is washed in a powerless darkness that seems so absolute I can't help but think that whatever that was ended the world as we knew it.

Everyone's coughing and choking on all the dust that was raised in the explosion. When we struggle out from behind our bunkers (read: more table-shields and some scaffolding), Eli's holding his head, and Ivy's staring at her sister with the biggest eyes she can manage. "What? I didn't do that! Look at the little brat!" Lily spits, getting to her feet, but Motor shakes his head so hard it's a wonder it doesn't fly off.

"No, it wasn't me! It was probably a backup generator that was busy powering this place til some leech knocked it over or something! I'm not even strong enough for something that big," he insists, which relaxes me since I can have some pretense that that thing was something normal. Then Voxel moans for our attention as she pulls herself to her unsteady feet to take away that pretense.

"Cielhomme! I saw it! The energy... it was a wave of energy being broken across this island and the Bay of Hudson from the direction of north, drowning us all present here before my very seeing organs!"

Ripvan suddenly looks at her with new eyes / seeing organs, blown away. "You are insane," he breathes reverently, turning it into the best compliment in the world. Voxel looks him up and down and flattens her clothes under his scrutiny.

"It does not do to call people crazy," she tells him with an edge to her voice.

He looks at the rest of us less approvingly, abandoning the energy wave thing. "The rest of you have not a chance to receive the prize. It is only worthwhile to the senile. Even if you wish to make your own teams, it is not in allowance—unstable minds only here on Fort Night. You have to be mad to commit yourself to the game we've cut ourselves off from the outside world for. It is too late for you."

I try and think of something to say to that, something about how we've cut ourselves out already and how we've already given our lives to one big, true Cops and Robbers game, but I don't have to. Jacques steps forward for me, and he's got that look in his eye that he wouldn't show before.

"And what leads you to the assumption that one mind in this room is stable? It matters not how sound one appears, for the deeper a scar is buried, the deeper it wounds. Each of us here has been cut out from welcome society, and it has been cut from us, deemed us lower than beasts when we rejected not only the Plexus but reason and virtue as well. To the rest of the world, we have no sieve, and therefore no life, no conscience, and therefore no mind. We are inhuman. We are cutouts and criminals, a combination that renders us black-heart one and all. We are the very definition of unstable."

The rest of us flinch away from thinking about our extractions and what they cost and what we've chosen to turn into since, but Jacques plows on.

"I cannot speak for the others, but as for myself, six years ago, when I had to abandon everything I had ever come to know and love for the sake of breaking free with stress not on the freedom here but on the breaking, I spent nigh three years brewing the perfect storm. Every minute of solitude and hatred became another dagger of lightning driving the wound deeper into my mind, and I embraced what I was and struck back. The time came for the storm to pass, when the pain could ultimately be shared, but alas, that shoulder has quit my side, and this storm has returned to me, as I could only elude it for so long."

He takes a moment to clench his fists tightly at his sides, a familiar sight that makes me think that he really is speaking for me.

"Now this storm threatens to consume me, and I shall be taken up in its fury with only the power that a lone sailor has to ride from a maelstrom. And I dare say that none whosoever walks this world is exempt from those adamant winds of Fate, that every one of us sails this storm-wrought sea without control of its tides. Its impending waves are never far from washing our skins with its madness until our very spirits are extinguished. And for every taste of that disaster, these spirits will twist themselves beyond recognition to conceal that pain, so that none that stand in this room are more than a shadow of the person they were hitherto, shadows holding knives and firearms and grudges and torches destined to die to darkness." Jacques puts his arms out at his sides to gesture to all of us, cutouts and pariahs who've been abused too long to have much sanity left. "Where, now, are your stable minds, Mr. Remington?"

Ripvan's mouth moves soundlessly for a second. Then he shakes his head. "It's still too late."

"Late? I've not yet heard the tolling of the midnight bell. There is still time ere the game, and we who turn vice into sport in mad attempt to flee our own shadows are fast determined to play."

Ripvan backs up slowly, his eyes flitting to each of us in turn, cornered. He seems even smaller in the dark that was caused by the power surge, though the rest of us aren't affected in the slightest.

"No odd numbers," he finally growls. "Either there are two teams or four. That decision is yours to make. Join up or split up against us. When everyone is where they need to be, the registration panels come up out of the floor at the far end. It poses a riddle that only the basket cases can answer. The answer is not a word, it is a shape, and you only get one chance. Get deluded or get excluded." The two in the doorway give each other a glance, look over all of us, and step out at the same time, shutting the doors behind them. I jump in the sudden blackness. The windows are so bad you can't see a thing in here until Jacques twists on his flashlight. Nobody notices Eli let out a sigh of relief.

"You heard the man!" Lily snaps, marching for the doors. "Come on, let's get to the other lodge, teammates."

"But the leeches!" Rex protests.

"Are you bleeding or metal?" He shakes his head, the dreadlocks hitting his shoulders making an actual sound. "Then you have nothing to fear," Lily concludes, holding back some insult about his hearable hair, and the others on her team follow her out the door, Ivy shutting it behind them.

"Nice knowin' ya. Okay, guys," I start. "We're gonna have to win this weirdo play thing if we want to keep the leeches away. I wish we knew a little more about this! What'd Lily think that stuff smelled like? What was with that energy surge? And how're we supposed to play, anyway? Who's heard of Tag with points?"

"We might as well be coming here all over again," Craw says, kicking some scaffolding in frustration. "We've got no idea what we're getting into, just that the prize is nice so we've gotta get qualified, and hopefully the rest'll get explained from there."

"We haven't qualified yet—the others have to get back to their lodge in time fast enough for all of us to play. With Rex, it could take hours," I add, all tongue-in-cheek even though I'm actually worried.

"They've a score of minutes ere the witching hour," Jacques says as he sits at the table, and we all turn to look at him for a minute, thinking about that amazing speech about proving us crazy—or more accurately, proving us blackheart.

Voxel, who was inspecting the back of the room for the panel Ripvan mentioned, tells Jacques, "You are poetry, my friend." He glances up, and in the darkness, I can barely glimpse some measure of the loss he's trying to hide, and his shard of honesty stirs me, so I walk over and sit next to him, not saying anything, but here for him, for whatever happens. I'm not good for much, but it's the look of the thing that counts, I guess.

Motor hops onto the table in front of us. "Hey, we're no replacement for flesh and blood, but we're here for you, buddy. Okay?" Jacques nods. Craw, Voxel, and eventually Eli all come over and sit down too, and yeah, it's no replacement for flesh and blood, but it's closer to the real feel of it than I ever got.

Craw snorts and smiles bitterly after a bit. "Sorry. I was thinking … They should've let us into this psycho Tag just cuz we were crazy enough to show up in this stupid bay! What were we thinking? It's all so crazy. No rules, no help, no certainty in sight. Man, now that I really think about it, we didn't have any idea what we were signing up for, did we?"

I shake my head. "No. And the worst part is, it's nowhere near over yet. We haven't even been here twelve hours. We're just getting warmed up."

He looks over at me. "Aw, c'mon, you couldn't even have done the 'this isn't over, it's just getting started' thing?"

I make a face. "Do I look like a thespian to you?" I ask with such sass it gets some chuckles.

"What does that even mean?" Motor cries, throwing his hands out in exasperation and posing on his knees.

"Check a mirror, Hamlet," I tell him because we could spend the next score of minutes in thoughtful despair over our lives, or we could spend them glancing at each other with shining eyes, trying not to laugh, feeling closer by the second. It's awkward and fragile because the situation's bleak, and we just awkwardly fumble from place to place with these random people, and we hardly know one another, especially me. I make it a point not to be known. But we try. Craw tells a funny story about a round of Sacrifice he played once, Motor tells a tall tale from his school, Voxel says something really odd and we get a hoot out of it. I make sure to catch Eli's eye at one point. He slips me a grateful smile. And so we do not wait in darkness in every sense of the word.

⟴

"—So I had to call in a horde of goblins to beat him up," Motor finishes with a nod. "Hey, what's wrong, Voxel?"

The woman in question looks up. "Mm? Oh. It's…" She scowls. "What the so-called madman spoke from his bad mouth. As if, er, mental unbalance is a good thing."

"Right? So fricking rude!" I agree. "One of my old gangsters—the guy came straight from Joanndu, carried a sword, wedged a 'la' into every paragraph, I swear he could steal the teeth from your mouth if you weren't paying attention, brilliant, just brilliant—he had an identity disorder, and after getting cut out to stop it when the meds didn't work, I was the only one he'd talk to about it. I mean, everyone's so carefree with the whole 'crazy' thing, and okay, that's fine, but there oughta be a line somewhere, you know? Sure, go ahead and risk your life and joke about it being insanity, we were fine with that, but hey, you start going around, making a game out of it, just know you're being a cretin, alright?"

Yeah, so much for making a point about not being known. The others share in one glance that make them realize that they've all been sharing up these bits of their lives, and here's me, being more of a nobody than Craw. There's a reason. I don't got the guts to spill. I pretend not to notice them.

"So," Craw starts, all innocence. "Just curious. When were you last in a gang?"

I think ahead because I know where this's going. "Almost four years ago. I got them all out of the way within about two years of being cut out. I was going for a record, went through twenty-five of them."

"Is that a lot?" Eli asks. Meanwhile, the others could not look more shocked if I told them I had twenty-five puppies and they all got sick and died in my arms.

"Hey, what'd I tell you about making me out to be a thespian?" I tell them, pointing a finger. "It's a lot, but I was young and bored and people had cool stories, so I traveled in search of them. Um... I kinda like to listen," I admit. "My life's divided into thievery and tedium. That's all there is to know. You're all pretty great."

As they look around at one another with smiles and wonder about my testimony, I tell myself, *Well, at least the last sentence wasn't a lie.*

⇹

Craw's halfway through explaining one of his wilder dreams after talking about the one he had last night (we've dissected it and come up with no meaning, but this one about a sock and a sentient throw rug is entertaining) when there's a sound. We all jump as one of the moldy boards of wood on the floor groans into the wall, and everyone turns to look.

A weird thin podium shoots out of the ground, a square panel the size of a dinner plate folding out of the top before it angles itself forward so it's not staring up at the ceiling. "Good, the Brigade made it," I say, getting up. The six of us run over as the screen blinks to life.

"So it's gonna have to be a shape? We're probably supposed to draw it on the screen," Motor says as black letters start making a box around the edges of the panel, so I have to tilt my head to read them.

"I could possibly get inside of its workings to either allow us in or uncover the answer," Voxel offers.

"How much time would that take?" I ask.

Voxel shrugs. "Ten thick minutes?"

I look at Jacques, who seems to have some way of telling time without needing a watch (it's too dark to see my Rolex). "And how much time do we have?"

"Five thin minutes."

"Alright, we're going to have to do this the real way." I bite my lip and can't help but think that Vici'd probably be able to do this the easy, surer way. She probably *is* doing this the surer way. Jacques has a hopeless look, and I guess Tom would be able to do this too, since he was the one with all the tech-knowledge. Voxel's just as frustrated with herself, Eli's right there with her. Even Motor's got his arms crossed because according to his stories, he's a hero who can do anything. Craw's the only one who looks normal, but he's more used to doing things the hard way, the real way.

While I wait for the letters to stop forming on the panel, I jealously wonder how it felt to get to *choose* "freedom" over the good life. Then the words reach back to the first corner and stop, and we lean forward to read them:

I'M THE ARROW IN YOUR EYE
I'M THE SALT IN YOUR TEARS
I'M THE ANGEL IN DISGUISE
I'M THE DEMON IN YOUR EAR
I'M THE PAIN THAT YOU PICK
I'M THE DEVIL THAT YOU CHOOSE
I'M THE MONSTER IN YOUR SKIN
AS YOU TIE MY NECKLACE NOOSE
WHAT AM I?

"You're song lyrics, first of all," Craw huffs, annoyed. "Those're the lyrics in 'Necklace Noose' by Spoon Carnival, except the whole 'what am I' thing at the end. That's all I know about it, though, not what it means." That makes me frown. Tersatellus has always been able to take info from the outside world, from Chuck Norris to who's at war with who, even though that's all Adamantration stuff. But Tersatellus never gets outside its Divide. That's always been its pride and joy, is that it takes in everything and gives nothing away. But hey, poetry's always had a funny way of defying boundaries, right?

"It's a shape," Motor reminds us, scratching his invisible beard in thought. "The words make a box. Maybe it's a square?"

"It can't be that easy," Eli says. "It could be a triangle, for the arrow, and because there's the urban legend of demon tails ending in triangles, right?"

"Or it could be a circle," Voxel muses. "Angels wear circle halos, and a necklace and a noose are all very much circles."

"We may as well scribble all over the panel in ilk of the madmen we claim to be." Jacques sighs, backing up. "This is impossible."

The word rings in my head and makes me think of more than one person who's got an allergy to the impossible. My eyes close for a second as a thought starts going, and when I open them again, I look at everyone in turn. They're still confused and frustrated but not showing it, because it's the wounds that cut the deepest that we cover the most, and each of us here knows someone who should be able to do this or someone who they should be able to do it for. And I get the feeling we all know the answer, we just don't *know* we know it yet—you don't know until you know. Yes, we all feel that necklace noose, binding us close to someone so they could be our anchors, whether that's good or bad, whether they're keeping us from going ballistic or drowning us alive under a stormy sea.

Something so sustaining can also be so destructive... It can bind people to themselves and to each other as easily as ripping them apart.

Without me noticing, my hand wanders up to my necklace, and I pull the little half emblem in front of my face, and I stare at it, breath caught in my throat when the realization suddenly hits me at full force. A bitter, reckless smile crawls onto my face as I look at all the frustrated people around me, brightening as I drop the half emblem and take a step forward. Under my finger, what's white on the screen goes black, but it's drawing, not going dead, and nobody tries to stop me as I use our one chance on a whim. My finger goes up in an arch, curves back down, comes to a stop at the bottom, then mirrors its way back up.

A heart. Because Ripvan was right—the answer is something that only crazy people would know, because only we are the only ones who feel this way about the answer, the only ones crazy enough to hold on to something that hurts us so bad. Because the answer is our love.

The screen goes blank, and everyone jumps a bit. My own heart's skipping beats left and right, freaking out because what if I got it wrong, or worse, what if I really did break the thing? But I luck out for once, and the screen gets more letters that spell out YOU HAVE BEEN ENTERED TEAM NAME HERE with a line at the bottom.

"Rat, you did it!" Motor cheers, dancing. "We get to play Tag!" He starts drawing our team name on the line.

"Cielhomme, I couldn't even figure out what it was saying when it wasn't a riddle," Craw frowns. "Some commas'd be nice."

"Regardless, it is done," Jacques says, solemn as a statue as the panel slides back into the ground.

Voxel's patting me and Mo on our heads in excitement. "I congratulate us for climbing the hill of victory after wearing the sad shoes of woe to this point of our second qualification in strange plays!"

"And not a moment too soon." The last one of us turns his bright-green eyes to the windows, and the rest of us follow his gaze, and the whole world seems to turn and watch. I feel it first, buzzing in my bones and in the base of my skull. The funny thing is, my watch beeps sharp and high before it happens, bringing our nervous impatience to a fever pitch until the clock finally strikes twelve, and midnight is upon us.

- IV -

Disclosure

"Where's that coming from, anyway?" Craw asks, and from the look on his face, I get the nagging suspicion he's worried my Rolex is as crazy as the rest of us.

Eli walks across the room and opens the door, sticking his head out. "It seems to be coming from the mountain. There's a bell moving on it, so I guess it doubles as a sort of clock tower, but without the clock."

"Hallelujah!" Voxel throws her hands up in the air. "An answer that is straight and narrow! After strange beasts of spinning appetites and strange kicking down of doorways and strange energy waves and strange plays with no explanation in the distance of sight or spit, such oddities are parodies of normality so that the real thing is pressed close to looking untrue!" Okay, her dialect's starting to bug me, but I get her point. It's nice to get a real answer about something for once. And you know what? They keep coming, whether we like it or not.

"Hello, Band?" Vici's voice suddenly throws itself in the room, and I perk up, but it's just from Eli's beacon. "We've got Rip and Rev over here making sure we don't cheat. As in, they're telling us the rules of this Tag thing. The other team's coming over to give you the lecture, so I suppose we've finally caught a break. We're getting some structure around here."

"So they made it too," I muse, grateful and on edge at the same time. If they beat us at this Tag thing, then I can't get immunity to those leeches, and if you think I'm not about to do everything in my power to not get attacked again, you're dead wrong. I'll steal the prize right outta their mouths if I have to, but I like the idea of winning too. "Who figured out the riddle for your team?"

Since I forgot about how these beacons work for a second, Eli has to repeat my question, and then there's a pause. "I did," Vici eventually says. "Rex remembered it was a song, so I looked up the lyrics and what they meant—there's a better Plexus connection here. Yes, we were pressed for time, so my team knows about me now, so I might as well tell the rest of you that I have some remnant of the mainframe left in me, and it allows me limited access to the Plexus."

It's so sudden I don't have time to stop her, and everyone in the room's eyes widen, ranging from amazed to untrusting.

"Listen, it's trivial right now. We're all strange, remember? The thing is, the lyrics weren't the only things I figured out from my trip to the Plexus. Remember that energy surge? It messed up nearly all of northern and eastern Tersatellus.

Everyone's freaking out because it came from outside the walls—from the north of Hudson Bay. They think it was some sort of attack, and they don't know why it happened, but Vastate is furious. It could be because it disrupted the *perfect* Plexus big time, and he's scrambling to fix it, while Tersatellans are having adverse effects. It could be because he knows exactly who's in northern Hudson Bay right now. Either way, our situation has officially worsened."

"Great, throw another log in that fire," Craw says, kicking some scaffolding. "And if Requiem's got anything to tell us, it's that Vastate is *not* the guy you wanna tick off." Me and Voxel go tense and nod.

"Who's Requiem?" Motor asks, and we all look at him in disbelief.

"You mean to express a lack of knowledge on top of the overbearing folktale of Requieminor?" Voxel cross-examines. "What other legends are you ignorant of? The Kill Switch? The Porcupine? Switcheroo? Sasquatch? Here, allow me to set it all straight."

"Don't tell him!" I snap, still blown away. That someone could not know.

Requieminor is the second-biggest childhood shock kids get (right behind learning that people die)—figuring out the man in white and gold who takes away the hurt isn't as nice as you think he is can get pretty dramatic. Requieminor's just the first of the dozens of people Vastate's razed when they oppose him. Layla Kael would be an example of a Req, as we call them. Most of the Reqs are cutouts that start trying to redefine Tersatellan life or turn citizens into circuit breakers or even cutouts, but they all have this in common: they go against Vastate, Vastate tries to change them with words (read: threats), and if that doesn't work, he sends in his rapture men to kill the Req and anyone close-by, then make their residency a crater to build something else on, and everything else they owned gets destroyed or examined and confiscated.

A while ago, we conveniently started calling that being Requed because it started with someone called Requieminor, and do we make fun of that name, you ask? The answer would be yes, we do. But the smiles are hollow and go away when the story starts. Like Kill Switch, who came years later, nobody really likes to talk about it in public, even though they have this unspoken admiration for the victim, who was still pretty young. Requieminor was just a cutout kid, a faulty citizen who was smart and wanted to go far but didn't realize when far became too far. Some people say that Requieminor *is* the Kill Switch, but it's all hearsay, I promise. The reality was a landmark case because people kinda liked Requieminor before his tragic, gruesome demise that involved a scrapyard and rusty knives and the convict's death coming last, after the relatives were killed first before his eyes, and he suffered long and hard. Strangely enough, it was for the same defiance that Vastate erased the Kill Switch for: allegedly, average crimes that both got wrapped in terrorism. But unlike the Kill Switch, it had live coverage all over the Plexus, so people got to watch Requieminor get shot down and left to die even though he told the rapture men not to record it.

Point being: don't make the Razor mad.

"At least we'll have Adamantration immunity when we get back," Spike says through the beacon, and from his tone, I get the feeling his cash prize will also go toward building an arsenal for defense.

"We have to get out of here alive, first," Eli reminds us. "We still don't know what *caused* that energy wave, and if it came from the north of the bay, then that's too close for comfort." I walk over and look out the window of the door, wondering what else there is out there I can't see, what else is going wrong. This time, no answer comes.

"We've seen nothing in this northern region that could provide anything near the amount of energy required to so affect Tersatellus," Jacques points out. "So there's little chance this was any casual accident."

By now, Eli's really got the timing down with the button on the beacon for us to talk to the other team with so it's almost a real conversation, but Vici hardly lets Jacques finish talking before she says, "That means someone was probably storing up a *lot* of energy for something highly suspicious. The wave was huge—either it really *was* an attack, or someone was planning for one, and it went wrong."

"That's a pretty hostile assumption," Eli comments.

"Well, I don't think Hilda's saving up a stockpile of liquid lightning to replace her candles for whacked lightbulbs," I point out.

"I'm just saying that I don't think she's got electrodetonation missiles, either." I shrug, not about to admit I'm wrong, and the air starts tightening with the smell of an incoming altercation with no purpose except to blow off steam about not knowing the answers to anything that matters anymore.

"Requieminor is a funny name," Mo says quietly, coming from left field, but hey, it'll get us just as far as launching into my upcoming argument about some seven-syllable word I've never heard of before.

"It's one of the common naming things some parents do," Craw explains. He picked up on the things-are-about-to-get-ugly vibe, so Motor's distraction is welcome. Facts don't get angry. "You know, same way most Tersatellan surnames are just words or words with vowels thrown in there, they've got methods for forenames even today—they either pick something normal that already exists, or the other option is usually to take a word and throw any letter they want at the end, chop parts of the word out or mash two words together. They call that a bridge name, and they do it with words, too, cuz people're that original—the Adamantration is a bridge between adamant and administration, though there's a story behind that. Requieminor is a mix of requiem and minor, which is a pretty dark combo if you ask me." Not to mention it sounds pretty whacked.

Motor thinks about it. "Then is Erratica really erratic with an A?"

Everyone looks at me, and it takes me a good three seconds to remember my name, and when I do, I shrug. "Yeah, even before I was cut out, I knew it was weird, and people would just call me nicknames."

Everyone stares at me for that, for casually throwing out something about my life and name, which is supposed to be real personal. I do it to get their attention away from Jacques, who's gotten all interested with the window since Macabreak is a bridge name for macabre and break.

Our quiet gets broken up when he steps away from the window and motions that someone's coming, so we break out into that unfocused susurration again as some creepy sound of laughter rises up in the distance, the kind of laughter that only really old people're capable of. It's almost as unnerving as the hissing, and I swallow, but I wait by the door anyway to meet our rule bearers and figure out what I'm supposed to do so I don't have to face the hissers again.

The door jerks open fast, but it doesn't fly in all the way, just wide enough for a wrinkly jack-o'-lantern of a head to pop in, with huge glowing eyes and this absurdly wide grin. They say "Boo!" and start cackling again while they let themselves right in without any invitation.

She—I'm pretty sure it's a she—she's shorter than I am with her stooped back, and she keeps on those wide eyes and smile all the time, like she just told us a great punch line and she's waiting for us to get it. There's not a strand of hair on her head, nothing but a red cap jammed on there to cover the baldness, which almost adds to her fierceness. Cielhomme, no wonder they always lose! "Um, salut?" I ask, raising my voice since I assume she's part deaf or something.

"Hello!" she yells back between fits of laughter. "Who're you?"

"We're the Filler people, and we've come to be a part of your nightly play," I explain, gesturing to the others behind me, who look less and less sure of this plan every second. This was supposed to be a game of Tag, not a fossil hunt. "We want to know how to win so we can get the immunity."

"Oh, no," a small voice groans behind her. "More players, less chance of winning."

Giggling up a storm, the dinosaur puts a finger to her lips at me and shuts the door behind her. It's not locked or anything, so of course it easily gets pushed back open by the other person outside. He trudges into the room with his head down so his thick hair covers his eyes, but even in the dark, I can see tear tracks running down his face. The boy comes to a slow stop with his hands in his pockets behind the lady, sniffling every second. He comes up to about my ribcage and looks hardly older than Motor.

"What's his problem? And what're you so happy about?" I have to ask for some reason.

"I'm Melodi Verto!" the crone likewise finds a need to say something random. "This is Harmoni Verto Wescott Stroud, traitor boy of Elyssandra! His problem is juvenile sadness, and my happiness is elderly elation, and I made both of those up!"

"I am held captive by amazement. Consider my breathing arrested. Now, could you please pour forth words of instruction and not jubilation? The whole night isn't available to be spent so frivolously," Voxel huffs.

Melodi laughs some more. "Oh, but young'un, you've got to stop and smell the roses sometimes! That's a good one, smell the roses!"

Craw palms his forehead. "Cielhomme! Quit it with the laughing already! It's not funny anymore!"

When she just stares at him with a vacantly pleased look, I stop him from palming her own forehead in a violent way called slapping before I turn to the bag of bones, squaring my shoulders and putting on my cheesiest grin. "*Hey*, friend! Are you ready to have some real fun tonight?" Melodi bares her toothless gums even harder in what I hope is still supposed to be a smile. "Because I sure am! But my problem is, I don't know how, but I really, really want to, and I was hoping you'd help me out! It'd *really* make me happy."

She kind of sways back and forth for a few awkward seconds, and I *really* don't think she heard me until she lifts up her arm to point at something. I turn, letting the stupid smile off my face, and notice a metal box sitting where the panel stand used to be. Eli gets there first (quelle surprise) and pulls off the top, holding up some sort of offspring between a plastic squirt gun and an assault rifle. "Taggers!" Melodi squeals, clapping her hands together.

"It's easy," an incredibly sober young voice says, and we all turn to look at Harmoni, who's lifted his head up, at least. He pulls out his own tagger for a demonstration, and a pellet explodes against the wall behind me with a POP. "You shoot people. One person starts out as It, but nobody knows who, not even It does, and whoever gets shot by It turns into It. Whoever's It at the end of the play loses five hundred points for their team and the team with the most points by six early wins. But when the sun rises, the islands get power again, and the defense kicks in and zaps the prize into acid, so the winner has to get it fast before that happens."

"Well!" I sigh, relieved. "You're right, that does sound easy!"

"And it gets even funner with everyone trying to rip you to pieces!" Melodi cackles. "Come on, come on, we're wasting moonlight! Nobody's allowed to shoot or slice in the bases, and it's no fun that way."

As if to emphasize the point, a chainsaw screams somewhere far away along with the rising sounds of hissing. Everyone in the Band looks at one another in a silent message that we almost forgot that this's war. But I grab a silvery tagger and head for the door, anyway, taking a deep breath to try and bolster something that might resemble courage if you don't look at it too hard. "Alright, then. Fun, it is."

And this time, *I* kick the door open.

Melodi flies out the door first, whooping with joy, and doesn't get ten meters before whipping around and pointing the barrel of her tagger at me. I barely manage to duck under the pellet, and it makes a daunting sound against the other door. "HAHAHAHA! WELCOME TO THE PLAY, SHEEP!"

"Sheep?" Voxel questions as everyone presses out of the door behind me, which is harder than you'd think because I haven't moved very far yet—I can only stand here and stare in awe at the retreating figure of Melodi Verto.

"Sheep're sacrifices," Harmoni says as he trudges out after her, sniff-sniff-sniffling. "You're all gonna die."

"No, we're not! Everyone's gonna live," Motor assures him. The two kids stare at each other for a bit. "Are you okay? Here, wanna cookie?" Mo pulls one of the cookies out of nowhere and holds it out as a peace offering. Harmoni looks at it for a second, and then there's a POP as the cookie explodes in a million pieces and a tagger pellet hits Motor's chest. He staggers back with a shocked "Ow!"

The other five of us all act instantly, returning fire so fast, you'd think nobody'd have time to react, but Harmoni springs into the air, flips, and lands a few meters away so only one or two pellets hit him. After he struggles a second for footing, he shoots us all a watery look and dashes off to the left, disappearing into the maze of valleys.

As fast as they came, they're already gone, but their words still echo off the walls of my skull, making me shudder. In a way, they weren't just talking about the play. It reminds me that this isn't just some innocent game of Cops and Robbers. This is extermination.

Welcome to the play, sheep.

You're all gonna die.

⇹

Even though I haven't been up for too long, it already feels like I've always been awake, alert, all senses firing, so it hits me fast and hard that we don't have a lot of options. We're new to everything here, and we're up against people who've done this their whole lives and are willing to go through us to get their prize, so we're going to have to make some changes if we want to get out of this thing in one piece. "Okay, guys, we're up against three teams here, and if we stay massed up this way, then we'll be a bigger target."

"Pairs again?" Craw guesses, and Voxel immediately grabs his ear and tugs him to the side so he winces. "Guess I've got my partner. Aw, Rat, you're not gonna save me?"

"Don't associate me with heroic verbs," I snap.

He pouts. "What're you gonna do, call me a thespian?"

Jacques floats back over to Motor, who breaks out of his confusion to beam up at him. I look at Eli. "That leaves the two of us, then."

"That it does." He makes some adjustment on his tagger. "I'd prefer to be able to watch over all of you at the same time, but I don't seem to be worth much doing that, so we'll have to see how well I handle partners. Shall we take the south and search for that river?"

"I am in agreement with the plan of Eli," Voxel says even though it doesn't exactly concern her. "Craw and myself will cross the valleys nearby the spike rock and tend to the west. You two males go north, where we arrived, then." The woman gestures in the general direction before marching off west with Craw, still pulling him by the ear. He puts a hand against his chest and uses the other to wave, and I could punch him. As they disappear into the valley, Motor gets all settled on Jacques's shoulders again, this time with his tagger ready as an effective sniper/lookout, and they set off without a word. Melodi was right. We're wasting moonlight. If we want to get that immunity and survive those leeches, we're going to have to start getting some points here.

So this is life outside the Divide. Huh.

"How good can you see in the dark?" I whisper as the two of us left slink along the edge of the chasm as quietly as shadows, which is something I get from years of being a rat, and it's something Eli gets because that's just Eli. *Maybe he'd make a good bandit*, I start pondering then shake the thought from my head.

"Just as good as I can see in broad daylight. Why's it matter?"

He's starting to talk more like me too. Sweet Cielhomme.

I hesitate. "Because most people can't see as well in the dark. That's why our pupils dilate, to let in more or less light, but it still doesn't do much, so we don't see stuff as easily. Some people get reforms to fix that, though, and it lets them see better too." *You're not the only one who's mechanically altered to see better.* Wow, I'm so comforting.

There's a stretch where the only sounds are low, distant hissing, some popping sounds, and the hush of the wind. Then, "It seems that every time we talk, something about this comes up. The Mech thing, you know. Now, I understand it's strange, but for the sake of time, let's not pursue the matter and say we did. Pretend it's normal."

I frown. "Okay, but for the record, I was explaining that cuz I figured that being stuck doing nothing for all that time means you wouldn't be able to ask questions about normal stuff, so somebody oughta explain things to you. It's not fair you might not know some other stuff everyone thinks you're born with knowing."

I mean, someone had to explain it for me.

My eyelids flutter a little in shock when I realize I just thought that. Eli stops and stares at me for a long time with an expression I haven't seen on him before, one I can't interpret in this light. "Right," he says slowly. "But . . . someone tried to. Once. While I was still out. You remind me of her. Um. Do you remember anything about being in a factory a few years ago, maybe six or eight? Maybe you were stealing something from one or something?"

"I only got cut out less than six years ago," I snicker. "And before that, I don't know what I was doing. By the way, I know you're asking if it was me—you've got a way to go in the art of subtlety. And no, I'm pretty sure that couldn't've been me. I was a normal kid, in a manner of speaking. Should've asked Fracture, the scrawny guy, he knows more about it than me. I don't remember much before turning twelve."

"Alright, but I mean, meeting the undying brother of… of Jaden R. Steele would probably be memorable—"

"Eli." He catches my tone and looks at me. "I *can't* remember much before turning twelve."

Oh God, I just said that.

Thespian.

I look away and try to shrug it off, going on, "Stealing from a factory isn't too rare, anyway. Could've been anyone, but I was too young to be doing that stuff. What'd they do, sit there and explain how to tie your shoes?"

"Never mind about that," Eli says, and the pain in his voice is profound. "What do you mean, you can't remember?"

I mean to snap at him, but it comes out too tired. "I mean I can't. Pretend it's normal."

"Okay," he tells me with a nod, and I can tell he understands. Some of the tension in me ebbs away.

We drop the subject and keep walking. I search for something innocent to talk about because we're not handling talking about personal stuff real good, so I nearly bring up the whole electrodetonation thing when I notice he's still messing with the tagger. "What're you doing?"

"Figuring out how this thing works to see if I could silence it or find a way to determine who's It or something useful. I've got a knack for figuring these things out. Whoa," Eli breathes, coming to a stop as the cliff to our right cuts in front of us and shows off the cracked valley floor, which is blanketed by the deep shadow of the mountain and by tons of black-and-blue bodies.

I try not to let myself freak out on the outside, but I can't help shrinking back against the tree line. Memories of their talons sizzle against my skin, and I notice how my leg aches even though the wound's scabbed. "What about what Revany said?" I mutter under my breath, peering over the cliff at them. "If we shoot one of them, do we get double points?"

"If we shoot one of them, we're liable to end up as a midnight snack."

I shudder. "Good point. Leeches are bad enough without being annoyed." Eli takes a step closer to the edge, and I frown at him. "What're you doing now?"

"They're so… still," he says, his eyes flicking back and forth over the valley. "Hardly any of them are moving, even. They don't sleep, do they?"

"Who knows? Who knows anything about them? Are they some animal that the rest of the world knows anything about?" Eli shakes his head. "Then nobody knows anything, so anyone's guess is as good as the next guy's, so I'm going to guess they don't sleep and that they're playing dead for us. They're getting smarter, that's what I think's happening. That's how we criminals think—expect the worst, because overestimating people is better than underestimating them."

"That's a pretty bleak attitude."

"I'm not famous for my optimism, Eli."

Still, he backs away from the cliff. "What do those instincts of yours think about crossing the valley to get south faster?"

I scan the valley. "My common sense thinks we're going to have to cross the valley at some point, anyway, since it's kind of right between the east and the south. Hey, whatever happened to ladies first?" I joke, moving for the cliff as he swings his legs over the side. If you can't tell, I'm pretty desperate to get across as fast as possible, before the leeches decide to stop being lazy. There's a clear spot that should be nice, and if they wake up and attack, then I can always just keel over and die.

"I thought it'd be better if we put the shield before the knight," Eli says.

I've never heard that one before, and I realize he just called me a knight and I'm about to yell at him about the heroism thing, but when I drop down onto the low ledge by the lip of the cliff and a pellet shatters against the rock beside my head, I figure out that the analogy makes sense in some way.

"Down! We're in the open!" He slips quietly down off the ledge with two feet and one hand against the rock, the other hand on the tagger, aiming, and I scramble after, not even bothering to try and have enough control to do anything faster than roll out of the way as popping sounds hack at the quiet of the night. The rocks turn smaller and darker the closer we get to the bottom, which comes fast because the first few meters are near-vertical before it starts sloping out toward the valley. I plant my feet down in the slide and try to get steady enough to shoot, but let's face it, I'm tumbling, and there's no such thing as steady. My free hand scrabbles for something, a plant, a big rock, anything to slow me down, but I keep picking up speed anyway, so the best option is to roll myself up in a ball and try to minimize damage.

Finally, we get to the valley floor, which is still sloped, but it's flat enough that I roll to a stop. "Ugh. Are we having fun yet?" I mutter.

Eli grabs my arm and yanks me to my feet as rocks start shattering where I was, crumbling into even smaller pieces under the assault of tagger pellets. I whip my head around, trying to pinpoint the popping sounds, hoping we're not surrounded. The valley's covered in gravel and other little rocks along with really big chunks of rocks, and from here, I finally notice the cliff's weird, curved formation—whoever was here first probably bombed the valley out for something, maybe trenches. Well, if it was trench warfare they wanted, it's trench warfare they're getting.

I dive behind one of the big chunks of dark rock and press my back against it, listening to the gunfire go quiet behind me. Off to my left, Eli's ducked behind his own boulder, and we look at each other before he grabs a rock from the ground and throws it out. The firing starts up again before they figure it was just a rock, and Eli holds up two fingers. I nod, since I heard two people too.

Faintly the sound of crunching on gravel and rocks reaches my ears, which feel a hundred times as powerful because of the adrenaline, so they start picking up the sound of hissing and whirring as it picks up. If I was on high alert two seconds ago, I'm near omniscient now, or at least I'm trying to be, wide eyes flicking around as the leeches slog around, flicking their tongues and getting up again, curious, but nowhere near strong yet. Most of them still sit on the valley floor, almost lifeless, but the ones closer to us're stirring, so they must smell dinner. I clamp my mouth shut as I realize something in there's bleeding from the tumble and quickly check all over for any scrapes, but I can't find any broken skin thanks to the jacket, and besides, they don't look too interested.

I'm just getting around to wondering if the people crunching over here will ever find me and if we're going to play the carousel game around the rock until the leeches eat all of us when laughter breaks over the valley.

There's a pop and a grunt and the sound of gravel going everywhere under a falling person. The laughter picks up. "Hello, children!" a scratchy voice hoots between giggles, and I wince, looking up at the lip of the valley to see hunched ole Melodi standing there with her tagger, which is bronze.

And I can't help but think that that's the exact shade of the unofficial color of the gangs of western Tersatellus. I take a split second to notice my tagger is painted silver, the color of eastern gangs, and I wonder if the other teams have corresponding colors and what that'd mean.

Then the relic starts shouting "THEY'RE BEHIND THE ROCKS, LITTLE SHEEPIES!" and shoots the tops off mine and Eli's rocks. Melodi disappears as our stalkers' crunching picks up again, and I fly out from behind the rock just as a flash of gray turns the corner, firing at will.

"No, no, go for *him*!" I hear Lily demand, too close for comfort, so I try to run backward while firing at her until I can get halfway around the rock from her, watching both sides closely with rapidly shifting eyes so I can always move away from her pursuit, keeping the rock between us at all times. When she sticks her arm around the rock with the gun, I duck to avoid it, but when I move to try and get her, she's the one to move in the other direction, so the carousel's started. "Oh, stop being a coward and face me, Mouse!" she jibes from around the rock even while she ducks from my sight. *Hypocrite.* As if calling me what I am is gonna do anything for her.

"You can't trick me into coming out," I say, carefully working my way to the left around the rock. Fun fact: I can throw my voice a little. "I'm not as stupid as you are."

"Neither can you entice me out with mere words. I'm not Siridean, you know."

"I know. You don't give any axels about what I say, right?" There's a cold silence as I continue walking, planning, watching my left. *Bloods are worth one point. The team with the most points by six early wins. Winner by six early gets Bruise immunity the next day.*

To me, there are no rules. Only ways to win.

Finally, out the corner of my eye, I see a figure of white and red paying too much attention to Eli and none to me. There's enough time for me to be surprised by the fact Lily picked *Rex* to partner with before he gets shot in the back.

With a gasp, he hits the ground a second time (Melodi hit him the first time a minute ago) and Lily shouts "HEY!" and starts running around the rock after me. I scramble around, but she's a lot more graceful on this slippery gravel than I am, so I have to figure out something else before she gets to a decent shooting point. On a spur-of-the-moment decision, I hook hard to my right and use all the juts and grooves on the rock to get to the top of it. So I'm not as graceful as Motor. It still gets me out of Lily's crosshairs. By the time she stops running around and thinks to look up, there's a barrel in her face.

"Now, I know you think you're something special, so don't worry—this won't kill you, not even this close up. But I'm willing to bet it'll hurt and rearrange your pretty head a little." She lifts her own gun up at me, but I smile. "Yeah? If you fire, I fire. That's how this works. And I don't think you're getting help anytime soon." Rex's having trouble aiming at me from the ground, and he can't exactly get up since he's given up from getting shot at so much, and there's someone standing on him too.

(Eli shrugs as if to tell me, "What? It was the easiest way I could think of to hold him down.")

"I'm sure you wouldn't hesitate to fire, but I'm willing to bet you don't have the aim to take my eye," Lily says, and I figure out where her barrel's pointing. I try to move, but she keeps it trained at my face, plus I don't know how to work my tagger too good yet—the only guns I've ever worked with were our LPGs back at the residency and a few things in some gangs—plus this is a pretty tall rock, plus it's dark out, and I mean *really* dark because another cloud rolls over the moon. So no, I don't have any sort of accuracy right now.

"She might not, but you of all people can be sure *I* have the aim to take out your teeth one by one from a kilometer away," Eli calls from his perch on Rex's back.

"Oh, I'm sure you could and would. And to bolster your confidence, why don't you say another empty prayer, Machine?" Lily snarls, and with only a tiny glance at me in warning, she dashes to the right, and I fire, but she caught me by surprise, so all my pellets hit rocks on the ground as she swings her gun arm forward. All three of her shots miss their intended target as he whips out of the way fast enough to turn into a blur in my view. The problem is, he has to get off Rex in the process. The albino jumps off the ground and fires at point-blank, so a pellet shatters against Eli's shoulder. I try to distract Rex with my own volley, but he ignores me and keeps shooting, so Eli starts shooting Rex's ammo out of the air, the capsules exploding against each other in midair.

"Y'gotta be stickin' it to me," Rex mutters.

I change targets too late, firing at the back of Lily's head a split second after she fires. Wherever I end up hitting her, the impact knocks her to the ground, though, where she gets hit three more times before Eli turns and runs. He seems okay, so even though I heard her shoot hit him, it mustn't've been bad.

"Rat, let's go!" Eli yells back at me, and I leap off the rock, hitting the ground running, but I don't get very far before something hard goes CRACK against my shoulder, sending me flying a short distance before I fall back onto the sharp rocks, where I stay, gasping and clutching my shoulder in pain. Lights explode in my vision, but my good left hand searches for the tagger that I dropped, the tagger that gets kicked out of my reach before I get lifted up by the collar with one hand. The other hand is wrapped tight around a black wooden bat.

Rex doesn't even flinch his furious red eyes as I kick at his arm, trying to get him to let me go. "So, y'wanna fight *that* way, huh? Y'wanna go shooting people in the back that stood up with you in the beginning?"

"You left," I spit, still struggling. "So don't pick on my loyalty when you've got nothing to stand on yourself. Besides"—I grin with a cough, getting some blood on his hand, as Eli runs up from behind and grabs a fistful of dreadlocks—"NO RULES!"

I drop to the ground and grab my tagger as Rex gets jerked back, but he doesn't fall, so I grab his shoulders and shove him to the side before he can do anything so he stumbles toward one of the rising leeches. The sight makes me stop for a second to stare in horror and awe at what I did before I can find the sense to turn and run. But sense or not, I glance back at him, whacking at the leech for all he's worth even though the bat keeps going straight through, and I notice the leech isn't even interested with his hand or eating him or anything. Instead, it pulls out its tongue and licks the back of his hoodie so he makes this high, disgusted noise.

"The pellets," I breathe, skidding to a stop as it clicks into place in my brain. Some of the other leeches are licking at the ground where the ammo hit and two of them are messing up Lily's hairstyle. "The ammo must have metal in it!"

My voice makes Rex stop in his useless battle to look at me, and at that exact moment, the leech finishes cleaning off the back of his shirt and starts spinning its teeth wildly, probably picking up the blood by now. *Blood has iron in it, too. That's all the leeches care about, is the iron.*

Without thinking, I let a test round off at the leech. Sure enough, the pellet doesn't go through, but hits dead-on so the ragdoll spins, its long limbs going everywhere, and it's almost funny until it whips its head toward me, emptying its hollow tongue in a scream of rage. My heart drops as I think, *Dinner is served.*

But hey, at least the little score counter on the side of my tagger goes up by two.

Eli grabs my arm, and we start flying deeper into the valley. Another glance back tells me Rex's okay and hightailing it too, with Lily right behind as the regenerated leeches split themselves between us. They still aren't as strong or fast as they used to be, and nowhere near as graceful—the way they move is they do this skating thing where they glide on the ground, whipping their arms back and forth, and their legs shorten and lengthen while they skate to absorb the shock in this bumpy landscape so they stay even, probably the same way the pump-suspension on a mobile works, except I don't know enough about mobiles to be sure. The thing is, they aren't so good at that now, and our main pursuer, the one I shot, trips and falls on its face. I have to laugh before I turn my head back around and keep running, even though it's closer to getting dragged.

"You were hit!" I yell over the wind with the point that the leeches probably want to eat Eli now. *Get tagged by a leech, and you lose your life.*

"I know, but maybe we can get out of their range!" he yells back, running between boulders. The clouds keep covering the moon, getting more frequent and thicker so I can hardly see my leader, so it's not that surprising when my foot catches on something and I stumble, weakening Eli's grip on me. The rest of his grip disappears when there's a POP in the distance, louder than it should be, and the pain in my bad shoulder gets reawakened, sending me back into the ground. It reminds me of the time some kid in a gang stabbed me with a dull pencil, but now it hit a tender target, so I can't focus hard enough to do much more than breathe. Someone curses—it's probably Eli—and I squint in the dark at my shoulder, finally noticing it's at a funny angle. It's not quite dislocated but not normal, either, and I grip my teeth and punch it back into place, which hurts for a second before it relaxes. Then the hissing picks up again, and I feel my blood go cold as I realize I've been hit, and they can smell me now.

Run.

Eli hauls me to my feet again now that I've fixed my shoulder. "Come on, the river's not far from here," he says between gunfire. He doesn't need to tell me twice, and he has to scramble to catch up to me.

"Who's shooting at us?" I ask breathlessly as I squint through the dark. My feet barely touch the ground between steps. That is, until we spin out in a hasty stop again as I hear rocks spray everywhere right in front of us, something landing on them with a THUD.

"You *jumped* from there?" Eli cries in shock as he pulls me away, and I blindly back off, wishing I could see.

"No, I came outta a cloud." The sarcastic voice is unmistakable, but in case I'm not scared enough, one of the clouds in question rolls aside enough for me to make out Spike's towering figure. Then it gets dark again. "Why don't you keep talking so I can get a better shot?"

The suggestion gives me the idea to crouch down to be a smaller target, putting my thumb over the dim score display on my tagger. Right before the clouds came back, I saw that Spike's tagger was deep gray (southern gang color), so they probably *are* modelled after our colors. That means the inside and the outside of the walls aren't so separated as we're supposed to think, which disturbs me more than any of the other secrets the Adamantration's kept from us so far.

"If either one of you tries to make a move at me, you're dead," Spike continues, and I hear him heft a much bigger weapon that's certainly no tagger. "You're not making it outta this valley to the south."

"You mean they set you up as guard dog?" I ask snidely, feeling the rocks on the ground slowly so he has a hard time seeing me moving.

It's hard to tell, but I think he turns to me and aims something at me. "Let's see how confident you feel when I direct your attention to the army of leeches that's about to eat you alive." The sounds of them get closer, but instead of looking back at their beady red eyes coming for me, I stare forward, running my thumb along a rock before picking it up and getting it comfortable in my hand. "You think you can run away fast enough when I'm standing here in your way?"

Hoping Spike sees in the dark as bad as I do, I motion Eli at him and then at the river while I say, "At the risk of being cliché, I don't have to outrun them." The cloud moves away from the moon again, and I get my eyes as wide as they go, trying to take up every bit of light as I can before launching forward. Spike makes a move to shoot, but someone ten times as fast as me knocks into Spike from the side, so he's distracted enough not to pull the trigger on me. Big mistake. I lash out at him and feel my rock scrape across his cheek. He doesn't even notice, just reaches for me. Then he changes his mind about his targets at the last second and turns around so sharp that, combined with his already lost balance, he almost falls over, but the marksman manages one point-blank shot with his real gun straight at Eli's face.

The gunfire's followed by a shattering sound and an electric ca-ca-ca-CRACK that makes sparks fly everywhere, blinding me for a second. Spike finishes his fall, and Eli goes down right after him, screaming something, something I can't define in my panicking mind as the leeches (who were getting drawn dangerously close because of the blood on Spike's cheek) suddenly start screeching again. Panic. Run again.

"Come on, come on!" I urge, and this time I'm the one to lift up Eli—he doesn't weigh as much as I expected him to—and pull both of us along while Spike's down and we've got a chance. Eli barely manages our fast stumble. One hand's locked on my arm for balance, and the other hand's pressed against one side of his face. Behind us, the leeches pounce lethargically at Spike, and I don't even bother glancing back at him, some mixture of disgust and hateful satisfaction gathering in me when I think about him getting eaten because of me.

Ahead, the valley takes one last dip, and sparse plants shoot up here and there around a wide, glittering mass that I take to be a river. This one's a lot faster than the ones I'm used to, i.e., ones that don't move on the surface. Off to my right, the valley swoops back up and out of the ground as part of the mountain, and to my left, it arcs up more gradually until it flattens out, and I can hear waves from there. Up ahead, there's a cross between the two slopes, and the valley ends in a lopsided crater that could only be the cause of explosion. There's a big carved rock formation up at the top that's probably the southern lodge, which almost seems to be a part of the rocky beach sticking out of the ground where the river meets the ocean. Sitting on top of the river, there's a bulky whirring metal thing. That's where I head, ducking behind a nearby boulder that gives us protection against the north and east, even though the moon's shining right in on us so we might as well be targets. We're not here for a second before Eli hits the ground again, still clutching his face.

"Hah! Think we... got away. What happened?" I pant, breathing heavy from all the running.

"My... my eye," he chokes and leans against the rock. "I can't believe he actually hit me in the eye."

I swallow. "What do you want me to do?" Eli just shakes his head, so I scoot out of the rock's pretend protection and give the area a quick scoping. "The leeches beat it. Either they're too interested in Spike, or they don't like it here, so we should at least be safe from them. What... what're you going to do?"

His green eye watches me with a look in it I've never seen before. "I don't know," he says, dropping his voice. "I'm afraid I've gone half-blind, but I'm even more afraid to figure it out for sure." He slowly takes his hand away from his face anyway, little bits of glass sticking out of his hand. There's a blackened hole in his face where his left eye used to be, and inside it, I can make out an intricate mess of tiny wires, bits of glass and bullet and twisted rods of metal that're impossibly thin. It's easier to see because of the way the wires spark so much, plus a pulsing red light comes from somewhere and gives everything a scary glow.

The sight makes me feel sick to my stomach, and it must show in my face because Eli turns away, putting his head down, probably assuming it's the mechanicalness I'm disgusted about. He jumps a little and looks at me in surprise when I put my hand on his.

"Spike better get eaten for this," I rumble. "That hurts just looking at it."

Eli shrugs, turning to hide his humble surprise. Probably thought I didn't believe he could hurt. "Do you think it'd help if you pulled the bullet out?"

"I don't know if that's a good idea for me to do that," I say, trying not to sound tense.

"Oh, right, it's still sparking. Well, I might be able to do it..." He reaches for it with the hesitation of someone who really doesn't wanna do this, flinching, then stops. "Maybe if I had a mirror or something."

"You could try the reflection on the river or that weird metal thing," I suggest. With the leeches gone, it feels safer to venture out. Even though there's still the possibility of getting sniped, ambushed, or nuked out of nowhere, it might as well be a library out there now that we're not about to get eaten. So I help Eli up to his feet again, and from there, he's okay to wander over to the mass of metal by himself while I hang back, keeping watch (read: not going anywhere near the scary whirring machine).

"I wonder what this is," Eli says quietly as he tries to pull stuff out of his eye. His whole frame shudders, and something small hits the rocks. "The ... the others seem to think ... it's part of the riddle."

"Could be," I reply, not really paying attention to anything except this great headache that's blooming in my head, and I move upriver so the breeze hits my face again. "Hey ... it probably is, since there's no leeches around here, while they should be attracted to the metal. That'd explain why the river under metal makes them go away. You know what? Maybe it has something to do with the water. They all stuck around in the ocean during the day, but maybe they don't like the freshwater." Even if that's not the answer, it gives me an excuse to flop down by the side of the river and splash water over my face before giving up and plunging my whole head under. I come up gasping for air, frigid water tickling my spine. "Cinnamon!"

"Um, is that a curse I don't know about?" Blushing, I shake my head. "Are you okay?" Eli asks. He's leaning against the dam or whatever it is with both hands now, done with picking the bullet out of one eye, so the other one watches me and the distance between us.

"Yeah, I kinda, uh, I really don't like that thing's whirring. It's giving me a headache." Still, I grit my teeth and walk over, observing it. "Okay, so if the riddle's just talking about the river and not the metal going over it, then fresh water's probably the thing to use against our hunters. So it'd almost be better if these *were* squirt guns," I add to myself. "Hey, you look a little better now."

Eli tenses, looking back at the dam thing (joke intended). It's a box that stretches flat against the river at its mouth, so the water goes in one end and comes out the other, and it makes a relaxing water sound that almost covers up the annoying hum that comes from anything mechanical. The cities roared with it, which is why I picked a residency farther from the center. "I find it comforting," he admits, his voice almost covered by the combined sounds.

"Well, we're all entitled to our opinions," I say, pretending it's normal and not pursuing the subject and all that. My boots're still soggy from the ocean, and besides, they're dirty from all the running, so it doesn't matter to me when I walk into the water up to my ankles, checking the dam out, or at least pretending to. Eventually, though, it gets to a point where I have to walk away upstream, holding my head.

"You know, it's not making any sound."

"It is to me!" I snap, covering my ears. "Maybe I do have something whacked with me after all, and I can hear things that don't exist. Wouldn't be surprised. Are you almost done? I'm sick of looking at this thing."

"Alright, we might as well—" He stops when a cloud passes over the moon again, suffocating the valley again. In the darkness, everything seems quieter and louder at the same time, if that makes any sense. "Oh. That's how it looks then."

"What, what's the matter?" I ask, waving my arms around in the sudden veil.

"Um ... my left eye was my better one. Or I suppose this one was my better one because it didn't need so much, you know, modification. It doesn't have the night-vision or zoom or anything. It's, you know ... normal." I stare through the darkness at him for a few amazed seconds before I hear him sigh. "Whatever, I can guess where the rock is. Better there than out in the open." Then there's a crunching of gravel—the world is just sound now—and I follow him until I bump into the rock. The only light comes from the yellow score counter on my tagger. Nine, it says. I have nine points for all my troubles.

We'll need a lot more than that to win, I think, and it makes my limbs itch to get up and keep hunting in spite of the fear and exhaustion. *Immunity. Victory. Win. Win.*

A few minutes of silence and darkness slide by before I start, "Well, the place seems pretty secure. We should be able to look around in peace. I really wish we had a way to carry around that freshwater! It must be the second part of the riddle."

"A river under muscle, they taste to hunt you," Eli recites slowly. "A river under metal, they taste to hide from you. To advance, the first, you must conceal, and the other, you must steal by mastering the masters that hunt hunters. The masters must be the locals here, since they're the only ones stupid enough to hunt the leeches, and if we beat them at this game, then we get this strange immunity. But that means the immunity should have something to do with the second river, shouldn't it?"

"Yeah, but the prize is gas in vials, not a river, remember?"

"That's right. You need a *liquid* to make a river, don't you?" My brow furrows as I start to come close to making half a guess about where this is going. "Harmoni says that when the sun rises—when the solar panels start working again—that some sort of defense turns all the air in the vials into acid. That conclusion must come from some evidence that the liquid it generates after coming in contact with electricity is volatile."

I have to get to my feet again as dots start connecting. "Wait, you know what, that could be why they could never come up through the track to get at us during the day: they don't just need night, they don't want to touch the track because it's electrical! And that wave of electricity could be what knocked them all out! And that's why they don't like this dam thing, because it's electric! That's probably why they ran away both times you started..." I drop off, hesitating as his eye sparks again. If I continue, he might get edgy like Craw, not sure if we're going to demand him to hurt himself to make the leeches go away. By now, the things freak me out so bad it's tempting, but I don't keep going with the thought. Still, I can't help remembering the relief I got when all the leeches scrammed when one of them scratched through his metal protection deep enough to draw blood. *Well, not exactly* blood, *but...*

Wait. That's it. The realization hits me right as the clouds part to cascade silver down onto the valley, and the both of us look at each other and say it at the same time.

"A river under metal, they taste to hide from you."

Our blood was the first river. So it makes sense that the second river should be...

You bleed liquid lightning?

... His.

"Well, this is a rather disturbing development," Eli sighs, kicking a rock.

"Why? Fat load of good it'd do us to make you bleed to death to keep the leeches away. We won't make you protect us like that, I promise."

"That's not why it's disturbing. I got the idea when I remembered what Voxel wanted to talk to me about during our search for the lodge. She asked about 'what energy method I use to sustain myself' and that sort of thing, and now I'm wondering if she already had the idea and wasn't sharing it."

I've barely gotten over the shock of figuring out the riddle when Eli's new concept of Voxel's betrayal sucker punches me in the brain. "Maybe she just didn't want us to try and prove her wrong. Come on, we should tell the others. Or I should with *my* beacon, since that way, it won't get to the Brigade. After what they've done, I don't care if they *never* figure out the riddle."

"Except for Vici?"

I wince as I take another blow to the loyalty. "Yeah, except for Vici." The beacons don't give off any light so it doesn't blind me as I push the button and ask everyone to get somewhere safe so I can tell them something important. Craw responds right away—apparently, he and Voxel've had a boring night, lucky suckers—but after a solid minute, Jacques and Motor don't reply at all.

And I start getting that criminal instinct telling me something's gone wrong.

After a few more failed attempts to get contact, I really start getting worried, and Voxel and Craw don't sound too calm, either. "Alright, that's it. Everyone that can hear this, meet at the north base. At, not in. It's a good vantage point. We'll go from there." I shut the beacon off and look at Eli. "What could've happened *this* time?"

"Anything," Eli replies, which doesn't help me feel any better. "But I'm confident in Jacques's ability to handle it until we get to them."

"The only question is where they are now," I mutter. We can only hope the boys heard us and just can't respond and they're at the north lodge waiting for us so we don't have to go looking for them. Not walking into an ambush would be nice too, but we'll see. "C'mon. Too bad I lost my flashlight."

We get out from behind the rock and start running back across the valley, dashing from boulder to boulder to be seen as little as possible. In this low light, I'm all but invisible. Eli does what he can. When he can afford to, he tows me some more since he's fast, but you don't walk away from getting shot in the eye that easily. It takes what feels like hours, but we make good progress through the rocks, avoiding the masses of black-and-blue without even getting shot at once.

On the way, I get this glorious image in my mind where we show up at the lodge, and the whole rest of the Band's there, waiting, and Motor's and Jacques's beacons were broken or something innocent, and we all group back up and win Tag and get the immunity. And because it's so ridiculous I keep feeding it, imagining Vici coming over to my side again, and the other team disappears after Lily has a change of heart and shares the secrets and dies right after, and we all have a grand old time here in Hudson Bay before we get out. Vici gets crowned the Champion, and I steal the money, and we're all rich, and we stick together afterward because that's how it's supposed to be, everyone having each other's backs and nobody keeping secrets. It's such a strong image that I half believe it. But only half, so that only makes it my third and a half delusion of the night.

When we finally get to the lodge where we first hunkered down, the lights're off and there's nobody nearby. The only sounds (besides us) are the beating of the waves on the shore. After a good five minutes of shouting and looking around to no avail, I ask, "Think we should look inside for them?"

"It's as good a place as any to search," Eli says and starts for the door, but I tense. *Mm, yeah, sabotage*, my inner suspicions say.

"Hang on, I take it back. Let's not go in."

"The lights aren't even on, Rat. It's empty." With that, he jostles open the doors and steps inside. "No signs of life."

Still suspicious, I follow him into the gloom.

Right when I step inside, a young voice from the back room calls, "In here!" My shoulders relax with relief, and I walk the rest of the way in, heading for the door that leads to the supply room. *Thank goodness, they're here.*

"Motor!" The dark door swings open, and I squint inside, smiling. "I'm so glad I—"

The Flashfire gun in the kid's hands makes a huge crackling sound that interrupts my sentence. Shock fills me from head to toe when he pulls the trigger, but right before the wave of electricity and pain pulls me out of consciousness, a flare of light ignites the doorway so the last thing I see is Harmoni's face. Everything slides in my vision until I'm on the floor, where it all starts fading down to his dark, glittering eyes that tell me that things are about to change for good.

Sabotage. Called it.

- V -

Treason

One eye opens to reveal fuzzy light raining down from above and I groan, wondering, how could *I* possibly be going to heaven? That's when it all comes flying back to me and I squeeze my eyes shut in shame, appalled about walking into an ambush *I predicted.*

If I had a headache before, it's a migraine now. I'm on one of those cold verticontrol tables that creates a small field of tilted gravity, so even though I'm right-side up with my feet pointing at the ground and everything, I'm lying down, cuffed by the wrists and ankles to this thing. It's machinery, so that's great for my head. "She's awake," someone next to me says, and I jerk away. He sniffles.

"Where in the name of fire and brimstone am I?" I demand, forcing my eyes open to scan the room. It's pretty simple, with rock walls, one white light, a verticontrol table across from me, and a bank of computers to the right. The table across the room takes up most of the wall, same as this one, but it's littered with tools and bottles. On the far left is a thick door that makes the place seem pretty important. And oddly advanced. This isn't a place I'd expect from a little island with a bunch of valleys and a mountain. It's strangely comforting, though. The machinery still presses in against me from all sides with its whirring boring into my brain, but I've always lived in cities, where me and the other rats belong. That makes me want to know where it is even more, though. Did they haul me off to some other island while I was out? And how long was I out? "You, kid! Harmoni, right?" The boy yanks his hood up over his head and turns away. "Hey, I'm talking to you! Twerp!" I add because Outmode used it against me all the time. "Where are we?"

He's getting ready to not answer me some more when a response reverberates through the room from somewhere high above the ceiling, the deep BRONG following straight after the vibrations. *So we must be in the mountain! And it's one in the morning, so I got the whole time question answered too. Look, I'm a genius too. Take that, Jacques!*

Jacques. The name and a band of others march through my mind, so I struggle against the cuffs holding me down (or holding me against the wall, depending on how you look at it—verticontrol tables twist gravity around so the wall becomes the floor to anything that's touching it). "What've you done with the others?" Harmoni takes another step away, trying to duck out of my field of vision with a sob. "Look, you little freak, if you don't answer me, I'm gonna give you something real to cry about!"

"No, you won't. You've been made fast." I whip my head to the door as it slides open, and none other than Victoria Oile walks into the room.

My eyes bug out of my head. "Vici! What're you doing here? What'm *I* doing here? And what's the little brat for?"

"Haven't you ever heard of an alliance before?" she asks coolly, pointing the crying kid out of the room. Then her bronze eyes search me for a long time. "You're here because you're being held hostage by us and the western team. I thought that was obvious."

"Come on, Vici, what're you doing?" I shake my head, wishing I could understand, but ever since we split, everything I thought I knew about her's been thrown out the window. "We've had years together—okay, a year and a half? I've been there for you through thick and thin, and I accepted you when you knew none of the gangs would. Nobody else would hardly even tolerate you. I can understand if you hate me because we disagree on something, even though I never saw you as that kind of person, and I can understand if you're through with me. I can understand if I misunderstood you all along, sure, it happens, life's a tragedy and we're all thespians, but still, this is the thanks I get for all those years?"

"I learned a lot from you, Rat," Vici says. "You told me a lot of things. That we're all special snowflakes, and we all fall down, and the only way to be different is to go up in the world. That you go up by stepping on people or taking the lift. You thought you were my liftman, but you've been mistaken. You're my staircase, and I understand that seems low of me, but you taught me first and foremost that we all start somewhere. And now that I'm getting along, I'm figuring out where my loyalties lie," she finishes in a careful way, looking me right in the eyes as she seriously pulls the middle finger on me.

And just in case I haven't told you before, that has double meaning for the two of us, a code that means to start acting because there's cameras and people watching.

Ha. The girl still loves me after all.

I twist my victory into a sneer and snarl, "That's real mature. If that's how it's going to be, then…" I stick my tongue out, one of our signs for understanding. Vici's eyebrow twitches, then she steps away and walks over to the computers.

"We heard your little comment over the beacon systems, by the way. Ivy's beacon can hear everyone still, the same way Eli's does—we're not fools. So why don't you tell me the important thing you wanted to tell your team, or else I'll figure out what kind of torture techniques these things are capable of."

I've taught her how to sound convincing. A shiver runs down my spine at the words, but I say, "Sure. You want chocolate chip pancakes with that?"

Vici gives me a look to ask me how I could be so carefree as if everyone knows that chocolate chip pancakes are one of our operational codes. "To go, please," she allows herself and dramatically puts her hand up in the air and jabs an option on the screen, and "accidentally" sets me free.

The cuffs sink into the table, and I, along with a couple other tools and things, drop to the floor. Vici feigns shock as I run for the door, spirits soaring, and pull it open by force, ready to get outta here as fast as possible.

Then it shuts back up without anyone touching it.

I pause, staring at it, and yank it open again, but it shuts again. Then I get frustrated and use both hands and get ready to shove it so I can be in the way of it stopping, but it flies open all by itself. Okay, do you know those horror games where you check over your shoulder a bunch of times and nothing's there until the next time you look, and then there's suddenly this lifeless body coming at you? That's what happens to me. There was nobody in the hallway the first times I opened the door, but now that it opens without me, Ivy's standing in the doorway, as lifeless as that dead body we were talking about.

The sight of her makes me yelp in surprise and scramble back into the room, and she drifts in after me, somehow shutting the door behind her without ever taking her eyes off me. Her mouth opens slightly, and I hear her take a deep breath as she points to the wall.

"Back on the table."

Her voice is not the sweet and melodic thing I thought I heard every now and then. This voice is the sort that wants to lock around your throat to keep you from replying.

The bottles close to the table fall back onto the table as it hums back to life, but I'm far enough away to be out of range. "Yeah, right," I scoff, "as if I'm going to let you poke me for answers when I'm not getting any in the first place. Go back and ask your sister if you can tell me to do something else, why don't you? You might need permission to breathe while you're at it."

Whether her look is hurt or thoughtful or she's imagining me in a noose, I can't tell, since I can't read her. "I said get back on the glitching table," she repeats, the words hammering into me. I wince and take a step back.

In the background behind me, Vici looks around frantically on the other verticontrol table until she finds a weapon to her liking, one that doesn't look that far from the LPGs we had at our residency. She flicks a switch and pulls the trigger, and a thick black cord goes flying out the barrel and wraps itself around Ivy, who squeaks in surprise. With a silent plea for forgiveness, I swoop down, pick up a screwdriver, and wham the big end into the side of her head so she falls over, dazed. Vici nods at me, and we run for the door, which she shuts as soon as we're out in the hallway.

"Can you lock her in there?" I ask, totally unnerved by Ivy by now.

"No. I could, but she'd be able to escape. She can still control... never mind, I'll try to explain later, but she'll be out any second, so we have to get out of here. The more you know, the scarier she gets, trust me," Vici says. Those two last words make me stop a second and look at her. Whether or not it was an accident, she's asking me to trust her again. And suddenly, I need to show her I'm worthy of that trust.

I take a deep breath. "Can I get the short version of how she could open the door even if you locked it?"

"Her mainframe fragment still has command functions in it, so she can still open doors and work most machinery indirectly because most of it here has Plexus availability—we're thinking that some Tersatellans have been here before. Why?"

"So if the door didn't work anymore, then she wouldn't be able to open it?"

"Yes, Rat, but it's a useless point, now we need to go!" Vici's getting frustrated, but I'm not done.

"I can stop her, then, if you promise not to ask or tell anyone."

Vici frowns but promises, and I turn toward the door and press my hand to it, feeling sick again. There's all sorts of mechanisms going on under there, ready to receive signals demanding to open the door, but I concentrate, and my headache gets worse as the mechanisms wreck themselves slowly under my hands behind the metal. First they start misfiring, then the electricity escapes all the wires and everything meant to keep it stable, so it starts messing everything up, with the signals getting shredded and eaten. Then the wires and boards and whatever the heck else is in mechanisms writhe as they slowly disintegrate, their brutal destruction giving me this savage sort of pleasure and satisfaction, lifting my headache for now. Fists beat against the door, and I step away, sweating. Vici's staring at me without even pretending to hide her amazement. She just watched me reduce a brilliantly technical door to a slab of metal in the wall.

"There, now you know." I sigh, unable to meet her eye. "Don't ask. Please. Because I don't know. I really don't. It just happens, it's always happened, ever since I can remember. I just, you know, wreck stuff, and I don't know why, and I never asked for it, so don't ask why it happens, and don't ask me to eat a battery."

Vici watches me with a strange expression on her face. "You keep changing so much it's almost as if I'm meeting you for the first time every time," she says in a measured tone. "But that's the way it's always been and I'm starting not to mind. You know I can't come over to your side, Rat, but I want you to know I didn't mean what I said in there, at the end, at least. You've been my liftman, and I wanted to thank you and, well..." She looks around for witnesses then sticks her hand out. "Friends again?"

"Forevermore," I half smile, and we shake on it. The world seems to shiver because criminals don't shake on conventional things, and I taught her well, and

I know that we're not on the same ground we once were. She wants something. But I'll wait to see what it is.

Vici steps back. "All right, now let's get your teammates." She starts down the hallway, opening and closing doors as we go, and for a second, we're back on that sidewalk together, laying out the procedure before we rob a place. "Lily will forgive me for letting you go if I get some information from you that could be deemed important and if I don't end up siding with you, so I'll try to help you however I think that I can get away with, but no more. In the meantime, tell me something you thought would be important enough to tell the others in person and not via beacon, where the conversation could be tapped. That's what Lily thinks happened, is that you figured something out, and she wants to know what it is."

I think a second, still not ready for the Brigade to know about the liquid lightning thing. In fact, I don't even want them to know about the whole deadly-iron-ammunition thing, even though they've probably got that figured out for themselves. "Well, the truth is, Spike's probably dead, eaten by the leeches," I pick to say. "That's something I'd want to discuss in person. It's my fault, after all."

"It's a fair enough claim, but so you know, he's not eaten. I talked to him on my beacon a few seconds before walking in the room."

"What a shame," I growl. "I'd like him better dead by now."

"Don't say that, Rat. You don't know enough about him to say that." I snort but don't challenge her—instead, I ask where we're at and where we're going. "This is the research area of a factory of sorts in the mountain," Vici explains. "They put you in that room by yourself with Harmoni, that sad boy, until I could come along and figure out how to entice you to spill the information, which everyone thought I was best fit for. Your teammates are in another room together, except for Eli, who's in another separate room, and Motor, who broke away when Tim put up a fight good enough to distract Lily, Rex, Melodi, and I."

"Tim wants to be called Jacques again," I say, filling with pride as I imagine what a great fight he must've put up.

"Well, if we were still in Tersatellus, he might prefer we skip straight to calling him a medic. Nobody goes that hard against four people armed as well as us without getting some, ah, scratches," Vici admits, looking away. "Especially not with Rex there. His adrenaline situation is incredible, though it didn't save him from getting hit pretty hard in return. Speaking of battle scars, what on earth happened to, um, Eli?"

"Spike happened," I reply, dark again. This is a mess! The Band should've never split up! "Why's he separate?"

"Why do you think, Rat? Lily wanted a special audience with him. He's down the hall through that door there. It's unlocked—this door isn't. Your friends are here. I'll get you through, and then I'm out of the picture, alright?"

"Got it. Vici?" She stops typing in things on the keypad to look at me. "Thanks." She purses her lips in an almost-smile before tapping the door open then starts running down the hallway. I watch her go, wondering if it's too good to be true, then slip inside.

"Rat!" a bunch of people (read: two people, what a welcoming committee) cry at the same time as I step into the room, giving it a quick glance that tells me that nobody's here guarding them, and they're all cuffed to the same verti-control tables I was—in fact, the whole room looks almost exactly the same. I take a confident stride for the computers, remembering how it was the purplish icon that Vici jabbed to set me free, but I never get there. The door slams closed way too hard for comfort, and I whirl around to discover I was wrong about the room not being guarded. Maybe I should've included the area behind me in my quick glance.

"It was a trap," Craw offers pointlessly as I back away from the barrel of Lily's gun, hands up. She looks even more furious with her hair still messed up by the leech.

"I figured that Vici would be weakened into caving for you instead of the other way around," Lily seethes, never taking her eyes off me as I back up even more. "So here I waited for you, and sure enough, you arrived and are now caught as a rat in a trap." She breaks the number one rule of comedy and laughs at her own joke when nobody else does.

I turn in a circle, giving the room another scanning. "Where's Eli?" I demand then do a double-take, and my heart goes into my feet, air locking so hard in my lungs I can barely manage to breathe, "*Jacques.*"

He's sprawled limply on the table, his white clothes torn up and stained crimson in several places. His only movement is this slight trembling and an opening of his blackened eyes so he can see me. My mouth flaps open and closed, dumbfounded by his crushed look, and his eyes slowly close again. I whip around to Lily, fists clenching. "What, are you trying to get us all killed now?"

"I'm sorry, I was under the impression you understood that people would *die*, considering this is a competition created to kill everyone who enters." A thoughtful look crosses Lily's face. "Maybe after he perishes, we can somehow use his body to bait the leeches."

Oh, that does it.

My knuckles go pale around the screwdriver I'm still holding as my self-control goes out the window. "That's it, you sick little dog, you're gonna die!" I scream and rush her, lashing out with the pointy end of the screwdriver. She tries to fire but for once my street arts get there first, and I knock the gun out of her hands, giving it a mighty good dent in the process, then kick her in the shin as hard as I can, and that's how the two of us start dog fighting, kicking, screaming, biting, scratching, pulling each other's hair, punching, elbowing, the whole bit, with no such thing as decency or anything, oh, no, just make her hurt. The boys watch in total awe as we go at it until she manages to whip out her tagger and jam it against my forehead, pinning me to the ground with her knee in my stomach and her free hand smashing my jaw.

"Your best friend pressurized this thing, Mouse, so if I fire, you're going to get a rather rude plastic surgery, though I daresay it'd be an improvement!" Lily spits, blood dripping down her chin.

The metal's cool on my head, and a deep, primal fear radiates through me, but I cling to my indignation so it doesn't show and work out past her hand. "Hey, point thah thing ah my eye so I don' godda lookacha!"

Lily flicks an unpromising-looking lever on her tagger. "You're going to be the first leech food, Mouse. Say good night!" I coil in preparation to fling her, and she's prepared to fire, but none of that happens because the door flies open *again*. There's a flash of light, and Lily collapses on top of me so I have to push her off with a disgusted grunt before I can sit up and look at my rescuer.

You'll never guess who's standing in the doorway with Harmoni's Flashfire and the angriest look you can hold in one eye.

"Cielhomme, that felt good!" Eli rumbles, giving Lily a kick in the side for good measure before pulling me to my feet. He's breathing heavily, twitching with frantic energy. "She stuck her glitching thumb in my eye, you know! The right one, I mean, and that was after she practically *stabbed* my dead socket with a wrench! I could kill her, I really, really could!"

"Save it. We can't kill her without getting rid of our ticket out of here, so calm down."

"Calm down! Always telling me to calm down right before I commit a real murder," Eli mutters to himself, real subtle. He's hyper on the pain—I've been there a few times, and it's not fun. I might as well be trying to tell lightning to calm down, but he takes a deep breath and lowers his volume and violence level. "Fine. Give me something else to do, or I swear I'll just keep shooting her with this thing."

"Help me get everyone free," I tell him and move over to the closest person stuck to the table and use the bloody screwdriver to start working the cuffs off. Eli goes over to the computers, leaning heavily against the desk. "Try the purple icon."

Voxel, who was on the other table on the same side of the room I'd been on, drops onto her feet with a cry of relief. A few seconds later, I get Craw free the manual way. He gratefully wraps his arms tight around me, sending heat searing through me again, which I wasn't expecting, and it almost makes me drop my screwdriver.

"Thanks, both of you," he says shakily, and it doesn't take a genius to tell he was freaking out. Unable to say anything in return, I go over to where Jacques is still cuffed and carefully unscrew the bolts so that when the gravity field gets broken, I'm ready to support him, or at least I thought I was, but he doesn't even make an attempt to stay on his feet, so the best I'm good for is helping him to his knees. I count a bullet hole in his side, a nasty grazing right where his shoulders meet his neck, and I guess the bouquet of scarlet right on his chest without a hole is a knife slice or broken rib, which means there could be more, probably courtesy of Rex and his club. The sound of him trying to breathe is almost enough to scare me out of my skin, and I don't know how Craw could deal with being next to him for so long. All this, minus the little injuries: a black eye, a split lip, a bunch of bruises.

"Jacques," I whisper, "Hey, can you hear me?"

He slowly lifts his head up and squints at me. "Did... did Motor escape?" he wheezes.

"Don't worry, he got away," I promise, and Jacques closes his eyes again, leaning against the wall. "Save the theatrics, thespian, you're not dying. We gotta bail."

"Ahem!" Voxel coughs, and I turn to see Lily picking her head up with a groan. Then there's a flash of light, and she collapses again. "Lovely, but I am still believing that we should take our own escape from the hands of this strange place. It teems with the ants we call enemy."

"Escape how? We have no idea where we are," Craw says.

"Not yet, we haven't." Voxel cracks her knuckles and walks over to the computers. "However, friends, considering that we are within my realm of tact, we will not be hungry for ideas for long. And if I cannot provide the proper feast, we have an expert scrounger who is known to worm her way free from tighter fixes."

While she sets to work, I refer to my subconscious map of the place and turn back to Jacques. "Do you think you can walk if we help you?" He manages a nod. "You know, that was really brave, what you did. Thank you."

This gets no response.

Long minutes pass before Voxel can conjure up a 3-D model of the place on the screen. "Here we are! It has the appearance of some sort of factory. We're within the research and development wing, and below us is the factory floor. Despite how those words sound simple in your ears, in truth, the place is a maze. Even if it were possible to take this with us, it would be hard as finding the combination of a padlock to decipher, and I doubt that others will refrain from pursuing us."

"So what're we supposed to do, run around like chickens without heads?" Craw asks. "We can't sit around doing nothing. We've got two people dying here!"

"I'm not dying yet," Eli says, even though he's holding the side of his face again.

"Technically, you have already died," Voxel points out.

"Don't go there. Nobody else is going to die tonight until I do, for a second time," he adds so Voxel's satisfied. "We need—"

Not even bothering to wait for Eli to finish his sentence, Lily springs out of her unconsciousness and grabs her beacon, jabbering into it, "Everyone there's an emergency in room 205 I'm being—AAH!" She collapses under a third shock, but it's too late. The message's already sent, and reinforcements will be on us if we don't split, pronto.

"Alright, now we really gotta bail," I order, fitting myself under Jacques's arm to try and get him up, but Craw has to come over and take the boy's other side so he doesn't pass out from the effort. Tired, starving, and wounded make for a bad combination, and I start worrying about how much longer he'll make it. Voxel clicks off her computer thing and strides for the door before all of us, and she just about makes it when it slides open without her, the way all the doors seem to prefer doing today.

And standing in the doorway is the other Alice with Motor's arm in her porcelain grasp.

I almost hit the floor from sheer despair before I notice the mischievous look of triumph on the boy's face. "Hi, it's the emergency people, and we brought a mini ambulance!" Motor chirps, pulling out a brand-new medicine kit, one of the really professional kinds they keep in dangerous places (in factories, for a random example) for almost any kind of injury.

My jaw drops as I look between the two of them in the doorway. "But... but..."

Ivy ignores me and lets go of Motor to step into the room, hungrily grinning at Lily's crumpled, bloody figure on the floor. She gives me a nod of approval for beating the tar out of her sister. I look between the kid and Ivy, who's finally got some life in those glassy eyes of hers, and I glance around to make sure everyone's just as stunned as I am.

"Motor?" Craw starts carefully, "you do realize that *she's* part of the group that stuck us here, and that Jacques... fought to keep you out, right?"

A profound look of darkness covers Motor's face. "What, you think I came back on purpose? I got out to the shore before *some*one buzzed me again and dragged me back here. He's strong for a kid like me! But I woke up and bit his fingers, so he let me go, and I decided while I was here, I might as well be useful. And besides, Ivy likes me." Ever since he started talking, Ivy's drifted over to Lily and has been kicking her gently but relentlessly. When Lily's eyes fly open, the kicking stops, but when she gets buzzed again, Ivy does that demon-flute laugh and keeps kicking. I'm so busy trying not to be horrified or sick I'm slow on the draw to help Jacques to the ground so Motor can come over with the industrial kit with painkillers and bandages and a whole hospital of medical stuff. I've heard people can stitch an arm back onto someone with those kits. They've been required in all the places where humans still work after the Safer

Factories Act a few years ago, but I didn't know the kits carried out into the rest of the world.

I refuse to think about what that and the Tersatellan-colored taggers imply about the certainty of the Divide.

We get Jacques's shirt off without much hassle—as a cutout with full nerve capacity, I'm telling you that I took one of those painkillers once, and I was numb for a solid hour. Me and Craw help wherever we can, but Motor's small and fast. "Dr. Michael Senior worked as a medic for Paramount Mobile-Auto, and he brought me with him lots, and somebody'd always be getting hurt by their stupid mobiles, so I caught on quick," he explains proudly.

Craw glances at me. "Do you think you could do anything for Eli?" he asks for me since I'm still mute. We have nobody on the outside now. Nobody on our side knows how to get out of here. I'm probably trapped in a room with a psycho and her sister, Eli's half-blind, and Jacques is bleeding half to death all over me, and leeches, leeches, leeches—

"You don't have to keep doing that, you know," Motor says when Eli goes to shoot Lily again. "I can stop her connection to Ivy, so she's not much of a threat." Great, the psycho and her sister are magically connected now? Bloody fantastic. Eli's on my page: he shoots Lily with the Flashfire anyway. Motor stops bandaging to squint at him with a tilt of his head to silently ask why he fired despite the relief on duty, and after a couple seconds, the kid gasps. "What happened to your eye?"

"Shot." Eli shrugs, still leaning against the table. "By Spike. Don't take offense, but I was just wondering, do you need opticorrection?"

"Um... I think so. Dr. Michael Senior says I'm kinda colorblind, and shortsighted in one eye and farsighted in the other, but I can't remember which's which. It's kinda helpful, really, especially now." So that's why he's working with one eye shut. "Hang on another minute, I'll help you next." The room goes quiet again, with the only sounds being Voxel tapping on the computer again, Ivy kicking away, Jacques's scratchy breathing, and Eli's eye crackling every few seconds. He paces and gladly keeps Lily from waking up anytime soon.

I keep my head resting against my knee the whole time. The longer I sit still, the louder the whirring sounds, but my limbs feel heavy, and I don't want to move. There's just... so much...

When my eyes decide to open again, Lily's all tied up with the cord that used to be around Ivy, and Motor's moved on to Eli. I'm still holding on to Jacques for some reason. For the first time, I thank God that Tersatellan bodies heal faster, even though Jacques's probably going to wake up hungry enough to eat a warehouse of food. Still, he's so beat and wrapped in so many bandages I keep my arm on his shoulder, half scared that if I let go, he'll fall to pieces.

Motor comes back over and asks me something, and I guess I understand because I pry my fingers open and hand him the screwdriver, and he goes away.

Craw watches me with a frown, and his lips start moving, but I don't hear him, so he waves a hand in front of my face, and I blink, focusing again. "Okay, Rat?" Craw's voice floats into my awareness.

"I hate being in powered buildings," I growl so bitterly Craw jumps. "How the heck's this place got any power, anyway? And how do you fit a factory in a mountain?"

Voxel turns around with a dazed look on her face. "One who puts a factory under the cover of a mountain must have one goal in mind: to hide it. And if what my eyes have caught is correct, then the person who put this here must have had every intention of hiding it, and they would be fully capable of powering this place. Friends, I'm afraid we reside in a Section 86."

My eyebrows jump at that. S86s are areas outside of the Divide where people or companies from Tersatellus have managed to get to and set up shop—pretty much the most illegal places on the face of the earth, considering how hard the Adamantration tries to keep the inside in.

"And since it is a factory, you have the capacity to formulate a hypothesis of which company this is, or at least which company supported this place." Even though she's nervous about so much as touching the screens now, Voxel zooms in on a huge metal-cutting machine that must be downstairs, and sitting in the corner of it is the small logo of Surgam. You can tell it's old because it's still got the initials J and R on the sides of the S, when those got edited out years ago, and if this place's that old, that explains how Voxel could snoop around the system so easily. And by easily, I mean she got in at all—if this place is owned by Surgam, it explains how it took her longer than anything to get into.

"And here I was, thinking the Porcupine managed to get off clean-handed," Craw says, chuckling. "I guess all us cutouts're lawbreakers, after all. Hey, what's the big deal, Voxel?"

The woman's gone from dazed to pale, and instead of answering, she scrolls over to another room labeled Security. Inside it, there's a whole bunch of something you'd find in any Surgam security room: ground-type MechGuards. And the bad news is, they're turning on. Top-of-the-line gunners start whirring to life all at the same time.

"They know we're here?" I ask Ivy, who shrugs, looking as freaked as I feel. Gunners are basically nonhuman discipline ops with no heads, tall chests for storing ammo, and four arms, the ends of which are guns. They're strictly for defense, though, so the public only hears rumors about them, with only a few pictures that float through the Plexus before the Adamantration shoots it down. I get to be one of the first Tersatellans to face one in person. Lucky me.

One of the gunners on the screen goes to a box on the wall and fires at it. Voxel's computer screens're the first things to go. Right after that, the rest of the power goes out with that sickening FWWooooooo.

And that's when I know we're sunk.

"Everyone!" Vici's voice comes back from Eli's beacon, and we stick close together and listen, huddled up against the sudden mass of darkness. "I'm getting word from the Plexus that Vastate's ordered an investigation into Hudson Bay about the energy wave. He's discovered Mechs on this island and is using them for the investigation. There's rumors all over the place about him taking over the Tech Sector, defenses and Mech programming and all, and those rumors are running rampant because the Plexus is in chaos. This sort of thing was never supposed to happen, and Vastate practically has to reweave the Plexus. As for him, angry is an understatement right now."

"So much for perfect!" Eli scoffs. Motor's at least got the wires and stuff aligned, so his eye's stopped sparking for the most part. It's still a black-and-gray hole, but it's an organized one. "And now we don't even have any Adamantration-immunity days to avoid the wrath that's about to crash down on us. This is nothing but an excuse for him to go back on his word and interfere with the race. If he's really controlling those Mechs..."

"Then we're history," I finish.

Motor gets to his feet and crosses his arms defiantly, a storm building on his face, and for the first time, he really looks seven years old. "I don't *wanna* be history," he complains. "I didn't break the rules and bite someone's finger and run around this stupid place, didn't fall in an *ocean*, didn't have people try and *kill* me, and didn't lose my favorite bike getting here just to be *history*! I came here to race, live, and win, so Mechs or not, I'm gonna do it!"

"Motor, stop!" Voxel cries, leaping for the kid, and I let go of Jacques to leap too, but even though we were the closest to him, neither of us make it in time to stop Mo from belting out the open door and turning a corner. I scramble to my feet and look frantically in the dim red emergency light that's turning in circles above me, but there's no other movement in the hallway.

"Gone," I say, wondering what on earth Motor was thinking. Wondering what on earth *I* was thinking. Voxel looks as horrified as I feel. "Jacques's gonna kill us when he wakes up." She nods with a gulp then creeps back into the room. Now that Motor's gone, Ivy's gone all nervous and stays away from Lily. Heck, now that Motor's gone, the whole room's tense.

Now that Motor's gone, I start seeing sense again, and my fists ball up at my sides. Coldness runs through me, and I stop giving a care about what Jacques thinks of this. I care what *I* think about it. Screw everyone else.

"Motor, what the heck are you doing?" Craw's asking his beacon. He squints up at me in the darkness. "He's not responding to anything."

"He'd probably respond to Jacques if he was awake," Eli says. Our wounded comrade doesn't even seem to be close to waking up yet, and it's probably for the better. The blood's started to show through the bandages, and you can tell by the way he's breathing that things are still busy knitting themselves back together, so oblivion is the best place to be. But maybe we don't have to wake him up.

I look up at Craw and smile. My coldness is seeping through, so he misinterprets it and takes a step back before I say, "Do we need Jacques if we have his voice?"

Craw thinks about it, looking between Jacques and the beacon under the light. "Then he'd kill me *twice* if he wakes up. I'm kidding, but still, does it make a difference who's asking?"

"Motor seems to trust Jacques, so he might be more willing to respond," Eli explains. "We might not be able to get him back, but you should at least try asking what he's doing."

"Alright, alright." Craw clears his throat and presses on the beacon. "Motor?" We all jump because he sounds so identical to Jacques, proper and gentlemanly and hurt and everything, it's uncanny.

"I'm not coming back!" Motor finally replies. "So don't try and talk me into it!"

"Fair enough—I don't pretend to expect that your mind would be so easily changed. However, I do hope you might tell us what your intentions are in running off so suddenly."

"Blue Lou," someone in the corner breathes before getting buzzed again.

Motor hesitates this time. "I'm hiding. By myself. Gunners target by sight and sound and everything, and I wanna live, so don't come looking for me cuz everyone else keeps getting in trouble. I'm hiding real good, okay? I've got a better shot by myself cuz you're all too big and troubly." My jaw tightens. "You guys hide somewhere too. It's not that bad down here—some of the Mechs are leaving, I mean. There's a bunch of them that left out this big door that won't open for me, so they must be searching for the thing that caused that shockwave. Until they figure it out or leave, I'm staying gone. Bye, and not good-bye, either!" There's a click that tells me the beacon on the other end is off, and the conversation's over. My fists clench harder than before. *He left me.*

The memory of me sitting there on the track with him when we first figured out about his haywiring flares through my mind. My kind of people are tough and distant, and we never embrace for trivial reasons—we hardly ever touch at all, but I was there for him. I held him to me. I . . . I let him get too close, I guess. *My mistake. I'm prone to those, aren't I? I'm broken, remember?*

And when they break you . . .

"He's lying about something," I decide, awarding me all sorts of looks. "I don't know what about, but he sounded too choppy to be telling the truth. There's something he's not telling us."

"Your trust is so comforting, Rat," Eli retorts.

"*Your wariness* similarly settles the worries of my brain," Voxel tells him in my defense. "I'm not attacking or judging, but it would satisfy me to put the opinion in everyone's ears that the knowledge that our protector's metal heart is too soft to suspect that anyone would wish to wrong it gives me anxiety."

"Cielhomme, guys, this is Motor we're talking about, isn't it?" Craw asks in his normal voice again—then again, nobody knows what his real voice is, now, do they? "I wouldn't expect him to try and hurt or lie to any of us, either. He's only seven, for crying out loud!"

"Yeah? You really think he gives two axels about us if he could bail on us so easily? Besides, don't we have another kid trying to get everyone hurt for no reason?" I demand, and I can tell by the way they all tense that Harmoni isn't on anyone's good side. "Last year, a faulty citizen walked out of her first grade class and pointed a gun at me. This isn't just about Motor—you can't trust *anyone*!"

"I think there can be exceptions, though, can't there?" There's hurt in Craw's voice, but I miss it. I'm missing everything. I don't care anymore. Vici was right! Where'd this pathetic, touchy-feely Rat come from?

I'm coming back and taking my rightful place again and shouting, "Of *course* not! How could there be? How could there be exceptions when my best friend skipped out on me just because I sided with *him*?" I gesture at Eli. "How could there be exceptions when I'm a cutout whose own clan of relatives rejected her just because she picked freedom? What kind of cutouts are you when you can still trust anyone?"

"You're going too far," Lily warns me. She doesn't get shocked, and she doesn't get noticed. I'm on fire now. Icy fire.

"How could there be any exceptions with my trust when everyone's keeping secrets about their extractions, huh? How could I ever give my trust away to a bunch of professional offenders, especially when one's a hacker that's literally insane—yeah, crazy, cry about it—one's a kid who can spawn black holes of destruction and runs off for no good reason the same way all the other glitching relatives did, one's famous for being ruthless, cunning and enigmatic, and *you* almost *kissed* me! I risked my life for yours, and then you almost *kissed* me, and now you're walking around thinking it's *nothing*!"

The Nobody puts his hands up in the air. "Calm down, Rat, that's just the way I am!"

"Well, that's not the way *I* am!" I fire back, almost screaming now, really on a roll even though that is the way I am, but no, I shut down that thought and say that Rat who'd pinch people's pockets while suckering them is a different Rat than me. "Don't you get that not all of us out there are you, that not all of us go and have one dance and one kiss for one night before flitting off to the next victim, that this is at least a little bit *serious* to some of us? That some of us want to *matter* to someone for a while instead of just being some passing interest? Did it ever occur to you to at least *say* something to me instead of pretending nothing ever happened so I didn't feel the nothingness that you were supposed to get rid of?"

"Look, Rat, I'm really sorry. I didn't know it'd make all your trust in me come crashing down so fast," he says, and I'm not sure whether it's supposed to be an apology or sarcasm.

"There was no trust to begin with," I snap, whirling around to face Eli. "And don't even get me started about you."

"I won't," he promises, getting to his feet with a look that kicks over my music box of memories and brings the panic and shock right back.

The fact that he's about to abandon me stabs my entire being. Of course. I deserve to be left. I'm ballistic, and it'll never be okay, but somehow, I never thought Eli'd do it, and some-other-how, I can't let it happen. "If you're leaving, then I'm going first!" I say, and stalk out the door as if it's possible to run away from getting abandoned, as if I could turn my back on getting betrayed.

Craw's the second one out of the room. "And take your attitude with you!" he yells after me before disappearing behind a door. Eli storms out third, and he actually jumps up and rips a hole in the ceiling and leaves through that, the sound of screeching metal grating against everyone's eardrums.

Ivy quietly unties Lily, and they talk in quiet tones before shaking hands so their handcuffs touch. Then they walk out, hand in hand and side by side, as if one isn't in subtle yet total control of the other.

A few seconds after everyone's gone, Jacques slowly wakes up to a dark and empty room, wondering what in the name of fire and brimstone is going on.

I shove open a door and slam it loud enough behind me for everyone in the building to hear it and scream angrily. How could I let myself get surrounded by such idiots?! None of them are mature enough to think for themselves! Forget leader, I practically have to play Mommy and keep everyone in line! Why's it gotta be me? I never asked to be the fricking martyr!

WHAT was I THINKING? I was almost TRUSTING people again! Since when's THAT worked for me? And I thought they trusted me back enough to not go running away! I had the gall to believe that Eli was right, that not everyone's the same, but THEY ARE!

Ugh, what an idiot! What else was I planning on doing, giving them a heartfelt display of my true colors? Didn't I learn the first time that it never works? The truth didn't set me free; it made me set you free. You told me I was a freak, and that's what they'd say too. I told you what I could do. You, my brother, the only one who stuck around after I couldn't remember anyone or anything else, and I told you I was getting cut out because it's not just the Plexus I screw up, it's not just my mainframe I made useless, it's everything, it's glitching everything, and I didn't want to hurt you. And I told you, and I didn't care if you didn't get extracted too, but I was hoping you'd tell me not to go. I was hoping you would come with me. You were old enough. We could've made it. We could've grown up together in that red house at the edge of the city and live happily ever after like you said, like you promised.

I got you to stop walking away for that one little second. Do you remember that? Did you feel something for me in that Plexusy, mindless haze after all, something that made you stop, that gave me one last spark of hope so I could say, "Listen, I promise I'm still the same person. Trust me. I'm still the same sister you took on walks and took to the pool for her birthday and taught how to swim and taught a whole bunch of other cool stuff and…" And I didn't really say it. I only thought it because I was too scared, and whatever it is you felt for me must've ended there because you started walking away, and that, my friend, is when you really broke my heart. You didn't look back, you didn't say good-bye, and I was just there wondering, "Oh, for Pete's sake, Statice, what'll it take to get you to trust me?"

And right before you disappeared, you took me in those stormy eyes of yours and said, "I don't know. I don't know anything for sure anymore. I don't know what to do, I don't know what to tell you, because I don't know *you*. Why don't you eat another battery, Erratica?"

Yes, you were confused. You were at a loss of words, and you were getting all sorts of things from the Plexus, but the bottom line is, you left me, left me alone with the taste of battery acid and tears, and you never came back. And here I am, about to start *trusting* again. But don't worry, I've learned my lesson well, my friend.

I'm so busy fuming, I almost pass up the hallway that leads to the room where I first woke up in, but then I stop and backtrack and sneak down the hallway. The door's busted open, and I slip inside, being the ideal shadow as I sneak through the darkness and feel my way along the opposite verticontrol table. The way they work is they create a temporary gravity field (it's got something to do with magnets and a bunch of complicated stuff I'd never understand) when they start up so that everything nearby gets pulled onto it, and then clamps come up and grab everything touching it. Then the whole field focuses solely on the things it's holding on to, so people can pull stuff off it without getting pulled into the field themselves, unless it's holding people, because then it won't let go until you break all the clamps. Even though the weak red light hardly reaches here at all so it's pitch-black in this part of the room, I have no problem finding what I'm looking for. It's glowing faintly with the number 9. My fingers curl around it, and the wall lets me have it, dropping it into my hands. The cool material relaxes me, and I pull it into position, a smile crawling on my face and a feeling blooming in my chest.

Suddenly, there're no teams. That's clear enough. At least to me it is. Back on the curb with a mainframe in my hands, broken me against the big world. No teams, no rules. Just get the points, and don't be It by the end of the play.

Sounds like my kind of game.

I decide to work my way up, since up is probably where the prize is going to be, and I think I'll end up stealing it anyway. Ripvan said that the prize was at the top of the mountain, which we're in, so up sounds pretty logical. But there's something real interesting about this place I should've got before, something I'm only figuring out for myself now since I wasn't listening before: this place is a maze. I must pass the same doorways a bunch of times, but it's impossible to tell because there's hallways that lead to other hallways, and that goes on and on and on until I'm using the emergency latch on every door to check inside for some sort of landmark, but everything's covered in darkness, which makes this even *more* fun. Unless you memorize every scrap of this place, get ready to get lost. There's something about the way the lights're positioned on the ceiling that makes me think they're supposed to help, but it seems as random as the hallways. A map wouldn't even help. This isn't even a maze, now that I think about it; it's a bowl of noodles someone threw on a table and used as a floor plan. Who builds a place this way, anyway? Oh, yeah.

After wasting a good fifteen minutes doing nothing but getting in some cardio, I'm ready to explode. The mystery of the lights is driving me up a wall, and I'm telling myself how I'm going to pick a room and hunker down when I pick up the sound of footsteps coming from the doorway to the right. My mind goes into robbery mode as I press myself against the wall, straining my ears. There're two pairs of footsteps: one pair's a careless thudding against the metal floor, which tells me the owner isn't worried about getting caught. Size-F rubber-soled boots, probably the kind they use in construction. The other pair of footsteps is equally confident but softer and longer, which means they're lighter, and they're walking heel-to-toe.

Spike and Voxel, I decide, smiling when I remember the conversation I had with Rex when I told him I could figure people out by the way they walk. Then my smile turns into a frown when I start wondering what the heck Spike and Voxel are doing together.

"Dumbest thing they ever did," Spike's saying as I creep down the hallway toward a door that's open too far to have been opened by emergency latches. Not that it would've mattered, since the shutdown included the sound system, so there wouldn't be an alarm, but it still bugs me that someone was here before me, and they pulled the door all the way open so it won't shut. "There was some great players on that team, and they just split up? I mean, yeah, I get how Shortstop and the Nobody probably won't last the night, but I gotta give the devils their due: there were three geniuses there, and two of em were superhuman. And we all know Death can't even find Mouse. The saying's true, I guess. Thinking really is old-fashioned. These idiots're gonna end up blowing the roof off this place, blast a whole new world of pain into space just for us."

"Except for you," Voxel notes quietly as I use the light of my score counter to slink around the room. There's this freak structure that I think might be for torture before I recognize them as stairs. My heart leaps into my throat, mixing with relief at the stairs and panic when I realize the footsteps are following in mine. Holding my tagger tight in one hand, I go over to the other side of the stairs—they're detached from the wall—and latch on, pulling my feet up to the other side so I disappear under the steps.

"Hey, I can still feel *some* pain, okay?" Spike snaps, and I can tell he's stressed by something. "You know, I had a clean extraction. I was one of the lucky ones, except I had to go back to the med center a few years later so they could knit me back together cuz I got run over. They gave me the option of dying or getting half rechipped so I can't feel much pain, taking a week to heal the normal way, sucking up all my inheritance to pay the Health & Medical Sector. Or I could let them totally reweave my Plexus and rebuild me so I'd never hurt again for nothing down, but that wasn't really an option, so I went halfway. That's why I can't get hurt unless I get attacked by Shortstop or electrified."

"You were run over?" Voxel asks as they walk into the room, beaming flashlights everywhere. Her voice bounces up the stairwell, strained in a way I think means she's trying to talk normal. "How did you manage such a thing?"

They stop at the bottom of the steps, and I hear Spike sigh. "You know that scene in the flick *Countless* where Gene jumps off the bridge after Last Adam cuz the idiot jumped in the river trying to kill himself, so Gene was trying to save him from drowning? Well, I figured out that if you try that in real life with one of the traffic bridges, it goes over as good as a hopper with a fan, okay? And so my brother is dead, and I am not."

His heavy boots start on the stairs, and Voxel follows close behind. "What makes you think the others will make the roof leave the building?" she asks as they walk right above me. Spike's boots almost knock me out of the underbelly of the stairs.

"Think about it, Vox. We're in a factory. We're in an illegal Surgam factory. We're in an illegal Surgam factory with a bunch of idiots, psychos, and robots. Add it up. If those bugs of yours heard Rat right, and all of the other info you got from Eli and I got from the clones last night is all right, then we've got this riddle figured out, and that prize they make here is thunder, so this whole place is a ticking time bomb. Because not only is this an illegal Surgam factory full of idiots, psychos, and robots, but it's old. Not only does this place have thunder, but it's bound to leak eventually cuz of the oldness and all the idiots running around shooting stuff. And since this thunder stuff is such a good conductor and goes Code Red Biohazard when it hits open air, all it's gonna take is one little spark to make it all light up. Sure, it'll all blow in one fast shock, won't make liquid lightning, but it'll be enough to kill anyone inside."

Half my blood goes cold at the prediction, but it doesn't get as much attention as it should because the other half's too busy boiling over something else. Gripping the side of the stairs, I swing down and push off the wall hard enough that I can scramble onto the stairs. The grace and ninja skills I display won't win me any awards, but it gets the job done. I get to my feet on a step and fling my arm into shooting position at the flashlight someone was dumb enough to bring and fire at will.

Metallic PINGs tell me two shots miss, one shot ends in a thud without a reaction, and two end in thuds that make Voxel scream and drop the flashlight. It rolls, illuminating me for an instant before flickering out and throwing us into darkness again.

"RAT!" Voxel shrieks, and I duck down, feeling crosshairs on me. "What on the skin of this world are you doing?"

"What're the bugs he's talking about, Voxel?" I demand, moving side to side so it's harder to guess where I'm at. "You were spying on us, weren't you?"

She struggles for a second before the truth forces itself out. "It's your beacon. I make it so that I claim the option of listening to anyone's beacon I wish to draw ears to, whether or not it is on or activated. I intended to use it for our purposes—"

"You're a traitor," I growl. "Even when we *were* a team, you were spying on us. And what's with Spike? Were you talking to him before we all split up too?"

Now it's Spike's turn to speak in his calm, everyone's-about-to-die voice. "Look, it's nothing serious or anything. It's just that knowledge comes with destructive abilities, and she likes knowledge, and I like destruction." Right after that word, there's the BANG of a gun, and I've got enough time to do nothing before a pellet explodes at my feet. I moved, but not far enough, and I jump and end up falling down the stairs all the way to the bottom, where I land in a mess of bruised limbs. It was just the tagger, which must mean he's worried about making a thunder leakage.

"Oh, great, now I've got Buster and Lovie against me," I spit, and they must've seen the flick about two gangsters who fall in love because it flusters them for long enough that I can run while I've got the chance. The opening I gave myself gets even bigger when they don't notice me sneak out—they start a dispute about their relationship, too busy arguing to spare me any attention, and I grin to myself, glad I know what to say. In fact, I'm so busy congratulating myself that I almost run right into someone at an intersection outside of the stair room.

I jump back in shock as they step out of the adjacent hallway in front of me, but my heart leaps when the face registers: "Vici!"

But the happiness doesn't stay long when I register the face of the other person who's got Vici by the arm.

Straight from the frying pan…

I'm so caught off guard I laugh out loud and wave my fingers cheekily at him and say, "Hey, Craig."

And into the fire.

The rapture man scowls at me. That's not a rare thing to see them doing if you're a cutout, but it never gets any easier to look at. Craig's irises flicker fast enough to make me feel sick, but they stay trained on me when I back away. I'm sure they've got some sort of targeting system, so he doesn't even have to look at his DC-5 to know it's aimed right at my forehead. In case I forgot to explain, the DC stands for demi canon, but we call it the Decapitator.

"Don't move," Vici warns me. She looks calmer than I'd ever be. "It only helps them see you."

"Thanks a lot, Vici, but I think he sees me." My mind's flying all over the place. *How'd a rapture man get here? When? Why? How many are there? Are they trying to kill us even though the Adamantration promised they wouldn't intervene? They promised! What's going on?*

"Indeed, I can see you, convict," Craig says. "You are to come with me to the factory floor, where the other contestants are being directed. As an order from Sir Adaman Vastate, we are here to gather information about the surge of electric energy that occurred two point four hours ago."

I keep my tagger low and stay still. Rapture men only shoot if you give them a reason to, but they take a lot of things as a reason. "You know the way out of here, then?"

Craig winces. "Please follow me to the factory floor. Don't ask questions."

"He has no idea," Vici translates.

"Please don't conspire amongst yourselves."

"Rat, come on, with this guy, we might be able to figure out something about what's going on," Vici's saying, pretending Craig's not even here, but I'm not giving either of them my attention. Out of the corner of my eye, there's a gun barrel poking around a doorway. Uh-oh. The frying pan's come back to hit me in the head.

I grab Craig and push him in front of me and Vici right before Spike fires, but Craig has enough time before hitting the floor to get off a round of his own. Then he falls to the floor and doesn't move again.

The world stops for a second. I'm staring at a dead rapture man.

I literally watch the light leave his eyes. He's gone.

Vici gasps. "You killed Craig!" she cries, and at first, I think she's talking to me, but then she pulls out a tin can or something, pulls the tab, and grabs the handle that shoots out when it telescopes into a meter-long Death shooter, the end of which gets pointed at Spike.

"Why don't you blame your friend for shoving everyone in the way before you go accusing *me* of murder?" Spike asks before she can continue. He's got a hand clutched on his arm, and blood soaks between his fingers. Did I do that? Maybe I should fire blindly more often. "When you think about it, it's not *my* fault he's dead."

"Um, humans? I'm not vertically beneath the impression that these are the correct seconds for some deep conversation about the taking of life," Voxel says, pointing at Craig. Under his shirt, next to a bullet hole in his chest, a red light blinks at a steady pulse.

"So they didn't give him any armor, but they made sure to know where to find him when he's dead," I retort. Or maybe it's a ping, maybe he's not dead, maybe—but there's no time to think about it.

Vici takes a step out of the hallway. There's clanging sounds coming from down there. "I don't think it's so the Adamantration can find him," she says slowly, giving me the two twisted fingers that tell me to run. "What the…" She pretends to be super interested in whatever's down the hallway so Voxel and Spike go over to look too, while I slip right behind them and shoot back the way I came.

Spike yells something, and gunfire breaks out behind me as something booms into the hallway. I skid to a stop and turn around to see a streak of metal bound in over the rapture man, spreading out its four long arms for balance. The red emergency lights glint off its chest as it turns to Spike and lets out a whir as its hands all turn into little cannons. "YOU'VE GOTTA BE *KIDDING* ME!" he bellows before the gunner pounces.

"Vici!" I shout, and she tears her eyes away to run after me. Two more gunners go flying into the hallway, and Spike and Voxel shoot crazily, but the things're barely fazed enough to hold back from ripping the duo apart. One Mech turns toward us fast enough to make me jump out of my skin and back. I grab the door and try to pull it shut, but some idiot opened it up all the way, so now it's stuck with just enough sticking out of the wall so I can grab hold of the handle, but I can't pull the door open, not even when Vici helps me. The gunner lets out a mechanical ring, and the two of us scream at the same time.

Then there's a flash of red and light and everything goes dark as the door gets forced shut by some strong ghost. I stumble back from the sound of metal hitting metal, then it's metal *screeching* on metal as gunner claws scrape the other side of the door, letting in shards of bloody light. A hand locks around my arm and sweeps me up the stairs. From the surprised shout to my right, I know the ghost's got Vici too, and while they might've saved me, I still have no idea who they are in this darkness, which is a problem. By the time we're up the stairs, I've wiggled myself out of the grip and spun myself to a stop. "Who's there?" I demand as the scraping gets worse below us, driving me up a wall.

"The boogeyman! Who d'you think it is?" a familiar voice snarls, moody as ever. "You coming or d'you wanna get ripped up by those things? I really don't care, cuz I need some new laces, anyway."

"We're coming," Vici decides for us, and Rex flicks on a penlight so we can see. Both me and Vici jump away, and he covers the light a little, thinking that's what surprised us, but then he notices how we're gawking at him and rolls his eyes, which probably hurts: forget a broken nose, someone must've tried to rearrange his face with a hammer.

"Don't act all scared, y'know what happened," he says, turning around. "This was just one hit, by the way, and it's better than before cuz Melodi fixed it for me so I can at least talk without sounding like an even bigger idiot. I'm not stupid, though, I didn't and I'm not going back for more, don't worry. You don't glitch with Jacques, I learned that fast."

Rex keeps trying to go, but I stay put and cross my arms. "Did you break his ribs?"

He does his annoyed circle march and nearly falls over. "Ugh! I shoulda known it doesn't even matter I nearly got my head knocked off, who cares, I'm just the freak!"

"I didn't say that, Rex. I just want to know who almost killed Jacques."

He sighs long and hard out his broken nose before jerking his head and eyes to face me. Between his ashen face and crimson eyes, he looks ghoulish in the light. "I don't *almost* do anything," he says quietly, twirling the penlight to show off the emblem on the end of it. That's a rapture man's penlight, complete with bloodstains on the side. "If I want a guy dead, he'll be dead, ain't no almost about it. And before you go judgin' me, why don't you go ask Spike and Voxel what they think of you getting people killed?" Everybody cringes as another gunner hits the door and tears open a hole big enough for them to get in. They both try getting in at the same time, though, so that buys us a few extra seconds. "Run!" Rex yells, but nobody needs an invitation.

There's only one door to go into, so that's where we go, slamming it shut behind us. "They only target people that were involved in killing a rapture man," Vici explains as we go down the hallway, giving Rex a pointed look as he ingeniously keeps the light on while we run, so my eyes start hurting. That, along with the spinning emergency lights, almost makes him disappear in the white and red.

"Naw, they must go for anybody—ain't my fault, I took this off some unconscious chap," Rex admits, sounding sort of embarrassed. "So don't go blamin' me! Oi, Melodi, where you at?" he calls down the hall. A peal of laughter responds, and he turns into the room ahead, but I hesitate, slowing to a stop.

"That woman freaks me out," I admit to Vici as the robots hit the door behind us.

"I don't like her, either, but she's smarter than you think, and this room's our best bet, Rat," Vici says, pulling me to the door, but I pull myself back.

"I'm not staying in the same room as her! Rex is bad enough. I don't need another bat to add to the belfry!"

Vici sighs, searching me as the gunners scratch at the door and someone from the room asks if they're being insulted. "Rat," she says sternly, giving me the tap-of-her-ear signal that means I'm supposed to follow her.

"Give me a good reason," I order, crossing my arms. Maybe a few hours ago, I'd be tripping over myself to follow her to the ends of the earth, but why? Why even pretend I could ever trust someone with my feelings that way? People only get close to you to cut your Thread. They say they've got your back, and then they stab you in it.

"Maybe because it's better than wandering around the place aimlessly," Vici suggests, equally moody. "What's gotten into you?"

"Nothing. Fine, I'm coming." I walk after her, keeping my arms crossed. The door slides shut behind me, and by door, I mean a wall of concrete a decimeter thick, so if I tell you I think I've made a really dumb decision, take it as an understatement.

Still, there's something comforting about the familiarness of the place, with the way every bit of the wall's smothered in maps and diagrams and blueprints and plans and anything else you can think of that goes on paper, crinkled and yellowed with age. Some drift up because they're covering a vent, and they overlap each other, so there's so many layers I couldn't guess what color the walls are. It's so unexpected in this building, so untechnical, that I'd be relaxed enough to flop into one of the ugly plastic chairs if they weren't so ugly, and if it wasn't for Melodi. Her bald head glows orange as she drifts around the room with a match, pulling candles out of her hat and setting them on tables and chairs and the floor, so I freeze because one false move would set me on fire. Suddenly, the paper walls aren't doing it for me anymore.

"When the power goes out, you light candles!" Melodi cackles as she tries to mount a candle on my arm.

"Rex," Vici says even though she's glaring at Melodi, "What makes you think this place is safe?"

"I thought the giant door gave it away." Rex does his famous eye roll even as his dreadlocks come dangerously close to a candle on the chair he sits in. The giant door now makes me feel half as safe. This room has turned from a bunker into a fiery tomb.

"Melodi, quit it with the candles," I snap, still standing in the doorway without moving a muscle. "Didn't anyone ever tell you not to play with matches?"

The relic stops with her arm halfway to a candle, silent, watching the flame on the match sway. "Ernie told me not to play... with matches," she breathes, her milky eyes looking somewhere far, far away from here. That distant stare's always been there, just hiding beneath layers, and it's something you might call crazy, and maybe it is, maybe that's the point. But I'm looking at those eyes now, and in the flickering light that reflects off their surface, I can see bereaved gemstone eyes searching a distant shore. I can see ancient eyes looking for some spark they've lost so easily and so often, I can see albino eyes watching the world for a way in, and I can see gray eyes watching the mirror for a way out. And I remember that crooked heart, black on a white screen, that proved the abnormality of my mind as words now dance in the back of it: *none whosoever walks this world is exempt from the adamant winds of Fate.*

I manage to get over to Melodi without going up in smoke, and I set my hand on her shoulder. She looks up at me with those distant eyes of hers, and yeah, it might be insanity. But I read somewhere yesterday that the course of love never did run smooth, and lunatics and lovers are the same breed, anyway.

"No," Melodi mouths when the match flame blows out. She drops it with an airy laugh and searches her pockets with shaky hands. "When the power goes out, you light candles. He said so. He told me so. One more. We need one more. A hundred and eighty candles to bring the lost home when you are out of power."

First I frown then pull the lighter out of the woman's hand when she takes it out of her pocket and tries lighting it. "Hey, Melodi? I don't think this is a good idea, okay?" Vici relaxes since she guesses *someone* in the room has brains, but Melodi's hands start shaking, so I hold on to one of them, grabbing a lit candle with my other hand. "This way," I tell her, and her other hand takes hold of the candle, so we both light number one eighty.

"How's that any better?" Rex asks, and Vici looks just as confused and annoyed, but she's got too much of a pride to keep intact to ask.

I hold the lighter up to my face. It seems so innocent, just a faded blue lighter, and so vintage, it's amazing it's gotten this far, amazing how such a simple design could survive in this techy world, and for a second, man, I want a smoke. But it's not innocent, no, it radiates disaster, and I slowly work out what my suspicion's telling me: the simple design makes a spark, which wouldn't be so bad except sometimes, one spark is all it takes.

Take now for example: a spark of a thought leads to a chain reaction. Now that I'm thinking of lighters and I remembered Tom and Hilda out of nowhere, everything starts lining up. I hold the lighter far away from me, up where everyone can bask in its simple, deadly glory. "Ladies and gentlemen, feast your eyes on the item that broke half the Plexus in Tersatellus."

"Great, they both lost their marbles," Rex mutters, and Melodi starts hooting again.

"Hang on, I can explain! First, Vici, tell me everything you can about liquid lightning. Not everything," I amend when she gets that sciency look. You might want to skip to Melodi's mollified summary of Vici's explanation, because when she gets that look, whatever comes out of her mouth makes people's heads explode, but I prepare myself. "What can you tell us about its other forms?"

Her eyes glitter with the Plexus. "The real name of the element involved is insipidly defined by the Adamantration as Tersatellum after various . . . sorry, useless information. States of matter, section three. Its states of matter are unique in the fact that they are determined by what they come in contact with, not so much to do with temperature as most elements. If it bonds with hydrogen, which it will do in water or in air automatically because of its high electronegativity, it stays gaseous as dihydrogen Tersatellum, or 'thunder.' When forced to bond instead with oxygen with the presence of heat to catalyze the reaction—this is also known as burning—it takes the form of a solid, but when unexposed to any element but itself, it remains as a gas until the vast amounts of electrical energy it requires to mysteriously strengthen its polarity is given, at which point the intermolecular bonds are strong enough to turn the gas into a liquid."

Vici doesn't look convinced by the explanation, and she also doesn't know where I'm going with this, but I motion for her to continue reading.

"Because of these strange state changes, each state has its own properties, closer to different elements than states of matter, especially in the ways they conduct electricity: Tersatellum has so many electrons that every state is practically materialized electricity, but as a solid, the potential electricity is inaccessible and can only be burned back into a gas to change state again into something usable.

"As a liquid, the electricity is conserved as long as it doesn't come close to a conductor or reacts with hydrogen, because then it releases the energy of its intermolecular bonds and turns into a gas. As a gas, the dihydrogen Tersatellum somehow has the ability to take electrons from any surrounding atoms in the air to attempt to make a balance when the polarity of one molecule of the hostile gas changes, catalyzing a mass imbalance of any dihydrogen Tersatellum involved.

"It's considered to be a sort of superconductor due to the way the imbalances carry a charge across the entire 'cloud' of gas. And those sketchy facts are basically all that is known about Tersatellum."

Rex flattens his hand and whooshes it over his head to convey how much of that he absorbed, straight-faced and everything, so Melodi breaks out of her giggles into whoops of laughter before grinning at Vici. "My dear, you got that word for word from Ernest Orlov's article on Tersatellum, so by no means is it sketchy!" the bat chuckles. "Boy-child, this is what the dear meant: there's tiny bits of stuff in the world called atoms, and some of it's Tersatellum, and they've got three ways to make themselves. Solid, it's useless. Liquid, it's got great potential to power all your little cities and cars and whatnot. Gas? Gas clouds in the open air? One spark and ZAP! You're dead!" Melodi screeches something that might still be laughter.

"Uh, thanks," Rex mutters.

I hold up the lighter again. "Spike made a good point I overheard a while ago: this place is old, and if we're all running around, shooting each other, something's going to leak. Also, as a solid, this stuff *isn't* useless. No matter what form it's in, it's the second river of the riddle—the leeches hate it, or at least the electricity. That's why smoking it keeps the leeches away."

Vici works it out. "The vials! The prize vials are full of Tersatellum! These people burn the Tersatellum to make the solid, then lighting the ends of that on fire must somehow turn it back into a gas that the leeches despise! And the defense turning it into acid when the power comes back on... that's just electricity liquefying it, and that's why the riddle says we need the second river to advance—it's liquid lightning for our mobiles!"

That hits me hard, and all my triumph fades. We can't use the prize for leech immunity or else we won't be able to move tomorrow, and this is losing its racing quality fast enough as it is. "Anyway, that's not what I was getting at," I say, sullen because that botches my whole protection plan. "When you burn the stuff, it turns into gas again, right? And that gas goes all electro-crazy when you give it any electricity, right?" Everyone nods politely without having any idea where I'm going with this, and I turn to the relic this time. "Hey, Melodi? Where'd you get these candles?"

"Dagur's Island, of course, since that's where I'm from," she sniffs. I thought so, since she's bundled up the way everyone else from that island is. "They make lots of candles, good candles, but half of them reek, and Ernie won't come home to that! Nobody comes home to that! Not even..." The bat goes still for a second then starts giggling again. "Not even beasties."

Rex sits forward. "You mean the leeches? That's what that nasty stuff Hilda was burning was s'posed to do, keep the leeches away cuz they don't like the smell of it burning?" I nod, waiting for him to make the connection. He thinks about it. "Well, I can't blame em. What's this got anything to do with that, though?"

I examine the lighter he pointed at. "Remember when Tom gave Hilda one of these when we left?" I ask slowly, and Vici gasps. Rex frowns and concentrates so hard his head might fall off, so after a couple of silent seconds, I continue, "Hilda was burning that Tersatellum stuff, which turned into that bad-smelling gas, which makes a huge wave of electricity at the slightest *spark*." Everyone jumps when I scratch my nail on the lighter, imitating clicking it.

"Oh, *dang*," Rex mutters to himself, standing up and putting his hands on the sides of his head to keep the revelation from spilling out his ears. "She musta been burning that junk when she used that lighter to light it up, and that's why that giant fricking wave killed half the Plexus in Tersatellus!"

Me and Vici nod, since that's exactly what we were thinking. But we're not there; we're outside looking in through a weird lens, so we don't actually know what's going on. I'll give you a hint—it's not as true as we think.

⟴

One Craig far away in a building carved in the shape of a tree stands up. He's alone with one other person in the dark room, which is devoted to incredible amounts of complicated machines that only one person could ever understand the functionings of. The place is known as the Loom Room with a nod to the Plexus.

"You were right, sir," Craig says. "According to the diagnostics, the shock absorbers in the mainframes still operate fine, so the electricity shouldn't have fazed anything, and according to these diagnostics I took here, there are traces of that destructive chemical we were talking about—the traces are all over the Plexus machines. This is why the Plexus was nearly unraveled abroad. Someone somehow managed to break in and attack. We still don't know about the energy wave in Hudson Bay, but this was terrorism on our own soil. If you hadn't been so quick to rewire the system and reweave the damaged codes of the Plexus, then it might not work at all right now, and..." Craig shudders at the thought.

"Then it's a lucky thing I happened to have plans for new Plexus programming on hand. Yes, my friend, new programming. Things are about to change, and for good," Vastate promises, turning for the door. "As for this horrible attack, I believe we both know the only man in Tersatellus who has the resources and capacity of violence to attempt such an appalling deed. I never imagined he would try something so utterly heartless, and I apologize for inviting him to meet with me anywhere near this apparatus. My point of our conference was to see if I could salvage some humanity from those immoral remains, but this only proves such a thing is useless to try. I'm afraid I've underestimated an unfiltered man's faculty for cruelty. Lock him up. He'll still be in the room in the Criminal Resolution Sector Headquarters where he chose to stay, and he'll resist your efforts, claiming innocence. Do not believe it. For the sake of bringing justice to our nation, bring our friend Jad—ah, Sir Adaman Steele to the dungeons below us with all due force."

- VI -

Jailbreak

"They've been at it for a while, haven't they?" I growl as the gunners keep working at the door. They're quiet since the door's so thick, but their scratching's been going on ever since we got here, and the longer we sit, the louder they sound, and the more my head hurts. "And what's with these ugly chairs, huh? Whose idea were they?"

"Rat," Vici says in her warning voice she gives me when she knows I'm going to nose my way into something I shouldn't, but the warning's more of a plead. She knows how I get, and some savage part of me is glad she's scared. She should be. I keep pacing and kick a chair, and she flinches.

"Heck, the whole island's whacked! Whose idea was it to dump a bunch of nuts into a bowl and let them come up with this stupid Tag thing? Who's putting Tersatellum in the vials? What's with this place?" I stop pacing with my fists at my sides. "And WHAT is with ALL this PAPER?!"

"Cielhomme, what's *wrong* with you?" Rex demands as I start ripping papers off the wall.

"It's probably the Mechs," Vici explains sheepishly as she yanks papers from my hands the second I get them off the wall. She's got the look of a mom who's using second nature to put stuff back on the shelves when her kid keeps grabbing it, hoping they don't find a bomb. "She gets antsy when she's by machinery too long."

"Antsy? I've got a headache, that's all! How can I concentrate on being a perfect stupid angel for you all if my head's falling open? I'm no electrode and nothing's perfect and I should be allowed to complain sometimes!"

"I'm really sorry," Vici apologizes to everyone but me, thrusting a stack of paper on Rex so she's got free hands again. "Rat, please calm down!"

"Calm down? Are you serious? We're being overtaken! Overwhelmed, outnumbered!" All sorts of other conspiratorial nonsense about machinery pours out of my mouth after that—it always happens after too much mechanical exposure. I grab a bunch of old designs and tear them down the middle. A rip off to my right makes me jump and turn.

"Now you're talkin' my language!" Rex grins, halving more papers. "It'll be the Metal Insurrection but without the good guys."

"If even lighters aren't safe, then what is?" I go on. Vici watches the two of us helplessly, and Melodi laughs her head off. "It's only a matter of time.

Machines will conquer the world! When the Plexus didn't tip everyone off, the distilling units should've."

"Exactly! No privacy!" Rex shudders at the thought of those stupid things before shredding more paper. "All this junk they throw at us that's s'posed to make life better, I hate it! This is what I think of their stupid perfection!"

He flings the confetti into the air, and Vici runs over and tries to catch the pieces, screaming. My vision's going blurry, and I'm going numb, but I'm laughing, I think, and throwing the paper around too. "I uphold my right to remain violent!" I choke out with a Melodi-grin on my face before falling forward, knocking candles everywhere. Not that it makes a difference. The papers were already catching, anyway. My vision's flickering like I'm sitting inside my head and watching the world through a bad VDU. Each pulse is an explosion in my head, and I don't know if it's supposed to have a rhythm or anything, but it doesn't.

"Why would you encourage her?" Vici's scolding Rex, trying not to hyperventilate as the room starts filling up with smoke.

Rex, who didn't seem to know that paper caught fire, shoves his hands in his pockets. "Well, how was I s'posed to know this would happen? What's wrong with her, anyway? Is she doing that same thing you did?"

Vici frowns then takes a better look at me and drops to my side, officially freaking out. "Rat? What's wrong? Say something!"

"Something," I spit. I can't even see her by now.

"Alright, she's okay for now." Vici coughs as she stands up again. "Now we need to figure a way out of here." More paper catches fire, making the little room glow with it, and outside the only door, the gunners make a great effort to get *in*side the only door. Melodi points to a vent, half laughing, half coughing, and Vici manages to get over without setting herself on fire. "Too small," she gasps, sucking in the fresh air the vent's giving. "None of us could fit. Well, Rat could find a way, probably."

"No time for admiring Mouse and her escapabilities, we gotta put out this fire!" Rex looks around for some magically placed bucket of water, and when he doesn't find one, he starts spitting at the flames. Everyone's clothes're starting to catch fire, and there's more smoke in the air than oxygen, and here's me on the ground, giggling while I burn. Melodi, who's burning too, watches me, and I think I know why she laughs so much now. I'm only laughing because it's the only alternative to crying. The sounds fade as this ringing sound reaches a fever pitch in my skull, and I start closing my eyes and letting it fade, guessing that this is it. Whatever.

Then, clarity. The ringing disappears. I gasp for the smoky air, sitting up straight. *What's going on? Why's everything on fire?*

"Rat's back." Vici works her way over to me, feverishly patting out the fires on both of us. "What happened? Did you abandon all sense? Why on earth did you throw that paper around?!"

I shrug, unable to look at her. "C'mere, there's more air down closer to the floor. Stay away from the walls and you should be fine," I tell everyone, kicking all the candles away from me. Rex and Vici huddle close, but Melodi stays where she was sitting, swaying and smiling and burning. "Come on, Melodi!"

She shakes her bald head. "Ernie wants me back," the relic breathes.

I start to protest, but she won't listen. Vici watches me intently. "Rat, what just happened to you? Do you even remember?"

"The Mechs are gone," I say simply, looking around again. "So I feel a little better now. And yeah, I remember, but now's not the time to talk about it, okay?"

Rex slaps his head to extinguish his dreads. "The Mechs're gone?" he repeats. "How'd *that* happen?"

In answer, there's a roar and a spinning blade eats through our door. Everyone's head whips to watch as it carves a hole in the door, and three good kicks force it open. Smoke gets sucked out of the hole as Revany swings herself in, chainsaw in hand. "What're y'all cooking in here?" she yells, grinning, and I stare in disbelief.

"Rev, you came all this way to save us!" Vici stands up with gratitude all over her face, and she's about to ask how Revany knew where to find us when five metal pellets explode against her.

"Y'all think Rev came all this way to *save* y'all? There's no saving in Tag, folks, there's only winning," the woman sneers and holds down the trigger, firing tons of tagger pellets into the room. There's nowhere to duck for cover except behind the ugly chairs, and Rex and Vici do that, while Melodi grins and bears it while I take aim with the tagger I've had out ever since Revany got here and return fire.

Revany staggers back when she gets hit, a shocked look on her face. "Yeah, that's right, get back," I say to the woman with the chainsaw as I stand. Two gunners lie in pieces at her feet. "How'd you get into the factory? Who came with you?"

"Rip came with Rev," she replies. "And Rev came in through a wall with her chainsaw." Oh, of course, the chainsaw. Shoulda seen that one coming.

I look behind me at the others. "So there's a way out!"

"I'd like it if you used the way out of this room first!" Vici coughs, and I scramble out, shooting at Rev to make her back up. She shoots me right back, and she's got better aim than I do, so my arm's getting a pretty good bruise by the time Rex and Vici're out. "Come on, run!" The two start running back down the hallway, and I start to follow then dive back into the burning room, which is so thick with smoke even Revany won't go near it. Idiots find hiding spots where psychos dare not tread, I guess. My plan's working—with Revany avoiding the room, she picks someone else to follow, so here's the best place to wait for her to get gone.

"Melodi, you alive in here?" Holding my breath, I creep between the flames and go over to where Melodi's collapsed on a chair. "Oh, no."

She rolls her head to face me. Her eyes still glitter with laugher, and she puts a burned hand on mine. "You'll turn out okay," she assures me with a toothless smile. "Ernie would approve. If only you would…"

I glance behind me a fifth time to make sure Revany isn't coming, and to wait out the storm a while more, I put my hand on Melodi's. She's slipping. "If only I'd what?"

"Be the choir," Melodi whispers all secretly then, with one last laugh, goes still.

I stare at her. "I'm surrounded by thespians," I mutter and start shaking her cuz I know she's not dead, but then a pellet shatters against the side of my head. *So much for my plan!* I think as I angrily turn and shoot Revany about a million times.

"What's wrong with you?" I yell at her, stomping away from Melodi. I don't miss her much, if you can't tell.

"What's wrong with you?" Revany mocks me, snickering. "Y'all're losing, by the way. And Rev gets the feeling y'all don't wanna lose. Y'all should tag more Bruises, or else y'all don't stand a chance."

I straighten up. "Wait. Bruises?"

She catches my tone and nods, giving her chainsaw chain a few tugs. "Rev let em in right after her, so blame Rev, not me," she smirks before turning and running down the hall in search for leeches, and I start to hear them at the far reaches of my hearing—hissing, shrieking, hunting for our blood.

Boy, this just gets better and better.

Vici unpresses herself from the wall and walks over to me. She's brushing metal dust off her shirt, so I guess Revany was chasing her for a while before she decided I made an easier target. "All right, you need to start explaining right now."

"Explain? What is there to explain? Machines drive me nuts, okay? You already knew that! Now isn't the time for this!"

But Vici shakes her head, frustrated. "That's the problem, Rat, is it's never the time for this. You never tell anyone anything. We worked together for years, and I thought these things merely give you headaches, not made you abandon all sense and shred papers and set rooms on fire! Melodi is *dead* because of you! If I'd have known this happened to you, perhaps I could've done something to prevent this! Don't you ever think of the repercussions of your actions, of keeping all your troubles to yourself until something leaks out and gets someone injured? Why didn't you ever tell me?"

My fists clench. "And why should I tell you?" I scoff. "You think you're some kind of angel or something and I'm supposed to dump all my life's secrets on you? What makes you so special that you deserve to know anything about me? I'm the real robber who could steal the Plexus out of the air if she tried hard enough. You're just a girl that's good with technology and falls to the floor sometimes."

Her jaw drops, and I can see she's seriously offended. "Where'd *this* come from? Do you have some personality disorder I didn't know about too?"

I give the question a wave of dismissal. "Don't take it personal or anything. I'm being a bully to all you poor, precious heroes because I've remembered I can't trust any of you. I am just stairs to you whether you know it or not."

Vici throws her arms up, shaking her head. "So I suppose that all those years we worked together, all those heists we went on, all of that time I thought we were friends, it was a lie, it all means nothing."

"I don't know, Vici. You tell me. You've made that decision already." I take a step forward as the clock strikes three above us. "You were the one to pick Lily over me. You were the one who kept shutting me out even after that. Keep in mind I kept trying to come back, and you kept giving me the cold shoulder, and if you were half the friend you thought you were, you'd know that doesn't sit well with me. You betrayed me first," I snarl, and before she can react, I tag her. "I'm just returning the favor."

Vici looks at me in horror for a second before shaking her head and turning and running and running and running away. I drop my arm and watch her, a laugh bubbling up in my chest. It's a funny kind of laugh because it comes out my eyes in a form called tears and hurts so good I don't stop until I sink against the wall, numb and hollow. The path I'm on stretches out ahead of me, and I think about it, watch my push turn into shove until I end up getting everyone killed, and I don't care. Some part of me planned that all along.

Some other part of me knows I'm supposed to get out of here before something or someone finds me and gets me killed, but I don't care. The thing us, I kinda want to care, but it won't come.

Maybe it's because of the electronics, I reason and pull out my beacon and prepare to chuck it, but it turns on, so I settle against the wall since the beacon's got something to tell me. A bunch of messages're left because I didn't look at them. While I read in the awful light, the others on the beacon system talk to each other about something I don't listen to. The first message says that there was an electricity problem that's getting corrected, and the rapture ops're coming into the bay to investigate. Then it says that the problem's been fixed and the next pirate's being chosen to come after us. Then there's a screen that tells me someone named Emily Swift has entered the bay. And the last screen tells me that Emily Swift has been exterminated.

I don't care.

I hit my head against the wall, unable to think about anything. Not about what to feel. Not about where to go. Not about what to do. Well, when in doubt, why don't I eat another… never mind.

"She was honestly the last person I expected to crack, but she went first not too long ago," Craw's saying on the beacon system, and I start listening in a removed way, sitting forward and holding the beacon in my hand. "When Motor bailed, she flew off the handle about this whole trust thing and ran off." There's gunfire in the background, and he doesn't sound relaxed. Good.

"She nearly got Spike and I killed many times afterward," Voxel adds in. "I don't believe she finds interest in getting everyone out alive anymore."

"Pardon my doubts, but this all seems highly unlikely to me," Jacques says, but even the smoothened sound of his voice doesn't move me. "Why would she do such things?"

Oh, but Jacques, you know why. Because when they break you, you have to break them back, not for revenge, but to hide how bad it hurts.

"Because she's a brat, that's why." The fact that Vici could alter the beacon system so fast to include herself in their conversation doesn't surprise me, but the venom in her voice does. "She's nothing but a temperamental, selfish brat. She doesn't really care about any of you, and she never did—all she wanted was the protection."

There's a general chorus of bickering before one voice cuts through them: "Come on, everyone, don't be that way. I know from experience that people have reasons for even the maddest things they do, trust me."

"Funny word choice you've got there, Eli," I comment, and I can imagine everyone jumping guiltily, realizing I was listening to all this. It's okay. People talk about me behind my back all the time, and they don't even know it.

"Rat! Where are you? We're trying to get everyone down to the lowest floor, the factory floor, to try to find a way out of this place. We need your expertise right about now."

"Expertise? I'm good at breaking into residencies and being a shadow. You don't need me for anything," I assure him.

"Well, then, we *want* you here. It doesn't matter if you think you're worth it or not, what's a band without a choir?"

I laugh at that. I'm taking Melodi's place as the laugher. "Oh, really? Maybe you should've thought of that before we all split up. What, did you get hit over the head or something? What made you change your mind? Cuz I honestly thought you hated me." The look on his face before he left flashes through my mind, and I wince, and I'll admit that it hurts because I told you I'd be honest. The only thing I like less than machinery is getting abandoned. You should know.

"What? No, that's not what I—I wasn't going to leave, I swear—"

"I saw that look in your eyes. You were gone."

"Well, you're wrong. You read me wrong." My eyebrows jump at this possibility. "And I just ran afterwards because I got mad, which was stupid. Look, it's just, I... I'm not perfect, okay? I'm sorry. I guess I let my anger get to me. It's happened more than I'd like, so it's something I need to work on. Can you let me have that chance?"

My eyes slam shut, and I exhale the same way I saw someone do in a flick once when they got stabbed in the gut. *I* never had that chance. You never let me have it. So why the heck should I let someone else have it?

On the other hand, *why not?*

Would I really wish that hurt on someone else? Maybe, maybe not. I don't care. I really don't. But a sound at the edge of my hearing makes the hair on the back of my neck stand up, and I get to my feet. Unearthly hissing rises in the distance, pressing toward me through the tendrils of smoke that dance slowly through the air.

"C'mon..." Eli sounds shaky about this. "Stop being such a thespian!"

Holy sticks, he really just said that to me. Priceless.

I choke down a smile. "Fine, I'm coming, but just so I can get out of this place. To me, the only thing this factory's cranking out is headaches and life threats." I hesitate then decide to add, "Keep an eye out for the leeches, everyone. Revany let them into the factory."

"Thank you for that piece of information. I hope it is something greater than a random fancy in the dark whirlwind of your negative emotion for us," Voxel says. "Allow me to assist you to the factory floor where a few of us presently reside. No matter what things happen to you, don't leave your beacon—it's how I'm tracking you."

"Alright, then, tell me where to go." I stand up, sore but ready. "Please."

Voxel's voice softens when she starts giving me the directions. I get moving, back the way I came and into the dark stairwell again. Lots happened when I was in the candle room, apparently—torn Mech hulls and wires lie here and there, and rapture uniforms are everywhere, but the bodies are missing, and for a while, this's a mystery to me. Then I start noticing how the hissing is getting closer, and how the walls look melty, and I realize it might be their acidic spit eating through the metal when they're licking up rapture man blood off the walls. Heck, they probably started trying to eat the walls, from the looks of it. The walls and everything else they could find. Hunger's getting to all of us.

My jog turns into a run that turns into a sprint, but the sounds keep pressing close. The numbness flies off me in layers as I start panicking, remembering those horrible teeth and tongues and the thought of all of us working together to fight off a horde spurs me faster. Give up the grudges! Survive! Survive!

"Am I close?" I pant into the beacon as I fly.

"Turn left and you'll almost be on the correct floor," Voxel tells me, and I take the left, glancing over my shoulder to see a blur of black-and-blue. And metal.

The power starts coming back, and lights flare on and off as I careen into another stairwell and almost fall down all the steps, but when something mechanical lets out a freaky warning behind me, there's nothing almost about it. I jump off, landing hard enough that my pounding head almost explodes, but the Mech that found me has the same idea to jump off, making me scramble so that it doesn't land on me. It follows me easily, considering I can't get more than a dozen meters between us—I'm too tired, too hungry, my head hurts too much for me to get any sort of lead on the thing. But when a good five leeches drop down behind it, screaming and flicking their tongues hungrily at me, I find the strength to kick it into high gear.

"They're on to me!" I yell into the beacon, and I'm about to say something else, who knows what, when the disc gets shot out of my hands. "NO!" I dive off into a room to the right after the beacon without even thinking that it's going to end up getting me cornered.

The lights flash again and start strobing irregularly as I back away from the door, scanning the room for anything, and the vent catches my eye. With shaking hands, I grab the first tool-looking thing I can find on a table and go for the vent cover, ripping it off in record time.

"CATCH!" I scream, throwing the vent cover at the Mech, who shoots it about fifty times so it falls to the floor in a holey heap. It turns to do the same thing to me, but I'm already worming my way through the vent. "Voxel, you hear me? Oh, please respond," I beg the wounded beacon as I crawl.

"Yes, Rat. I'm recalculating your route. Your best option is to GET OUT RIGHT NOW!" the woman interrupts herself, and the light coming from the room behind me gets blotted out by a very angry leech. Imagine a foreign-sounding curse go through my head in curly letters. I scrabble through the darkness until I see another vent and bust it open on the third kick, dropping to the floor hard. The leech comes out right on top of me, and I freak out, swinging my fists and tool thing at the leech, and something kinda crazy happens: my fist goes right through, but the tool gets stuck, and the leech flies off me, screaming.

"Metal," I gasp, getting to my feet. "That's, what you eat, cuz it's the only thing, you can touch!"

Speaking of metal, you'll never guess what busts through the door behind me.

I hit the floor, hands on my head to squeeze myself into a smaller target, but the instant the gunner starts firing, the other four leeches start pouring out of the vent and on top of me. Three of them turn to the giant hunk of metal and start swarming it for a meal, but one of them still goes for me, and I don't have anything to defend myself with anymore except for my tagger, so I fire away into the thing's mouth in the hope that it gets satisfied enough to stop trying to eat me. No such luck—it just gets annoyed and whips out its tongue, and it eats my tagger and that's the end of that.

"Rat, the pellets make them target you, and your jacket's been hit," Eli reminds me, and my mind flings that hint together before really thinking about it, so before anyone can imagine how dumb this'll look, I rip off Craw's jacket, throw it on the leech's face and run. Sure enough, it stays away from me, but I'm not free for long.

One of the leeches from the Mech looks up and follows me with a hiss, nearly licking me, so I stumble as I shoot down the hallway. The lights keep flashing, so my eyes don't have any time to adjust and my legs are turning into slush and I'm still coughing up smoke from when I set the room on fire, but I keep running, keep clinging to this hope that maybe I'll last another sixty seconds. Story of my life.

"Go right!" Voxel demands as I feel a machine coming at me from the left, and I skid to the right, bullets blowing right past me. There's two gunners this time, and I know they're missing me for the same reason I'm almost falling over every step I take: we're all suffering from my headache. More leeches find us, lashing their tongues at the Mechs, but they don't stop so I keep running. "Almost there! Hold on! You're going to make it!" Voxel promises, but I won't. I know I won't.

Finally, a bullet grazes my side, and the leeches's screaming grates so hard on my head along with the pain of the scrape I stumble bad, and the Mechs get too close. They're too big. It's too much. My skin goes ice cold, and I fall with a shudder, collapsing on the floor right in the doorway of a huge room with iron bridges, metal cutters, and gigantic glass spheres. A memory skitters across my mind and crashes into the dark somewhere else. Gritting my teeth so hard they'll probably go up into my gums (then I'll really be the new Melodi), I do the fastest crawl you've ever seen into the room.

"GET AWAY!" I bellow as someone comes running toward me. *I just want to die alone!*

"Let me help—"

"NO!" I can't think! I kick and punch at anything close to me because anything I don't understand gets categorized as a threat and I don't understand everything so it's all trying to kill me! There's no friend or foe at this point! It's just live or die and everything's trying to get me to die so everything has to die so I can live!

"Rat, calm down!" they shout again, hurling one of the Mechs away from me with superhuman strength, so the haze in my head clears a little. The other Mech keeps trying to come for me but can't get close enough—every time it gets to the point where my head might crack open if it gets any closer, it backs away, affected by my own circle of destruction. The first Mech is busy fighting the person. It stops shooting when it figures out that shooting doesn't work, and it caps up its guns and starts trying to dent the tar out of my defender.

"Die," I mouth at the leeches as I kick at them, out of air by now. The fight near my feet doesn't stop when the lights flicker on and off, each hit sounding as loud as gunfire, and I can hear quiet cries of pain, and I wonder if someone's losing the fight of their life, or maybe it's me they're dying for. But that can't be. But it doesn't matter. The gunner finally gets up the guts to get closer to me, and I shudder and go still, and it starts spazzing out. The person, who's off to my right by now, sees the gunner jerking and gets the idea to shove the Mech closer to me. I swallow the whole world of air as coldness shoots through me, and I breathe, "That's it," and the balance tips.

Usually, it takes a while before I can start crashing stuff again. I guess I have to charge it up or something, and until that happens, there's just this mutual malfunctioning between me and machines that leaves me with those great headaches and leaves them messing up the same way Motor does when he haywires them. But apparently, if they get too close and touch me, it doesn't matter how charged I am, the scale tips, and they can kiss their functionings good-bye.

The Mech drops to the floor, spasming right next to me under the flashing light that rains sparks down on us, giving it this ethereal feel as dark pleasure rushes in to half replace the migraine. But only half. There's still the other Mech, and it's backed away from me, its antique artificial intelligence letting it figure out I'm some sort of threat to be close to, which I find funny. It doesn't understand me, so it sees me as a threat. And so the circle of life comes full swing, and here we are at the end, sparks raining down from the popping lights on the ceiling, a gunner about to shoot me, and leeches barreling toward me if the gunner isn't enough. I squeeze my eyes shut, trying to focus on the gunner, wondering, *If I focus, can I do it on purpose, can I stop it, can I do something, anything, please? This life ain't much, but it's all I got...*

That's when I hear the footsteps.

There's gunfire, but my eyes fly open when I don't feel any of it hit me. The gunner's going nuts, even though I'm nowhere near it. At first, the leeches only focus on the Mech, trying to eat it, but then they all whip their heads toward the footsteps pounding closer from my right. "BACK OFF!" a huge voice thunders, and all five of the leeches scatter away.

"Yeah, shut it down!" a much smaller voice cheers to my left, from the hallway I came from, and the last Mech drops down in a heap on my other side. It must not be operating anymore, because suddenly, I can breathe easier than I've been able to in too long, and I sit up halfway, squinting through my shuddery haze. Someone small dives into the room just as a fleet of rapture men turn the corner, glaring so hard I almost believe they've got laser vision. They charge, but something that looks suspiciously like a shoe flies above my head and explodes in front of them, so they all stumble to a stop, fazed. A fish-shaped gadget follows the explosive, and wire flies around in a circle, and the fleet gets bound together so nobody can shoot, and before any of them can protest, the door to the room slams shut, and we're left alone.

Long seconds of echoing pass before I sit up the rest of the way, gasping for air. Someone comes over and tries to help me up, but I growl, "Stay back, I can get up myself." Then Melodi's words about being the choir thing ring in my head, and I sigh and let a bunch of strong hands lift me to my feet, wondering how Melodi knew about the band. Once I'm up, I turn my head and look at them all, Voxel with a new screen thing that probably worked the door, Jacques looking sore but better than before with more fish-things in one hand, Craw rubbing his throat, Motor breathing heavy but smiling all the same. And Eli. Hurt from the fighting but holding me up so I pretty much just have to live and I'll stay up.

I bite my lip, giving the group a skeptical look. "Okay, what happened?"

"To make a long story short, we all figured out real quick that we've got enough problems trying to stay alive without splitting up," Eli explains, shrugging his arm so I can see something blew half the skin off it, showing off darkened metal underneath. I try not to stare, even though it's one of the crazier things I've ever seen, and being a robber and all, I've seen some pretty bizarre things. "Alone, each one of us is only barely capable of scraping by."

"Yeah, there's no balance in a solo," Craw jumps in. There's an awful gash on the side of his head that's been leech-licked shut. "We need everybody in the band to keep it all toned right, offset each other's weaknesses, you know?"

"That's worked real well so far. You're saying we should stick together just for survival purposes?" I ask.

"Well, that is only one slice of the pie of truth," Voxel admits. "Though some of us are still cross about the explosion that occurred between us in the room, there are still sentimental flavors that are hinted in the pie."

I glance at them all again, not ready to believe anything. "Alright, let's start at the beginning. Motor, you'd better have one heck of a reason for showing up again after bailing on me." Nobody seems to notice how I took it personally.

The kid shuffles his feet and looks at the floor. "I just … didn't wanna get anyone hurt. I thought I was the one that made the power go out, and I remembered this one time, when we were having a party, and I lost this game, and I got really mad, and all the power went out in the room, and I thought it might be another part of the haywiring thing, and I wanted to try it again now, and I didn't wanna get anyone hurt, though, so I made everyone mad at me so you wouldn't look for me, and I went and found some gunners, and I tried it and I figured out I can kinda make stuff, you know, shut down." He taps one of the lifeless Mechs with his foot. "For good."

My fists clench and unclench a lot. "You still should've told me. This should've never happened. Nobody should've left anyone. This was supposed to work. We *chose* each other."

"Then let us all choose again," Jacques says solemnly. "Perhaps this was a necessary evil in which one must leave solely to return, to make the harmony all the sweeter and the bonds all the stronger. Apologies are in order, and if amnesty follows, then we will know that we are united once more."

"I'm sorry," I announce before anyone else can, and they all look at me in surprise as I step forward, swallowing my pride and grudge. "And none of you should be. I was just in a mood, freaking out, being stupid and reckless. You know I'm not the head of the anger management department. The whole half-cocked betrayal thing was bull, just forget about it."

"Rat, we understand the whole trust issue is out of our countries to you," Voxel tries to explain. "You've been passed through the digestion of twenty-five—"

"Eh, eh, let's not go there," I interrupt. "No teary backstories, no lame excuses. Let's call a spade a spade. I'm no thespian, I'm just an idiot, and I'm sorry. Motor, I guess what you did makes sense, so I won't blame you. Sorry for insulting you guys too. I mean, if you can break into Surgam systems and shut down Mechs just by looking at them and scare off leeches by screaming at them and hold your own in a Brigade attack or a MechMassacre to try and save a fellow bandmate, then who cares if you've got a few screws missing or if you're still a kid or if you've got a scary reputation or if we don't see eye to eye on everything?"

Craw finally breaks out into a smile. "So, hath I been pardoned for appearing strange to thou?" he asks theatrically.

"Sure, you're okay for being weird. We do have to talk about that, though." I turn to Eli. "You, I'm still scared of."

He doesn't get my sarcasm. "Fine. Scared, I can deal with, so long as I know we've all been brought back together, and I can have another shot at helping you."

Everyone watches me expectantly, and I get the feeling they think it's up to me whether or not the band's back together. There's no way I'll make them all suffer just because I'm too stubborn to put faith in people, though. "Okay. So long as nobody pulls a Rex, consider us a team again," I announce, and they let out their breaths and smile and pat each other on the back. "Now, let's get the heck outta here."

There's sounds coming from behind the closed door, things begging to get in as escape plans start flying between us, and I take a step back away from them and away from the door, aimlessly watching one of the giant spheres with my arms crossed, wondering if I made the right choice. But hey, it happened again—the world was falling apart, but we came together, and that was enough to stop it. *For now*, I think with my lips pursed.

"Hey. I really wasn't going to leave."

Eli starts toward me, and I come back into focus. "Before you start trying to flatter me into putting faith in you again, I want you to know I won't be needing any of your help. You've done enough. I don't want to ask anything else from you, and if you offered it, I probably wouldn't accept it."

The lights flicker back off, so I don't see his reaction, just hear his sigh. "What makes me different from everyone else that you can't rely on me, Rat?" he questions in the tone of someone who's got a specific answer in mind.

"It's not about that or anything, I just don't think it's fair to you," I dodge. "We all oughta pull our own weight. You see it works good."

"C'mon. I want to talk."

Emboldened by the dark, I give him the answer I think he's looking for: "Well, to start with the obvious one, I'm a cutout, and you're half machine."

"Thanks for that. You don't mean it. What else?"

I think a bit, putting my reasons in order instead of arguing. "Second of all, you murdered a rapture man just to get here, and you keep coming close to ripping someone else's head off."

"Hey, he died because I walked out of the residency, and about fifty of them fired at me at once, and one of them ended up shot and they needed someone to blame. My plan was to get to Zenith before twelve and throw a shoe at a certain alabaster Headquarters to qualify for the race. And as for my temper, I'm working on it." It's true—he sounds pretty calm lately, but he's pretty calm about a lot of things. It's the special things that turn patient mountains into volcanoes. "Anything else?"

"Yeah. You're not a Next with the rest of us. You've never had to look over your shoulder every five seconds you walk down the street, you've never been betrayed by the gangs, and you never had your clan of relatives point you out the door. You did the leaving, and you've never been left behind, so you don't know how to doubt stuff. Maybe Vastate was right and we do suspect every ambiguity we face, but it's better than thinking nobody'll stab you in the back if they get the chance. That's too close to electrode thinking for me to feel safe with you."

The lights blink back on, and I see Eli's got his hands on his hips, watching me keenly with that one green eye. "So you're telling me that you can't trust me because I trust too much? Then it's a vicious cycle! How am I supposed to break it? What'll it take to get you to trust me?"

My inner reaction to that last question is so huge it changes the atmosphere of the room, and everyone off to the left who was ignoring us and trying to figure a way out of here turns their heads at me, while I just stare at him and think, *You told him more than you've told the others. You don't think so much about what you say to him. You sided with him at the start of this. It's not because he doesn't matter. It's because he's the one who keeps his hands on the table, because he's innocent like you used to be. The Erratica in you already does trust him, but you're so busy being Rat you can't admit it.*

You're not the same girl Statice took to a pool and taught how to swim, but you know a piece of her's still inside of you, and you know this guy reminds you of him, of the only one who didn't leave when you forgot.

Tell him. Tell him why you're scared of him leaving. Tell him why you want him to stay. He will.

But my outer reaction is just, "I don't know. You're a Steele, aren't you? Figure it out. That's what you're good at." I start heading over to the cluster of people, and they all stop staring at me. "Where're we at with this?"

"We've decided against taking the Brigade with us, if that's okay with you, but we haven't gotten much down on how we're gonna go about doing it," Craw explains. "Jacques figured out how the hallways work, and Voxel can get up a basic floor plan, but neither of those seem to have any way out. We found out where those campers went, by the way. When this place was a prison, it got abandoned then bought by Surgam after the last extermination, and a bunch of the prisoners worked here. That's why this island gets supplies even though it hasn't been used in a while because of some of the prisoners doing this stupid game thing, and we could've asked them how they got in and out except the rapture men kinda cuffed them, and the leeches finished off anyone left. This's top-tier treason, what Surgam's pulling here, and none of the operatives're happy about it. I'm pretty sure the whole squad and their prisoners got out more or less alive, believe it or not, and bailed once they figured we wouldn't come quietly. The only ones left alive here are us, the Brigade, some ops and the other two teams."

"Well, then it's simple, isn't it?" Everyone looks at me with big eyes. "We were the only ones dragged in here against our will. Everyone else in here knows a way in and, therefore, a way out. So all we have to do is take one of them and—how'd she put it?—torture them for information."

Before anyone can decide whether or not I'm being sarcastic, a voice from above calls down, "Oh, you're going to?" In the flashing of the lights, the dark silhouette of Ripvan Remington leans against the railings of one of the bridges above our heads. "I'm hoping you know that we are the individuals that *invent* torturing for information, lass. Just ask the last Filler batch." I step back as he leaps over the railing and drops down, landing on his toes and fingers, with that wolfish grin on his face. "Oh, how I hate them!" He laughs. "How we hate the whole lot of them! How willing we are to strap them to the tables they themselves invent and smuggle over here, how we relish in dragging knives across their skins and filling them with gasoline and lighting them on fire! And how willing the others are to watch."

I swallow, realizing that we keep throwing this whole torturing thing around without ever really thinking about what it means.

"Oh, but don't hesitate now! Cheer, cheer, now, everyone. This is the only real entertainment I get in this Devil's pit."

"How's about you tell us where the hole Revany cut in the wall is, and we can leave you alone to your play?" I suggest. "No torturing included. Everyone's happy."

But Ripvan shakes his head, slowly walking toward us so we all step back toward the doors that the leeches bang against. "The play is not enough. Give me another Lucky—the others want to punish him for keeping the secret against them. So we take bare wires and whip him to oblivion." My mind flies to Lily, and I can almost hear her screaming as Ripvan takes another step, settling his eyes on Eli. "Give me another Dark Horse—before Lucky, they wrongly accuse Dark Horse of having the secrets, and we force-feed him the electric acid left from corrupted prizes." His manic gaze finds me, and a laugh shakes his body. "Give me another Queen of Hearts to doll up—she sacrifices herself, lets me draw with razors on her skin as her friends take the opportunity to retreat."

"Oh, so that's what being crazy's all about, then?" I ask now that I have his intention, and he circles close to me, eyes drifting along me as if he's already planning what words to stab in. "Avoiding the past tense at all costs? Attacking people for no reason?"

"Yes, yes!" Ripvan cries in delight. "I'm a sociopath and always have been! Oh." The smile falls off his face when he realizes he just used a past tense verb. "Er. I mean…"

"And by the way, *sadist* is the word you were searching for, though in your case, *loser* would work just as well," I offer.

Ripvan stands a little taller, trailing a hand on my arm. "You can't torture me with your words, lass."

"Wasn't trying to." I shrug. "Just kinda doing a sacrifice thing to occupy your attention. It's called a distraction, lad." His eyebrows pop up, and he looks behind him, right into the lead pipe that smashes into his face.

"Faker!" Voxel yells and hits him again. "Disgrace to a true problem! Good night! Ow, my humerus…"

"It's okay, I think he's out. Nice hit, and thanks for taking your cue right," I tell her. "Well, since he's passed out and we can't get any info out of him, we might as well move on with the escape plan. I've lost my appetite for even pretending to work facts out of people. Jacques, what'd you figure out about the hallways?"

"In each intersection, there is one light in the ceiling for every direction one could go. Following routes with even-numbered protective bars over the lights will guide you down more hallways, while going in the direction of a light with an odd number of bars will lead you into a dead-end room. Each light has one screw on its casing, and this screw always points in respect to the light towards the stairs, and on this floor, they all point towards this place. This is all without fail."

I take a second to be blown away that he figured all that out, and that anyone ever planned something so canny. "Okay, that means this is the most important place, which means the way in and out should be around here somewhere. Voxel, can't you get anything better than a floor plan? And where'd you get that screen thing, anyway?" I ask, turning up my nose at the electronic. It's too small to affect me much, especially since I took down a great big hunk of metal, so I don't have the charge to be bugged yet.

"Craw did the talking that was smooth to the girl that is gray-haired and won me this prize," Voxel explains, and Craw shrugs. I should've known from how amazed Lily was about Craw's Jacques imitation that she would ven up to his talking skills. Maybe his charm's useful, after all. "And I cannot get anything better than a floor plan because if I try to crack the code, then I get the blue screen of Death."

My brow furrows. "Blue screen of Death? Lemme see. And hurry," I add when more leeches find another door to bang on. "I'm not sure how much more time we've got."

Voxel's fingers fly on the display unit, going down a menu to the floor plan after typing in a password (it's thirty-two and a half characters long, since she somehow uses her nail to cut the bottom half of the last symbol off). Then she pulls up some sort of option tab that's supposed to let her search for stuff specifically in the original reconstruction plan—entrances and exits, for example—but it's thumbprint-lock protected. "Now, if I remove this backing here," she starts and uses her marker-tool to remove the backing of the unit, "and move the operation cell into modification mode and connect this wire to it, which only I and Marker have ever been able to accomplish, then it *should* give me the option to edit the coding so I won't need a thumbprint, but no matter what I attempt, it refuses to let me inside of its brain. So I've been forced to try all means to try to break in the real way, but my use of fingerprint replication leads me to the Death screen." Hesitantly she pulls out a vial of watery stuff and dumps a drop on the screen. It shifts and glows, spreading itself out and making itself into a fingerprint that seems long and thin enough to be Steele's. The words telling you to do the fingerprint thing fade off the screen, along with the thumbprint box, but new words replace them right away:

"Really, Voxel? A third time? What would Gregory say?"

"This is why it gives my insides the ants of anxiety! Gregory was my teacher," Voxel clarifies shakily. "Nobody knew about him except for me and himself. The first time I attempted to break into the Surgam database to see if I could discover anything worthy to use for extortion, the president told me that I should try something more in my league or go home. In case I was lost, he gave me the exact address and coordinates of my top-secret gang base that had been formed two point three hours before."

"Real subtle. Nice brother you've got there," I mutter to Eli, who half-smiles.

"Well, he's got a few sharp edges, if you know what I mean." We all laugh a little at that one since it's the closest thing to humor we've heard in a while. "Even I can't make anything of this, though. Any ideas, anyone?"

"Can you go back to that thumbprint screen?" I ask, and Voxel shuts the thing off and back on, working faster as one of the leeches starts screaming for blood, probably mine. Craw offers me Ripvan's handkerchief for the wound on my side, and I take the moment to apologize for losing his jacket before turning back to Voxel's device. I hover my hand over it for a second, trying to see if I can either damage it or get a feel for how it works the way I do with people, but my finger must touch the box because the screen changes again and says, "Oh, now you've got Rat trying to get in, too? I'm sorry, but considering that I can't tell whether or not there's a rapture man with a gun to your head telling you to do this, I'm not about to let you into the Surgam system so easily."

"Ugh, we're not trying to get in against our will, we're trying to get in so we can get out of here!" I yell at the stupid machine as if it'll hear me.

Guess what? It must hear me.

"In that case, I'm confident you can figure out the password if you take on the right perspectives," the blue screen says before going back to the thumbprint screen. I catch it instantly and smile, shaking my head as I read the same boring script that tells you to scan your thumbprint. Why would he tell me to figure out the password if you're supposed to scan your thumb? "Give me this," I tell Voxel and take the screen, tapping on the P icon in Thumbprint. Sure enough, the letter appears in the box, and it rotates to stay upright when I tilt the screen, so I get the A and Ss from Scan then turn the thing so the M in Thumbprint turns into the W, use the O and R from Your and turn it upside down so the P in Thumbprint turns into the last letter of Password.

"Good job thinking outside the box," the screen reads next, and it's weird that someone hundreds of kilometers away is unconsciously congratulating me, but it's kinda cool too. "Sorry for the bad pun, I couldn't resist". The old Surgam symbol blinks on the screen before it turns into a whole new list of options.

"You're incredible, Rat," Voxel breathes as she takes the screen thing back, dashing her fingers across it. She holds it at an angle so it's harder for us to see, and I frown. The blue screen of Death shows up again in about three seconds.

"I thought you were escaping, Voxel."

It exits the screen and goes back to the menu, an arrow pointing at detailed construction overview option. "Oh, fine, I'll figure you out later," Voxel scowls and goes back to what she's supposed to do, which is good because a blue finger finally manages to spear its way through the door.

A tongue burns through the steel and starts poking through, and I realize that if this place wasn't made of metal, the leeches wouldn't have to touch it, they'd just go jellying through any crack or crevice to get to us and we'd probably be dead by now.

"Aah, hurry, self!" The hacker rapidly scrolls across the screen, searching for the closest exit as the leeches slowly leak in through the hole in the door, distracted by pieces of small machinery lying around so they don't notice us yet. "It claims right here that everything within the factory floor is coated in some chemical so that hunters won't be attracted by the metal it's made of, so I'm scared that we don't have much time before they find interest in us instead!" Shaken by the presence of the leeches, Voxel searches more frantically and less efficiently and I'm scared she's gonna miss the exit, but then that blessed arrow pops back up on the screen. All of us gathered around the screen tell her to follow it as if she doesn't take the hint that it's going to lead her to the exit we were telling it that we needed to find.

It's too far up off the ground for Motor to see, so he's stepped back from the excitement and watches one of the giant metal-cutting machines with a long conveyor belt spitting out the side. "Uh, guys . . . ?"

"There!" I point at a vent shaft close to the floor on the plan.

"Rat, that's a vent shaft, not an exit," Craw tells me with a shove.

"Those're synonyms in my language."

"GUYS!" Motor yells again, and we all look up just in time to see another kid come leaping out from behind the metal-cutter with the grace of an acrobat, aiming midair and firing a round right at the display unit. It hits, cracking the screen and sending the thing flying out of Voxel's hands. The screen flickers off as it hits the floor.

"No!" Voxel drops to her knees and picks the device back up right when all the lights shut off again, pitching us into total darkness. By the time the emergency lights're on, Eli's trying to help Voxel with the screen thing, Ripvan is trying very hard to make a comeback with a pistol, Jacques is holding him down, Harmoni's in tears for no reason, Motor's stomping at him with all his seven-year-old anger pent up on his face, and me and Craw blink in the red light and try and figure out what the heck's going on.

"Why'd you do that, huh?" Motor demands, his voice hitching childishly. "What'd we ever do to you?" Harmoni says nothing, just stands there crying so Motor breaks the kid code and shoves him. "You're such a crybaby!"

Harmoni's mouth drops open at the scathing infantile insult, and he returns fire with a harsh juvenile jest of his own: "You're a meanie!"

"Mama's boy!"

"Poophead!"

"Chicken!"

"Jerkface!"

"Sissy!"

Totally offended by now, Harmoni decides to drop the bomb: "Well, you're a big, fat, stupid BULLY!" Motor's taken aback as it is by the double blow of the BFS and the bully but Harmoni goes on, "And you've got cooties, and you're ugly and nobody likes you!"

Motor crosses his arms with the most force arms have ever been crossed with and answers, "Then why don't you cry us an ocean and we can both drown in it?"

Everyone turned to look when Mo dropped out of innocent mode. "Whoa, where'd *that* come from?" Craw mouths at me before stepping toward the fight, but it's too late. The damage is done, and Harmoni screams in rage as he hoists up his tagger and fires away.

"Missed me," Motor taunts when the storm's over.

"I wasn't aiming for you," Harmoni sneers and I look in the direction he shot to see a freaky crack riding up one of the glass spheres. Eli, who's abandoned trying to revive the broken device, starts forming something that might be a curse, but we never find out because of the CRACK that reverberates throughout the room. Sparks fly out of the dead machinery that holds up the sphere. The power flashes again so the machinery's useless to stop the gas from leaking out as the cracks keep snaking up the side of the glass, which wouldn't be so bad except all the leeches suddenly start screaming and flying off.

"It's thunder," I breathe as I watch them go. Eli must understand because he gives me a panicked look before diving for Harmoni, but the kid does his crazy backflip out of the way, landing on top of another sphere and pulling out a lighter. He clicks it, and a shudder runs through everyone in the room with all the power of a static shock. That was an omen, a warning of what's coming if we stick around. Harmoni won't hesitate to shock us all to death as soon as the air's saturated enough for the shocks to kill us. "We've gotta get out of here before it's thick enough to get any worse!"

Jacques wrenches the pistol out of Ripvan's grip and fires at Harmoni, but he disappears in another brief blackout that seems caused by the gunfire, like the pistol turned off the world for a second, and now it's back on without Harmoni in it. Some part of me hopes he's dead. "Get everyone out, now!" Jacques growls, slinking toward the sphere and keeping his gun trained where he expects Harmoni to be.

"The vent," Eli says then turns to me. "Get them out through the vent, and keep them away from the mountain."

"Wait, where are you going?" I demand, fists bunching.

"I'm going to see if I can get the other team out. The electricity shouldn't affect me, but the rest of you need to go."

"You're leaving me!" I yell before I can stop myself. Another wave of static, stronger this time, almost brings me to my knees. "No, it's okay, that was just instinct. What I said, I mean. Go, I'll do my best."

"Rat." Eli's voice stops me, and I look him in the face. His intense green eye shoots right through me the same way it always has, unweakened by the lack of a pair. "Believe it or not, but I'll be back for you. I promise. Now, go."

Without even a nod or anything, I turn and run, trying to visualize where I saw the vent on the construction plan. What if it's not there? What if it was in the plan but they forgot to build it? What if it's too high to reach? What if it's too small? What if we can't get out, and we all die here?

"Jacques, c'mon, I'm not losing you too!" I holler to my right as I find the corner where the vent should be. Guess what? No vent cover. Nothing but sheet-metal walls.

"Great, now what?" Craw asks as he runs up to me. "There's nothing here!" He's frustrated enough that he stomps once to let it out, which is such an unusual reaction to me. I look down. His foot made a weird sound against the ground, and I stoop down close to it as the power flashes on, letting me see the part where the floor meets the wall better. There's little gaps in the edge, and when I stick my hand into one of the shallow gaps, I feel moving air, and there's another wall a few centimeters back. This wall is only a few millimeters thick.

"It's a fake wall," I say, standing up. "But why?"

"To double the protection," Jacques suggests as he comes up behind us. "And so that none whosoever has the proper tools might simply decide to use the vent shaft to take a vacation for the day. In other respects, having the vent grates everywhere would be unsightly. This would allow for air to flow into the room in the most effective way, considering it's at the floor so the good air can only rise. There's no dust in the corners this way, either. Many factories have this design. I thought more people knew."

I shake my head. It's simple, elegant, and genius, and it's going to get us killed. Sums up the whole dang factory, now doesn't it? "*Now* how are we supposed to get through this wall?"

"Excuse me, but do you believe a chainsaw will work?" We all whip around to see Ripvan limping at us, a communications device in his hand and Revany by his side. "We don't have possession of a Death wish, so that's reason enough to help you."

I hesitate, doubtful about this being about survival, but then there's a third wave of shock that makes everyone drop to the floor, and I decide that whether or not this's about survival to them, it is to me. "Go for it," I grunt, helping Revany to her feet, and she gives me a nod of thanks before starting up the chainsaw and tearing a square through the metal. Its roar fills me with some ghost of confidence, insubstantial but comforting, and I can see why it's her weapon of choice, especially if it can cut through walls (maybe I should invest in one of these things). Even with the cruddy light, I can see a dark hole in the corner of the square she cut. *The vent cover!* "Do some more over there."

"With pleasure!" Revany laughs, grinning with all her might as the saw eats through the steel. It's so sharp, and the teeth have such a precise angle, it hacks slowly through without sending sparks everywhere. I've never been more grateful for someone's interest in sharp, pointy objects.

When the vent's totally in sight, I scramble up and examine it. There's no grate or screws or anything—seamlessly welded bars over the hole connect right to the wall. They somehow resist the hardest pressings of Revany's chainsaw, but Voxel's not the only one who came equipped with trade secrets.

Yeah, yeah, very convenient, but what did you think I did to get a reputation for escaping stuff, teleport? No, I'm the sort that doesn't step foot outside without an arsenal and three emergency plans, and my paranoia is justified, thank you very much.

I reach into a pocket on the inside of my jeans and dust my right hand in some floury powder, spit on it, and rub the bars furiously on their tops and bottoms where they meet the wall. Nothing seeable happens, but after I dust off my hand, I can grab a bar and pull, and it slowly starts coming out of the wall like it's nothing sturdier than half-dried clay. The people watching let out an amazed cheer, and everyone grabs at the grate. Jacques alone ends up pulling out three bars before I get my one out, so before I know it, the vent's open, and there's a pile of iron bars on the floor. "Careful, guys, the ends're sharp," I warn as I pull myself in. "I'll go first in case we meet trouble—me and trouble, we're bosum buddies. Hurry!"

Motor springs in after me, fitting easily. The others after him have a harder time, but they manage to get in after a chainsaw and a few other weapons get left behind (more than one of them looks less psycho-killer now). I crawl as fast as I can up the slight incline, scared every second that another spark's gonna kill us all or that a leech'll follow us in here in its own desperate attempt to escape. A distant, unexplainable explosion adds to the sense of urgency, and I try to go even faster, probably getting me some good bruises on my elbows.

It's stuffy in here, which makes me realize that I'm thirsty as a horse along with being hungry and tired, but I'm thankful the shaft's big enough to fit everyone and it's not going in crazy angles. Most other places have vent shafts that twist all over the place to meet up with machines that do certain stuff to the air, but this place leads straight out with gentle mechanisms to purify the air embedded in the sides of the shaft, small enough that none of them hurt my head too bad, and nobody's clothes catch on them. Some even have tiny green lights on them, so we're not crawling around in pitch-darkness. It almost makes me think this place was designed with escape in mind. Minus the iron grate. Kind of a deterrent for escape, that.

"C'mon, guys, we're almost there!" I shout behind me as I come up on another grate that shows the beautiful outdoors. I've never been so glad to see it and never more scared to see it behind bars.

Behind us, an angry sob echoes up the shaft, along with a soft clicking sound that tells me someone's trying to kill us and the only thing that's stopping him is the faultiness of unmodern technology.

There's no time for more miracle powder. My mind flies into a frenzy, so my heart's pounding, and maybe that pulse is what makes me notice I'm still bleeding from where that gunner's bullet grazed my side. I'm not the only one who notices the blood—outside, the sound of hissing picks up, and something that might be considered a plan flies into my head.

"Guys, if this gets me killed, tell Vastate I ate a bowl of his Plexus for a snack. I've always wanted to see what he'd say to that," I call behind me before pressing my hand to my bloody side and shoving it out the grate. "HEY, UGLIES! COME AND GET IT!"

Nobody even gets any time to argue with me before a black tongue flies at me, and I whip my hand back with the tongue right behind it so the dark thing slams into the bars. The leech furiously winds its tongue around the grate and whips it off in one mighty heave. While it's distracted with eating, I scramble out, but instead of helping anyone else out, I turn and run. Motor pops out next, probably wondering if I've turned into a hypocrite who's going to abandon everyone. He gets his answer when I keep waving my bloody hand around. "C'mon, uglies, over here!"

Hypocrite? No, I'm going more for Queen of Hearts. The valor ran out long ago, but I get away with pulling stupid sticks like this because I've survived too much, and my instinct to survive sometimes gets shouted out by my heart going, "Eh, screw it, we're immortal, let's show off!"

It works. The leeches nearby ignore the people tumbling out of the shaft to go for me instead. Most of the leeches were in the factory, so only two more come to join the one I've already got the attention of, but three's a crowd, and a crowd of leeches is more than enough to match me. They scratch and scream at each other over me, and one of the newcomers lunges at me. I manage to dodge it, but the other one whips its tongue out and wraps the end around my wrist and pulls, so before I know what's happening, I've got my shoulder in its face and my whole arm in its tongue and mouth. It feels disgusting, and I shudder and struggle as the wet, gelatinous tongue muscles squish down on my arm, washing it in that acidic saliva, and its teeth start turning. My arm's skinny enough and those teeth're far enough apart that it makes a circular cut all around my arm without tearing it off, which stings real bad because of the saliva. The taste of my blood makes the thing even madder.

Man, I shoulda taken that lead pipe with me. My boots that usually do the trick are not helping.

"Rat!" Craw cries as he stumbles out of the vent, and the other two leeches that were about to join the feast back away from his voice.

"Help the others, I'm peachy!" I demand through gritted teeth, choking as my arm sizzles. One of the leeches gets some guts and licks at my side, making it hurt so bad I almost hit the ground, but I stop myself just by sheer terror of getting my arm sliced off by this leech's teeth. "Hey! My arm! Give it back! Sticks, sticks, sticks," I curse as I pull, digging my heels into the ground.

To my left, my team helps Ripvan out of the vent, and he drops down to help out Revany, who's last. There, even if I can't yank my arm free and it gets sawed off, at least everyone else's safe.

What's the tally now? Four and a half delusions? Well, I'm half dead, so I'm only half responsible for these things, so let's keep the tally at four.

Something happens right then to shatter our safety into a million pieces. Something that makes every leech in sight gurgle and scatter for a few meters before dropping to the ground. Something that I can feel from out here. Something that makes the others stagger back from the vent, something that makes Revany's eyes go wide as she screams and writhes and then goes very still. Something marked with the classic VVVVZZZZZZZZZ of static electricity rippling through the air, crackling through hundreds of bodies, living or dead or mechanical, roaring through the mountain made of steel and dihydrogen Tersatellum. Something big happens, something big enough to change lives, to end them, something big that started small, with a single innocent spark.

The electricity sears through me, and I drop to the ground, twitching as my whole body hums. We didn't get far enough away from the mountain to avoid getting a little shocked, but I still think most of us made it out alive. My heart pounds and my head pounds and I curl up into a pounding, painful ball on the ground, just letting the wind wash over me and starlight shine down on me for a long time before I can crack my eyes open and look at my arm. It's got a new tan, and there's no hair on it anymore, and there's a very stylish scab going in a circle by my shoulder, but it still works. The beacon in my pocket beeps, but I ignore it.

Something small tackles me, and I freak out before I realize it's Motor. "Rat! Are y-you ok-k-kay?" he stammers, and I don't know whether he's asking because of the shockwave or because he fell on me, but I nod either way, and he starts trying to pull me to my feet. "Help m-me! They're s-st-stuck!" My head whips to where the others were, and I scramble over. Jacques's the only one standing.

"You alright?" I ask him, searching Voxel for a sign of life. She waves at me but won't open her eyes and keeps hitting the side of her head.

"Merely disoriented. It'll pass. Come," Jacques summons and I go over to where he's holding down a thrashing figure. It's Craw, and there's a look of complete terror on his face as he goes to pieces.

"I can't breathe!" he mouths, no air coming out, and his mouth keeps moving to form the same words over and over again. There's nothing I can think to do except what I've always done; I pull my jacket from around him and tuck it under his head and hold him down and pray it ends. Motor stumbles over and watches us with his huge, frantic eyes that beg us to do something.

"C'mon, Craw," I whisper, taking deep breaths like I'm showing him how, and put a hand on his chest, pushing. Too bad I never learned a thing about CPR. He's calming down, but I can't tell whether it's because of me or it's because he's turning blue. I'm about to start trying CPR anyway because he's calmer now, but a ragged voice interrupts my compressions.

"Excuse me, but do you think this would work?" Ripvan pushes himself away from Revany with tears on his face and holds up a Flashfire. "I've got the power turned down."

"We might as well try it," Motor says, so I take the Flashfire and settle the end on Craw, who couldn't care less at this point.

"This'll probably hurt a bit," I admit apologetically and start pulling the trigger, but I get interrupted again, this time for a good reason.

Craw finally lets out a "GAH!" and rakes in such a big breath I'm not sure how there's any oxygen left in the bay. Everyone sighs in relief as he stops fighting and relaxes on the ground, stealing all the air. "Ugh… thanks," he gasps, and I pat him on the shoulder in response.

"Still can't see," Voxel grumbles, banging away on the side of her head. Her eyes pop open every now and then, but then slam right back shut. "Wait… no, that's Transportation Sector Headquarters surveillance. I am regretting many things…" It's hard to tell whether she's having flashbacks or if she can really see the security tapes she's talking about. That'd be one cool power if it didn't make the rest of your vision disappear. "That's the museum… oh! There! Hello, humans!"

"Welcome back, Voxel." When I'm done making sure Motor's okay, I hesitantly go over and help Ripvan pull his charred teammate out of the vent. She was still touching the metal, so the electricity got her bad. I shiver as we settle her on the ground outside.

"Nobody inside lives through this," Ripvan chokes, putting a hand on Revany's cheeks. It looks so weird, seeing her without her shark smile or crazy eyes. "Leave us. Now." Ripvan lifts Revany off the ground and starts carrying her away, so I drift over to the edge of the cliff we're on and sit down, dropping my legs over the side. Below me, the gray stone slopes down and stretches out in front of me, wrinkling in a huge maze. Hundreds of leeches lie paralyzed in the valley, but I can see some moving ones in the distance, closer to the other end of the chasm, where broad-leafed trees wave in the breeze. We must be facing north. Someone behind me—I don't even bother identifying them—wonders out loud if anyone else survived that, and someone else hopes so. It'd be unthinkable if the six of us were the only ones left alive on the island.

Six. And only five of us are Tersatellan. So much for us being hotshots.

But I can't believe that. I lean back on my hands, thinking Lily's team knew how to get out of there, and even if they didn't know about the shocks, they'd wanna avoid the leeches. Plus Eli…

I don't know what to think about that. But I decide that whatever he's doing, he's alive too. We're out. The leeches're down. The Mechs're down. The ops have mainframes with shock absorbers, so they'll be fine, but something tells me they won't be after us for a while. We're okay. Well, Revany isn't.

Footsteps crunch over to me, generic sneakers that manage to find good balance on the awkward slope of the mountain. Craw. He sits down next to me, swinging his legs out into the chasm. "Woo! That was a close one. Guess I owe you one, or a hundred. Lost count already."

A gust of wind blows, and I lean into it without caring about almost falling off the cliff, without caring about anything. Coldness fills me, making me feel icy and stagnant. "Is it bad I don't feel anything right now?" I ask without looking at him. "You know, about…" I jerk my head back at Ripvan, for all the deaths and disasters he stands for, for everything we've had to endure already in our short time here in Hudson Bay.

Craw doesn't say anything right away. "It's not that bad, I think," he finally tells me, looking out into the valley with those jaded eyes of his. "We've all got our ways of coping with the bad stuff. One way's to go numb and not feel anything, so it's not bad, it's just coping. You'll feel it again later, when you're ready. Besides, we didn't know her too good, and what we knew wasn't good." He gets a crooked smile. "Want a little help? I could kiss away your mental boo-boo. You'll feel something. I still owe you that, anyway. Or do you really hate what I do?"

I snort. "I'm no better. I had my first kiss when I was a little older than Motor, and me and the other kid were pretending to get united. Then he moved away, and I only saw him again yesterday, and he ran away again when he saw how ugly I was. After that, my flings were limited to schemes. I'd buy poor suckers a drink and flatter them and pretend to be interested and run away with their beacons and jewelry. At least you're honest and just do it for the heat."

"No, not sweet ole you," he teases.

"That's what I wanted to talk to you about. I've got this false identity as a timid cutout girl named Laisha Horne you might have met."

"That was…" He trails into silence, face falling. I nod.

A few seconds pass. Then he slaps me. I let him cuz I was expecting it, and I sorta deserve it—his beacon had a cool fifty primes on it, and it all went down the drain in the name of gourmet dinner.

We're both laughing about it for a while. "Boy!" he snorts at one point when it dies down. "We cutouts have some pretty weird romances, huh?"

"Tell me about it," I mutter then kiss him.

I like to believe that we cutouts don't ever kiss on anything amorous. For us it is distraction. I do it to get square. I do it to sit back and breathe the smell of basil, hold that close to me instead of the sight of Revany wriggling and dying before my eyes. Hold on to it because I'd rather that fill the hollow tune in my music box of memories than images of Baldur with a hole in his head or Craig with a bullet in his chest or all those cutouts dying at the hands of the rapture men on their way to the Castaway Point. Hold on to it as a shield against the thought of Siridean falling into the ocean or Gypsy dying in her sleep or Tom getting eaten alive. So in a way, it's nice being a cutout, because we've got nothing to lose, so when it boils down to a mutual need for camaraderie to fight away the emptiness, we have few reservations and fewer regrets. What can I say? Misery loves company. But so does trouble—you see, a downside to being a cutout is that there's no rest for the wicked.

One shot of a tagger echoes behind me, and I almost fall off the cliff as the pellet pushes me forward. Craw barely manages to keep me from sailing, and I scramble away from the ledge, half of me freaking out, the other half wondering if I'm EVER gonna catch my breath. "What was that for?" I yell, twisting around to see Ripvan standing solemnly in the middle of our cliff, a tagger at his side.

"For getting me hit on the head, that's what. Do you still have these?" he asks. Voxel, Motor, and Jacques pull out the taggers they've managed to hold on to. "Then heed these last words of advice. There is a reason the northern team always wins the play—we may be a team, but the rules say nothing about teams, only that Bloods are worth a point, no matter which Blood it is." He flicks a lever on his gun, and it goes gray with the number 9 in the score counter, and he throws it to me (I drop it, real smooth, and have to dust it off after picking it back up). "You'll have to forgive the lack of points. This is where your tagger last saves. It isn't that difficult to regain your points, however, and regaining your points is in your best interest, considering the defense kills anyone who's not on the winning team if they try to steal the prize. Unless, of course, you're Dark Horse, but I don't suggest being Dark Horse. It turns out rather ugly," he sniffs and pulls out a flask. "A toast to the end." The flask hits the ground when he's done drinking. "Alright, lass, the play is over."

My eyes widen, and I dive to the left, and maybe I'm dodging, maybe I'm trying to get in a good shot, but whatever I was doing, it doesn't work. One fire of a real gun echoes through the night, and Ripvan goes to his knees then falls the rest of the way forward so we've got a clear view of Clementine McHarper with a smoking gun in her hand.

Hmm. Maybe I shouldn't have ignored that beeping in my pocket.

Harp lowers her gun slightly, her eyes glazing over all of us in one swoop. She's a bright young woman that tried to get extracted and turned scary after her son was murdered three years ago. I didn't see her yesterday at the Castaway

Point, so maybe they just recently figured out she's a hired assassin. Not the kind of person you wanna get stuck on an island with when you'd like to see the end of the week.

"Put the guns down," she growls, and everyone slowly sets their weapons on the ground as she waves her DC-3 all over the place. It's the same thing as a DC-5 but smaller. "Um . . . good morning, or evening, or whatever you want to call it. My tag's Harp, and apparently, I'm supposed to be some kind of pirate. I want somebody to start explaining stuff right now, or there's going to be trouble."

"Okay, okay, we will. Relax," Craw starts in such a calming voice, Harp lowers her gun even more. There's something about that voice that makes me think he's not just doing it to make sure Harp doesn't shoot. I strain my ears and wait for him to talk again, but it turns out I don't have to—it clears up that he's stalling when I hear fast footsteps off to my left. Craw keeps explaining worthless stuff to keep Harp busy, while I search the darkness to the left with wide eyes, but we're at the top of one of the random slopes of the mountain, and I'm on the ground, so I can't see downhill.

Harp notices me not paying attention and flicks the barrel of her DC-3 at me. "Hey, what're you looking at?" she snaps, and I crawl backward, trying to get out of her crosshairs. It's too late—she already followed my gaze and opens her mouth to say something then starts to fire at me, but it's too late for her too. Before she can react, the shoe flies into her face and explodes, knocking her to the ground. Her gun fires as her consciousness gets whacked to the moon, but because of the attack, the bullet bites the dust by my side and I'm alive, I'm alive and I've never been so aware of that until now when it hits me for the first time that it won't take much to get me dead. But I wouldn't count on that happening anytime soon if I had half as much trust to give as you do.

I scramble to my feet and watch him as he rises up over the hill, one-eyed, one-shoed, and totally unstoppable.

"Eli."

He gives me a smile and answers, "I told you I'd be back for you."

- VII -

The Recidivist

The clock strikes five, and Motor groans, flopping on his back. "It's only five? I thought we've been doing this since forever," he complains. We've had this little circle thing going on ever since Eli got back where four of us tag each other (so I guess it's more of a square) while one of us sits out and pretends to rest, even to fall asleep if we're feeling nervy. Eli gets the glorious job of knockout duty again, since he's the one with the Flashfire.

After he showed up, he explained where the Brigade's camping out, and Craw thought to ask something that was bugging me too: if the Brigade didn't go to the mountain by force, then they knew where the exits were, so why'd they need to be rescued? Honestly, if I'd been in Eli's explosive shoes, I would've just saved the Band and left the Brigade to save themselves—after all, the teams *were* formed because half of us didn't want Eli's help. In this case, it's a good thing I wasn't in Eli's shoes. It turns out the Brigade went into the factory on their own will, but they went in blindfolded by the northern team so nobody knew for sure where the exits were.

Lily and Ivy made it out with their talents, but they weren't doing so good at getting the rest of their team out via beacon, so Eli stepped in. Vici kept refusing his help but she couldn't stop him from telling her about the password thing. Spike was the next to deny any help, so Eli stole (yes, stole, I'm so proud!) one of his many explosives and blasted a hole in the wall so Spike would have to be an idiot not to go through the makeshift door. That was the explosion I heard in the vent shaft. Rex was a bit harder to find, but he didn't protest getting towed out the hole in the wall, so everyone got out alive before the last wave turned the factory into a Death zone.

But since Eli didn't know they were led in blindfolded, the next question was *why* he went off to save them, anyway. In answer, he shrugged and guessed he had a sixth sense too, just a little different from the rest of us.

And now we're here, Eli zapping Harp so she doesn't wake up because we don't know what else to do with her, Voxel taking a break, and the rest of us shooting each other with metal pellets as the leeches start stirring again.

One more thing: the Brigade sent off Eli with a message that if they win the play, then we can consider ourselves stuck on Fort Night for another day, because they're not sharing.

"It'd almost be better if we lost," Craw muses, yawning. "If we let them get away, then they can't bug us anymore. It'd be nice to have the island to ourselves. We'd have everything in the lodges and wouldn't have to share with anybody." By now, food and water's turned into a big question, and nobody'd mind having a safe place to sleep, either.

"Yeah, but then we couldn't keep an eye on them anymore," I point out as I reach four hundred points. "You know what they say. Keep your friends close and your enemies closer."

"That's dumb. Then they can bite your nose," Motor says as he tries to tie his shoes with the short laces. Apparently, he almost lost his shoe in the vent shaft. I excuse him from our circle until he's done. Tied shoes are important to me.

"Rat, could you help me enter the Troy of this security system?" Voxel asks from where she's leaning against the mountain. She got the screen thing working again, even though it's still cracked and sometimes flicks back off. It actually got mad at her for the damage. That thing's got the most artificial intelligence of anything I've ever seen.

I sigh and get to my feet, dusting off my jeans. "Alright, guys, we might as well all take a break. If the Brigade figures this out, we're toast, anyway, and if they don't figure it out, then *they're* toast." The boys gratefully relax, and Voxel waves me away because the screen flickers off again, so she has to fix it for the hundredth time, so I end up drifting over to Eli instead.

He stops humming when he notices me coming over, but not before I catch it. "What're you humming?" I've gotta ask, being a pretty curious rat.

"And why should I tell you?" I cross my arms at the sarcasm. "Your cutout chorale," he admits eventually. "Though I'll guess you'd say I don't have the rights to even hum it, considering the last line."

My eyebrows jump since I didn't think he'd know about our little battle cry. "You mean the 'some believe' one?" He nods, giving Harp a shock. *Tags*, the anthem in question, has a bunch of verses since people use the same first three lines—"Some believe we've crossed the line / We've lost our touch we've lost our minds / We're never in our place we're never on time"—and then there's a lot of options from there, so it takes me a while to guess which last line he's talking about. "Oh. 'So call me criminal if being human is a crime'?" (All the last lines ask you call me a name if/because of something). He nods again, looking at the valley, the sky, Harp, anywhere but me. "Where'd you learn it from?"

"Jaden sung it a lot," Eli admits after hesitating then snorts. "He couldn't hit a note to save his life, but it never stopped him from trying. Other times, he'd recite the words, which was easier to listen to. You'd like him, I think, if you got to know him, but that never happens. He's still a mystery to me, and I've lived with him for seventeen years."

Now it's my turn to hesitate, watching the leeches in the distance get up and wander around weakly. We'd better get out of here soon if we don't want to get eaten, but I figure I've got a few minutes, and besides, the Band needs some time to rest before we get moving. "He really brought you back to life." I shake my head at the thought. "So … how was it? How'd you know what to do?"

"People explained a few things. Jaden did some tests, some simulations so I had some sort of muscle. I think I always knew what to do, how to move and everything, but I couldn't before, until suddenly I could." The memory of the frustration passes from his face, and he smiles. "It's a funny story, actually. The very first thing I did was open my eyes, of course, so the first thing I saw—I don't know if you noticed it, but Jaden, being, well, Jaden, had taped up this strange picture to the ceiling, a picture of this cliff by the ocean, and sitting in the middle of that cliff was something very out of place. Thus, the first free thought I had was, 'That's an odd place for a piano.'"

"And after that?" I prod, and his smile fades.

"After that, I grabbed the beacon from off a nearby shelf and began to let the message play. It didn't even give me a chance to push the button or anything—I had to run from the residency before anything could catch me, but even so, the mass of rapture men were waiting for me. Maybe there were some discipline men there, I don't know. I just know Jaden didn't qualify, so they were ready to shoot. So many of them fired at once, it was inevitable that one of them was hit in the crossfire. Then they seemed to pause for a second before they blamed me, but a sentence of murder was my ticket to Hudson Bay, so I took it and ran."

"It must've been overwhelming, suddenly getting tossed headfirst into life like that." He nods in a way that tells me overwhelming doesn't begin to describe it. "Still, you probably weren't the only one in shock. I mean … he brought you back to life," I repeat, since I can't even imagine it, but I'm coming from a different angle this time. "That must've taken some … time, must've cost him something."

"Oh, it did. Jaden gave me everything," Eli says, respect and sadness in his voice at the same time. The way he can use the guy's first name tells me they've got something special, if I didn't catch it in the homesick way Eli's staring into nothing.

I turn to face him and ask slowly, "Then why did you leave him?"

Eli puts his face in his hands, sighing. "It's … not all black-and-white, Rat. It never is. You said it yourself, and I quote, 'sometimes, we've gotta leave behind who we used to be and everything we've ever known so we can get to everything we can be.' I couldn't stay. What would I be if I stayed and did nothing? Some secret kept from the Adamantration forever, some abomination locked away in the shadows? Then what would that sacrifice mean? That's why I ran, to make it all mean something. I'm lost to be found, left as nobody solely to return and come back as somebody, somebody that helped a bunch of criminals survive extermination, but somebody all the same, somebody better than 'good enough.' Jaden could only rebuild my body. It's up to me to get the rest of my life back together." I jump when Eli's hand appears on my shoulder. "Rat, I'm sorry to say that I know how the bereft and abandoned look. You fit the bill, and I don't think it's all about Vici or even the gangs. But whoever it was that left you, what if they're like me, and they left because they were scared of not being worth staying, they left to try and make your sacrifices worth it?"

I grunt, turning away. "There weren't any sacrifices. I don't do that for people. Besides, he's never coming back."

"Why not?"

Eli shrugs at me when I give him a complicated look. "You know, you scare me sometimes, Mr. Omniscient—but in a good way," I tell him, standing up to rally the others and try and come up with some sort of plan. The leeches are rising again, and if their hunger makes them hunt better, then we're asking for trouble. Still, something inside of me makes me look down at my wrist and unlock the Rolex, pulling out the steel wool bracelet. That same something in me makes me glance back one more time and softly let slip, "Statice had one green eye too."

In that special way of his, Eli knows that random comment means something more than I care to admit and replies, "Thank you. What happened to the other eye?"

"It was gray," I say with a shrug then go and kick Voxel on the leg. "Hey, wakey, wakey."

"I'm not sleeping!" she yawns, sliding the display unit underneath her. "What's vertically above?"

"We've gotta figure out a safer place to go before the leeches get us."

"What about the factory?" Motor yawns as he sits up. "It's full of that stuff now, so they're gonna be too scared to follow us in." Nobody wants to own up to being freaked out by the graveyard the factory's turned into, so we all agree. "But what're we gonna do with the pirate?"

"Um, I'm afraid we aren't going to get a say in the matter," Eli says as he keeps pulling the trigger of the Flashfire, but nothing happens. It must be dead. I grab Ripvan's Flashfire and try that one, but it's totally fried. "Great! Now what do we do with her?"

But again, we don't get a say in that, because Harp picks that moment to do the same thing Lily did and jump out of her pretend faint to lunge for where we stuck her DC-3. Half of us all jump for her, and the other half ducks for cover, and the second half was smarter because she makes it to the gun before we reach her, and yeah, by "we" I mean to tell you I'm in the first half because I'm an idiot. Harp fires away at anything that's got eyes to aim between, and thankfully, she doesn't quite get her mark, but she does manage to cut part of the skin off my arm. In the distance, the leeches go nuts, and their hissing surges over us in layers.

"STOP, those things eat metal and anything with blood!" I yell, pressing my hand against my arm.

"Well, lucky me," Harp snarls. "They'll be too busy with you to go after me!" That said, she runs for the vent, firing somewhere above her as she slips in. There's nothing to do but watch in horror as a landslide of gravel spills and covers the vent in seconds flat and keeps coming right at us. The factory's suddenly no longer an option.

"Run!" Craw spurs us as bigger rocks start pouring down after us. At first, I panic, stuck between an avalanche and a valley of leeches, then Jacques grabs my arm and pulls me for the ledge as a good-sized boulder rolls for where I was, big enough to break my legs if I stayed there.

"No, don't run," a voice says, and we all turn to see Lily standing off to the left. When she got there, I have no clue, but she was obviously watching us, waiting for the right time to show her face. Her hair refuses to glitter in the starlight as she walks over to us, totally calm about the line of gravel pushing us back toward the cliff. "If you do, I'm sure that nothing under heaven could save you from being eaten by that horde of hunters. And even if they don't, well, I've got other ways of keeping you here. Missiles trained on the valley floor, for example. And don't think I can't do that. I've got this whole place under my thumb." She smirks, beckoning her sister up next to her. Ivy looks sick and sad and shakes slightly, sparking something that might be pity in me. "You see, my sister here has not only kept her machinery-control part of her Plexus, but she's honed it well. The entire factory is at her command, and if you step foot in that valley out of my proximity, she'll command it to blow you to bits. You're staying here."

I look hard at her eyes. *Are you bluffing, westerner?* I wonder, but it's impossible to tell.

"What do you want, Lily?" I growl as the rocks keep sliding closer. The rest of the Brigade watches from a distance—I can see the top of Spike's head out of the corner of my eye.

"What do I want? I want to win the play," Lily replies fiercely. "That's why I helped the landslide shut in that freak McHarper. That's why I came to stop you, and by you, I not only mean this whole team, but you personally, Mouse. I've figured out you're a bigger liar, a bigger Next than I first believed, and you're the biggest threat on this island, no matter what the others believe."

A smile crawls on her lips, and I step back away from her, my blood going cold.

"You see, on the randomized list read off to declare who was going to Hudson Bay first, I found that the top three on the list all sided with the glorious protector without even including him. With Vici's excessive digging into Plexus systems with more malice than Voxel, I wasn't surprised to find that she trumped Eli's murder out of spite, and I wasn't interested enough to see what Rex had done because I was too curious as to how *you* of all people topped the list. I mean, I knew you were a thief, and I knew you got away with a lot of stuff, but I wondered if that was all it took to get this bad. And my curiosity was rewarded." She laughs the same way she did when I walked into the factory room that I hadn't known she was guarding, and I swallow. *Caught as a rat in a trap.* "Why don't you show us the tattoo on your back, Mouse?"

"What tattoo?" I fire back, wishing my hair was still longer or that I was wearing something better than this stupid tank top. She doesn't look confident enough, so I know she doesn't know what that ink says, doesn't know the whole story, but she knows enough to start turning people against me in ways that'd get all of us hurt if I don't do something.

Lily looks calmly at the coming landslide then back at me. "Well, I have almost an hour to wait, if you're in denial. Unless you want me to tell them for you? Shall I read the charges of your scroll?"

I look nowhere near calmly at the landslide and the leeches and the curious, maybe hurt faces trying to figure out what I've been hiding, and the cold realization of what I have to do shoots through me. "Alright, don't tell them anything, just tell me what you want me to do! I'll do it. Anything."

"Rat, what're you talking about?" Craw asks, but I don't even look at him.

"Anything?" Lily repeats. "Just to save face?"

"You think that's what this's about? Dignity? Try survival. They'll kill me if they know." Everyone exchanges looks after that one, but Lily's eyes glint.

"Then why don't you come over *here* and see how well *I* can protect you? I'd love to know how you did it, Rat. I really would love to know what's hidden in your bag of tricks. Come on, you get Vici back, you get away from this loser crowd with all their faults, and you get my oath of silence, all for the low price of whatever's left of your loyalty. What do you say?"

I hesitate a second then slowly start walking over, sparking a chorus of gasps and murmuring behind me. "As for the rest of you, keep playing!" Lily barks at the Brigade, who all leap forward, taggers ablaze, and the murmuring turns into shouts of surprise. "One way or another, that liquid lightning will be ours! Now, Rat." She smiles her viper smile as she turns back to me. "Come along and let's see if we can't open up that heart of stone yet."

"You're gonna keep me safe from the leeches too, right?" I prod in my calmest voice as I hear the scrabbling sound of what must be someone going off the cliff. The struggle turns into a fight behind me, and there's yelling from both sides.

"Rat, wait! What're you doing?" someone cries, but I don't even look back. That's rule number one when running away. Don't look back.

"Oh, of course," Lily overrides them, taking fast strides down the steep side of the mountain so I almost have to run to keep up. We get a good distance away before a sharp pair of footsteps breaks off the main group, and I stop with my fists bunched as Lily turns around to do the answering for me: "Ah, the can opener's come running back! My apologies, but you're not invited to this party, robot."

"What've you done to her?" Eli demands, and I shiver at how strong he sounds. How... angry.

"What have I done? Nothing. It's what she's done that should matter. Be happy for our friend—she's leaving behind who she used to be and every pathetic sap she used to know so she can get to everything she can be with me. Smartest thing she's ever done."

Someone back up the hill starts screaming Eli's name, and he pauses, torn. Half of me begs him to leave, prays that my own play's successful, but that's the voice that distracted Siridean while the others escaped, the voice that stole the leeches' attention so the Band could get out of the mountain safely, the voice that doesn't explain anything to anyone because of the repercussions it'll have, because silence is the only way to get minimum damage. There's another voice in me that's scared, a voice that's sick of being on damage control all the time, a voice for the half of me that wants nothing more than for Eli to take me away from the graves I keep digging for myself, to be that support for me so I don't have to be alone all the time. But I have crossed that line already, so I stay silent as he decides to let me go.

"You'll pay for this," he warns. "Both of you." My eyes close, and as I listen to him run back away, I also hope with both halves of my heart that it isn't as final as it feels.

Besides the fighting, the night's quiet for a few seconds before Lily walks in front of me, smiling gently. "Would ya look at that. We got a lil' actor here, don't we, Queen of Hearts? Giving me something to do while the rest of em run from the western markswoman, yah. Real sweet, it is."

So she knows what I'm doing. But even if she's not fooled, everyone else is, and even though there's no pretend-pact keeping the two of us together, we each want something from the other person, which puts us on the same level.

"I was going for the Motor approach too," I explain casually as we start walking again, more careful this time, two strangers walking the same path with plain faces on top and an arsenal hiding beneath. "If they don't want me, they won't come looking for me. If they don't love me, then they can let me free and let me go, so if I should die before I wake, then nobody'll care. They won't get hurt because of me, not now."

Neither of us relax, even when we walk into the factory through a gaping hole in the mountain. She starts leading the way then, beckoning me through another giant factory floor full of unconscious leeches and down a red-lit hallway. We're two bats out of Perdition, stupid enough to go back. It's a fine setting to start playing the game, start getting some cards on the table. "You said you needed to win this Tag thing. That was when I noticed you've got two letters instead of a score, and I figured out you needed someone new to be It."

Lily nods, tapping her tagger at her side. "And when ya worded Vici at the Castaway Point that this was about survival, I knew you had something up your sleeve, but I dunno if they'd *kill* ya for it, nah."

"I'd say anything to get them to like me less." I shrug. We walk into another factory room full of metal-cutters and giant globes. "How'd you get the race list?"

"All I can word is: *thank* you, Larry! Oh, what a shock it was to see your name and one crime next to it that my mother seemed to have missed. Let's see, yadda, yadda, grand larceny, embezzlement, shoplifting, burglary, piracy... attempting to destroy the Plexus?" Lily shakes her head, snickering. "Never quite took ya as a terrorist. Y'know, in all history, there's only been three other tries to wreck the Plexus. The first was a few years after you were borned, and the last was a coupla hours ago. Somehow, ya must've iced outta their fingers. How'd ya do it?"

"Oh, you know," I say vaguely, stalling. "It was an average crime that got blown out of proportion, really. I kinda... seized something they didn't really like me taking."

Lily laughs then swings around, and I anticipate a blow but she pins me hard against one of the giant metal-cutters before I know what's happening instead, and I feel that she's stronger than me. Her purple eyes stare into me so hard I get this crazy feeling she's about to jump down my throat and rip me apart from the inside if the machinery behind me doesn't tear me to pieces first. Its influence starts reaching for me, making my whole body ache, and from the look on her face, I think Lily must have some clue that what she's doing to me hurts more than it should. "Now, now. Why don't we start this off on the right foot by being open with each other?"

"You want openness? Why don't you tell me the race secrets, Outlier?" I spit, struggling.

"Why don't *you* tell *me* the secrets, Dream Girl?"

"I don't have them!"

"That's right, because I do, and I'm keeping them," Lily says with that wicked smile. "Of course I have them. I wouldn't let your friends consider torturing me for information if I didn't have the secrets, now, would I? I wouldn't put myself at that risk, would I?"

"You tell me. We're all con artists today."

Lily studies me for a good long time, and I watch her right back. Neither of us are telling the whole story here. Something in her tone makes me wonder about what else she's hiding under her sable handcuff, what's going on between her and Ivy, what's up with her and the secrets and trying so hard to get on everyone's bad side. But that's nothing compared to me and how I topped the Adamantration's hit list, how I've been there ever since my extraction.

"You're not going to tell me anything, are you?" she asks softly.

"Nope." I give a little smile. "All this thievery business takes a little magic to do it right, and a good magician never reveals her secrets."

With that, I finally work a hand free of Lily's grip and lie it flat, blowing across it the way Motor does when he's saying good-bye to the dead, and a fistful of floury powder flies into Lily's face. She staggers back, screaming with fury, and I take the moment of her distraction to get away and get my thoughts in order. For some reason, she really wants to win this whole Tag thing, since she's willing to hunt us down for it, and she made it a point to let us know she won't be sharing any of the prize. Is it a trap? Does she just want to make us play hard to trick us into wasting our time or something? Or does she desperately need that liquid lightning for something she's not telling us about?

Whatever it is she's going for, she's ready to kill for it. That much's obvious enough by the way she lunges for me, claws bared, and fires her tagger against my head even as she tackles me. Between the pellet and the floor, my head rings so bad there's nothing I can do to stop Lily from grabbing my own tagger, which has IT on it instead of a score, and cracking it over her knee.

"There," she pants as her eyes water from the powder, "You're finished. Even without knowing what makes you so bad, I could still use you for my original intended purpose, so the others won't mind, so long as you're It." The two halves of my tagger fall to the ground, and Lily's emptied hands ball into fists. "You're *hopeless*. So *tell* me. What do you take that must make you so powerful that you can call Plexus destruction an attempt at an average crime? What modifications have you undergone that you can attempt something that's only been tried by legends and get away without anyone knowing? What mutations are in your blood that you can work your way to the top of that list without even trying?"

"*You're* a mutation!" I fire back insolently, and I get a slap in the face for it.

"TELL ME! I WANT TO BE POWERFUL!" Lily screams. "I WANT TO BREAK IT! I HAVE TO BREAK IT!"

"Break what?" I wonder to the world in general since I know she won't answer me. Then my eyes go wide. "Wait, that's it! That's why you need to win! You know that wave of electricity made by Hilda's Tersatellum accident-bomb shut down half the Plexus, so now you've gotta win to get some to try and destroy it for yourself!" My brow furrows. "But why?"

Lily's mouth opens and closes, and she shakes her head. "You know what, I'm sick of her. Kid, let's have it." She pins me to the floor with the threat of a real gun as Harmoni falls from a cloud or something and lands silently beside me, tears running down his face as he looks at me.

"You lived?" I sputter, half shocked, half disappointed.

"You won't," he promises and pulls out the lighter again, flicking it.

The spark explodes, and I buck painfully as electricity shoots through me, frying me alive, so I can't help screaming even after it's over. Some of the

Tersatellum's leaked out by now, so the shocks aren't lethal unless he chains them together. When the wave ends, I lie here in a gasping, sizzling heap, trying to scrape my brains off the sides of my skull. Lily and Harmoni both look unfazed.

"You're... sick people," I choke, mind flying in every direction. "I'd tell you I hate you, but I already... won the... understatement-of-the-year award... when I said... going into a room with paper walls, Rex, and a psycho with candles... was a bad idea."

It's fulfilling to see Lily boiling because she can't break me. Oh, she will, I bet, but not yet. Not before I figure her out, get inside her as easy as a residency with a distilling unit vent. I grin when I catch her mistake and get ready to make her pay.

"Your... eyes're glowing with Plexus, Lily. You've still... got your chip."

Her eyes darken. "Again," she commands, and another shockwave sends my conscience flickering. It makes sense now—she's not affected by the electricity because mainframes have shock protectors. How Harmoni isn't effected and how half of Tersatellus *was* effected, I don't know, but that's a question for a later day.

"Who're you talking to up there in the Plexus?" I work out, and really, it's much more butchered than that. "Your girlfriend?"

Lily almost comes back with a snotty comment of her own, but my answer comes running into the room. "I'm here," Harp announces as she skids to a stop. "Nobody's dead yet, but we're winning, and there's less than an hour left."

Lily tries to shush her, but the last part gets out, anyway. "Until what?" I question. Harp gives me a funny look, probably wondering how I don't know, and starts to explain, but she gets tagged right in the kisser and shuts up.

"Until the end of the play, genius," Lily hisses, motioning for Harmoni to go for it again.

"Wait! Why'd you have to stop her from saying that? Something big happens then, doesn't it? Something you can't tell us about?" I guess.

Lily lowers her arm and weighs her options for a second. "What, Rat, do you honestly think Vastate would activate a bunch of Mechs in some illegal factory and then do nothing about the illegalness? After he sent a bunch of lawbreakers here to be killed so viciously? This place is set for demolition at six sharp. So either you tell me how to destroy the Plexus so that order doesn't get sent, or I'm going to do everything in my power to make sure me and my team have enough fuel to haul out before this place goes sky high."

⇹

The truth hits me hard enough to knock the air out of my lungs. If I don't think of something fast, then everyone on the island'll get blown to bits. I can't let that happen.

That's the whole thing. It's about survival, it's always been about survival, but not mine. When I told Vici about that, I was talking to her. I told her I needed to protect *her*, not me. I followed Lily in here to try because she's not stopping for anything; she'll let everyone get killed without batting an eye. She's the ruthless one, so anything I can do to distract her, slow her down, I'm gonna do. Motor still has a whole life left to live and give, and everyone always knew he'd give it because that's who he is. Craw still has a world left to set on fire, because that's what he does, make people feel something, get rid of the emptiness. Voxel still has a vision to carry, this bold (if crazy) vision of truth and justice to see through to the end. Jacques still has oceans to sail before hitting shore, still has things to figure out and a heart to put back together. And I'd have to be some new flavor of jerk if I put my life above Eli's second chance. Me, I'm just sodding immortal, just the rat. We're good for eating our way inside only to sneak right back out, and that's exactly what I intend to do.

(Then again, intentions don't matter much when you get the right cue.)

"Great, just when I had something I was ready to nobly die for, you go and give me a reason to escape." I sigh. "Thanks. I'd hate to go down as a hero."

Lily focuses back on me instead of her visions of everything going kablooey. "Oh, you're not making it out of here alive, Mouse," she purrs and motions for Harmoni to flick the lighter again. The electricity comes before I can do anything, and even though I fight for consciousness, the pain pulls me under long enough that the three of them can somehow get me into one of the spheres of gas without me fighting. It smells kinda like the candles in Hilda's house, so the first thing I think of when I wake up is about how bad it reeks, but then I let the anger encourage me to my feet, and I bang my fists against the glass.

"She's awake!" Harp yells—they didn't get very far—and Lily orders them to run, probably to join the game of Tag to make sure her team wins.

"Sorry, but I'm a sore loser, so my team's winning this!" I call after them, digging into my left-inside-pant pocket for another spit-activated miracle powder and planting my feet against the glass. The powder sizzles against the side of the container, and I climb right up the wall because of it, coming out the top of the fishbowl-shaped thing and sliding down the side. When I hit the floor, it jostles me enough that I stay there for a second, dazed. Then a bullet lodges itself in the glass behind me, and all my limbs that want to stay sodding immortal start scrambling without me needing to tell them.

"Battle stations, everyone, get her!" Lily roars. "The Band can't win!" She backs onto a lift and kicks it into gear and then ducks behind the half-shield made by the controls and safety bars. Harmoni somehow springs up two stories and lands on a bridge, and Harp dives behind one of the broken spheres. It occurs to me that they all look like snowglobes, and to an outsider looking in, we're a bunch of shrunken people fighting to the death in a souvenir cabinet.

Some of the black-and-blue ragdolls in the cabinet start coming to life as Harmoni fires his tagger at me, giving everything a hundred new shades of deadly. I duck behind a globe and glance at my enemies through the cracked glass. One has a tagger, one has a real gun, Lily has both, and I'm dead terrified of those leeches, considering I almost had my arm sucked off by one not too long ago. And all I've got is wits.

Sounds like my kind of game.

"Are we really going to play cat and mouse?" Lily snickers as I circle the globe. *Laughing at her own jokes again.*

"Wow, Lily, that was so bright. I'm blinded by your brilliance," I cue as my fingers find the wires they were looking for. Paying attention to those construction plans really helped—after memorizing them, I remembered where a certain power panel is, and now I grab a lead pipe and swing it into the thing for all I'm worth, sending the room into darkness. By now, I'm almost used to getting shocked, so I can pick myself up off the floor real quick. Even the emergency lights're out now, but a good rat doesn't need the lights. I've seen the place enough.

"Ah, she's hiding in the shadows now," Harp smirks, and when I turn to the source of her voice, I can make out her glowing irises in the darkness. Without a sound, I scamper up a ladder for her and decide to go for dramatic effect.

"Nope," I whisper right next to her so she jumps and screams, firing where she heard me, but I'm not there, I'm behind her, I'm grabbing her arms and hitting her DC-3 over the railing. She ends up forcing my pipe down there after it but not much else. "I *am* the shadows." With only the smallest twang of guilt, I shove her off after her gun, and she doesn't make any sounds after hitting the floor.

"Guess what can see in the dark?" a quiet voice sniffles from across the room so I can hardly hear it, but the tagger-gunfire gives me enough of a hint. The pellet explodes against my shoulder and I think fast as the hissing picks up, glowing red dots eyeing me hungrily.

"Guess who doesn't have to see in the dark," I return as I drag a nail down one of the railings, coming up with a gob of chemicals made so that leeches don't start eating the factory, and rub it against my shoulder as I slink down the bridge, planning to go for the kid next, but footsteps on metal off to my right tell me I don't have time for that right now. I run for the sound, dropping a pocketful of pretty rocks from Hilda's house down so they crack against the metal factory floor. Lily unloads her gun toward the sound, so I hear exactly where she's at and dive at her.

"What are you doing?" Lily asks angrily when I end up grabbing her ankles. Oops.

"Uh … arresting your feet?"

I roll to the right just in time to have my head not blown off by a bullet then get back on my feet and finger the darkness for the gun. She dodges me, slapping at my hands with her own free one, but eventually I grab her sleeve and yank her arm down and reach for the gun with one hand. It doesn't stay in my hand for one second before she pulls it free, presses the barrel to my forehead, and pulls the trigger.

I'm quiet even when I'm hitting the floor.

Lily lets out a gasp and everything's still for a few seconds as horror settles down like dust. Then a laugh bubbles inside of me as I lift up my hand and slowly let six bullets drop onto the metal bridge. "Oh, Lily, I thought you were a weapons dealer. Didn't anyone ever tell you not to dry-fire a gun?"

She tosses her blank gun over the railing, disgusted. "I may not have weapons of Plexus destruction, Mouse, but I've got more than one gun," she growls, and in a way, she's not lying. Her tagger is technically a gun, and it's supposed to feel the same way a real gun does against my forehead, so I play along for a sec and go still as the quiet footsteps of her reinforcements come up behind her.

"Oh, yeah?" I challenge when the steps come close enough. "Then, YOU'RE ARRESTED!" Lily yelps in surprise when I grab her ankles again and tug so she falls to the floor right as Harmoni fires, so it's her he hits. Multiple times. Before she can stop him, leeches come flying from all directions, and I stumble away, searching for the ladder from before. Harmoni comes out of nowhere and tackles me, trying to get in a good shot, but I manage to keep his arm away from me and get in a great well-deserved punch that not only lets me get away, it gives the stupid brat something real to cry about.

"RAAAT, *I'LL* DESTROY *YOU* FOR THIS!" Lily screams, and I let myself turn around and eat one more hole in her.

"Get it right, Leadhead: I didn't destroy the Plexus. I stole it. And as long as we're being open, you might as well stop calling me Rat too. You're the first one to catch me." I smile. "So you might as well call me what I am before I gnaw my way back out. Go ahead. I want to hear it leave your lips. I dare you to try and say it without all the fear I'm due. Or haven't you guessed who I am yet?"

Lily goes silent for a few seconds. Even the leeches go still (she probably figured out the whole chemical thing to keep them away or took off whatever pieces of clothing the taggers hit), so the gravity of this moment scorches its mark on everyone here. Below me, Harp picks her head up and whispers, "Oh, Cielhomme. No. They're dead..."

So their suspicions have been confirmed. Now they know. And while it's not all my secrets, nowhere near all there is to know about me, it's still something nobody's known before, so for a second, I'm just as overwhelmed as they are.

Harmoni screams in frustration off to my right, ticked about being left out of an affair that's strictly Tersatellan. My feet barely touch the floor before the kid's footsteps start running for me, so I search the ground with blind and frantic fingers. He slips on the rocks and stuff I threw down before and sits for a second, crying, which buys me the time I need to find Lily's blank gun on the floor and slide in the ammo.

"Payback time," I mutter to myself, and Harmoni doesn't get in spitting distance of me before I fire. The bullet hits one of the bases of the spheres, and sparks go everywhere, and even though most of the Tersatellum's been burned up by now, it still gives the factory one last mighty shock.

When the wave ends, I saunter over to Harmoni and take his tagger in case I need to turn someone into a leech target. "H-h-how?" he sputters from the ground, and even though he won't see it, maybe he'll hear the creepy beads hitting each other as I wave his anti-electric chain above his face. That's how he avoided the shocks before, is with this stupid little charm. Jewelry ain't so useless, after all.

"Don't tackle a thief if you've got anything valuable on you. On a scale of dumb to ten, that's as bad as kicking a thug. You asked for it." Harmoni's startled eyes search the darkness for me as he gropes his neck for the chain. "What? You think that one second isn't enough time to split six bullets or some stupid necklace? Why do you think they call it a split-second? Besides, I've had bigger . . . seizures."

I get up and start heading for the exit, and even though I know I'm going to have to figure out how to tell this to the others, I can't help feeling high about it. Not good, not bad, just intoxicated by this staggering fact. One of the biggest things I've worked to keep in the dark has been kicked into the light, and there's no path back into hiding. The others will need an explanation. That much is inevitable. But I don't feel defeated. No, somehow, I actually feel relieved by the thought, if dizzied, and maybe a bit . . . unstoppable.

Someone lands behind me with a gasp. The leeches still haven't followed her yet, and she's a safe enough distance away that I can run away if they start chasing her again, so I turn around and watch her. As she takes one shaky step forward, the emergency lights flare on, igniting her hair in a glowing frame around her head, so the shock on her face is clear as day. She almost looks betrayed. It's so huge, and it seems painful, even impossible for her to try and fathom. "You," she breathes. "All this time . . . everything that's happened . . . I can't . . . you're . . . y-y-you're . . ."

"Yeah. I am." Lily gapes at me, and Harp looks between us with rising turmoil on her face, the same turmoil that I feel, but I bolster myself anyway. I've been figured out, so I might as well be the one to announce it—my life's about to change for good, but it's going to be on *my* terms. It's time to declare to my audience with arms open wide, "Ladies and leeches, you bear witness to history today. A legend rises from her ashes. So let's all stop trying to keep me down and add another act for the Kill Switch."

Then I turn my back on the oncoming hunters and their flabbergasted prey to start striding out of the graveyard, crossing the chalk line that I never dreamed I would come back from. But here I am, returned from the darkness to the spotlight.

"Now, if you'll excuse me, I've got a play to finish."

- VIII -

Guilty Minds Think Alike

It takes long minutes of running around aimlessly through the black-rocked valley to find anyone on my team, and when I do, it's because I trip over them. There were enough Brigadiers out there, sure, but either my team's dead, or they're just really good at hiding. The first person I find is in the second condition, blending so well in the shadows with black-and-camo that if I didn't run right into them, I'd never notice they were there.

"Rat!" they hiss, and I forget my scraped elbows a second, sitting up to look at him.

"Jacques!" Suddenly, I realize I really *was* worried the Brigade did something really awful to everybody, and I almost reach out and wrap my arms around my teammate, but I hold myself back at the last second. My brain flings together an explanation. "Listen, I know what it looked like back there, but—"

"Say no more," Jacques stops me with his words and hand, and I swallow, backing away from his burning eyes. "Do you take us all for fools?"

"No, of course not, but..." I trail off when the starlight glints off his smile. "What?"

"My brilliant young friend, you may consider yourself pardoned. Whether you willed it or not, we have learned enough of you to know you would never forsake us without reason, so no matter how clever your ruse, we saw through it. I only hope we played our parts as well as you did yours."

I'm too shocked to do anything but stare for a few seconds, then there's no stopping it this time. I tackle-hug him, laughing or crying or something. "Y'know, if I'd known all along it felt this good to be understood at least a little, I might've tried it sooner!" A little. As if knowing my act of betrayal was just a show for distraction gives my team more than one tiny piece of my puzzle.

"It does my heart good to hear it. Now, would you care to enlighten us on your purpose for this charade? Everyone is listening, by the way. You caught me in the middle of a conversation."

"Hi, Rat!" Motor giggles, his voice coming out of Jacques's beacon. "The beacons're broke, so we've all gotta listen to each other all the time, buttons or not. Ivy did that, but she can't get the Brigade's beacons to hear us."

"Oh. Hi, everyone," I say nervously. "Are any of you somewhere you're hiding so I need to be quiet?" A chorus of responses comes up from everybody except one. "Eli?"

"I'm fine. Just explain, would you?" he snaps and the corner of my lip twitches. So not everybody knew it was an act. I've still got some apologies to give, but that's something you do in person.

"Alright. Lily's gone ballistic, guys. If you haven't noticed, the Brigade really needs to win this Tag thing for some reason. They're concentrated way too much on it for it to be harmless, and it's driven Lily up a wall, which I think might be affecting Ivy."

"She did seem a bit vertically beneath the weather," Voxel comments, and somehow, it makes me glad we can all talk the free way we could if we were all together instead of needing to hit buttons all the time. "But why is the she-devil so hectic?"

"Because that prize means a lot more than we thought. Staying here isn't an option anymore, everyone—if we don't get that fuel and we're stuck here, it's all over. Turns out the geniuses back home figured out this's an S86, and they're set to nuke the place at dawn."

"Okay, *not* good. The Brigade smashed us out here, Rat," Craw explains. "Their guns're reformed, so they shoot freaky fast, and we kinda ran into a problem: out of ammo. We're defenseless."

"But they didn't figure out the shooting each other thing," Motor points out, full of hope. "We should still have enough points to beat them! Don't worry, we're really good hiders, so they won't get us anymore."

"What of Lily?" Jacques asks. "You claimed she was being rather… obstinate."

"She is, big time. But I've got the leeches distracting her now, so she shouldn't be a problem, and I think Harp's broken a bone or two. How much time do we have?" My Rolex can only be called well-done after all this zapping. I think it still works, but I can't see.

Jacques looks at the sky as if the answer's written up there, but I get the feeling it's more for concentration. "We have about a half of an hour." How he knows that is a mystery to me, but we're all entitled, and now's not the time to ask.

"Alright, we've got two options here: a surprise attack or puppy-guarding. We either hide, spring out at the last second, run with the Tersatellum and hope we can get to our mobiles before the bombs hit, or get to the top of the mountain, guard the prize until six, then run with it and hope we can get out our mobiles before the bombs hit. Either way, it's got more running and more hoping than I'd like, but we can't exactly take vials of gas, so we'll have to wait until six, when the defense turns it into liquid lightning. That's the only way you put it into mobiles, right?"

"Yeah, but maybe we don't need the defense to make it into liquid lightning for us. Maybe we could just grab the vials before the Brigade knows what's going on and make it into fuel ourselves," Motor suggests. "They'll never see it coming!"

That's stretching it, but I think it's a sturdier plan (even though we don't know *how* we're going to get the electricity to make liquid lightning), so I admit, "Sounds better than options A or B. Much less luck involved. Let's regroup by that big tree on the north side of the mountain. It's in the shadows, so we should be hidden getting there. Everyone know where I'm talking about? Good. Let's go."

Jacques pockets his beacon, and I start going, but he stops me a second. "Hold. How *did* you manage to top the race list?"

I bite my lip. "Later, okay? When everyone's back together. It's kinda hard to explain, but you won't really kill me for it, I hope. Now, let me try and teach you how to be a shadow."

A peek around the rock shows Spike's dark outline in the distance right where I saw him last, so they're not hunting; they're patrolling. All it takes is a well-thrown rock to make him run away from us after the sound of it hitting a distant boulder, and if Jacques doesn't throw well, then nobody does. With Spike distracted, the two of us slink across the valley floor. My feet've found their place now and skim on the rocks with ease. We start going slightly right toward the tree, which is when I spot Vici up there. "Sticks!" I hiss, ducking back down where she can't see me. She doesn't hear me, and I can't hear her, so I look for rocks and angles to hide behind as I slip closer. Jacques watches me, probably wondering if I'm crazy, but I give him a thumbs-up and scan the valley. When I spot the two people I'm looking for, I point them together and invent a bunch of hand signals until I hear Vici's beacon crackle to life.

"Everyone! Abandon your sentry post and retreat to home base," Lily's cold voice commands. "We can't risk one of them growing brains and getting more ammo. If we don't win this, it won't be me to give everyone a few Perditions to pay!"

Vici gives the world another good look before dropping out of the tree and running quietly for the Brigade lodge. After giving her a minute to run, I climb up onto the ledge and under the tree, which is so soaked in shadow I can hardly see the hand in front of me. Jacques follows me up just before Craw and Voxel get back, beacon and marker-tool in hand and smug grins on their faces. Ah, to be criminals with superpowers. "Good to see you back," Craw smiles, and I decide to give him a hug, and Voxel too—I'm really having a sale today, after all.

"Me too!" Motor shouts excitedly as he bounds up over the hill, locking his arms around my legs. "I heard the shock things, and I was scared I lost you."

"Well, you could say I'm lost to be found," I say, straightening up as Eli slowly walks into the shadow of the tree. We watch each other for a minute, but it only takes a second for the look to disappear into nothingness.

"Nice job, Rat," Eli tells me and starts trying to move on to the plan, but I interrupt.

"Eli, I'm sorry."

He lifts an eyebrow at me. "I thought 'nice job' was a compliment, not a request for apology."

I put my hands on my hips. "Listen, I know how walking out on someone looks, and I'm sorry to say I fit that bill. Even if you're expecting it, the first time's always rough. I was hoping you wouldn't have to go through it—all this time, I've been kinda jealous—hence, I'm even sorrier that it was me that did it," I admit, throwing my arms open. "So c'mere and get your hug if I'm totally pardoned and everything."

Eli resists for a second then breaks out into a smile and walks over, and I grab him and just crush the guy against me. "You had me going for a minute there. I guess I must be gullible, because I really thought you weren't… weren't coming back. You terrify me sometimes, Rat," he mutters in my ear.

"Yeah, but you came back first." I shrug. "I'm just returning the favor."

"Uh, sorry, but… 'Kill'?" I turn around to see Craw looking at me confusedly, along with everyone else. "That's kind of a morbid tattoo."

Whoops. I'm sort of back into the light over here, and Eli's hand moved my hair outta the way.

Craw's comment is a cue, and when I search everyone's patient faces, I can't find a way out. No way I want to take, anyway, and there's no good way of explaining. So I decide to get it over with fast and hope they don't have any questions.

"That's just half of it," I tell Craw, motioning for my jacket back so nobody'll be tempted to stare. "The whole thing's Kill Switch. And it's not just a fan thing."

This awards me with a whole minute of silence before Voxel snickers. "No *way*." I nod, and she starts laughing. "Then there is a lack of presence of hard feelings between we felons for you being higher than me on a special list! Cielhomme, Rat! How'd you *do* it?"

"Pardon me, but time wears on in spite of our curiosity, so I'm afraid this conversation must be forestalled to a yet a safer time," Jacques warns, pointing at the horizon. The sky's getting brighter, and stars're fading. An hour ago, that sight would make me cheer up, but now my heart sinks at it. Time's running out.

"At least we've got the biggest name in the criminal business to help us split that fuel! C'mon, guys, let's go!" Motor urges, running toward the top of the mountain.

"NOT SO FAST!" a livid voice booms down on us, and we all turn our heads to see two figures up there, black silhouettes against the lightening sky, one with long hair that almost shines in the predawn light, one with a braid. The second one pulls something out of a tall ragdoll that sinks to the ground with a spine-chilling chattering sound, but we don't have time to wonder if Vici really just killed a leech. "Set it!" the first one snarls, and Vici turns away from her victim and gives something an almighty tap.

BRONG. BRONG. "Welcome to an early dawn!" Lily sneers. BRONG, BRONG goes the bell, and the horror of what they're doing crashes through me. They're trying to activate the defense early so they can run off with the Tersatellum and leave us all behind to explode. "Playtime's over, kids! And you can consider yourselves the losers." BRONG… BRONG.

"That's not true!" Craw yells up at her, since he's the only one loud enough that his voice would carry that far—Lily's got some kind of cone that's making her voice louder. "We had a strategy! *You* lost!"

"Oh? Then how come I can do this?" It's impossible to see what she does that distance, but from the glint off the glass, I can guess, and my heart stops. She's got a vial, despite the defense. "If you're confused, you might want to ask *It* how one loses the game of Tag."

"Sticks," I mutter, kicking my brain into action. "Look, the defense hasn't been activated yet. She still has to keep those vials there until six, or until the losing team tries to take it, or until my excellent friend Vici figures out how to make it shock the stuff faster. I've got this anti-electric chain thing from Harmoni and a lighter from Melodi, so if we can get those vials, maybe we can get into the factory and make some fuel if there's any Tersatellum left—we could break another globe or something. But I don't know if we'll have time to fight our way up there and through the factory and out onto the beach, or how the heck we can get to the vials if that defense'll shock us to death if we touch them!"

"Well, you've got that chain thing, don't you?" Motor points out. "So that's how you get past the defense!"

"But what about the rest of it?" I ask helplessly, searching the two objects in my hands like a necklace and vintage technology could save us. Then they disappear, and I look up to see Eli putting the chain around his neck.

"I'll do it," he steps up, "since I'm the fastest, and I could take on Lily and Vici." He's looking intensely at me in a way that I know, that I've worn—he's not just volunteering; he's asking me to let him live out his second chance.

"Are you kidding? This is the Kill Switch we're talking about!" Craw scoffs. "She stole part of the Plexus! This'll be a piece of cake for her!" The others nod in agreement.

"But…"

"Yeah, Rat could rescue me from the leeches, remember?" Motor pipes up. Eli opens his mouth to protest then turns to go anyway before anyone can say anything.

"Wait!" I demand, grabbing his arm so he's forced to face me. He desperately searches for reasons, for words to defend this need to do more than enough, to be more than good enough.

"Rat, please, could you—"

"I do trust you," I say, looking him straight in the eyes, one electric green, one steel gray. "But I'm not letting you go. Not before saying good-bye and good courage."

Gratitude and something that's probably relief washes over his face. "You too" is his solemn reply, and we shake on it before he turns and sprints off. For once, though, watching someone fly away doesn't make my blood go cold, because criminals never shake on anything conventional. And considering that all our possessions could pretty much be carried by the clothes on our backs and the bags under our eyes, a trade isn't something shallow.

The early morning wind bends the corners of the paper in my hand, a faded, crinkled picture that holds a vault of memories in the seemingly safe image of a piano on a seaside cliff. And as Eli climbs the mountain, he dodges bullets, and he puts on my third and original exception to the no-auxiliaries rule: a steel wool bracelet that a special green-and-gray-eyed boy wove for me a few days before the world changed, a bracelet with a secret message woven into it. One of those gray strands of steel wool is dyed ruby red, and that strand was the long one that you used to tie the ends together as if to tell me, "Erra, no matter what anyone tells you, remember this: blood runs thicker than water." And I'll tell you the truth, since I told you I'd be honest. I took it as a hint, and I held on to that thread of hope that you really did leave me just to come back someday.

But don't worry, my Rolex's secret compartment doesn't go on empty. The picture's carefully rolled up and tucked inside with more confidence than you'd imagine, and then I turn. "C'mon, guys!" I spur when I notice everyone staring at me.

"So where's that Rat that never trusted a word anyone said?" Craw jokes.

"Oh, not this again!" I laugh curtly and start running. Jacques pulls Motor onto his shoulders, and the kid adjusts his goggles over his face as they go, and the rest of us start picking up on the cue—Jacques pulls up his bandana over the bottom half of his face, Voxel twirls her marker and draws on her war paint, Craw flings the ends of his scarf out of his shirt, and eventually, I give in and pull my hoodie off and tie it around my waist so my tank top shows off my sable, the tattoo on my back that nobody's gotten a good enough look at yet to know that KILL SWITCH isn't all that's there. Between/behind the two words, there's the symbol that was drawn in blood on rusty metal by Requieminor as the world watched him die, the symbol that I blacked into the data codes of the Plexus, the symbol hiding in the shadows of the very emblem of our nation, the symbol that blazes against the shadowy metal of the tallest tower on the planet. X for cutout, for the wrong answers, for the lost causes, for the blackhearts who look at all that is good and just and say *no*.

In New Arctic Circle, that symbol still endures in the dark before the dawn, even while every floor, every invention, every success and failure and dream inside of the Pylon is finally razed to the ground. Masses of papers that would put the room I saw in the factory to shame go up in flames, smoke pouring out of them as thick as tears, while the promises of a better future curl and blacken and disintegrate. Machines waiting to change the world are blasted to pieces. Criminal Resolution mobiles' sirens wail into the dark. Black-and-yellow tape makes senseless patterns of stripes, stretching around the Pylon as if everyone's trying to suffocate it. Ashes cough out of the doors, and the whole structure shudders. Nearby citizens scatter away, warned by the Adamantration that the head of that Headquarters is responsible for a terrorist attack. Rapture men have moved all the important systems out and take control of the defense control units and set a time and date for destruction of Fort Night, which has evaded the eye of the law for long enough. People need to be taught that there are rules in place for a reason and that there are consequences for breaking them.

⇹

"YOUR VICTORY IS FORFEIT!" Craw bellows as we dive into the valley, Brigadiers not knowing whether to open fire or scatter or correct his grammar. We storm them, but they get themselves together eventually, and one of them calls for splitting up and covering more ground, so we have to do the same for the third time all night. Craw and Voxel peel off to the left, Jacques and Motor go right, and I keep running as fast as my feet can carry me, spying on the target.

"HEY! WHAT KIND OF A NAME IS DOUGLAS, ANYWAY?!"

"It's not gonna work that easy with me," Spike smirks, turning away from his sniper spot on a rock to relax in front of me. "But I need to restock my own word-war room, so feel free to try."

I shrug. "Actually, I'm done. You just missed Voxel and Craw ditching the valley." The two haven't really left yet, but Spike doesn't see them duck behind the rocks, so he swears. "Thanks for letting me distract you, genius. Now, if you'll excuse me—"

Before I can slip away, Spike grabs me by the arm, which I practically had to wave in his face so he could get it (ugh, you can be the best actor in the world, but it won't matter if the audience doesn't take their cue). "You're not going anywhere," he growls. Voxel and Craw're still sprinting across the barren valley floor, so I stall, struggling against Spike until they get to the tree line, where I can barely make out Craw giving me a thumbs-up.

"Spike, what're you doing?" Lily's voice demands from his beacon in his pocket (I think it's kinda funny how good Craw can mock her). "Don't think I can't see you! Stop fooling with Mouse and kill someone already!"

"With pleasure," Spike snarls, letting me go so I run, shrugging my hoodie back onto my shoulders. "Ha! How far do you think you can run before I shoot you down, little girl?"

"Pretty far!" I call back, pulling one of his guns out of my hoodie and waving it in the air. Spike's eyes light up in fury, and he starts after me, but I'm already chucking it as hard as I can to the right. A shadow rises out from behind a boulder, and I must've thrown the gun too high because Motor has to catch it and hand it down to Jacques, who nukes the rock Rex was trying to snipe us from. The albino runs off in panic, Spike retreats before getting attacked, and I scramble to catch up with Jacques so we run together for the other side of the valley. Boy, we're all suddenly marathoners! This really is a race! But soon enough, there's no Brigadiers in sight, so despite all sorts of discomforts that I won't even bother listing by now, I grin with relief. The plan's going great. "Hey, we might actually make it outta here without a problem after all!"

And that, my friend, is my fifth and final delusion of the night.

Suddenly, all the hair on the back of my neck stands up, and I skid to a stop, turning in horror, praying it isn't true. But it is. The sound of hissing laps against my ears as the leeches come out of their hiding, skating for the mountain. One flies right past me at breakneck pace, faster than I've ever seen them, louder than I've ever heard them without screaming.

"Wow, they must be hungry," Motor comments.

"And Eli is wounded," Jacques adds, and I go pale, remembering that metal under the gash. They want steel more than blood, and they can smell it from scary-far away. "Motor, can you see the top of the mountain?"

The kid opens and closes each eye until he figures out which one's far-sighted. He'd got a better point of view too. "Yeah. Um ... Lily's shooting at Eli with the tagger. I think he's got the vials, but the leeches're coming!"

"Tagger," I breathe, and pull out the tagger I stole from Harmoni and fire a random shot toward the horde, then a closer shot, and closer.

"What're you doing?" Motor asks, wondering if I've gone nuts.

"Leaving a trail of crumbs. Go! In the least Death-alluding way possible, I'll see you on the next shore," I promise as the leeches turn their heads and start following my pellet blasts, since that's closer to them than Eli. They lick at the ground furiously, moving so fast I can hardly keep up in my shooting. Jacques runs into the trees with Motor, and I step back, watching the huge horde that's coming right at me because I run out of ammo so I can't lead them away. All my mind can think of when I see them is pain and Death, so I close my eyes, locking my shuddering breath inside me.

Come on, I'm Kill Switch, the new Queen of Hearts, enigma and martyr and sodding immortal! Let's see what I can do!

The brief memory of Vici pulling something out of a leech's head on top of the mountain flies out of my music box, making my eyes blink back open with hope. Most of the leeches aren't even half a minute away from me now, and when I try to force down the panic, it keeps pushing back. *Maybe Vici didn't kill one. It was dark. It could've been a ruse. It'd be some standard trick that I myself taught her. Maybe Revany Remington was wrong, and nobody's ever killed a leech before. They were created by the Adamantration to kill us. What if it's impossible to kill one of them?*

Then again . . . you don't know until you know.

By now, they can smell the blood right through my skin and rush at me in such a frenzy I can't make out individual bodies anymore. They move as one unit to the left when I start running on the valley lip, the mass of them moving fast enough to overtake a truck, but I've got a head start, and they're taking the long way down there, where they can trip on the rocks in their craziness. They're so hungry their shock-absorbing legs aren't working the way they should, and they've got a hard time getting up the slope, so I'm better off up here.

Long minutes of running pass, and the first light of dawn streaks the sky before I finally see the southern lodge. It gives me a burst of strength, and I scramble as fast as my aching legs'll carry me back down into the valley.

"Some believe we've crossed the line," I pant to try and control my breathing, or else I'll break my lungs from breathing so hard and fly across the threshold, slamming the door behind me. "We've lost our touch, we've lost our minds." My hands tremble as I nose around until I find a flashlight and throw on layers and layers of jackets, which I find in the back room. Even my head has to be covered eventually, so I'll be going in blind, trusting only what I remember about the unforgiving landscape. I'm nearly baking under all the clothes, but the leechs've stopped trying to break the door down after me, which means they can't smell me. So of course I'm about to go back out there. "We're never in our place, we're never on time." Last but not least, I find what I couldn't at my own lodge: some sort of multitool that's nowhere near as good as my old one, and it takes twice as long to find it as it did to steal my old one, but it's red, and it fits great in my hand, and it's metal.

The multi hides deep under my layers before I start for the door, unscrewing the flashlight. Who needs light if I'm gonna go in without my eyes? No, it's not the light I need—instead, I reach in, hold my breath, and stick the battery in my mouth.

As it dissolves into the taste of battery acid, I walk out into the entourage.

Even under the layers, they can start to smell what's going on, which I kinda hoped for, anyway. They're just interested enough to follow me over to the dam.

The battery helped, for sure, but it doesn't hold me long, and the headache starts up soon after I climb to the top of the giant metal structure. I have to peel off a few layers from my face and stuff after leeches start losing interest, which is good because I'm drowning in here. Sweat pours down me, and honestly, not all of it's because of the heat.

"C'mon, I'm counting on you," I mutter even though nobody'll hear me. Leeches start licking at me curiously, and I squeeze my eyes shut, the fear and other things making my head pound harder every second. "Ugh … I don't feel anything. Fifty-three out of every hundred die in extraction. Eight more will die in the first day. Fifteen more will die in the first week, and twelve more will die in the first year … that leaves twelve survivors. Not fourteen … but not zero … twelve."

Twelve of us can beat the odds and survive a year of being a cutout.

Why not one week?

But for every second that passes, Saturday feels further away. *This was not a well thought-out plan*, I realize as sparks explode in my vision. The dam whirs underneath me, louder than bombs, louder than the leeches, louder than anything. Somehow, touching it makes it worse, so I shakily start stepping off it but end up collapsing, so I have to crawl. What comes then isn't really relief; it's just less pain that's coming slower, but even that's flawed because then some of the leeches get out of the water to follow me, and I need them *in* the river, so I grit my teeth and climb back up onto the thing, waiting for my head to explode.

It never happens. There's rustling off to the right, and silver hair gleams in the early light, making my heart sink until I notice how short and blinding it is. "Ivy?" I croak, and I think she nods, but I can't see. She points at the dam, and I weakly manage a thumbs-up. Yep, I'm crazy.

She hops up right next to me, and I feel the power of the machine fade to nothing under her command. "You were with him to the end," Ivy whispers to me, putting one of her hands on mine. "Thank you." Then she disappears, and the real end begins.

Somewhere inside the mountain, one spark ignites a Tersatellum cloud big enough that the shockwave reaches out of the mountain. Most of it disappears in the air or does whatever electricity does, but water's a pretty good conductor too, so the charge carries downstream. The leeches scream in agony as the shock runs through them, and I strip off the rest of the extra layers so I have as much movement as possible. Electricity ripples through me, but I feel fine—there's a chain around my neck that's stopping it from doing anything. What? Did you think we just exchange sentimentalness when we shake hands? We criminals, cutouts, and comrades are practical people, so if one of us realizes we'd actually kinda benefit from a good charging, we pawn off useless volt-rejecting jewelry back to where we got it.

When I flick out the multi, the leeches scream even more. I pick the nearest one and do a total leap of faith, falling down on them with a glint of steel and a prayer that I'm the third person to ever kill a leech.

The blade slices into their head, and we both fall into the river, where I get up, and it doesn't move. "HA!" I cheer, then it reverses to an "AH!" when the thing's tongue wraps around my ankle. That little cry's the last thing I get out before I get pulled under the current.

Desperate, I slash out with the multi, gripping on to it so tight that none of them can rip it out of my hands. Five of them wrap their tongues around my waist, lift me out of the water and slam me back down again so my head hits a rock. They're weakened by the electricity, which was the plan, but they're stronger because they're hungry, and they'll do anything for my blood at this point.

With a mighty hack, I manage to lop one's arm off, but it's not even fazed. Nothing stops them anymore. Stabs in their chest do nothing, stabs in their legs, in their hands, tongues, nothing! They don't care! The only thing that's keeping me from getting eaten's the fact they're weakened! And who knows how long that'll last?

Not long, it turns out. A straggler that didn't get shocked comes up from the top of the valley and empties its tongue of air at me and tops the list of loudest things I've ever heard before it lunges. Its tongue wraps around my ankle, and it pulls my whole leg in its mouth, and I feel myself start to sizzle as its teeth start poking into my thighs.

What a way to go, I think and grope the river for anything to help pull myself away.

Then an ominous vvwwoooOOOOOOO fills my ears, and all the leeches turn their heads to the sky, chattering to themselves before spitting me out and skating for the shore. I lie on the bank of the river, gasping for air. Then I pick the best swear I can think of and scream at the top of my lungs. With that priority taken care of, I can shakily sit up.

At the spot where the river meets ocean, there's a solar panel tree sticking up out of the rocks. Beyond that, the ocean's getting covered again in sweet black track, and leeches dive beneath it, disappearing so fast you'd wonder why they ever came out in the first place. But it's not six yet. The bombs haven't come and blasted us to pieces, and the sun hasn't even reached the solar panels yet. They shouldn't have power.

It's a mystery to me until I hear the footsteps. "Guess you weren't tasty enough for them," Eli calls as he walks toward me with a less extreme look of exhaustion than he wore the first time he charged the track—the shockwave probably helped. Even though he's smiling slightly, I can tell something's wrong. "Don't worry, I got the fuel, and I left half for Lily's team. She seems pretty surprised about that. Most everyone's at the beach now, ready to go."

"Then what's the matter?" I ask, standing as he comes to a stop beside me. I'm tired enough to stay sitting for the rest of my life, and I have so many questions and so many things I'd rather talk about, but I'm on my feet anyway, ready to go.

"Are you okay?" he counters instead of telling me then doesn't wait for an answer, just gives me his magical support. "Here, have a gun, I'll tow you again, and we can make it to the shore by six. You shoot at anything that moves, got it?"

"Pft, have you seen my aim? Eli, c'mon, what's wrong? What'm I shooting for?"

He gives me a complicated look before giving in. "Gunners. Most of them survived the electricity. It might've actually helped them. I saw them running out of the factory, and they don't look like they're on automatic anymore—I think they're being controlled, and by someone who has pretty much *no* idea what they're doing, which might make them even more dangerous. It doesn't matter if you were the rapture men's best friend, they're out to kill anything with a life to take on this island. We don't have to worry about the Brigade, anymore, though. They're busy enough on shore with everyone else."

"The gunners are on shore too?" I try to swallow as we start running. How're we supposed to get off this rock in time if there're gunners trying to kill us?

"Not yet, they aren't!" Eli yells over the wind. "We've got some new problems. Sir Adaman Isic Wheel's got one more surprise in store for us. The mobiles won't start."

⇹

Bang. Bang. Bang.

I try not to focus on anything except for shooting. Only half the masses of metal I aim at get hit, and I've only got one of them down so far, but I'm not shooting to stop them from coming as much as I'm shooting to stop myself from thinking.

Bang. Bang. Bang.

They're firing back, and their aim sucks as bad as mine, but some teeny-tiny part of me wishes one bullet would hit true if it means I don't have to feel myself get blasted apart by some bomb. It's such a cruel way to go, blown to bits in no time flat. You're nothing after that. There's no funeral or burial or burning or anything; you're just left to rest in a lot of pieces that don't even resemble a body anymore.

Bang. Bang. Bang.

How could this happen? How could that guy make it so our mobiles wouldn't start at exactly the time we needed them to start? Is it happening to all the mobiles? Is anyone safe?

Bang. Bang. Bang.

We shoot up the slope and into the trees, where a blanket of shadows wraps around us, pinpricks of dawn filtering down through the leaves. They'd be much nicer for running on if I'd gotten used to them, but I haven't, so I slip and slide, and it's all Eli can do to keep us upright. Somehow, we manage, and I keep shooting at the gunners as they get closer and closer. They can never get us. They keep tripping or doing wonky things that make it obvious that someone's button-mashing out there somewhere. They're trying to make the gunners shoot and run and see the way people do, maybe the way a rapture man does, but the angles and the size is all wrong because gunners are Mechs, and Mechs are inhuman.

That doesn't stop them from trying.

Bang. Bang. Bang.

"Almost there!" Eli shouts back, which is good because this is the second gun that I run out of bullets with. At least Spike had more than one. The trees thin more and more until we break the line and hit the shore, where the black expanse of the track sits on the ocean so you'd never even know there was any water down there. Everyone's going nuts on the beach, tearing stuff up with their mobiles. "Anything yet?"

"I can't find anything wrong with the engine or the SANTA clause or eval modem or anything!" Motor's working on my truck since his bike got swallowed by the bay.

"Did you—oh, gosh," I wheeze, standing with my hands on my knees, trying to catch my breath. "D'ja check out, the, the fuel thingy? Maybe the trap has something to do with everyone running out of fuel."

"Aye, we've already looked over that," Jacques says gravely as I stagger over. "Everything's sound."

(On the other half of the beach, a special western Tersatellan whips her head up in venning and words, "Blue Lou, even words *aye*!")

"These mobiles should be in the ideal state of operation!" Voxel yells, kicking the tires furiously. "ISIIIIIC!"

I hop inside my own mobile, sinking into the seat, and throw my battered beacon into the holder, which usually makes the truck spring to life, but nothing happens. Nothing I press, poke, prod, or punch does anything. Not even the horn works! "You guys already put fuel in these things, right?"

"No, that slipped our minds," Rex says sarcastically, coming out of *nowhere* to look at my truck.

"Hey, hands to yourself!" I growl at him and get back out, running my fingers through my hair. "What're we gonna do?"

"Whatever it is, we'd better figure it out fast," Craw says, pointing into the morning sky. I can make out tiny black dots in the horizon shooting toward us. Some random thought must tell me I can get away from them just by backing up in horror, because that's what I do. *Maybe we can run on the track to get away. If we could get even one mobile working, we could all carpool and escape. I don't even care if it's not my mobile. As long as we make it off of here alive, I—*

I scream a little as a hand grabs my arm and yanks me back, but their other hand wraps around my mouth. "Shut up, would you? I'm not about to get caught cuz you're a sissy," Spike growls in my ear as he drags me to where the Brigade's parked.

"And you're a BFS bully. What do you want from me?" I demand from behind the hand. He tastes like metal and grease.

"See what you can do about this," Spike says as he dumps me by a giant open door that shows the inner stuff in his tank and points at a bunch of black wires. "There's a gray one. It's not s'posed to be there, and it's not s'posed to be seen, either, but you don't go around wearing sunglasses all day without getting some night vision. I already tried knifing it, but it takes something stronger, and I've got this nagging suspicion that you've got something stronger. Go on."

I hesitate, but something tells me that asking "Or what?" will get me punched in the mouth, so I tug the thick wire closer to me and (making sure he doesn't see what I'm doing) bite down on it, weakly hoping that whatever I do to machinery takes over. Electricity fills my mouth, and I spit, grossed out, but the mobile rumbles awake, so quiet that nobody else notices. My eyebrows hit the clouds. We were both right.

Spike gets me to my feet. "Good job. Now, go help the rest of your team since you know how."

"Wha... why'd you let me know what to do?" I ask, since I'm sure he could've figured out a way to bust a wire by himself, no radioactive saliva necessary.

"Because that's how you make something called allies, if you wanna sugar-coat it," Spike explains, smirking at me. "Listen. Leadhead was right. Playtime's over. Once these teams split, we'll be gone for good, enemies til we're six feet under. That's a problem for me since I happen to be on a team whose enemies include a cyborg and a mystery girl who can somehow top the criminal list." He leans close to me and drops his voice. "I don't know who the heck you are, Mouse, but I can deal with another mystery if I can get some power along the way. So now that I let you know how to get us off this rock in one piece, why don't you be a good little spy and give me a gun back? Cuz I'm sure you don't want me as an enemy, either."

I realize I don't have a choice. It's do or die, and by die I mean find some untimely, gruesome end whenever Spike sees fit to take his revenge against me. By die I also mean the option where I have to get him out of my way. Which I can do. I am not helpless. But being on top of that situation would require murder. The dead don't speak, you know. But I like to think I'm not a killer.

He grins when I put a gun in his hand, but I feel cold and hollow. *A good little spy*. Suddenly, I'm a double agent. It's so sickening to think about I've gotta stand in the sand for a second with the sea breeze at my back, dancing on the tattoo I won't show anyone, before I can get up the nerve to walk over to my team again. They didn't even notice me leave.

"What's wrong, Rat?" Motor asks, but I don't say anything, just look under the hood of my truck where he's working again until I spot the gray wire.

Seconds later, the truck roars to life, and everyone's heads turn. "SHE GOT IT TO START!"

A cheer swells up, and it feels so ethereal to watch them all jump back into hope, to tell them what I found out, like everything's a flick I'm watching out of someone else's eyes in slow motion with the sound turned low. That girl behind those eyes, that traitor that nobody suspects yet, she can't be me. No. I don't do that sort of stuff. When it comes between murder and treason, two sins that even cutouts acknowledge in our principles, I don't have a choice, so I literally make one.

A smile screws on my face as the first real rays of day shoot against the world, and the shrieking of the missiles reaches us. No, I'd never do that sort of stuff, never get tricked into traitorhood. I'm a rat, but I'm no spy; I'm just one sneaky shadow.

"C'mon, Motor, you get shotgun!" I shout as I pull myself into my truck. The kid leaps in the side after me, beaming, and I beam right back at him. Jacques pulls up in Tom's sleek black mobile right beside me, Voxel coming up from behind, and Craw to my left, rolling to a stop with a blast of his horn. "Alrighty, Band," I say through the beacon as Eli hops in back with a thumbs-up. "Let's bail. Monday's not the day I want to get blown to bits." With that said, I floor it.

Off to my right, the Brigade shoots out, not far behind. Lily and Vici fly out in front, top down, heads forward. Rex stays by Spike's tank, which's morphed so the top's down on that mobile too (good Lord, a convertible tank), and it's also got a passenger. Ivy's hair cape streaks out behind her, and Spike drives with his gun still in one hand, not even looking at the track, and the longer I watch him, the more relieved and freaked I get as the deadly glory of what I really did breaks over me in waves. He doesn't notice what I've done yet, so he shoots me a smile and brings a beacon to his face. The beacons must've gotten changed again, because surprisingly enough, everyone hears his comment: "Impact in three, two, one…"

Bang. Bang. Bang.

Three missiles hit the island behind us, and the tops of mobiles close as the blast mushrooms up, and the visible shockwave starts racing for us. I panic, thinking we're not far enough and we're not gonna make it, but for once, we're as safe as it gets. The sound rocks the truck. Flames and rocks spray into the sky, and pebbles shoot down on us in an apocalyptic rain, denting everything, but even that passes, and we're clear. There's smoke behind us, but there's nothing but track ahead of us. I let out a breath I didn't even notice I was holding, and Motor whoops and high-fives me. "We made it!"

"Guys, we're alive!" Craw hails over the beacon, and I'm so relieved I bust out laughing.

"Day one, check! What'd I tell ya? This'll be a piece of cake, best holiday of our lives!" I promise them all, and this time, I half-mean what I say. Even though I'm keeping secrets, it's not as bad as it was before. Even though they only understand me a little, it feels so good I lean back and close my eyes, smiling. Even though an island got nuked behind us, we weren't on it, and I feel the best I have all day.

It doesn't last long, though. The beacon beeps to life and reminds me that this is a war, and surviving the first battle doesn't guarantee a thing.

CLEMENTINE MCHARPER HAS BEEN EXTERMINATED.

"Hey, at least she's in a better place now," Spike chuckles. "In fact, she's in a lot of better places. You know, over there, over there, maybe some of her's over there..."

"Shut up, Spike," I growl and shut off my beacon. Motor looks shaken already and gives the beacon a disturbed stare, so I tell him it'll be okay, to try and comfort him. Because he's my real bandmate, and I'm the one with the voice, so it's my job to use it.

Beyond him in my window, Spike mouths "Whatever you say, ally," at me and salutes me with his gun, the gun I gave back to him, but I don't respond, and I don't tell Motor when it'll be okay, because I don't mean it one bit.

After all, the gun Spike's saluting me with is totally blank.

But for now, me and my people are thick as thieves, and I, my friend, am content to be misunderstood.

See you on the next shore

CONGRATULATIONS. YOU HAVE HEREBY SURVIVED THE FIRST DAY IN HUDSON BAY.

STAND BY FOR DAY TWO OF YOUR EXTERMINATION.

About the Author

Jessica Shubert lives in an outer suburb of Chicago, Illinois. She is a fan of science fiction and fantasy literature herself and has always enjoyed reading and writing. Her works of fiction and poetry have been selected and featured in various places, like her college's liberal arts magazine. She plans to continue writing about Tersatellus and other stories.

CPSIA information can be obtained
at www.ICGtesting.com
Printed in the USA
BVOW09s1200201117
500905BV00002B/308/P

9 781640 271005